From where the age of men?

Sun, soil or will.

From where the form of men?

Boundless space, happenstance or reverence reshaped.

From where the thoughts of men?

Distant light, Darwin's flight or heaven's might.

To where the path of man . . . ?

# THE
# BASTION
# PROSECUTOR

## EPISODE 3

AJ Marshall

*MPress books*

The Bastion Prosecutor
Episode 3

First published in the United Kingdom 6th June 2009 by MPress Books

MPress Books Limited Reg. No 6379441 is a company registered in Great Britain
www.mpressbooks.co.uk

British Library Cataloguing in Publication Data
A catalogue record for this book is available from the British Library.

Where possible, papers used by MPress Books are natural, recyclable products made from wood grown in sustainable forests. The manufacturing processes conform to the environmental regulations of the country of origin.

ISBN
0-9551886-7-9
978-0-9551886-7-1

Typeset in Minion
Origination by Core Creative, Yeovil 01935 477453
Printed and bound in England by J F Print Ltd., Sparkford, Somerset.

# AUTHOR'S COMMENT

Through the ages, civilisations of planet Earth record the number "three" as having both significance and reverence. It occurs in the natural, artificial and spiritual world with uncommon frequency. It has the "power" to shape the dimension in which we live and the dimension that we believe in. Architecture in the ancient world seemed liberated by it – the symmetrical triangles of the Egyptian pyramids spring easily to mind; whilst the "trinity" has formed the cornerstone of a great religion for more than two thousand years. Symbolic multiples, particularly six, nine and twelve, also appear to have a mesmerising authority in our world if we stop to look for them.

My *Kalahari Series* is a futuristic trilogy. Significantly, however, this episode of *The Bastion Prosecutor* is itself one of three – a trilogy within a trilogy. In this book, the quest to find a power source to replace oil and other carbon-based fuels continues against an historical backdrop and unfolding environmental calamities. The players, earth, wind and fire, and blood, sweat and tears, all have a part and there are others like these in the story line should you wish to look for them – you may be surprised at their relevance. "Three", the so-called "universal denominator" weaves like a thread through the tapestry of this story – I hope very much that you enjoy the read.

Finally, I should like to make note that the timings of actual historical events mentioned in *The Bastion Prosecutor* are accurate to the best of my knowledge; however, by nature of being set in the future, the tale and the characters therein are entirely fictional.

Be prosperous and of long life.

# INTRODUCTION

**The story so far ...**

Lieutenant Commander Richard James Reece is the survey leader for Osiris Base, a permanent encampment on Mars. The year is 2049. There is also a longer established and larger base on the Moon, called Andromeda. Richard Reece is a former military and space shuttle pilot, having previously served on Andromeda Wing; he is British. Appointed to Mars for three years, he envisaged a quiet, uncluttered time. Two things happened, however, that would subsequently change his life forever: meeting Doctor Rachel Turner, Osiris Base Principal Medical Officer, and finding, in the wreckage of a remote, long abandoned alien spaceship, a flight log. The writings in the log bear an uncanny resemblance to those of earth's ancient civilisations. Richard Reece studies the text and succeeds in deciphering it.

Close to the wreckage, Reece also finds a number of strange, fractured, crystals. They contain latent energy of enormous potential. Knowledge of the discovery, and its implications, soon reaches earth and not only the government agencies for which it was intended, but also unscrupulous, corrupt, multinational conglomerates. Their aim: to gain possession of the crystals, harness their electricity-generating potential and hold the world to ransom. The race is on.

Earth's natural resources are almost exhausted. Anxious governments press into service an experimental spaceship before it is ready. Capable of incredible speeds, *Enigma* reduces a Mars retrieval flight to mere weeks. However, its highly sophisticated systems computer EMILY, has another agenda. Major Tom Race, an American and the ship's commander becomes embroiled in a prophetic struggle against synthetic intelligence.

Misplaced trust and eventual betrayal allow the International Space and Science Federation to secure the first valuable consignments, but impatience and political conceit degrade their potential. Now the remaining crystals must be retrieved from Mars. The race sees new competitors, but there can only be one winner.

**The Bastion Prosecutor – Episode 1**

Richard Reece has been incarcerated on earth pending court martial. He is accused of misappropriating ISSF property – namely the flight log of the crashed spaceship *Star of Hope*. Called to London by the British Secret Service he survives two attempts on his life. The first is by agents of a corrupt international conglomerate, and the second by a sinister figure dressed in a monks habit. During the subsequent meeting he is offered a deal: Help recover an ancient Ark believed to contain a lost crystal, and in return all charges against him will be dropped. He also discovers that his fiancée, Rachel Turner, lives a double life. Emotionally devastated he accepts the mission. Thereafter, ancient text, historic monuments, agents of the conglomerates and their deadly machines and a beautiful, mysterious woman, manipulate his destiny until his mission becomes a quest.

## The Bastion Prosecutor – Episode 2

Whilst inside the Great Pyramid of Khufu, Richard Reece begins to realise that his beautiful guide Madame Vallogia and her unlikely aide Asharf Mukkoum, have a hereditary role as mysterious as the monument itself. He is unaware that mechanical predators have sealed the entrance to the pyramid and now stalk him with a directive to interrogate and then eliminate. After a near-death struggle, Richard and his party escape the mausoleum and begin to assimilate long lost and seemingly meaningless clues that coax him south, first to the deserted Valley of the Kings near Luxor in southern Egypt – more particularly the tomb of the Pharaoh Rameses II – and then, after a another narrow escape, to the ancient kingdom of Kush – a region now known as the Sudan. During a briefing in Khartoum, given by his MI9 controller, Richard is confronted by more evidence of wayward and illegal computer programming: an astonishing hologram. The encounter confirms the existence of the so called "Ark of the Light" and directs him east to Eritrea and the ancient and long forgotten seaport of Adulis.

Meanwhile, Tom Race who is onboard the Federation Ship *Enigma* for the Kalahari crystal retrieval flight to Mars, has forged a dubious alliance with EMILY, its autonomous and self-aware systems computer – a relationship based on misconstrued human traits. After an incredible voyage through the solar system and with the ship subsequently established in orbit around the red planet, Tom visits Osiris Base – only to find that both the consignment of crystals and the flight log are missing. A secondary mission to explore the pyramidal structures on the Plane of Elysium sees an attempt on Tom's life. By his own resourcefulness he survives and upon his return, he is able to point a recriminating finger at the base Security Officer. This, in turn, leads to the recovery of the lost items. Along with the cargo, Tom reluctantly agrees to return the officer to earth. However, EMILY sees opportunity in this incarceration.

*The Family*

# ACKNOWLEDGEMENTS

Penning the manuscript to this novel was the fun part. Bringing, subsequently, the three books that comprise this work to fruition, involved the efforts of other people. To mention their names and offer my sincere thanks is both a pleasure and a privilege. I take this opportunity to do so. Firstly though, to my family: Sandra, Laura and Aron, for their unconditional encouragement, and again Laura, for turning the first page. Also, to my mother Beryl, for being at the centre of things.

**Brenda Quick**
For an indispensable critique.

**Core Creative: the team**
Awesome design, despite my determined interference.

**Sarah Flight**
For careful editing and valued opinions.

**Andy Hayward and colleagues at J F Print Ltd.**
Essential for the essentials.

**David Marr**
For an honest critique that only a good friend can give.

**International friends and colleagues**
For linguistic translations.

**David Brown**
Continuity check

**Carol Waters**
The final eye.

**Temporary Temples**
Image of Highclere Hill Crop Formation

**Gilbert Park Photography**
Image of Meroe Pyramids, Sudan

# FACT

**Throughout** the second half of the twentieth century and particularly during the cold war, secret government agencies, funded by their proponents, pursued programmes of research and application using techniques of extrasensory perception. One such technique, known as *Remote Viewing*, entailed the use of trained psychics or "RVers" to "travel" using only their minds; distant and often inaccessible locations being "surveyed" with startling accuracy. Research information, results and their consequence, remain veiled in secrecy.

**Lying** under a Cairo suburb, Heliopolis was once the supreme religious centre of ancient Egypt. Believed to have been established long before its first mention in historical records, Heliopolis was a wonder of the ancient world. It was also the principal religious centre of the Pyramid Age, and its theology inspired and motivated the construction of the great monuments on the Plateau of Giza. The mysteries of the all-encompassing, omniscient Egyptian gods were celebrated by generations of initiate priests at Heliopolis, as they serviced temples to the Great Ennead. This enduring priesthood was famed for its learning and wisdom throughout the ancient world: many of their secrets still lie undisturbed.

**The** earliest detailed images taken of the Martian surface by an orbiting satellite identified two areas where clearly defined structures appeared "artificial". Within a region known as the Elysium Quadrangle appeared pyramidal features – two large and two small. Subsequent images have shown the same detail. In the region known as Cydonia Mensae, another series of structures have seemingly significant features, one of which appears to be a five-sided pyramid.

**Recorded** over several centuries and throughout the world, complex and beautiful markings continue to appear. Not just in arable grasslands, but also in reed beds, forest tops and even sand, many of these "crop circles" have distinct and striking features. Tending to manifest on or near ancient, sacred sites, acknowledged in the past as places of power, many of these formations have blatant mathematical connotations and symbolic implications. Each year more arise, particularly in southern England. As increasing quality, intricacy and size continue to astound, deciphering their apparent encoded meaning is recognised by some as a prophetic necessity.

**The** ancient Maya stand alone as the celebrated civilisation of Mesoamerica. Although isolated from continental Europe and certainly the eastern Mediterranean – human contact is thought to have been almost impossible – the Mayan culture displayed astounding similarities to those of Mesopotamia and ancient Egypt. Their pyramid-building prowess, pictogram script and initiate priests serving all-powerful Gods in lavish temples lay testament to confusing commonalities. Like the Sumarians, the Indus Valley civilisations of India and the Egyptians, the Maya tracked celestial movements closely and created an accurate solar-year calendar based on their observations. They also made mystical connections between earth and sky, positioned and constructed their buildings using complex mathematics and became great farmers and traders. Even their legacy: ruined temples, astonishing artefacts and stone-carved graphic script, exemplify this stark reality.

**Worshipped** in the "Mansion Of The Phoenix" in the ancient religious city of On, or Onun, the Benben stone is believed to have been of meteoric origin. Only much later, did the Greeks call On "Heliopolis" and their documentation sheds some light on this most sacred of Egyptian artefacts. The Benben stone's supposedly cosmic origin and most particularly its "conical shape" has justified a great deal of conjecture that this stone was an "oriented" iron-meteorite, and that its shape subsequently inspired the designers of the first, true pyramids. Items of space debris that fall to earth, often with spectacular effect, and are recoverable, are called meteorites. The sun-like display of such a happening would surely inspire stellar symbolism, and clear evidence of this is found throughout the religious beliefs of the Egyptians and many other ancient civilisations.

**The** history of ancient Africa features more narratives of similar complexity and sophistication than any other ancient civilisation. Yet almost without exception, it is only Egypt that receives substantive consideration. The Kushite Empire, arguably the pinnacle of African civilisation aside from the land of Egyptian pharaohs, occupied territories now known as the Sudan. More particularly, the city of Meroe was foremost in that empire as a commercial, cultural and religious centre that bridged Southern and Northern African trading routes. The Meroitic language, which used hieroglyphic script, remains undeciphered today. Extensive ruins now pay silent tribute to this once vibrant city-state and these include substantial stone-built pyramids. The unique and strikingly angular architecture of these mausoleums differ considerably from those built by the ancient Egyptians and cite similarities to structures recorded elsewhere in the solar system.

**Ethiopia's** claim to the lost Ark of the Covenant is contentious. However, it is to some extent documented. Many do believe that the sacred Old Testament treasure rests in the ancient capital of Axum, exactly where the Ethiopians say it is. Indeed, it seems likely that the Ark did arrive in Ethiopia in the late fifth century BC, about five hundred years after the time of Solomon and Sheba. There is some evidence to suggest that it was first installed on an island in Lake Tana, where it remained for eight hundred years before finally being moved to Axum around the time of Ethiopia's conversion to Christianity in the fourth century AD. Also known as Aksum, Ethiopia's most ancient city has a history dating back more than three thousand years. Aksumite imperial power reached a peak some time after Meroitic Kush, which it finally conquered in the second century AD. Aksum, together with the strategic and fabulously wealthy Red Sea trading port of Adulis, became two of the most important cosmopolitan centres in the ancient world.

# THE
# BASTION
# PROSECUTOR
## EPISODE 3

# EPISODE 1 CONTENTS

| | | |
|---|---|---|
| Prologue | | 1 |
| Chapter 1: | Alliance of Necessity | 9 |
| Chapter 2: | Double Jeopardy | 43 |
| Chapter 3: | The Law and the Light | 53 |
| Chapter 4: | Brothers in Arms | 137 |
| Chapter 5: | Stark Reality | 151 |
| Chapter 6: | Aggressive Electronics | 159 |
| Chapter 7: | Ill-conceived Afterlife | 173 |
| Chapter 8: | Wasted Comrades | 193 |
| Chapter 9: | The Plot Thickens | 207 |
| Chapter 10: | Too Little Too Late | 225 |
| Chapter 11: | The Direction of Truth | 235 |
| Chapter 12: | Caught In Time | 275 |
| Chapter 13: | The Compass Points East | 281 |
| Chapter 14: | The First Deal | 289 |
| Chapter 15: | Awaken the Bygone | 301 |
| Chapter 16: | The Cross Connection | 307 |
| Chapter 17: | Unexpected Friend | 329 |
| Chapter 18: | Portal to the Past | 337 |
| Chapter 19: | Pandora's Box | 353 |
| Glossary | | 367 |

# EPISODE 2 CONTENTS

Chapter 20:  The Look of Love                          1
Chapter 21:  Knowledge is Power                        7
Chapter 22:  The Binary Plight                        23
Chapter 23:  Trail of the Ancients                    41
Chapter 24:  The Dark Side                            67
Chapter 25:  Perception Point                         89
Chapter 26:  The Long and Winding Road               101
Chapter 27:  Future History                          107
Chapter 28:  Back at the Beginning                   119
Chapter 29:  The Elysium Conspiracy                  159
Chapter 30:  Far Sighted                             221
Chapter 31:  The Second Coming                       247

# EPISODE 3 CONTENTS

Chapter 32:  The Right Woman                           1
Chapter 33:  Cause and Effect                         83
Chapter 34:  Belated Correlation                     125
Chapter 35:  Passage of Time                         239
Chapter 36:  Time and Time Again                     267
Chapter 37:  Medieval Mantle                         271
Chapter 38:  Founding Fathers                        291
Chapter 39:  Here Comes the Sun                      339
Epilogue                                             351
Glossary                                             357

# EXTRACT FROM THE DIARY OF ADMIRAL DIRKOT URKET – TRANSLATED FROM THE FLIGHT LOG OF THE "STAR OF HOPE"

On the eve of this final journey, I scribe these thoughts. Mostly for thyself, as I know many in kinship do likewise, but also for diarist, as destiny may this voyage foretell its course for my kind. This quest, at the least doomed, at most, the destiny of our souls, is as wanting as the light of a coming dawn. I am, I yearn, with the heaviness of heart that weighs with bidding forever farewell to my brethren, but blessed too with the smile of hope and gaiety of spirit that we may yet bring salvation to our creed. The history of my kind who abided on Homer, a fair body in the heavens of Zodiac, arises from the dusk of our mother place, the curtain of its lifelessness falling many myriad distant. Of all those that joyed on that most beau of celestes only four vessels set forth. Two from the land of Sapia, five score and ten from the north, fair of skin and fair of pride yet fierce that none would cross. So too a dozen less a century from the south, white of hair and blue for seeing. From Meh Hecoe fortune bestowed a full century and four score, their kind dark of skin with hair black as night. Graced the last to account their lives from the consuming fire, but two score and a dozen less one from Mohenjo, thin of eye and yellow their look. These four chariots of kind sought the heavens, only these from so many, their beginnings consumed. Many suns passed and as many bodies, monumental some, meagre others. Until after a full celestial epoch, the fairest place was befound and it was bequest them. In time, great places arose and prospered. The Sapiens of the north in Eridu, of the south in Atlantis. In Te Agi Wakhan the Mayans and in Mohenjo Daro the Harappas. All fairly multiplied. Ordained for two millennia all prospered, their numbers spreading the land, until in much less time fortune changed. Great movements begot Eridu and later vast waters to eclipse Atlantis. Of Mohenjo Daro, a mountain of fire scorched so naught remained, but of Te Agi Wakhan the stone of light snuffed, its civil just to disperse. Of the stone that lit Eridu, two fragments were redeemed. One used thereafter to light Babylon, its great gardens a millennium to keep homage to those, the lost. The other protected by a sacred casket, looked upon by angels until graced by understanding. Lo, over the annals of time the stone that gave Babylon life has too waned. So be it to those here gathered, entrusted by our brethren, the remaining to breathe life into this our last hope, The Star, should we be able to seek our kind and others for salvation. May Astrolias be with us, for in faith we will find the course.

# CHAPTER 32

## THE RIGHT WOMAN

The sea looked cold, grey and foreboding as the Tiltrotor swooped low and banked steeply to the left. Numerous tiny islands, part of the Dahlak Archipelago, dotted the seascape. The crystal clear, turquoise waters, that spring to mind with mention of the Red Sea, seemed distant indeed. Now its hue reflected that of the sky: bleak and gloomy. Richard sat on the left hand side of the cabin and in the turn, the high-wing configuration of the aircraft gave an opportunistic panorama of the coastline. He peered intently through the small window straining to see an airstrip in the murky weather conditions, but to no avail. Moments later, as the aircraft's wings rolled level, they crossed the beach line. The power levels of the engines reduced and so did the vibration that permeated the airframe. White sands stretched south as far as the eye could see, but their coral brilliance and broad expanse appeared muted, even desolate. Richard could clearly see several men fishing; some stood in the surf with long poles, patient and intent. Much further south, Richard knew, lay the straits of Bab al Mandab, the sea pass leading to the Gulf of Aden. At the head of the beach, where the sands gave way to rough scrubland, Richard could see a number of tin shacks that formed a small shanty village. A group of children played and then stopped to gaze at the aeroplane as its shadow passed over them. At just 150 feet, landing would be imminent. Richard tightened his seat belt and gestured to Naomi, who sat in the aisle seat opposite, to do the same. Passing 50 feet, the aircraft began to vibrate heavily as it transitioned into vertical flight mode. A minute later, they touched down.

Climbing from his seat, Richard scanned the surrounding area as best he could. He felt nervous. 'You had better wait here for a while,' he said to Naomi.

With a nod from the pilot in the left hand seat, Preston opened and lowered the cabin door. He took a few steps down, pulled from his pocket a set of digital binoculars and then methodically surveyed the landscape. He was expecting a vehicle, a contact, but there was nobody. He circled the aircraft cautiously and then carried out the same exercise, this time with an infrared overlay selected on the compact instrument. There were, however, no indications of body heat, no signs of life. Every animal had been eaten, he speculated.

After several minutes, Preston stepped back into the cabin. Richard was in the small flight deck talking to the crew. He overheard one of them say, 'Are you sure you want us to leave you here?' The question did seem ominous.

Richard finalised the pickup time for sunset the following day, with the proviso that if it changed he would call using a coded, military satellite link and then he backed out through the narrow doorway. He turned and looked squarely at Preston. 'Well?' he asked.

Preston's expression seemed to sum up Richard's own appraisal of the area: inhospitable and probably very dangerous.

'The place is deserted, Boss,' Preston replied. 'No sign of the contact.'

Richard nodded and glanced at Naomi. 'We are exposed here,' he said. 'Best we move out to one of those buildings and wait. The crew want to leave as soon as possible. Quite frankly I don't blame them!'

Preston pointed behind him. 'There is something suitable over there.'

'Okay, let's get the kit.'

The kit comprised three rucksacks, one of which was overly bulky because Asharf had filled it with what had become his prize possession – the Humatron's cape. Despite Richard asking him if it was now strictly necessary, Asharf had insisted that it might yet prove helpful. The men carried close-support weapons, enough provisions for three days and a backup communications device.

Naomi carried a *hydromix* water maker. Essentially, this is a lightweight, contoured backpack containing a tank of compressed hydrogen and a mechanism for mixing the gas, in the correct proportions, with atmospheric oxygen in order to produce liquid water. The unit could produce several thousand litres of freshwater.

Richard checked the integrity of his ISTAN and then replaced it into his shoulder holster, whilst Preston checked the charge on his sonic pistol. Naomi was the last to leave the aircraft and no sooner had she alighted onto the concrete runway than one of the pilots closed the door behind her. Preston indicated what he thought was the most appropriate building and the group hurried towards it. As they neared the dilapidated wooden building, the Tiltrotor climbed vertically, transitioned to forward flight and accelerated towards the southern airfield boundary. Dust and debris blew in all directions. Barely climbing above 50 feet, it was soon out of sight and moments later there was silence.

They entered through a rear door. Richard was not keen on the makeshift shelter. Should they need somewhere secure against an enemy, it would be difficult to defend. Warily, he looked out through a window and then crossed the room to another. This would be an obvious place to search should anyone come looking but at least it provided cover from the intermittent drizzle and he hoped not to be there for long. His wish soon came true.

'Someone's coming!' called Preston, as he put his eye

close to a wide split in the wooden front door and peered through it.

Moments later a large four-wheel-drive vehicle screeched to a halt outside. Partially obscured in the deep shade of the veranda and dark green in colour, including the wheel rims, it appeared camouflaged. The front door of the building was distorted and had swollen in its recess. With considerable effort, Richard wrenched it open, but having done so, he remained inside and eyed the man in the vehicle. The man's mouth moved as if he was having a conversation. A few seconds later his electric window slid open and Richard saw he had European features, although his skin was more a sunburned olive colour than native.

'Quickly . . . there are problems on the road. We must hurry!' the man shouted. 'The militia are coming!'

To Richard, the man's English had a refined quality with just the hint of an accent.

To be clearly seen, Richard stepped into the doorway. 'To search for the light . . .' he shouted back.

' . . .is to reveal Osiris,' the man replied. 'Now quickly!'

Richard needed no further encouragement. He turned and indicated to Preston to load up.

The vehicle had three rows of seats. Preston and Asharf climbed into the back row and Richard and Naomi took the next. Richard sat behind the driver. The man put his foot down but almost instantaneously slammed on the brakes. Everyone shot forwards.

'What's going on?' demanded Richard.

The man gestured. Richard followed his eye line. On the north-eastern perimeter road of the airfield, not five hundred metres away, a vehicle sped from left to right. It was an army vehicle, an Armoured Personnel Carrier. 'An APC,' Richard breathed in Naomi's ear. Khaki coloured and striped with darker brown, the deep growl of its powerful diesel engine grew louder until it negated any surprise provided by camouflage. Apparently unaware of their presence, the heavy vehicle continued past, its occupants concentrating on their mission.

'They know we're here?' queried Richard.

'No! Not yet, anyway,' the man replied. 'We have their operations frequency. They know an unidentified aircraft was seen in this area; it disappeared and was then spotted again heading south from the airfield at low level. That is where they go first, the southern boundary.'

The driver waited a few more moments until the APC was out of sight and then he floored the accelerator again. This time the electric motor whined. Soon they were making 120 kilometres per hour. He avoided the potholes as best he could at that speed, but the vehicle shuddered with monotonous regularity. Then he burst through a set of closed wire-mesh gates and screeched into a sharp right turn. Naomi clung onto her seat for dear life. They careered through pools of muddy water and several times the wheels spun helplessly, before renewed traction thrust everyone back in their seats again.

The driver put a hand to his earpiece. 'There are more

of them coming! I must get onto the main road before them,' he advised nervously.

'Who are they?'

'Chinese energy conglomerate, heavy handed military security.'

'I know of them,' Richard interrupted, nodding.

On this road, it would be obvious where they had come from. The T-junction loomed. At the last minute, the driver braked and then he pulled the vehicle around another right hand turn. They swerved across the wet road surface and the driver floored the pedal again accelerating south on the main road. Richard clung onto the driver's seat. 'Put your seatbelt on, Naomi!' he said curtly. It was none too soon. In the far distance they saw a large lorry coming over the lip of a hill. The metalled road was narrow and Richard saw how difficult it was to pass a small truck carrying a precarious load of tree trunks. Its driver was forced off the road so that the nearside wheels vibrated, bounced and kicked up dirt and debris on the unprepared ground.

The lorry now looked decidedly military and bore down on them bullishly, keeping to the centre of the road. The driver checked his rear view mirror. The small lorry had stopped off the road, tree trunks scattered. Apart from that the road was deserted.

'Heads down . . . into the foot wells, quick!'

They all scrambled from their seats. There was precious little room for Richard behind the driver. Preston, crouching out of sight, pulled his binoculars from his pocket. He flipped down a prism-shaped device over the eyepiece and then perched the instrument on top of the seat back. 'Tell me as the lorry passes alongside,' he said.

'Alongside!' declared the driver. 'He's not going to give an inch . . . hang on!' With that, the man wrenched the steering wheel to the right and pulled his vehicle off the road and onto the parallel track – at that speed he fought to keep control. The 4x4 bounced, swayed and skidded uncomfortably. Naomi gave out a gasp as she was thrown against the door – Richard pinned her against it with a strong arm. The heel of the driver's hand hovered over the klaxon boss in the centre of the steering wheel but he thought better of it. The military, olive-green lorry was now closing fast.

'Keep your heads down!' the driver warned again. 'Here he comes . . . standby . . . standby . . . now!'

Using the binoculars as a periscope, Preston sighted the lorry – an obsolete model with a long, drab-green tarpaulin cover that stretched over a high protruding framework. The cover flapped violently in the wind, particularly the open doors at the back through which Preston focused then enhanced his view of the inside. As it raced away from them he pressed a button to record the image, asking, 'What do you make of that, Boss?' and dropped the instrument over the seatback.

Richard peered into the binoculars for several seconds.

'Soldiers! They're oriental all right, twelve of them. Wait

a minute. How do I bring it up, Preston?'

'Button on the right, Boss.'

Richard peered again. 'There is a motif on their combats, a large T and something else that I can't quite make out.'

'You can come up now,' said the driver. 'The way is clear.'

Richard climbed back onto his seat; he reached down to help Naomi and then leaned across her to withdraw her seatbelt. He gestured for her to clip the buckle in place. He turned and looked over his shoulder at Preston. His expression was tense. 'Tongsei,' he said, 'There's no mistaking that motif . . . look!'

Preston studied the image and nodded. 'It's the same as the one emblazoned on the side of the mineral barge *Colossus* alright.'

Richard looked back at the driver, who by now had settled things down by returning to the centre of the metallic road. He sighted Richard in his mirror. 'They are everywhere. There has always been a presence, but outside the capital it has been discrete . . . never like this. Nobody rocks the boat these days – not if you want to live. Tongsei have enormous investments here, mainly in mineral extraction, but the last few years have seen yields plunge – what is left is deep underground and very costly to work. Militia numbers have increased considerably over the last week and there is no mistaking their resolve. They speak a dialect of Mandarin, from Sechuan Province, so there is no mistaking where they come from, either. It is quite clear that these *emissaries* are under new orders. They are looking for something and being very heavy-handed about it, as I said. Word on the street is that the government can do little about it. It seems that our friends are looking for something very, very valuable; the same thing as you, I assume, Mr Jones.'

Richard nodded thoughtfully. 'Interesting, yes?'

'By the way, I'm Charles Marretti, Charlie if you like. Sorry about the rough ride.' He smiled at them through the mirror.

Richard sat up straight and indicated behind. 'Preston and Asharf and Naomi here,' he explained, and put a hand across the man's shoulder to introduce himself. 'Rhys Jones,' he said. 'How do you do?'

'Pleased to make your acquaintance, I'm sure,' replied the driver, awkwardly shaking Richard's hand.

'So you're in charge of field ops in Eritrea?'

'Yeah. It used to be a quiet posting but things are hotting up.'

Richard patted his shoulder. 'I'm glad to have you on board and thanks for the fast pick up.'

Charlie shrugged. 'Stuff is happening, that's for sure.'

Richard nodded again. 'Yeah, and it's going to get worse before it gets better. Have you had a full briefing?'

'Uh, uh! All I know is that your assignment is critical. I'm to give you *red alert* assistance.'

'Good. I'll bring you up to speed on the way ... So, how

10

far to town?'

'Another fifteen to twenty minutes, depends on any hold-ups. There is food and water in the safe house.'

Most of the roads were unpaved, not that that was a surprise to Richard. Although only drizzling – and that sometimes intermittently – an excess of surface water clearly hampered everything here: movement, trade, day-to-day living and services. Puddles and depressions that littered the criss-cross of streets and side roads brimmed full of sloshing, orange-coloured water, or oozing, stodgy mud. Animals and vehicles alike ran the gauntlet. Richard could see that no matter which alternative street the driver turned down, someone or something seemed stuck. There was also a good deal of refuse littering the town and the unsanitary conditions seemed like something from medieval times.

'There are new faces here in town, Mr Jones, and my local man is reporting a lot of unusual activity,' Charlie said. 'We will have to be very careful. If you had come as little as a week ago, life would have been a lot simpler. Adulis is nothing more than a backwater these days, a shadow of its former self, you might say. Nevertheless, the natural harbour is still usable in parts, although most is heavily silted and has been for many centuries. Small coasters still make use of the limited docking and wharf facilities, but there is so much soil being washed down from the highlands that dredging operations go on almost continuously in an effort to keep a channel open to the sea.'

'Right,' answered Richard reflectively. 'I thought the six-wheeled *Terra Firma* would have been best for these conditions; the Embassy in Khartoum has them.'

'It's prudent to invest in Chinese built vehicles in Eritrea these days, draws less attention and you can get spares. Their engineering is good; this *Land Voyager* hasn't let me down yet.'

At that moment, one of the Voyager's rear wheels dropped into a deep puddle and lodged itself. Charlie put his foot down and both rear wheels began to spin. They spat out dirty, reddish-brown water and slimy mud at every passerby who came within twenty feet; many cursed and shook their fists. Charlie looked concerned. 'Can't afford to be stuck here,' he whispered, and selected a lower gear by pressing a button on the dashboard. He gently coaxed the vehicle forward, at one point all four of the wheels spun helplessly. A group of locals gathered and took shelter under the wooden porch of an adjacent shop front. They began to jeer and point, some even laughed and shouted spitefully.

'That's all we need.' Charlie tried again. 'This place is becoming a regular meeting place for cretins. Don't look at them! Look away! Eyeballing is taken as a challenge and this lot don't need any excuse.'

'We've got company,' said Preston, looking behind. 'Two militiamen . . . both armed!'

'Shit! Come on . . . come on!'

The vehicle began to rock forwards and backwards. The two rear wheels repeatedly reached the crescent of the water-filled depression before spinning again and falling backwards. 'Hide your faces!' Charlie ordered, as he checked his rear-view mirror. The two soldiers were approaching; one of them pulled his rifle from his shoulder.

'I'm in trouble if I splash them,' the driver explained. 'They would have us out!' He pressed another button on the dash, locking the rear wheels just as the vehicle rocked forwards. Then he prioritised the front-wheel drive mechanism and squeezed the accelerator pedal. Miraculously they gripped. Just as the soldiers were within mud-slinging distance, they moved off. Charlie Marretti wasted no time. He pulled into the centre of the street and disappeared around the first corner, breathing a huge sigh of relief.

After another 100 metres they passed, among others, a scruffy herdsman who was encouraging a heavily laden camel to stand. It seemed to be under considerable duress, having sunk up to its hindquarters in debilitating mud. The man kicked and cursed the beast but it wasn't responding. Richard watched as the vehicle slipped and slewed, narrowly missing the animal, and shook his head, feeling sorry for it.

'Almost there,' Charlie said. He took another left, opened his window to pull his wing mirror in and drove on. Moments later, and with a resounding "clunk", the nearside mirror was pushed hard against the side of the car by a wooden veranda post. Marretti held his line for another fifty metres and then turned right into a deserted alley. The surface was firmer. 'This leads to the back of our safe house. It is a private road, little used. At one time, this was the better end of town. We wait for five minutes and then we move – just to be sure.'

Richard nodded. Charlie briefly answered a telephone call. From the way he spoke Richard knew that he was using an online encoder. 'On the hour,' Marretti said, decisively.

Richard checked his chronometer – it was 09:57. They waited.

'Where are you from, Charlie?' Richard asked, breaking the silence.

Charlie seemed surprised at Richard's question and glanced at him in the mirror. 'It's not public knowledge, but as you ask, I'm from just across the boarder with Ethiopia, a place called Gonder, although my family line is Italian – we came over in the 1880s. I went to the English school in Addis; my father thought it the best. When I was thirteen, he sent me to England to complete my education. I went to a school called King's College in the west of England, in a market town called Taunton, I loved it actually.'

Richard nodded. 'Really?' he replied, raising a smile. 'I know King's. We played them regularly at rugby and cricket and occasionally hockey too; my school was in Wiltshire.

Always had a good game, I remember – and after that?'

'I read foreign politics at Oxford and a bit of law. Subsequently, went for a job in the city. That's where I was recruited, in London. Satisfied?'

Richard shrugged. 'I like to know who I'm dealing with!'

'You move into the safe house now.' Charlie handed over a key to Richard. 'Hole up there for a few hours until I get movement reports from my people, then I will be back to take you to where you want to go.'

'What's the address of this place?' asked Richard, ducking to see beyond the windscreen.

'The house fronts East Street, but that will do you no good, the street signs are in Amharic around here. It is not far to where we are going. Just be patient. Keep a good look out from the first floor window.' Marretti pointed. 'You will see me arrive and then you must leg it down to the car.'

'Okay, a couple of hours, then,' Richard agreed.

'*Grazie Signore,*' said Naomi, as she climbed from her seat.

'*Prego, Signora,*' came the surprised reply. '*Per favore. Stai attento.*'

'I am not sure, Signore Marretti, that this man knows the meaning of careful!' Naomi replied, glancing back over her shoulder. The brief smile she gave him lifted his troubled expression.

The rear facade of the house was of red brick. There were

three ground floor and two small first floor windows, all heavily framed in dark hardwood. The single door was low but wide and similarly of dark, heavy timber. The house was in a row; Richard counted nine. They were of different shapes and sizes, probably reflecting the architectural heritage of their original owners, as in its heyday, Adulis was a renowned melting pot of different cultures. The safe house was small compared to the others and its features much less ostentatious. For one thing, it was constructed of a local material, whilst the neighbours boasted their wealth and status by using materials drawn from faraway. The building to the right, although blemished, was clearly of a white limestone. In bygone days, this would have been a princely street and perhaps this house was the first, thought Richard.

Nevertheless, all the rear gardens were relatively narrow – barely twenty metres, and unkempt. Richard was soon turning the heavy iron key in the door lock. Cautiously he pushed the door open and stepped inside. At that, the vehicle drove off behind them. It was like a silent, stagnant time capsule, due in the greater part to metre-thick walls, and the heavy, distorting glass of the windowpanes. Red brick, laid edge first, formed the uneven floor and numerous ornate, circular patterns, some partly concealed beneath large, Persian-type rugs revealed a Roman influence. Some of these swirls boasted inlaid seashells having mother-of-pearl polished hues. There was an open door off to the left that Richard could see led into a kitchen; in the doorway, the brick floor had been worn into a hollow, reflecting centuries of use. The air was stale and damp. There was a spattering of "lumpy" African-type furniture and some of the chairs had cushions in a material that matched the floor rugs. A wooden sideboard had a dusting of green mould. Had he reached up, Richard could just have touched the wooden planks that formed the upstairs floor, whilst the beams that supported them sagged alarmingly towards the middle of the large room. Preston slammed the back door shut and locked it, trapping them inside. The noise drew a grimace from Richard.

Across the room was a single front door, again in heavy teak or mahogany. Richard walked over to it and checked the lock. In addition, a large iron bolt was firmly wedged in the adjacent doorframe. Carefully, he drew back a drab, straw-coloured Hessian blind that covered one of two windows that looked out onto the main street. For a backwater, Adulis, and more particularly East Street, seemed particularly busy. Perhaps there was method in the madness of a safe house in the middle of town, Richard considered.

'Asharf, take a look upstairs, would you?' Richard asked. 'And Preston, checkout the food situation please, perhaps something for a brew?'

There was a narrow, exposed staircase leading upstairs and moments later Asharf could be heard walking softly on the bare floorboards.

'There is a gas bottle and a hob, Boss,' shouted Preston,

from inside the kitchen. 'And some victuals. Tea or coffee anyone?'

Richard looked at his chronometer and then at Naomi.

'Coffee for me please, Preston,' she replied.

Richard gestured for her to take a seat. 'It could be a couple of hours,' he said, quietly. Naomi nodded.

Richard was impatient to get on with it. Asharf came noisily down the stairs, his boots leaving patterned treads on the polished wood. 'It is all clear, *Effendi*,' he said. 'Three bedrooms, two with beds – that is all.'

Richard nodded. 'Preston and I will go over to East Parade, Naomi. I would like you and Asharf to remain here.'

'But what if you need a translator, Richard?'

'The brief says that there is a curator, a man who speaks English. If I need you, I will page you, okay?'

Naomi nodded. Richard looked at Asharf. 'You have the alarm?'

'Yes, *Effendi*.'

'Okay, use it if you have to. It will make my telephonic pager vibrate and you can send a message. Go and buy a takeaway. I noticed an Indian restaurant just up from here. Here's some money.' Richard gave him a fistful of local cash. 'And then keep watch upstairs.'

Asharf returned with good spicy goat and rice which everyone enjoyed.

'*Effendi! Effendi!* The car, it returns!' Asharf shouted excitedly from upstairs.

Richard sprang up. 'Good, let's get on with it. You'll be all right?

'I would prefer to come with you, Richard, but I understand,' replied Naomi, with a special smile.

'Lock the door behind us. I hope we'll be no longer than two or three hours. Any problems, anything suspicious, anything at all, send me a message . . . understand?' Richard caught her eye and for an instant they were lost, then Richard tore his thoughts back to the moment. 'Preston, let's go!'

A minute later Richard and Preston were in the car. Charlie Marretti reversed back up the alleyway. 'The other end is blocked, spot checks by the militia,' Marretti explained. 'Normally, it's a short walk to East Parade, ten minutes, south end of East Street and through the Hanging Arch, but it is better we drive there. Keep your heads down.'

Richard slithered down the seat and unclipping his shoulder holster, he felt for his ISTAN. Preston watched him. 'Check the charge on your sonic pistol, Preston!' Richard ordered.

'Already have, Boss, and my static baton is on standby mode.'

The street remained busy and overcrowded for its entire

19

length. Despite the commotion and the melee of bickering, angry shouting and numerous vehicle horns, Marretti remained remarkably cool. He took his time and went out of his way to avoid struggling animals and roadside altercations. It took more than ten minutes to drive, but eventually they arrived at an ancient arched gateway that clearly formed an important access point through the original, defensive city wall. The crumbling stone wall, built in the main of exposed loose rock and debris, still stood over ten metres high in places, but it lay dwarfed beneath this impressive gateway. Constructed from large blocks of red sandstone, the gateway was adorned with carved figures, ancient symbols and contemporary graffiti, and appeared to be in remarkably good condition. Two huge wooden gates still hung on iron hinges, but they lay propped against the inside walls of the wide archway, their role clearly obsolete. The gateway was a bottleneck, but Marretti waited patiently for a break and when one appeared, he quickly took advantage of it. Not surprisingly, however, a water-filled depression occupied the centre of the road and as they passed beneath the arch, the big tyres of the Land Voyager caused a bow wave that was enough to make even the most obstinate walker jump clear or turn back. Marretti smiled apologetically in response to the barrage of insults and shaking fists.

There was a gradual incline to the road on the other side of the archway and conditions became a little easier. After no more than three or four hundred metres, the traffic thinned until only a few users jostled for space on the road's peripheries. Marretti kept his speed at a fast walking pace.

'Don't tell me,' said Richard flippantly, as he looked back towards the archway. 'That was the East Gate, a defensive exit point from the old city!'

Marretti used his rear-view mirror to look at Richard. 'That certainly was the *old* East Gate, Mr Jones, but your orientation is about face. That part of the town dates back only to the eleventh century, this part was already occupied a thousand years before Christ. It flourished during the years of the Aksumite Empire and was certainly thriving when Christianity first came to this region around the fourth century AD. During its heyday as the world's most important trading centre, this was where the wealthiest merchants lived. Some of these houses have their foundations at the original street level; the history is incredible here.' Marretti sighed. 'Sadly most has long since been lost.'

'Where is East Parade, then?' asked Richard, studying the old houses closely as they passed by.

'All of this is East Parade; number one is at the top. It is not particularly elevated, but there is a view over the old harbour. This area has a government preservation order on it; some quarters are also world heritage sites. You do not come here unless you have specific business. I have booked an appointment for you as a prominent historian from the *National Geographic* – otherwise we would have been stopped by now. Too many artefacts have been stolen over the years; local government is very suspicious of foreigners.'

Moments later the vehicle stopped. Ancient buildings surrounded them. Some were tall, reaching five or six storeys. There were numerous balconies; one example, on the other side of the square, was cleverly constructed with Romanesque features and boasted an ornate iron balustrade, but this seemed out of place and was clearly an addition from a much later period. Some of the buildings had clay-tiled roofs, while others were flat with castellated ramparts that brought the militant Knights Templar to mind. Some were restored, in good condition, plastered and whitewashed, but others were dilapidated with walls that bowed outwards precariously. There were a number of narrow alleyways, none wider than a metre. Richard and Preston simultaneously climbed from the vehicle watching for some ancient warrior in this historical quarter.

The quadrangle was impressive and the air of bygone days was almost tangible. There was a circular fountain, no water, but its marble-like stonework glistened in the intermittent drizzle and the surrounding area lay paved in a similar white, but porous stone that was well worn, frequently fractured or displaced and in the main, heavily discoloured.

'This way,' said Marretti, gesturing the two men towards an impressive house that was easily the largest in the quadrangle. There were five marble steps leading up to a

22

pair of dark wooden doors, each had several rows of black iron studs. Higher, on each side of the doorway, two large lanterns hung from black metal brackets. Marretti pulled on a slender bell pull that passed through the doorframe. They waited. He checked the time and they could see he was uneasy. Preston used the heavy metal knocker in another effort to give notice of their arrival. Worked into the form of a male lion's head, its reverberating thud rattled the doors; this time the left hand one opened slowly. From behind, they heard a voice.

'I have been expecting you. Please enter.' The man's voice was as old as the building, but Richard could not place the accent. As the door opened wider and Richard stepped inside, he saw a very old man.

'Good afternoon, Sir,' Richard said respectfully. 'My name is Jones, and this is my assistant, Preston. We are journalists. Thank you for this appointment.'

The man nodded knowingly, his expression open and kind. 'I know exactly who you are young man. I have been asked to help you. If I can, I shall do so.'

'I will park out of sight and then return to keep watch,' Marretti interjected. 'Do not leave this building until I am here to collect you . . . understand?'

Richard nodded in acknowledgement. At that, he scanned the area, raised a hand to say goodbye and quickly returned to his vehicle.

Richard towered above the man who had answered Preston's rough knocking. He wore a dark brown woollen djellaba with the hood laid flat across his shoulders and a belt of grubby white rope that looked like a piece of sailing ship's rigging; the ends were simply knotted and bound. His hair was wayward, wispy and completely white. His skin was weathered and brown and his appearance Arabic. Richard had a friend who hailed from Yemen, although he had not seen him for some years, their features were very similar.

Another man, an African, who had short, white, curly hair and was similarly dressed, walked silently across the cavernous hall; momentarily he seemed interested in the intrusion and then disappeared into the darkness of an adjacent room.

Richard shook the old man's hand; the fragile bones like the skeleton of a bird. Preston followed suit. 'Your English is very good, Sir,' Richard commented.

'I learned during the great days of empire, when the Americans ruled the world. Anyway, one cannot be an historian of merit without speaking English,' the man replied matter-of-factly. 'I am Banou, Chief Curator and you are my first visitor for three years. I was informed of your visit and we are pleased, very much, to open our treasures for you.' The man looked deep into Richard's eyes. 'I think we do not need to speak of the geographical magazine. I have known journalists, and one you are not!'

Richard was surprised. He nodded acknowledging the man's acuity and then looked down. 'No, no, Sir, you are quite right. I'm not here to write about what I find.' He looked up openly. 'So, this place is a museum; I was told it was a scriptorium?'

'Scriptorium, archive ... museum? What is the difference? Yes, we have a wonderful library, as well as many artefacts that we have treasured over the years. Now, what is it you seek?'

'We are looking for a record of a ship, or more precisely, a ship carrying a specific cargo. An important but secret cargo, identified only by its worth. It would have sailed from Adulis, bound we think for India or perhaps China.'

Banou's brow furrowed. 'When? In what century?'

Richard grimaced. 'I don't know. The only clue is that the year was marked by catastrophe on perhaps global proportions – a year without a summer.'

Banou's expression lightened. 'Ah . . . that does help,' he said. 'I know of only one year where the warmth of summer was absent; where blackened rain spoiled the land for every season. The year without summer . . . yes . . . the year after the first great eruption of Krakatoa.'

'Krakatoa! The volcano?'

Banou nodded. 'It is the only year without summer recorded in this place, and that was because crops failed and taxes were lost. Krakatoa was a volcanic island in the Sunda Strait, between Java and Sumatra. It erupted first in 1595, filling the atmosphere with ash and pumice, and choking out the sun. The following year, there was no summer.'

'But I thought that event occurred in the nineteenth century, Sir?'

'That was the second great eruption, young man; in 1883, and it was heard across the world. *That* was when the island disappeared, leaving only an ash cone above the sea – Anak Krakatoa, Child of Krakatoa!'

'So we look for the year 1596!' said Richard excitedly.

Banou nodded in a contained manner. He gestured for Richard and Preston to follow him. 'Come,' he said.

The house appeared to have a cellar as deep as it was tall. Richard and Preston followed the man down three flights of steep, wooden steps that frequently creaked and complained beneath their weight. It was dark, dismal and claustrophobic. The suppressed glow of a single electric light bulb did little more than illuminate the area around each stair well. As they reached the third landing, Richard leaned over the balustrade and peered downwards – there were at least two more levels. Banou pulled out an old aluminium torch from the pocket of his djellaba; again, its effect was of little consequence. 'We have a limited supply of electricity,' he said, in a resigned tone. 'Two hours in the afternoon, that is all, and batteries are impossible to find.'

Richard rummaged around in his rucksack and eventually found his self-charging photoelectric torch. He switched it on and offered it to Banou, who could hardly believe its luminance. His eyes widened and he gasped as long, angular shadows jostled around them, cast by rows of tall wooden shelves and stacks of books and manuscripts.

Within this labyrinth of records, history smelt of rotting paper and heady camphor from mothballs.

'You may keep it,' said Richard in a whisper, as if trying to avoid disturbing the sleeping ghosts of ten thousand scribes. 'The more you use it, the longer it lasts!' he added. 'But you should hold it here, so as not to cover the photoelectrical cells.'

The old man was so taken aback he was momentarily lost for words, but he bowed politely towards Richard and registered the gift with a broad smile and then he flashed the penetrating beam excitedly around the large room and over the blackened ceiling. There were dust-laden cobwebs everywhere inhibiting exploration of the corners and some strands, glowing in the light, stretched down from the ceiling and brushed lightly against their heads. Banou turned again to Richard with a smile of delight about his new toy and disappeared between two rows of box-lined, floor-to-ceiling shelves. Richard and Preston followed and almost collided with him as they rounded the next blind corner. 'An everlasting light from the new world,' Banou enthused.

The old archivist clearly had an idea of where to commence his search, but his subsequent progress along the row was laborious; all the while he was methodically scanning up and down. He focused on labelled box ends, occasionally dwelling for a moment to pull them towards him. In most cases the writing was faded, in some, completely erased. 'We have records of taxes, transactions

27

and commodities dating back to when Ethiopia first became Christian,' he said proudly.

'That was in the fourth century AD,' confirmed Preston.

Richard looked at him impressed.

'Quite so,' replied Banou. 'The rulers of Adulis kept their records meticulously, so that no tax should go unpaid, no revenues lost . . . you understand. The great trading port grew wealthy on such revenues and for centuries its influence dominated the entire region; here we preserve this legacy. Many documents are now damaged or missing of course. Records of the precious cargo you seek may well exist, but if you do not want to spend a lifetime in here, then you should be more specific.' The old man swept his hand over a number of box ends. 'We have the year, but now we need something more, Mr Jones, an owner, a ship, a name, something more, if I am to help.'

Richard stood silently thinking.

'You ask the impossible of history.' For several seconds, the old man looked quizzically at Richard. 'Do you know what you ask?' he said, eventually.

Richard looked at him blankly.

'Where else has your quest taken you, young man? What is the common thread?'

Richard rubbed his chin thoughtfully and turned to Preston for inspiration. Preston shrugged. 'The ancient Egyptians,' Richard muttered, after a lengthy pause. 'The pyramids . . . the great Pharaoh Rameses – perhaps his tomb . . . KV5?' Richard thought of Professor Simpson-Carter, of his hologram and his marked, dead body. 'What about the *Sacred Nine*?' he speculated. 'Yes . . . the Sacred Ennead . . . the Ennead!'

The old man stood almost to attention. 'Be very careful when and how you use those words; they are not to be spoken lightly,' he advised.

Richard nodded and said under his breath: 'How right you are.'

'Louder!'

'Try the *Ennead*, Sir. A ship called the *Ennead*, leaving Adulis in the year 1596, bound for the east!'

Banou sighed and turned to inspect the rows of wooden boxes that were behind him. He peered intently at one specific box, housed slightly above head height and re-read its bleached, crinkly label. After a few seconds, he pulled the box from the shelf; it was long; more than half a metre. Inside, there were a number of tightly rolled parchments. He offered the box to Preston to hold and the torch to Richard and carefully rotated each parchment, his ancient hands wrinkled, with fingers long and bony, until one took his interest. 'Yes, this may help,' he said.

Preston tucked the box under his arm whilst Banou very carefully unrolled the parchment. To Richard the writing seemed to be a type of pictogram. The old man nodded wisely. 'You have chosen well, young man. It seems that there was a ship called the *Ennead*. It is described here as being the fastest dhow to make the passage to the Yellow

River, a place far to the east. Revenues included silks and fire powder.'

'Wasn't the *River Yangtze* described as the Yellow River, I mean before it dried up a couple of decades ago? Could that be it? China! The Ark was taken to China!'

'Of more relevance is the owner,' replied the old man, warily. 'A merchant whose address is listed here, inside the old city and whose family name was Thutmose. We should find the records of this man's transactions. To own such a ship, he would have drawn and paid copious taxes. We must find the records of the port authorities. Come! We go back!'

The curator Banou was surprisingly spritely for his years. Soon they were racing across the entrance hall, the great room echoing with their footsteps. The fact that Richard and Preston had trailed the old man up to the ground floor in almost complete darkness was of little consequence, as their guide patently knew everything there was to know about the house. No cracked or protruding flagstone would catch *his* heels, as every nuance was ingrained in his memory. The old man took the first flight of stairs like a gazelle and Richard was grateful for the natural light that filtered onto the first landing. Clearly, the fact that his new "gift of light" was self-perpetuating had not fully registered, because he had turned off the torch. The staircase that led upstairs was quite different to the one that accessed the bowels of the house; for one thing, it was made of stone. It was also beautifully carved, curved and cantilevered, evidently an impressive architectural feature during the house's heyday, and marks on its white marble steps clearly delineated where, at one time, a narrow carpet or runner had lain.

Up they climbed, up two more flights of stairs, and on the third landing, a long narrow pole of light penetrated the gap between two half-open wooden shutters. Banou scurried towards a room on their right. 'This way!' he insisted.

Inside, the room was large and rectangular. Richard was growing used to the stale mustiness of the place. Nevertheless, it did feel remarkably dry, due, in part anyway, to the permanently closed shutters. Like the cellar, this room was filled with wooden shelving. Intermittent gaps between the long, parallel columns allowed only narrow access and both Richard and Preston frequently turned sideways to avoid protruding boxes and stacks of papers. The old man shuffled along several corridors scanning the shelves and periodically stopped to read a label. 'This section is sixteenth century,' he mumbled eventually, and then continued a little further. 'And this is where we should look,' he said, stopping short and looking back at Richard. The torch beam passed over several box ends, while its reflection cast shadows over the man's wrinkled features.

'What we seek is an artefact, Sir,' Richard advised sombrely. 'Its owners, or perhaps more accurately, its guardians, would have wanted to keep its existence an absolute secret. We believe that the artefact would have travelled in a protective casket, probably a plain, unpretentious box of some description, probably made of wood, and that the people who carried it avoided the authorities in Axum in favour of a resting place here in Adulis. We believe that it lay hidden here for many centuries. However, realising that this once great city was now in decline, the guardians decided to move it again, to a safer place, you understand . . . the East . . . hence the China connection. That is why our lead on the year is paramount. We also believe that, in order to avoid scrutiny by the authorities, the guardians volunteered taxes at the very highest rate, as if the casket contained Nubian gold or the like. After all, who in their right mind would pay revenue on *the most precious* of metals, if indeed that were not the commodity inside? What I am trying to say, Sir, is that the artefact itself will not be recorded, only the unusually large tax that would be due on its passage and the charge for its shipping from this port in 1596. It is also likely that a number of people, we think only women, would have travelled with the artefact. This in itself would be unusual, as freight is normally unaccompanied. These facts, and the year, 1596, are all we have to work with.'

The old man nodded. 'You should call me Banou, Mr Jones, though I appreciate your respect; however, I am not a Knight of the Realm of Great Britain.' He smiled broadly, causing a deep crow's-foot to appear at the outer corner of each eye. Then he turned, scanned a number of boxes, focused on a particular label, scrutinised it closely and withdrew the box from its rack. After almost the length of his arm he stopped and let the box droop four or five centimetres thereby securing itself in position. Then, with agile fingers and the experience of a lifetime, he flipped through papyrus-like paper cards. Mostly discoloured, some totally blackened with age and some having pieces missing, there were hundreds of them. Periodically Banou stopped and peered at a card closely before moving on. 'It appears that the Thutmose dynasty had six dhows, all revered for their speed, and for two generations at least, the *Ennead* was the fastest of them all!' he said, eventually.

Keenly interested, Richard stepped behind him to look over his shoulder and saw the text on the cards as Banou himself stopped to read them.

'It is hieroglyphic script,' Richard commented, surprised. 'But only a few of the pictograms are Egyptian . . . and those are early forms. Unusually, the *Ennead* set sail from Adulis only twice that year. Look, it says so there!' Richard pointed.

At that, Banou froze. Then he turned slowly to look at Richard. For a time, his gaze was penetrating. Clearly, he was shocked. He looked back at the text and raised a pained expression. 'You are a foreigner,' he grumbled. 'Compared to me at least, just a young man, and I am told, new to the ways of the ancients. They said not to expect . . . learning. Therefore, I should help in every way possible. I should offer advice, for in these matters you are without the great assets of scholarship and age. Now tell me, how on this precious earth, would you know of text such as this?' he asked, clearly astonished and very suspicious.

Richard parried the question by asking another. 'Is this Meroitic script, Banou? Is it?'

Banou nodded. His eyes darted to the cards in the box and then back to focus on Richard. 'Indeed it is, and to the rest of the world it remains undecipherable.' Banou paused thoughtfully. 'The uncountable documents in this house have been recorded in many different languages and as many dialects over the centuries. I have knowledge of a good many, and that through a lifetime of study. So how do you ... ?'

'I could ask the same of you, Banou,' Richard replied matter-of-factly. 'I mean there is no Rosetta stone for Meroitic script, is there?'

Banou nodded again and his expression lightened. 'There are a few who can still read this script; it is a closely guarded secret. The script is derived from a much older form; one that remains lost in antiquity.'

Richard gave a knowing gesture as he patted the old man's shoulder. 'It is a long story, Banou,' he said quietly. 'And one I don't have time to recite. I have studied a written language very similar to this, remarkably similar I have to say. Perhaps even the one to which you refer. With the aid of modern technology, it was made possible for me to decipher, and that is the truth of it.'

The old man gestured with open palms towards Richard; an encouragement for him to reveal more. At that moment though, Richard noticed a faded blue motif tattooed on the palm of Banou's right hand. Gently, Richard took hold of his hand and peered at the tattoo. After several seconds, he let go. His thoughts raced as Naomi sprang to mind, and what she had said but a few days earlier: *"There are others, they help where they can."* Was Banou, one of those others, he thought, and what does he know?

'May I ask what is the significance of that symbol tattooed on your palm?'

'It is the mark of an ancient religious order, Mr Jones, one long since forgotten, and long irrelevant to this world. In truth, there is not much to know, as nought remains of it – only that I am descended from it and with that, some knowledge of this text is passed.'

Damn! He doesn't know, thought Richard. 'May we continue?' Richard asked, taking the papyrus card from between the fingers of Banou's left hand and studying it intently.

There was some text that Richard could not understand, but incredibly, most of it, he could. After a few moments, he looked back at Banou. 'Would these records use the Gregorian calendar, our calendar?' he enquired, deferentially.

'The Gregorian calendar was introduced in 1582, if I recall, by Pope Gregory XIII. It was quickly accepted as the common system for trading throughout this entire region.

I should say that these particular records use that system.'

Richard looked again at the discoloured piece of card.

'Then we should look again at the records for the third day of the third month.'

Banou nodded. He found a suitable place in the box to start and began slowly rechecking through the cards.

'You know, the number *three* just keeps cropping up in all this,' Richard commented to Preston. 'By that I mean the number *three* and its *multiples*. I just can't help thinking that there is some relevance here. The image of the crop circle I saw in London, it appeared in a field of wheat on Highclere Hill in Hampshire, and again almost the exact image was discovered to be Mayan . . . thousands of years older. It had thirty-three rays. Then there is Naomi's lineage, with its thirty-three year cycle.'

Preston looked confused.

'Forget that!' Richard said, abruptly. He paused. 'And the *three* great pyramids on the Giza Plateau. However, there are *nine* pyramids in total . . . the other *six*, reputedly being the tombs of queens. Three to the second power, three squared . . . *nine*! The sacred *nine* . . . the Ennead! The triangle too, directly related, and the basis of astral mathematics and alchemy. Divine triumvirates too are known in many religions, for example, in Egypt – Isis, Osiris and Horus and what of the Christian connotations, the Holy Trinity. Surely this can't be coincidence?'

At that, Banou stopped what he was doing. He glanced sideways for a moment, gestured as if to speak and then continued his search through the cards.

'Twelve months in a solar year, 2012 . . . the termination of the Mayan Long Count Calendar,' Richard continued, inspired.

'Yes,' interrupted Preston, enthusiastically. 'And what about the three wise men?'

Preston's eagerness to help made Richard shake his head.

'Okay!' Preston ventured, defensively. 'What about six, six, six, then; the mark of the . . .'

Banou interrupted. He spoke quietly, without shifting his eyes from the cards. 'The *universal denominator* is of greater significance to us all than you can possibly imagine, my young friends. The binding force is *earth, sea* and *air*. Wait! I have something!' His face brightened. 'Record of cargo loaded onto the *Ennead* on the day you specified – a casket, measuring two cubits, by two cubits by three cubits.'

'Cubits?' said Preston, his expression confused.

'An ancient system of measurement, Preston,' Richard replied. One cubit is approximately equal to the length of a forearm. That makes this casket about three feet wide, by three feet high, by five feet in length, in old imperial measurement. Say, for argument's sake, that two cubits is approximately ninety centimetres.'

'There is more!' interrupted Banou again. 'The tax paid to the port authority was for the casket being filled with gold – a princely sum indeed. For the ship's owner, there would be more to pay. There is no other note of the casket's contents. Ah, this may be of interest! It notes a manifest. Nine women travel with the cargo, including three maidens!'

'That's it! That's it!' barked Richard. 'Where was the ship bound? Where did it go? Banou?'

Banou shook his head, 'the writing is all but faded; I cannot read it.'

'Ugh, no, please,' gasped Richard, in exasperation, trying to take the flimsy paper.

'Wait, it says the voyage is planned for six months – they sail far to the east!' Banou stared at Richard, his eyes fired. 'We should look for record of its return – in the month of September. It is all we have.'

Richard's frustrations were plain to see as he shook his head and squeezed the bridge of his nose between thumb and forefinger. Then, as if on cue, a suppressed digital tone disturbed the silence. Simultaneously, Richard felt his telephonic pager vibrate. He withdrew it from an inside coat pocket. It was an abrive from Marretti, it read:

> There is a militia patrol at the Hanging Gate. The situation is developing. I do not like the look of this. They know I am here and are growing suspicious. We are on government property, normally they will not enter. We do not have much time. Quickly!

Richard looked at Banou. 'We are running out of time!' he said bluntly.

Banou replaced the card and the box and then shuffled a little further along the shelf, running his fingers over several labels then he stopped, nodded and tapped a slender finger on another box end – his long, discoloured fingernail caught both Richard's and Preston's attention. Banou pulled the entire box from its rack, gave it to Richard to hold and delved into its contents some way along its length. He pulled out a card, read it and nodded, before replacing it and shuffling along the line a little more. He pulled another. 'I have it!' he said. His eyes darted to Richard and then back to the card. 'Record of the *Ennead's* return to Adulis, September 21st.' Banou read the card slowly and then he reread it. His expression changed. 'It was indeed an unusual agreement,' he continued. 'The *Ennead's* master was to receive full payment when the cargo and its charges reached their intended destination. There is a note that the dhow's owners themselves paid the full tax due to the port authority in advance of the *Ennead's* departure.' A brief smile flickered on Banou's face. 'Only a very beautiful woman could coax such an agreement . . . *cherchez la femme*,' he chuckled to himself and continued to read the card. 'I have something more,' he said eventually. 'Here the owners ask for a rebate from the port authorities, as the cargo was never delivered.'

'What?'

'It is written here.'

Richard exhaled loudly. 'Is there anything else, Banou, anything at all?'

'You must realise my young friend, that these are *not* chronicles. Nor for that matter are they historical annotations, as none exist. These are documents of financial transactions, meticulously made and by way of their official ownership, providentially preserved.' Banou paused, reading further only to himself. After a while, he looked up at Richard. 'It says that the *Ennead* was captured on the high seas near the island of Jedabah by a fighting ship. The *Ennead*'s master stated that the ship flew colours that were layers of red, white and blue and that sighting of such vessels had grown frequent in the southern ocean. Whilst he would always avoid them, this ship came upon them through the light of a rising sun. With no escape, he bartered his most precious cargo in order to gain release, which included the casket on which tax was pre-paid. That is why a rebate request directed to the Adulis authorities is recorded here. The dhow's master never received payment from his passengers.' Banou nodded knowingly. 'Yes, it says that the *Ennead*'s cargo was given over as ransom – it seems that they were pirated!'

'God! This is impossible, it really is – like looking for a needle in a haystack!' declared Richard, shaking his head in dismay.

'I know of Jedabah,' Banou whispered, unperturbed by Richard's despondency. 'It is an island in the Indian Ocean and lies close to the great southern trade route. Arab seamen used it for centuries, millennia even, as a food and water stop. It is mentioned many times in our records. A paradise with fresh water and a strange flightless bird that was easy to catch, as well as nourishing. The island, although visited frequently by passing seafarers, lay uninhabited until the sixteenth century. I have seen a record that describes men from the great ocean to the west setting encampment – thereafter the island was avoided. The foreigners did not stay. Nevertheless, the Arabs lamented its discovery, as it was never again regarded as a safe haven.'

Richard sighed. 'Is there anywhere else that we can look, Banou?' he asked, casting a wary eye at his chronometer, 'otherwise this is the end of the road.'

Banou rubbed his chin thoughtfully. 'Yes. Clearly, the authorities wanted a full explanation before any rebate was paid and witness reports too, no doubt. We should look in accounts ledgers for that period.'

'Do they exist?' asked Richard dumfounded.

'Some do, and I have been here long enough to know exactly where they are. Follow me ... quickly.'

Richard and Preston followed in Banou's wake, into another room on the same floor. To them, it looked like all the others – floor to ceiling shelving, dark, narrow corridors and dank, stale air. This time, however, the curator knew exactly where to look and within minutes, he was withdrawing a box from its rack. He flipped excitedly through the documents. Richard's telephonic pager vibrated in his pocket, another abrive; he read it immediately:

> They are coming in.
> Passing through the Hanging Gate.
> This is dangerous.
> You have 5 minutes!

Richard looked up at Preston. 'There's trouble outside, we haven't much time.'

'Ah . . . I have it,' Banou interrupted, in a satisfied manner. 'This is very interesting. Not for as long as I can remember have I made such a discovery . . .'

'What does it say, Banou? Hurry!'

'It says that the fighting ship was identified as the *Prince Nassau,* as its marking was recalled and a copy made by a crewman on the *Ennead*. This was later translated by scribes in Adulis, and the colours too were recognised as from the "sealand" far towards the setting sun.'

'And . . .?'

'It appears that the ship's captain was, to some extent anyway, a gentleman. It states that after stripping the *Ennead* of its cargo, he said that he could not be responsible for the safety of any of the women who insisted on boarding his ship.'

'So for them to remain with the cargo, would endanger their lives – that's what it means.'

Banou shrugged. 'It appears the captain's men had been

at sea for over seven months and had not seen a woman in all that time.' Banou looked up. 'Obviously, he felt he could not trust his men in such circumstances and would not vouch for the women's safety.'

'Is that all?' Richard was beginning to worry that their time was pouring through the holes of this sieve of an archive. 'There must be something else?'

Banou shrugged again. He looked at the next card in line. 'In truth I know not, for nothing else is written. What is fact is that this account carries the mark of a woman known as the "Elder". This forms part of a sworn statement given to the authorities by the *Ennead's* master. It seems that he continued east in order to trade. Only with a suitable profit from the voyage did he return to Adulis. There is further account of duty paid on fine silk and jewellery. The date annotated is 29th September 1596. It seems a rebate *was* paid.'

'What of the women, Banou? Is there any further mention?'

'No, there is none. We can only speculate. Nine women, three of them young and penniless . . . and there would be debts. Perhaps a period of service before release – with good fortune, perhaps they were allowed to return from whence they came.'

'Heartbroken! They would have been heartbroken,' commented Richard sadly. 'Banou, can I see the card to see if I recognise the mark of the "Elder"?'

Banou offered Richard the card. 'The mark is a simple

pictogram, probably an initial. Perhaps the mark of their house?' he suggested.

'Yes. It looks to be a very early Egyptian pictogram; a hieroglyphic symbol from the first dynasty,' Richard concluded. 'Interesting that in the sixteenth century, this woman would continue to write in a long forgotten form.' Richard shrugged.

'In any case, it is simply the letter "V".'

'There is nothing more,' Banou said sadly.

Richard paused, he looked at Banou and then at Preston. 'Wait a minute! I have stood before a statue of a *Prince Nassau*, even taken an image of it . . . as a tourist. Now, where was it?'

'There's a *Nassau* in the Bahamas, Boss. I've been there, it's a holiday destination . . . well, used to be!' Preston offered.

Richard shook his head. 'No, that's not it.' He rubbed his temples and then looked back at Preston. 'Your telephonic pager, Preston, do you have a signal?'

Preston pulled the device from his trouser pocket and stared at the tiny display screen. 'Yes, but it's very weak. We can't break the communication protocol though, Boss – it might compromise our position. On these models only abrives are scattered; you know that!'

Richard considered the implications for a moment. 'Yes, you are right. Look, Preston, we have to take the risk, time's running out. Open on the WorldNet, type in "Prince Nassau". See what it comes up with.'

Preston was in two minds, but his finger moved quickly on the keypad. After a few seconds, the screen lit up with a response. 'I have something!' he said excitedly.

'Go on!'

'Prince Mauritius Van Nassau – member of a Burgundian noble family who were made Stadtholders of Holland, Zeeland and Friesland, Counts of Nassau, and the Princes of Orange by Charles V.'

Richard smiled. 'Of course! That's where I saw it – the statue stands in Port Louis, the capital of Mauritius. Yes. The island *is* named after a *Prince Mauritius*, a Dutch aristocratic figure. The Portuguese discovered the island in the early sixteenth century, but it was the Dutch who set up the first colony and installed the first governor. That was some time later. Natural disasters, cyclones, flooding and the plague got the better of them, though, if I recall. By the early eighteenth century, they had abandoned the island and a few years later the French took possession. A French colony, King Louis XV . . . hence Port Louis!'

'Do you think that they took their contraband back to the island – the crew of the *Prince Nassau*, I mean?' Preston interjected.

Richard nodded. 'Seems very likely – after all it was their base port.' A wave of optimism swept over Richard's face. 'It is a good lead, I am sure of it!' Richard looked at his chronometer. 'We must leave.'

Banou tapped his finger thoughtfully on the card and then rubbed his chin. 'The island countless generations of Arab seafarers called Jedabah later became known as Mauritius; such enlightenment?' He smiled faintly as he replaced the index and the three men hurried to the stairs.

Richard still excited by their find said: 'It's a paradise, Banou. I've been many times and its history is fascinating. Back in those days, it was blessed with abundant fresh water and tropical forests. Fishing was easy inside the reef and food on the ground was plentiful.'

'Yes . . . yes, my young adventurer,' interjected Banou breathlessly. 'The strange, flightless bird . . . it was so simple to catch!'

Richard stopped on the step below and turned. 'Banou, you're right! The dodo! The bloody dodo bird! Long since extinct. A species unique to Mauritius . . . it evolved in isolation. It lost the ability to fly because it didn't need to; it had no natural predators. Its remains have only ever been found on Mauri . . .' Richard looked up at Preston. 'Send an abrive to Rothschild. Tell him we need a lift to Mauritius, absolute priority. See what he can do!' Richard then turned and continued down the stairs. 'It must be the best part of three thousand miles to Mauritius from here,' he said, over his shoulder. 'Much too far for the Tiltrotor, but we *will* need it for the pickup. Tell him to standby for precise timings . . . no, on second thoughts, tell him to liaise with Marretti!'

Richard, on the ground floor, offered his hand to Banou. 'I think we may be onto something.' He could not contain a broad grin. At that moment, two loud thuds reverberated through the entire house. Richard's eyes widened, he knew instantly the implications – somebody had come calling and they were not friends. Richard's pager vibrated; another abrive from Marretti:

> It is too late. You have visitors.
> Do not use the front door.
> Ask the curator. The rear entrance is still
> safe. On foot, I am waiting. Now!

'Banou,' Richard said, thrusting the pager back into his pocket. 'The back of the building, the rear entrance ... it's our only way out!'

'Follow me!'

Preston sent his abrive. They raced down and across the hall as three more loud knocks echoed. Somebody outside thumped on the door. They heard shouting. Down another flight of stairs into the cellar and along a number of corridors and through several doors they ran until they arrived at a back entrance. Banou quickly released four black iron bolts and turned a large key in the door; the lock responded with a clunk. He gestured for Richard and Preston to stand back out of sight and then just slightly opened the heavy wooden door. He gulped, taken aback as Marretti seemed to appear from nowhere.

'Follow me!' Marretti said, wasting no time on pleasantries.

Preston was out first. Richard turned to Banou. 'Thank you, Sir,' he said, shaking the old man's hand. 'Please, no heroics. If they press you or any of your people for that matter, you tell them where we went . . . agreed?'

Banou nodded in a kindly manner.

'*Come on!*' Marretti shouted back. Richard sprinted down the narrow stone path to catch up.

Banou closed and rebolted the door. 'Good luck my young friend and may the merciful one extend an open hand to you,' he said, softly. 'Something tells me that I have not seen the last of you. Before my days are spent, you will be back, *inshaallah*.'


At the far end of the path Richard saw Preston and Marretti bear right at a T-junction. He sprinted after them only to skid on the wet rounded stones and his foot caught one of two parallel grooves worn into the cobble by centuries of cartwheels. He felt a sharp pain in his ankle but he ran on. Ahead he saw Preston and Marretti hesitate. Charlie looked back at him, his expression anxious; their path was being funnelled by tall stonewalls on either side. Further along the road, Richard saw their route was blocked by a pair of imposing gates. There was no going back, not now. He ran on, his unbuttoned coat flailing behind him.

As he approached the gates, Richard could see a row of hefty metal spikes running across the top; with no idea what lay beyond and their lethal look, options were very limited. Then they all heard the faint sound of whistles being blown – they were going over the wall!

Preston positioned himself at the base of the old fortification to the left of the gates. As Richard neared, he could see why: two heavy iron buckles straddled them and were secured in place by large, rusty padlocks. The layered stone construction of the wall towered some two metres above Preston's head. He stood resolutely, with his hands cupped together.

Richard saw Charlie run at Preston. Clearly, they had already formulated a plan. Charlie put a foot in Preston's hands and with an energetic jump and an almighty lift from Preston, managed to scale the wall. With outstretched arms lunging upwards, Charlie reached out. He caught the capping stones and hauled himself up. In the distance, the sound of a siren and men shouting echoed around. In an instant, Charlie was on top of the wall; he crouched, turned, and checked what lay on the other side.

'Now you, Boss!' Preston shouted, gesturing at Richard to make the run.

Richard took a few paces backwards and launched himself, slamming against the weathered stones. Preston groaned with the effort. Richard reached out, his left hand found no purchase but his right caught a stone edge. He was close to falling but Charlie bent down and gripped his wrist. Richard caught a toehold in the wall and swung his body to the left. This time his flailing hand caught the edge of a capping stone and he held it. Beyond, a whistle blew excitedly; the shrill sound penetrating and haunting above a melee. Men shouted to one another. They were getting nearer.

Richard's woollen coat was a hindrance, but with a massive effort and with the help of Charlie – who now had a good hold of Richard's upper arm – he reached the top. The wall was thick, almost a metre, but it was crumbling with age.

The distant noise of a search team galvanised Preston. He ran at the wall and managed to find a purchase in the old stones and with agonising slowness climbed to within reach of Richard and Charlie, who were lying along the wall, head to head, to reach down for him. Richard's hand clamped round Preston's wrist and he held him as Charlie supported him under a shoulder; between the two of them, Preston was able to grasp the coping stones and pull himself up. Richard looked back along the alley to where it widened only to see two vehicles screeching to a halt; one was a canvas-clad troop lorry with the infamous red "T" emblazoned on its side.

A short volley of sublets ricocheting of the wall just metres away took all three men by surprise. The "ping" of rebounding, high velocity projectiles made them cower briefly. Richard looked up; militiamen seemed to pour from the back of the lorry, while others rounded the corner at the far end of the alley; they came from the direction of the house. Richard thought of Banou; was he safe? Another hail of sublets strafed the wall.

'Come on, come on, man . . . this way!' shouted Charlie

to Richard, who still lay flat on the wall, stomach down, his grip on Preston's trouser leg insurance against Preston falling backwards; he was in a precarious position. Gunfire rattled . . . *ping, ping, ping, ping* sang out as a line of sublets ricocheted off the stone; sharp splinters flew in all directions.

Preston clambered to his knees and turned, his eyes widened in horror. The advancing group, numbering at least twenty men, were no more than sixty metres away. There was an officer. He wore green serge and a cap with a red badge. He led the charge. He held an automatic pistol in one hand and a whistle in the other, which he blew and blew as if crazed. The men around him shouted unintelligibly and waved their batons and weapons wildly.

Preston was safe and crawled towards Charlie on all fours; Richard followed on his feet but bent double; the capping stones were loose and dislodged under their weight, some pieces crashed to the ground.

In full flight and now just forty metres away, the Tongsei officer raised his pistol and fired again. Instantly, sublets jounced around Preston's feet, Richard danced to avoid them. The sound of a machine gun ran out, but ill-timed and wayward, Richard heard the sublets penetrate the wooden gates with dull, alarming thuds. They had just seconds remaining.

On the other side of the wall a street bustled with activity. There was a long shallow ramp leading up to the gates; the general street level looked perhaps two metres lower than the side that they had scaled; it looked daunting. Further along there were a number of awnings; beneath were the street shops, part of the souk.

'Over you go, Preston, onto that blind . . . now!' Charlie shouted.

Preston rolled off the wall and onto the sloping canvas. Shots rang out again and the shouting became perilously close. Next it was Charlie's turn and over he went, leaving Richard to dive for cover. The awning made use of the wall for support and had wooden joists forming its sides and front and within this frame, soaked discoloured material sagged heavily with the weight of the two men. From below somebody complained bitterly in a strange language.

Alarmed by scrambling noises on the "militia" side, Richard needed little encouragement to follow his friends – but the blind would surely collapse with three and it was a long drop. He held off.

Preston, who had tumbled all the way down, appeared hampered in the sagging material as if in a loose hammock, but Charlie rolled only partway and then to the side. Meanwhile a round, oriental face appeared above the wall. Richard gasped. The man wore an olive-green metal helmet with the dreaded red T above a narrow peak. He began to scream, his eyes ablaze and then he dropped one hand from his hold on the capping stone. He was reaching for something. Richard was having none of it. He swivelled on his chest, recoiled his foot and gave the man an almighty kick. Down he went. Richard heard the dull thud and an accompanying groan.

Richard spun round again; he slid across the wet, lichen- covered stones to the street side and without delay rolled off the top. He had in mind Preston's difficulty and maintained his tumbling momentum until he crashed into the wooden joist at the bottom; adrenalin made him immune to any hurt. In one flowing movement he reached over and took hold of the frame from beneath and then he pivoted his body on it and was over. Realising that there was still a sizeable drop and an uneven surface on which to land, he eased down to arm's length. Charlie was on his feet and making appeasing gestures towards the irate shop owner, but Preston still hesitated. There the two men hung, somewhat precariously, for a few seconds. Loosened rubble and a heavy stone tumbled between them. More than a metre to the mud, Preston seemed discouraged by the unwelcome attention of a small, unkempt and vicious-looking dog that snapped at his ankles. Richard dropped, landed squarely and swung a kick at it. The shop owner started ranting again in protest. People stared. The horn of a passing car beeped. A startled camel reared up. Charlie pulled a wad of notes from his coat pocket and shoved them into the man's hand; he said something in the local dialect and then gestured towards a row of hanging djellabas. Preston landed. Unfortunately for the dog it was payback time, and Preston looked much bigger now; it yelped and scampered off into the shop. The infuriated owner cooled; he seemed placated by Charlie's offer and pulled three coarse woollen cloaks from the line. Richard heard the sound of tumbling stones above his head and stepped beneath the blind as more rubble fell to the ground. Charlie immediately handed over two cloaks and then in a practised flurry swung his around his shoulders, his head disappearing beneath its hood. 'Follow me!' he ordered, from the shadows.

Richard and Preston followed suit and then walked off in studied nonchalance. As they hurried past the two gates, metal butts and wooden batons smashed violently against the other side and militiamen shouted in frustration; the officer's whistle sounded clearly; like a magnet, it drew support. People, who had stopped and gathered, watched the three figures go, while others looked back and pointed accusingly. A nearing police siren grew ominous.

The din spooked another heavily laden camel – this one panicked. It snorted and reared as it slipped in the red, slimy mud, dislodging boxes from its back. Its Arabic-looking driver responded by pulling hard on its rein and with a whip in his other hand coaxed the animal to continue. An accompanying friend who immediately set about reclaiming the lost stores gave Charlie a look of odious disdain. Charlie gestured some form of apology to the young man and then rechecked the area; he appraised both directions and then indicated their way. The three men hurried on and soon disappeared into the throng of the busy street.

Richard woke with a jolt. Eyes wide, he stared at the sloping, watermarked ceiling. Cracks in the plaster that radiated like the tributaries of a river, caused him to think of the great Amazon delta and the awe-inspiring panorama common to the 'America South' re-entry profile. What he wouldn't give to be a shuttle pilot again, and back a few years too, when the sky was still blue and the brilliance of pristine, white, billowing cloud proclaimed his return to the living planet. Never again would he complain of the tedium of another routine flight from Andromeda to the Cape, nor at the enforced automated flight regimes that eroded his personal skills, or even at the absence of coffee when inconsiderate passengers demanded the undivided attention of his Flight Attendant. Just to sit on the flight deck of an S2 again; that would be enough.

A tiny spider scurried across a dust-laden web that straddled the corner not far above his head. It was so quiet in the room at that moment that Richard thought he could hear the arachnid's delighted squeals as it twirled an unfortunate fly with impressive coordination, whilst encasing it in debilitating strands of silk. Only then, whilst focusing on the reality of life, did Richard's senses re-register the pungent smell of rotting wood and damp, stale breath, and only then, seemingly, did his back complain, more a result of the hard wooden slats of his makeshift bed than the previous day's excitement.

There was movement in the room; Richard turned his head to look. It was Asharf, sprawled on a cushioned sofa; one that was clearly too short for him. Richard checked his chronometer: 07:08; he had slept longer than he had intended. Across the room, Naomi appeared fast asleep on the only proper bed the house had to offer, whilst Asharf too, despite his contortions, seemed silently contented.

Richard had slept fully clothed and left the room as quietly as leather boots on wooden floors would allow. He kept a wary eye below as he descended the narrow staircase. Downstairs, Preston sat in a chair adjacent to the window that overlooked the main street. For Richard's benefit he carefully moved the cutain and glimpsed outside again, surveying the street in both directions.

'It's getting light, Boss, and there's still no sign of Marretti.'

Richard nodded. 'We are wasting time here, Preston, precious time.'

'If he ended up driving to Asmara for another suitable car it, could be an hour or two yet.'

Richard nodded again. 'There must be something that we can do; I hate just sitting here, waiting! Did you get an answer from Rothschild?'

'All I know, Boss, is that he opened the abrive. But I got nothing back before Marretti told me to turn off all of our electronics.'

Richard walked across to the window and took a fleeting

look through the curtain at the street scene for himself. It was dank and miserable but a respite in the drizzle was encouraging. A few locals walked past and on the other side of the street a donkey, laden with firewood, struggled head down and bedraggled; a young man, seemingly with little compassion, walked behind and slapped it occasionally across the rump with a cane. Richard was sorry for the animal and shook his head. 'It looks quiet, deserted even. I might take a quick look outside, do a local recce, just to be sure.'

'Is that wise, Boss? Marretti said stay inside at all costs. The streets are crawling with undesirables and you just don't know who is who.'

'Yeah, but it should be okay at this time of the morning!' Richard rubbed his stubble and wiped some sleep from the corners of his eyes. 'Listen, I want to check out something down by the harbour. Two blocks down on the right I noticed a street called The Wharf. It's not too difficult to imagine it leading down to the harbour. I'll be an hour max, back before Marretti returns, definitely.'

Preston grimaced. 'I'm with you, but are you sure, Boss?'

'You stay here, an hour maximum.'

Preston sighed loudly. 'I'm not keen on the idea myself, and I am supposed to be your close cover. And what about our communication problem?'

Richard seemed convinced. 'Don't worry, Preston. I have no intention of putting myself in a situation where I need backup. I'll slip out the back door. You lock it behind me and keep a sharp lookout – Colonel Bogey theme to let me in. Understand?'

Preston nodded, reluctantly agreeing. 'Something to eat first, Boss?' he suggested.

'Ration packs?'

'Yeah, but special service issue, not the space packs. Actually, they're not too bad.' Preston raised his eyebrows and a smile of satisfaction crept over his face. 'In fact, I quite enjoyed my breakfast. I can certainly recommend the *protosoy* bar!'

Richard looked at a number of shredded plastic wrappings on a nearby table. He dwelt on them and on Preston's innocuous remark for a moment or two, before looking back at him. His expression caused Preston's smile to drop. 'In a year from now,' Richard said, prophetically. 'Unless you and I are lucky enough to be back on the moon, or Mars for that matter, there won't be much else to eat that's not in a can. I wonder if you will recommend the *protosoy* bar with such enthusiasm then, Preston.'

Preston shrugged. The corner of his mouth twitched.

Richard cast the brown and cream coloured djellaba over his shoulders. He fastened the white, animal bone buttons and pulled up the hood – only now did he notice its strong odour. 'At least I smell like a bloody camel!' he commented from beneath the folds.

Preston was too concerned to smile. He opened the

door cautiously allowing Richard to slip outside. Richard waited until he heard Preston turn the key in the oversized door lock and then walked rapidly down the garden path. He checked the alley, one eye peering round the corner, and then he paused, and checked again – clear! It had rained overnight and a heavy dampness hung in the air and pools of water dotted the ground.

Although overcast and dull, enough light filtered through to proclaim a defiant sunrise. He pulled up the folds of his hood, more against the cold than any prying eyes and decided to use the alley, which ran parallel to East Street, to his advantage and join the gently inclined main street much further up; after all, the direction of the harbour was obvious enough. He turned left and briskly walked some three hundred metres, checking periodically the crossing streets for militiamen.

Eventually, the alley broadened into a well-used but narrow road – although interestingly, its surface remained firm underfoot. Long, straight, clearly well drained, with signs of grooved stone gullies on both sides and evidently, at one time anyway, leading directly out of town, this new streetscape reminded him of Pompeii – although on a much smaller scale. As he progressed he passed numerous ruined buildings, adding weight to his supposition that this was originally a principal thoroughfare of some antiquity, maybe the main street towards the busy port. After all, he concluded thoughtfully, it was not just Nubian architecture that had influenced this region.

After another three hundred metres or so, the road terminated at an open area. The surrounding houses became smaller, more recent and shanty-like. This must have been a small park or a children's playground, thought Richard, as he warily began to skirt its perimeter in an anticlockwise direction. Now, however, as a climbing frame and a dismantled children's slide lay heaped in a corner, this area was clearly a keep for livestock – pack animals and the like. Richard carefully avoided a number of dung heaps and the rubbish that lay littered around and scanned the area further along and to his left. Twenty metres away, he could see a gravel footpath leading off between two houses and on further inspection, neither house appeared occupied. Richard hastened across the open ground. He paused for a moment within the relative cover afforded by the close-set houses. At the far end of the alleyway, an occasional pedestrian crossed the gap. Richard assessed this as a convenient place to enter East Street; he was certainly far enough away from the safe house to avoid compromising it. Anyway, he may only need to cross it, in order to find a better way down to the harbour. Keeping a wary eye, he quickly covered the alleyway's length.

Where the gravel path opened onto the main street there was a large puddle. A figure, which passed close by, having sidestepped the muddy water, startled Richard. Dirty feet in sandals kicked out beneath the grubby cloak and walking downhill with a face hidden beneath a hood, the man paid Richard no heed.

Richard loitered uneasily. For no apparent reason, other than perhaps the occasional passer-by who, despite his camouflage, stared curiously, Richard's heart began to thump. He leaned carefully around the corner of the left hand house to check for militia before crossing. First, he looked left, it seemed clear, and then he looked to his right and instantly gasped. He could hardly believe what he saw coming towards him. Instantly, he pulled back into the deep shadows of the alleyway. Surely not, not here!

A burst of adrenalin quickened his thoughts. He assessed his situation and made a decision. Pulling his hood well over his head he dragged his shoulder around the corner of the house and stayed close enough to the wall to avoid the deepest part of the puddle, then he stepped from his cover and walked towards the apparition. He watched its ungainly progress as they neared one another; sticky, slippery mud impeding them both.

The figure neared. It was tall and gangly and dressed in a loose, grey, fleece-like cape – it was this that Richard had recognised. Swallowed deep inside the folds of its ample hood, the figure's face was lost.

It lurched, making haphazard progress and frequently slithered in the mud. Occasionally, a misplaced foot sank, producing a footprint that was uncommonly deep and alien. Richard continued; he dared not turn; he dared not look up, not now. Within earshot, he heard it. There was no question. The buzzing, whirling sound grew louder, haunting him. An arm's length apart, Richard put his weight behind his shoulder as the figure gave no ground and seemed intent on barging past him.

Its body was solid and hard and it knocked Richard painfully against the wall. He turned and tracked the figure as it continued and watched as it splashed unconcerned through the deep puddle at the head of the alleyway. Richard noticed the reddened water run off the material of its cape without a trace, like droplets off a duck's back.

The mechanical noise retreated down the street. Thankful not to be recognised, Richard slipped back into the alleyway and stopped to reassess; yet another hazard to contend with. With extra diligence he retraced his steps.

Richard knocked on the door. No answer. He tried the shutters, which rattled but remained resolutely shut. He stood for a moment deep in thought, his heart still pounding from the shock, then he hit his forehead with the heel of his hand. Idiot! Colonel Bogey! That was what they had agreed. Da-da . . . da, da, da, da – da – da, he tapped secretively on the door with his knuckles. Instantly the door opened and Preston dragged Richard into the room and rebolted the door. In the candlelit room Naomi looked up from her seat, and Asharf, hurrying down the stairs, missed the last two steps and nearly fell headlong. Richard blew out the candle and released a shutter to look furtively up and down the street.

'What is it, Boss?'

'Trouble! I've just encountered one of our mechanical

friends, a Humatron.'

'Where?' cried Naomi.

'On the street, back along a bit.'

Asharf came over to the window to peer through the small gap and shivered. 'I had hoped never to meet one of those things again, *Effendi*.'

Preston's eyes widened as he looked at Richard. A sliver of light illuminated Richard's face. 'The same model you decapitated on the *Columbus*, Preston, before the *Enigma* took us out.'

Preston nodded. 'How can I forget?' he said. He glanced at Asharf, and could tell he was scared.

'Our encounter in Cairo, inside the Great Pyramid,' Richard explained. 'Shook us all up a bit.'

Preston seemed to understand and looked back at Richard. 'The HU40s that Rothschild mentioned during our brief.'

'Yeah . . . and he mentioned five. Two we stopped in Cairo; which means that another two units could well be wandering the streets. That robot is here for a reason, Preston . . . there is no doubt about that.'

'Where was it, exactly?'

Richard paused. 'Coming this way.'

Naomi gasped. Asharf's expression dropped as he moved back from the window.

Richard raised his hand in an effort to quell their anxiety. 'Making slow progress, though,' he offered, clearly considering the implications.

Preston's eyes narrowed. He sensed that Richard was formulating a plan and he was getting the wrong vibes. 'Then we button up and lie low until it's passed. Do you agree? Boss? Rothschild's brief was clear on this point. *We avoid Humatrons at all costs.*'

Richard shook his head menacingly. Preston began to look concerned; he went to speak, to reiterate their orders, but Richard interrupted. 'If one of those damned things is here, then so are the other two, I guarantee it, and probably a controller too. They are not looking for us; no, it's likely that they think we are dead, remember?' Purposely avoiding Naomi's stare, Richard scanned the darkened room and breathed a deep sigh. 'They are looking for something specific and the fact that they and we are here in Adulis is no coincidence.'

Preston fidgeted nervously. 'What are you thinking of doing, Boss? Better I know now.'

'We snatch it! An ambush and then we take it out.'

Preston's eyes widened in trepidation, 'Not again!'

'Richard, no!' exclaimed Naomi, clearly horrified at the proposal.

'Listen! In a few minutes, that machine will walk past this door. It's on its way down to the docks, I know it, and I mean to find out why. The three of us . . . Naomi, I want you upstairs – you will be our lookout. Asharf, the candle please.' Richard locked the shutters and said to Preston, 'We surprise it! Asharf opens the door, we drag it in, you pull its hood down and I take its head off with the ISTAN;

clean as a whistle . . . understand?'

Preston shook his head in reply.

'We have done it before, so no problem,' Richard added reassuringly.

Richard had briefed Preston on his specialist secret service weapon and the Humatron's cape – which he now knew was lined with Samite – on their flight from Khartoum. He waited for a response. Preston's palms began to sweat as he considered failure but he knew that there was little point in trying to dissuade Richard. Reluctantly he nodded his approval.

'Richard . . . please! It is too dangerous! Why can we not let this, this, machine devil pass? I am in favour of going to Mauritius, but not this!'

'*Naomi*,' Richard emphasised, turning to look at her. 'These things always seem to be one step behind us. Eventually, they *will* catch up with us again, and when that happens, we may not be quite so lucky. Something is going on here . . . it could be important and anyway, I have a plan. Please, Naomi,' Richard gestured upstairs. 'Give us as much notice as possible . . . then call at ten metres and again at five. As it passes the door, shout, *now*! and leave the rest to us.'

Without saying another word, but shaking her head more in sorrow than disapproval, Naomi turned and climbed the stairs.

Suddenly, Naomi shouted from upstairs. 'I can see it

Richard . . . thirty metres away!' She was watching through a tear in the curtain.

Downstairs, Asharf made ready behind the door. Richard had withdrawn his ISTAN and its green blade glowed menacingly in the darkness. Preston crouched; his left hand hovering over a thigh holster that contained a fully charged static baton. Like a police truncheon, but made of polytetramide plastic, the baton incorporated a powerful capacitor that could store a potent static electrical charge. With five settings, and the third able to render a man unconscious in an instant, the weapon was a good backup. However, he would need to be very careful before using it and press the discharge button only if he was sure that nobody else was in contact with the robot.

Standing away from the window, Naomi watched the hooded figure make its lurching progress towards them. As if transfixed, she stared and seemed mesmerised by some strange aura emanating from the robot that grew stronger and more intimidating with its approach. She had felt it during her previous encounter with these machines. There was a personality, like a life force, but afflicted, stunted and woeful. People avoided it; even crossing the street to do so. She watched a passing car, which, skidding helplessly in the mud slewed too close to it. In response, the figure lashed out, making a sizable dent in the vehicle's bodywork. The driver did not stop. 'Ten metres, Richard, ten metres!' Naomi shouted, anxiously.

The three men made ready.

'*Five!*'

Naomi pressed her face against the windowpane in order to look down. Asharf's hand twitched on the door handle. Preston made ready to pounce. Adrenaline coursed through Richard's veins. 'The hood, Preston,' Richard reminded, his eyes ablaze.

'*Now!*' Naomi screamed.

In that instant, Asharf wrenched the door open. The caped figure stepped into view, its head shrouded by a drooping hood. Richard reached out, put an arm around its neck and pulled. Completely taken by surprise, the machine was slow to react and it slipped awkwardly in the mud. Now Preston had hold. Richard put a foot against the doorframe and together the two men heaved the robot inside. The machine tripped on the threshold, half staggered through the doorway and in a flailing flurry, crashed onto the hard stone floor. Face down and restricted, the machine's head thrashed beneath its cape and it tried to extend its long neck. It pushed up with its arms, like a press up. Richard stabbed the back of its head with his heel and the robot responded with a piercing electronic howl – a penetrating, terrorised shrill that lasted for seconds and from his facial expression, clearly sent a shiver down the spine of a passerby who hurried past the door. Asharf kicked the machine's legs clear and slammed the door shut. The machine reached out and grasped one of Preston's legs, pulling him to the floor. Asharf dived onto its back. Preston, his face contorted with pain, kicked out wildly. Asharf stretched across the machine's bulk, trying to grasp the hood and pull it back. Richard, who also had a hold with one hand, tugged at it unsuccessfully. The machine sensed what was happening and pushed itself up. Whining electric motivators and loud mechanical sounds accompanied every movement. Richard tried to force the robot down, but it climbed to its knees, throwing Asharf off its back and into the window shutters, which burst open, letting in the light.

Richard scuffled with it, trying to expose a machine part. Preston withdrew his static baton. 'All clear!' he shouted. Richard jumped back. Preston lunged, jabbing the tube towards the robot's body. The robot reacted, firing out a hand that caught the baton and knocked it clear, sending it clattering across the floor. Preston fell backwards onto the tiled floor and a metallic fist crashed down perilously close to his face sending shards of stone across the room. The fleecy material of the cape was difficult to grasp, but Richard had hold again. With his right hand and with all his strength he heaved at the hood. In his left hand, he held the ISTAN high in preparation. This time he was successful and the hood peeled back to reveal the machine's x-shaped head. The robot's neck instantly extended out of Richard's reach and continued until it was too long. Its face turned to look down on Richard and seemed to register him. Two teardrop-shaped eyes glowed red and pulsated – it seemed to recognise Richard, as if programmed with his image; another piercing, warbling electronic tone reverberated around the room.

Richard stepped forward and took a swing with the ISTAN, but the machine responded quickly, moving its long neck clear again and then it too lashed out. Its metal hand caught Richard's forearm and the blow knocked the ISTAN from Richard's grip, sending it flying through the air into an adjacent wall with a loud thump.

Richard barely avoided another aggressive swipe from the machine and ran back to retrieve his weapon. The machine climbed to its feet and straightened up. Without hesitation, brave Asharf leapt onto its back again; with arms tight around the machine's neck, he hung on for dear life. Richard picked up the ISTAN and thought green, a blade appeared and then he turned back into the fray. A robotic leg, with its white cellulose skin protruded from beneath the cape. Preston saw his chance and like a footballer going for a sliding tackle, launched himself at the knee joint; his blow smashed it sideways. In that instant, the smooth but eerie whirring of motivators turned into a grating sound – there was damage!

As if in slow motion, the robot looked down at its distorted knee and then up again at Preston. Its *plasmoltec* face slowly contorted into a hideous shape and it leaned forwards towards him. Richard went for it, but the machine brushed him aside with a powerful swipe and then, with amazing speed its two arms darted out towards Preston. Metal fingers grasped Preston's neck; they extended around it and squeezed. With both hands and in desperation,

Preston pulled and tugged. Richard scrambled to his feet. Preston tried to release the cold, metallic grip, but in vain; his eyes began to bulge and he choked as his efforts were of no consequence. The machine watched intently as Preston's squirming began to subside; all the while, its red eyes pulsated rapidly – a kill!

Asharf, still on the machine's back, struggled and tugged. The robot extended its neck so that its face was close to Preston's; it focused sadistically on Preston's livid face and closed eyes. At that moment, came opportunity for Richard. He lunged forwards and lashed out with a wild swipe. The green, glowing blade of his ISTAN passed clean through the robot's neck just above its shoulder. Instantly the head and neck fell to the floor and then the bulky robot slumped forwards. Clear, oily-smelling fluid oozed from the opening.

'Ugh . . . uggggggh!' Preston gurgled.

Richard reacted. 'Quick! The hands! They are still locked around his neck!' he shouted.

Asharf stumbled forwards, grabbed the machine's wrists, held them up and presented Richard with a target. Like a surgeon, Richard sliced through the palms of both robotic hands, severing their structure. Asharf pulled the remnants clear. Simultaneously, Preston filled his lungs, sucking in air painfully, his neck a contusion of bruises. Richard breathed hard and held Preston up as he gasped.

Naomi hurried downstairs and stared at the disarray: Asharf climbing painfully off the back of the machine;

Richard trying to sit Preston by the window so that he could breathe more easily. She walked across the room purposefully, glancing at the bulk that was limp and lifeless.

'Thank the gods you have survived,' she said gently, putting a soft hand on Preston's shoulder and examining the marks around his neck. 'Can you speak?'

'Yes ma'am, just about,' Preston croaked.

'I have something that will ease the soreness,' she said, kindly. Her expression for Richard, however, was less endearing. 'Never should you underestimate these things, never!' She paused. 'Now, pray tell me, what good has this done?'

Richard smiled sheepishly. 'I do have a plan. Asharf, please, the cape.' Richard gestured.

Asharf stripped the cape from the robot, leaving its form plain to see. This was the Humatron Model HU40 and it was indeed a technological masterpiece. With a similar skeletal structure, only of Etheral alloy, and standing as tall as a man, its statistics were impressive. Naomi stared at it. In place of a ribcage was a rigid box structure that tapered at the waist. Within this, was the power plant: a combination of high capacity catholithium batteries and photoelectric converters, which, after thirty minutes exposure to white light, could produce and store enough electrical energy to power the machine for twenty-four hours. There was also an emergency power supply; a small cryptogenic power cell that, if the machine was closed-down to "retentive animation" power levels, could retain "body and mind" functional programming for twenty years or more. Also inside the boxed chest cavity were the primary memory processor banks and motivators, the latter being powerful electric motors providing mobility and immense strength. Covering the skeletal framework was a flexible celluloid skin about one centimetre thick, which provided bulk and impact resistance and sealed within this skin, under pressure, was an oily electrolytic fluid. Much like an inflated balloon, this fluid pressure gave the structure its humanoid form and in addition allowed electrical signals to pass from the "brain" to the numerous motivators. This was the warm fluid that seeped out from the robot's severed neck and dripped onto the cold flagstones, where it formed an expanding puddle around Naomi's feet.

The machine's arms were abnormally long and only the last two joints protruded from the cellulose skin that covered the four-fingered, claw-like hands. Richard leant over and picked up the robot's head. With some effort, he turned it for Naomi's benefit. Shaped like an X, but with a lower crossing point that formed two dissimilar sized triangles, it appeared disproportionately large at the end of a flexible, multi-faceted neck. Engineered with a greatly reduced diameter at the top, the neck was spliced into the rear of the head directly at the crossing point. The lower, smaller triangle was covered in a fine, silver-coloured metal grill, which itself covered two vertical slits. Richard pointed to the slits. 'Odour sensing, electronic vocal chords and, apparently, processors containing programming for several languages,' he advised.

Naomi shivered. 'It is the most evil thing I have ever seen.'

The main facial area – the upper triangle – was an advanced plasma display screen that could not only produce amazing three-dimensional images, like some precocious laptop computer, but also incorporated *plasmoltec* technology. Asharf became fixated with the last expression on the robot's face. With this state-of-the-art technology, the screen was like semi-molten plasticine; it could move, distort, stretch and contract. From a flat screen, a face – taken from just below the nose – could be conjured; moulded with all their nuances; expressions so created, fused from one to another entirely at will and also, it transpired "subconsciously" by the machine's "emotion" complex.

All this technology required power and to this end, the back of the head, together with the back of the trunk, was composed of an array of shiny, graphite-coloured photoelectric cells. Asharf prodded one of the menacing eyes with his finger; there was shape, but no light. The machine's eyes were essentially projections; images displayed on the facial screen. In liaison with Level 7 thought processes, manipulation of the screen's plasticity could produce contours that appeared to make the eyes real, even down to a "blinking" response; it was the eyes, their changing shape and colour that gave the robots their deathly, sinister appearance. Capable of infrared sight, giving vision even in the darkest environments, they glowed with an intensity that was proportional to the power levels of the machine's internal batteries.

Eventually Naomi looked up from the machine. 'It is horrible. It has no place in our time.'

Richard shrugged. 'Like it or not, Naomi, these things *will* have a part in our tomorrow, there's no holding back the advance of technology,' he said. There was thoughtful silence. 'As I said, I have a plan.' Richard looked at Asharf and then gestured towards the kitchen. 'Asharf, I need a wooden stick, something like a broom handle, please, check the kitchen.'

Asharf disappeared into the kitchen. Moments later, after causing a loud *crack*, he came out smiling. In one hand, he held a broom head and in the other, its handle.

'Perfect,' Richard congratulated, as he manoeuvred the long neck of the robot towards Asharf. 'Shove the handle up through the centre of the neck.' Asharf, who looked as confused as Naomi, did as he was asked. Pushing against each other until most of the handle disappeared into the ringed neck, Richard took hold of the remaining pole. He turned the contraption vertical so that the bottom of the neck was level with his chest and the head some way above his.

'Now Asharf, dress me in the cape.'

Naomi gasped. Asharf draped the cape over Richard's

shoulders and as Richard crouched low, pulled the hood over the robot's head. He secured the cape by a number of self-fasteners on the front seam. Richard's disguise was complete as the voluminous robe hung to the floor.

Preston who sat propped up against the adjacent wall felt his head as the feeling came back into his neck. 'Whatever you are thinking of doing with that disguise, Boss,' he croaked, 'I've a feeling that I'm not going to like it!'

Richard turned in Preston's direction and spoke from beneath the folds of material. 'I do what this damned machine was doing . . . I go down to the docks. Take a look around; meet a contact perhaps; if I'm lucky, learn something.' Preston looked unconvinced.

'Oh, Richard, why do you insist on such reckless behaviour?' Naomi asked, shaking her head.

'Because it's possible . . .'

At that instant, there was a huge crash against the front door of the house. Wood splintered around the lock. Then another deafening smash terrorized the senses and with it the thick door bowed, the hinges creaked, dust from around the doorframe filled the air.

'What the?' shouted Richard from beneath the cape.

'Someone's coming through!' Preston bellowed, and he sprang to his feet.

Moments later, as if a massive force had come against the door, it burst open. The doorframe buckled. Shattered fragments of wood and metal flew and part of the heavy black lock fired across the room and clattered onto the floor. The door smashed against the wall behind as if an explosion had ousted it and then a hulking figure filled the opening. Naomi, Preston and Asharf, taken completely by surprise, gasped in horror while Richard, only dimly aware of the situation beneath the folds of the cape, rummaged around for an opening in his cover.

The figure bent low, stepped into the room and then grew tall again. Dressed in a grey cape, it was instantly recognisable. The machine pulled off the hood to expose its triangular head. It was another machine, *another Humatron*!

Preston's face paled and they all froze, glued to the spot on which they stood. The machine extended its head. Slowly, menacingly, it rose until it touched the ceiling. It looked down on them with glowing, orange, teardrop-shaped eyes and with a wary motion it scanned the room, left and right. The *plasmoltec* face began to move, to form, to take shape, but the expression was still unclear. Then, as if selecting an emotion, its eyes narrowed and its cheeks bulged, as if to sculpt a sickly smile. From beneath the cape, twitching electric motors hummed quietly. A bony-looking metallic hand jerked backwards from beneath its cape and gripped the edge of the heavy door that now hung awkwardly on one hinge. With enraged aggravation and brute force, the robot pulled at the buckled door and slammed it shut against the distorted frame. Now ill fitting, broken light from around its periphery streamed into the room and silhouetted the eerie figure.

For what seemed like a lifetime, but could have only been a moment, there was a dreadful, pulsating silence. Were they to be killed by this inhuman alien? They hardly dared to breathe as they watched the Humatron's sightline lock onto Richard's shape as he fumbled, comically unaware of the danger and trying to indicate a message. And then part of the robot's dismembered head protruded from beneath Richard's cape. Immediately the Humatron issued a shrieking electronic tone and waited for a response. When there was no reply and the dismembered head hit the floor with a smash, the Humatron's gaze followed it to the floor. Richard's hands appeared on the front fasteners of the cloak and pulled them apart enabling him to see the danger clearly. He drew a sharp breath and as the hood fell to his shoulders he tried to indicate with his eyes, but his companions seemed frozen with fear.

Richard pulled open his cape and slowly slid a hand inside his coat as the Humatron's gaze shifted back to him. It was then that the machine seemed to sense the pungent smell of electrolytic oil and its focus was drawn towards the body of its mutilated colleague lying motionless on the ground near Preston, and it suddenly realised what was going on.

Slowly, the Humatron opened its own cape and allowed it to fall in a heap around its feet. There would be no restrictive clothing in this fight. Richard looked across at Preston again and unclipped the flap on his shoulder holster.

The machine's screen face flattened and a series of white lines appeared on it, they moved up and down and side to side, like the tuning lines on an old television set. The Humatron was assessing the threat – digitally calculating body sizes and estimating weights. Finally, after focusing on Naomi for a second or two and promptly dismissing her, it prioritised Richard.

With the speed of a striking praying mantis, the machine raised its arms, stepped forwards and lunged at Richard. It grasped Richard's cape and pulled him off balance. Richard slithered out and rolled clear. Asharf turned, picked up a wooden chair and launched it at the machine. The machine brushed it aside with such force that the chair broke into matchwood as it smashed against the wall. Richard withdrew his ISTAN, thought blue and aimed at the robot, but in an instant the machine was upon him and there was no time to fire. Preston scurried crab-like across the room and retrieved his static baton. He pressed a button on its casing; there was a barely audible buzz but the machine heard it plainly enough and its head spun round until it was eyeing Preston. Preston stood his ground, giving Richard time to step to the side.

The Humatron's eyes turned red and began to pulsate; its screen face contorted. Fully charged, a tiny green light flashed on Preston's static baton and he beckoned to the machine. Like a gladiator with a short sword, he crouched and made ready for hand-to-hand combat. Richard nimbly stepped out of the machine's reach. The machine's attention flipped between the two men and then like a cat, Asharf moved behind it. Preston lunged with his baton but missed, Richard lashed out with his green blade – the machine avoided it. Like animals trapped in a cage they shifted and manoeuvred.

'Naomi! Go! Run!' Richard shouted.

Naomi backed towards the door, but the robot realigned itself to her. Asharf hurled himself at the mid-section but the machine swept him aside with little effort and he slid painfully across the hard floor. Preston lunged again, this time successfully and, as he caught the robot's leg, he immediately discharged the weapon. The robot recoiled from the electric shock and its screen face distorted in agony. There was an accompanying, piercing, electronic shriek, but there was insufficient charge to do permanent damage and the Humatron counter attacked by trying to catch Preston's hand. Here was a chance for Richard but he narrowly missed the robot's arm. The machine lunged out at Preston again, also missing, but it managed to grab the flowing sleeve of the djellaba with such force the fabric tore off at the shoulder seam and the momentum sent Preston crashing against the wall where he lay, winded. Richard stared worriedly as Preston shook his head. He was clearly giddy and disorientated.

Richard attacked. A lash with his forehand and a swiping backhand – each time the robot parried its body out of range. Deftly, Richard took a few steps backwards to give him space; he thought blue and fired off a molecular blade, then another. With surprising fleetness of foot, the machine avoided them. Asharf threw another chair. The robot caught it mid-flight and launched it at Naomi, standing bravely by the door. She ducked and the chair splintered on impact with the wall behind her and then she darted over to where Preston lay, still unable to stand. In that instant she diverted the Humatron's attention, giving Richard a chance to make a sweeping blow at its legs. The robot was too quick for him and kicked the ISTAN out of his hand; it clattered across the floor. The machine punched at Richard's face. Richard side stepped the lunge and made a dash for the ISTAN but the machine intercepted him effortlessly, brushing aside a heavy table as it loped across the room.

The sound of whirring motivators and clicking relays seemed amplified now, they ran in unison, stopping, reversing, powering in an instant; by its adeptness the Humatron gained the upper hand.

Richard was defenceless and the machine knew it too. Slowly, with almost human vindictiveness, it backed Richard across the room until he could move no further. In his peripheral vision, Richard saw Asharf lying in a crumpled heap and Naomi and Preston somewhere to the side.

The machine paused and then shot out a claw-like hand to clutch him on the side of the throat. Richard, anticipating the move, grabbed the metal with both hands but the inhuman force slowly began to bend his arms backwards. He tried to hold it off, but it was impossible. Long metallic fingers closed around his neck. Richard kicked and struggled but the Humatron squeezed and with little effort, lifted him clear of the ground. Richard hung there, dangling, pressed against the wall like a piece of meat as the machine clenched its other fist and withdrew it in preparation for a blow that would surely crush his skull. The pain was excruciating and Richard tensed his body as the machine savoured the moment.

Suddenly, the Humatron collapsed taking Richard with it. The pressure on his throat released and Richard found himself on his knees looking up at Naomi. She stood like an avenging angel with the ISTAN held high and stared in disbelief at what she had done.

Richard pushed off the dead metal and got up unsteadily. On the floor lay the smoking ruin, cleaved completely in two. The Humatron was deactivated.

'Are you hurt, Richard?' Naomi asked with concern.

Richard felt his neck and moved his head in a peculiar way, as if realigning his bones. 'Pretty sore,' he admitted. He looked down at the machine and the fluid that now pooled beneath it. 'I don't believe you just did that,' he said, and gently took the weapon from her to replace it in his shoulder holster. He hugged her close.

Asharf climbed to his feet and walked across to take a closer look. Richard put a hand on his shoulder. 'Good hunting on Madame's part, eh?' His quip broke the spell of harm in the room and in turn helped Preston to his feet.

'Bloody hell, Boss! You reckon there are more of these hanging around?'

'Fraid so; at least one more.'

The smell of degraded oil made Naomi grimace with distaste. 'Can we leave this place?' she appealed to Richard's bent back as he inspected the debris of the machine.

'As soon as you tell me how you activated the ISTAN,' Richard replied, standing. 'The bio key to the operation of this weapon is unique. It is computed from my synaptic trace.'

'With your scepticism, Richard,' Naomi rebuked softly, 'you forget how close we have been.' She smiled hesitantly. 'Closer than any technician taking samples, and I have perfect recall.'

With that enigmatic statement, Richard had to be content.

## CHAPTER 33

# CAUSE AND EFFECT

'We have three cloaks and two heads, Preston,' said Richard, modifying his plan while gesturing towards the Humatron that Naomi had sliced into two. 'So we both go, cover each other. See if anybody stops us. These machines are expected somewhere.'

Preston shook his head. 'I still don't like it, Boss. Less now in fact! We could be walking into something. It's just too risky for my liking.'

'Yes, and I agree with Preston,' pressed Naomi, joining the conversation. 'I heard what Peter Rothschild said too – they accounted for five Humatrons but there could be more. We should make arrangements for our pickup and continue south.'

Richard answered. 'At least five.' He checked his chronometer. 'Crikey! It's ten minutes past seven. We have missed the comms window, clean forgot about it. Preston, quick, switch on your pager . . . nine seconds maximum, absolutely no longer. Use the emergency default channel, sat comm, Link 7.'

Preston unzipped an inside pocket in his waistcoat, withdrew his telephonic device and selected the channel. He opened the satellite link for nine seconds precisely to avoid a signal intercept and a possible back-bearing enhancement that would betray their position. The device beeped twice. Preston looked up at Richard. 'Two messages, Boss.'

'And?'

'The first is from Marretti. He says that he will be with us at zero eight hundred hours and that the airfield is now compromised. The take-off will be from a position half a k south-east of the King Piye wharf. He has given the coordinates . . . precisely zero nine hundred hours. We are to wait *here* for his arrival. It closes with J.J. Wilkinson. That bit I don't understand.'

A smile flickered across Richard's face. 'JJ Wilkinson,' he repeated nostalgically. 'Now there is a name I haven't heard in a long time.'

Preston looked puzzled.

'He was a rugby coach. Taught in the south-west schoolboys' league for forty years or more – famous as hell, and revered. I had the privilege of being coached by him, but that was a bit before Marretti's time, I would have thought.'

Preston looked more puzzled.

'Never be on the ball for more than thirty seconds; after that, do something with it. That's what he taught. It made the game flow. Everybody knew him for it.'

'My school played football, not rugby,' Preston commented, matter-of-factly. 'What does it mean, Boss?'

'It means that the area is hot. Thirty seconds – that is all we will have. Rapid extraction . . . the Tiltrotor will touch down and thirty seconds later it departs, whether we are in it or not. It means; be on the ball, and don't be late!'

Preston shrugged. 'Rugby . . . never had the opportunity,' he added, introspectively.

Richard nodded to reinforce his theory. 'The docks,' he said and checked the time again. 'We have about an hour I would say – time enough. We can recce the position while we are down there, but we need to get going. What of the other message?'

'It's from Rothschild, sent four hours ago from London. He acknowledges Mauritius and says arrangements are in hand. They are opening the official archives . . . that's it!'

Richard paused thoughtfully. 'Okay, Preston, a compromise, listen up. *I* will disguise myself as a Humatron and you follow me at a safe distance, agreed?' Richard turned. 'Asharf, can you get your hands on another djellaba, preferably of local material? Preston's is a mess.'

Preston stood with arms akimbo to show it wasn't his fault a sleeve was missing.

'There is clothing upstairs, *Effendi*.'

'Good.' Richard looked back at Preston, his eyes narrowing. 'First sign of trouble and we clear the area!' He raised his eyebrows to emphasise his statement.

Reluctantly Preston agreed. Richard eyed the severed trunk of the deflated Humatron and considered his options for a moment. 'Something else,' he said, and then he withdrew his ISTAN, lifted the machine's right hand and with one swipe parted it just above the wrist. He drained the remaining fluid from inside the body part as Asharf came stumbling down the staircase carrying a bundle of dark brown material.

'I have it, *Effendi!*' and threw it to Preston.

'Good. Let's get on with it.'

Richard spoke from beneath the cape, its hood pulled down over his face. 'How do I look?' he asked expectantly.

Preston and Asharf nodded and made impressive gestures as they inspected Richard's disguise.

Naomi shook her head, 'I do not like it, Richard.' She sounded worried.

'Naomi, everything will be okay! I will be back in less than forty-five minutes. Preston will keep a good eye on me. You ready, Preston?'

'Well, yes, I suppose so,' replied Preston, as he buttoned up his djellaba and pulled up the hood.

'Good!'

Richard stepped over the hulk of the first downed robot and approached the remains of the door. He held the broom head low, at belt height. Asharf, with some effort prized open a gap that was wide enough for him to slip through and peered into the street, checking in both directions. He pulled back immediately and nodded.

'Now, Asharf!' Richard ordered.

Asharf gave another hefty tug opening the door further. Richard stepped onto the street and joined the throng of people going about their daily business. He raised the Humatron's head and pressed the broom head against his upper chest with one hand. Thirty seconds later, Preston followed him. Asharf and Naomi pushed the door closed behind him.

Richard's shoulders were narrower than the Humatron's and as a result, his cape dragged in the red mud; but unlike the clothes of others there was no soiling; no sticky coagulant to hamper his movement; the staining simply ran off. The effect was noticeable.

Occasionally slipping, but making every attempt to maintain a Humatron's awkwardly stiff stance, he progressed slowly down the street towards the harbour. Preston kept him in sight, keeping a distance of fifty metres.

Richard inclined the broom handle and robot head forward, creating a penitent appearance. With his other hand he parted the cape between two fasteners to enable him to see where he was going. The effect was restrictive but just enough. He would rely heavily on Preston for cover and protection and that opportunity arose quickly enough. They were barely three hundred metres from the safe house as Richard stepped off a makeshift pavement to cross the street when somebody came alongside him.

'Where have you been?'

Richard's heart jumped; he was startled and made a jerky movement.

'Where is the other Humatron?' the voice continued. 'We have been looking for you!'

Richard kept his head down and continued to cross the street. He slithered in the mud, but regained his balance. Preston suspected something and closed the gap.

'Mr Rhinefeld is waiting. He is not happy.'

The speaker slipped, Richard felt him against his right side. '*Scheisse!*' the man cursed and then he seemed to regain his composure. 'Damned machine,' the voice blurted again. 'Follow me, this way!'

The man speaks good English thought Richard, and clearly they have retained English as the robot's primary language protocol but I can detect a German accent.

The voice mumbled something out of earshot and then it trailed away on Richard's right side. Richard waited for a few moments and surreptitiously opened a bigger gap in his cape to briefly check the surrounding area. Three metres in front of him a burly figure was leading the way, wearing a dark blue fleece and floundering through the mud. Richard followed him. Preston, maintaining a suitable distance, trailed them both.

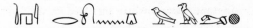

After ten minutes of difficult walking, the muddy road levelled off. The adrenalin in Richard's bloodstream had sharpened his senses. He knew that the quayside must be close. He peeked out through the gap in his cape as a vehicle drove past. Surrounding him were stone-built buildings that were square and of regular design. At a glance they appeared old and in disrepair. Richard quickly scanned a wider arc. The ground became firmer and the man in front quickened his pace. They progressed until the road led into a large open area like a square. In times gone by a bustling market would have been held there. The surrounding but distant buildings reminded Richard of the old residential conversions on the waterside in central London. Surely he was on the dockside by now. Richard heard someone approach from his right hand side and dropped his hand to close the gap in his cape.

'Ernst . . . only one? Where is the other?' a voice said to the man he was following.

'There is no sign of it!'

There was a pause and then the other voice continued.

'Rhinefeld will not be pleased. If I were you, I would be worried,' the voice mocked the burly man.

'Shut it!'

'Ah, I can see you are already worried.'

'I said, shut it! Ask it yourself, why don't you? The machine will not answer me.'

'Too scared, eh? I am not frightened of them, as you are.'

It was a man's voice. Higher in tone with a sharp refined edge. He spoke English with an Iberian accent – probably Portuguese. Richard smelled cigarette smoke as this man spoke. He must be right in front of me, Richard deduced, trying to intimidate the machine.

'Where is your tin friend?' the man repeated. 'Answer me, Humatron. Remember your presets.'

There was an awkward pause, Richard speculated feeling for the metallic hand he had in his pocket. If these people were like Richard, they would have a healthy respect for the robots. Richard hoped he could rely on them keeping their distance.

'I said, where is the other machine? Call it! Do as I say or I will deactivate you!'

Richard slowly raised the robotic hand until it protruded from beneath the cape, taking care not to show too much. He gestured behind in the direction they had come.

'What's wrong with you, can't you speak?'

Richard lifted the hand a little more and tapped the stick just below the robot's head.

The man turned. 'Its *vocallator* must have malfunctioned. This consignment, shit engineering . . . nothing but trouble.

Let's go, Rhinefeld is waiting.'

I'm in, thought Richard.

Due to the lack of cover, Preston remained marooned on the far side of the square. He lurked impatiently behind a corner until the three figures disappeared between two buildings and then he gave chase across the open ground. It was firm underfoot and he easily avoided the frequent puddles. Moments later, and with his back towards a red brick wall, he eased his way along the wall of a crumbling building until he reached the corner of a narrow street. Carefully, he looked around but to his dismay, there was no sign of Richard or the two men. He rushed down the street to the next junction, a crossroads, but there was still no sign; there was either left or right! He checked for tracks – there were too many and too much water. 'Bloody Nora, I've lost him!' he mumbled in exasperation. Short of combing every wharf and alley he would never find him. Richard was on his own. Preston tried to evaluate the situation, the damage limitation; desperately he scanned the area – there, not sixty metres away, he could see the harbour. Nothing for it but to make for the dockside, he thought, and ran off in that direction.

Richard trailed the two men by a suitable distance in order to keep a lookout through the narrow slit in his cape. They progressed east. He knew this because of the orientation of the harbour and the estuary that led to the Red Sea. Some ten minutes passed but the two men remained locked in heated conversation; clearly apprehensive, there was evidently some blame to be apportioned. The name Rhinefeld was familiar, Richard mused, and it bothered him. During his last briefing Rothschild had warned him of a Rhinefeld who was a secret service agent, an interrogator, believed to be working for the Spheron conglomerate. What had he got himself into?

The burly man turned, 'You, Humatron. Move!'

The men quickened their pace. They swung a left and then a right; it was like a rabbit warren. Richard splashed through a murky puddle. A vehicle's horn sounded in the distance. Intermittent drizzle became persistent as the men disappeared around another corner. Richard became confused.

'*March, schnell* . . . quickly!'

Richard quickened his pace and sighted the men again.

Finally, the street opened into a large dockside area where Richard's limited vision saw rain falling on the sea. A high, rigid security fence with barbed wire curled liberally along its summit blocked their path. Richard followed as the two men turned right and skirted the barrier until they came upon a pair of fortified steel mesh gates. On their arrival, there was the hum of an electric motor and the gate on the left opened automatically.

'*Schnell*!' the one called Ernst, barked again.

After a further fifty metres they approached a large quayside building. From occasional glimpses Richard made out bleached wooden boards built shiplap fashion then wooden framed windows in a construction with freight doors. Richard heard the squeaking of dry hinges. One last look, he thought. A step-over door was filled by a huge figure and the two men came to an abrupt halt. Richard sank under his disguise as the man said, 'Rhinefeld grows impatient. You know what that means? Where is the shipment? How long before it arrives?'

There was a pause. Richard thought the cadence of his voice made him sound very much like a friend of his who hailed from eastern China, near Shanghai. Richard was now counting the odds. Three of them, plus the infamous Rhinefeld – two to one against him and Preston. Things could get difficult. His heart thumped.

'Where is the other one, Ernst?'

'Do not worry about the other machine, Xuan, it will find us.'

'You lost the freaking robot!'

There was another pause. The reply had an aggressive tone.

'I told you the machine will find us. Leave it! Anyway, I have news of the shipment.'

There was another pause. 'It had better be good, or . . .'

'Shut up you two,' one of the men interrupted.

'Come inside . . . and *you*, Humatron, this way.' Richard recognised Ernst's voice.

Door hinges squeaked again and there was the sound of feet scraping on steel. Richard moved carefully. He put an arm out and felt the left hand doorpost run along his forearm as he stepped over a high threshold, his foot got caught under the cloak and he tripped and stumbled through the opening. He tried not to swear.

The sprung door closed behind him and the reverberating thud that echoed around him told him the building was cavernous. The surface was of smooth, flat concrete. After steadying himself and taking a few more paces, Richard regained his composure. In an effort to lend greater persuasion to his disguise, he slowly raised the machine's head until it was well in excess of a man's height, and then he stood, statue-like. His pounding heart sent adrenalin coursing through his veins. Stepping into this lion's den without a lion tamer was not such a good idea.

'Stay here!' Ernst's voice commanded him. The other men fell silent.

Richard listened as their footsteps faded and judged their distance and then heard talking. He risked a brief look and saw the three men had stopped in front of someone tall and wearing a long black coat and a wide brimmed hat. That must be Rhinefeld; an opportunity too good to miss, Richard thought, and he carefully turned to scan the door and nearest windows with open wooden shutters, although a few had drooped where the rotten structure had parted.

'*Ja*!' Rhinefeld shouted to the speaker. There was silence while he listened. Slowly, Richard turned back towards the four men. His view was, by necessity, narrow and restricted. He grimaced. There, close to Rhinefeld, another figure stepped into view. It was a bigger, broader figure clad in a grey cape – another Humatron!

'*Ja! Ja*!' Rhinefeld's voice boomed again and he nodded and looked in Richard's direction. '*Sie*! Humatron! *Kommt hier*!'

Instinctively, Richard dropped his hand and the gap in his cape closed. The menacing tone made his blood run cold and then he realised that Rhinefeld was speaking to him.

'You! Humatron! Come here. *Bewegen Sie es*!' Rhinefeld's authoritative voice resounded.

Carefully, Richard walked towards the men. He tried to replicate the Humatron's awkward lope. As he approached, he could hear their shuffling and he sensed them staring at him. He could hear the other Humatron's motivators twitching. Lacking such cover, Richard half exposed the robotic hand from beneath his sleeve – the ploy seemed to be working.

Rhinefeld asked. '*Wo ist . . .*?'

At that moment, a telephone rang; the tone was shrill and repeatedly ascending. There was a crumpling of leather as Rhinefeld retrieved his handset.

'*Ja!*' Rhinefeld half shouted, impatiently. There was silence for a few seconds. '*Gut*, tell me of zis new city . . . what does it mean . . . *die neue Stadt*?' There was an enlightening pause. '*Where* is zis new city? . . . *was sagen Sie*? *Sprechen Sie Englisch* . . . what are you saying?'

There was silence again as Rhinefeld listened. Clearly, he was speaking to somebody with better English than German. Rhinefeld answered. 'Zer information has been discovered in Rome and someone goes now to Lyon . . . I see.' Another pause; seconds seemed like hours. 'Michel de Notredame . . . no, I do not know of zis man . . . I see.'

Richard heard the man's voice, heavy and guttural coming through the speaker – his English wasn't much better. He caught the occasional word, but not enough to understand the conversation.

Richard kept half an ear to the dialogue but was more concerned by the Humatron. Its head swivelled this way and that as if trying to home in on him. The red eye monitors glowed with extra energy every so often as if the computers were gathering information. It went to take a step towards him but Rhinefeld, in mid conversation about Michel de Notredame, put out a restraining hand. Richard began to feel that he should make a run for it and calculated it was at least forty strides back to the wicket door.

'Zer great physician and astrologer . . . 1557,' Rhinefeld said slowly, evidently repeating words. '*Das war das* interpretation of his prediction. You are sure of zis?'

Rhinefeld continued and Richard listened intently. '*Aber wir müssen* . . . but first we continue our work in Adulis . . . *ja, das ist gut!*' With that, he terminated the conversation. Rhinefeld turned his attention to Ernst. 'Zer shipment! What of zer shipment?' he demanded.

Ernst shifted nervously. '*Gute nachrichten mein Herr!*'

'*Sprechen Sie Englisch!*' Rhinefeld chastised. He raised a sickly smile. 'For our friends, Ernst, you understand,' he explained derisively.

Ernst nodded apologetically. 'Good news, Mr Rhinefeld. When I left the Port Authority Office, the first shipment was already being unloaded. It should be here at any time.' A smirk flickered on Ernst's face.

'What of the other?'

'Not on the same vessel, Mr Rhinefeld for security reasons.

It arrives tomorrow morning. Everything is set.'

Preston was sweating under his djellaba. He had covered every alleyway that Richard could have disappeared down but there was still no sign of him. The last thing he wanted to do was draw attention to himself, but another course of action was necessary and in desperation he stopped a woman in the street. She carried a large clay pot on her head. 'Sorry, excuse me. Have you seen a tall man in a grey cape pass this way?'

The woman looked confused – she shrugged and walked on. Preston tried another one – with a bundle of firewood strapped to her back. This woman, who was unusually tall, stepped around Preston, trying to avoid him. Preston followed her for a few steps, asking again. The woman turned and dismissed him with a stabbing finger and a flurry of disdainful mutterings in a language unknown to him.

He sidestepped a filthy red pickup truck that had driven onto the street and surprised him from behind. Then he dashed across to confront another pedestrian, this time a teenage boy who led a laden donkey – there seemed to be little English spoken in this town. Two men passed by and looked at him suspiciously. Then Preston saw a woman dressed in western clothes further down the street, and he ran towards her. The woman looked frightened by his approach, so he put his hands up to reassure her. 'Madam, sorry,' he said. 'I'm looking for a friend. He passed this way fifteen minutes ago, maybe a little more. He was wearing a long grey cape . . . very tall.'

The pretty African woman nodded. She pushed back the multicoloured shawl that covered her face and looked up at Preston. Fine drizzle fell on her hair that was pulled back tightly off her face and she had striking brown eyes. Preston's expression changed to one of expectation, he forced a smile; this time he might be lucky?

'Yes, I saw someone' she said in good English. She

seemed to approve of Preston and returned the smile. 'I have come from the Abyad fish market, further down, by the quayside, although there is little to buy today. I did see a man like this, he was with two others, Europeans like you. I remember him because a car passed and splashed him; the muddy water simply ran off his cape as water does off a sea bird. This must be your friend.'

'Yes, yes, that's him. Where? Which way?'

'Keep this way, to the waterfront; you will see the old docks. Stay to the right side. Look there . . . less than ten minutes.' The woman indicated down the street and then eyed Preston and with the back of her hand she gestured in that direction. Preston turned, his eyes widened; a militia vehicle – an open topped lorry – was making slow progress down the hill towards him.

'Thanks!' Preston said, touching her hand and with that, he ran off.

The woman seemed disappointed.

**Meanwhile – in the safe house**

There was a knock on the back door. It was barely loud enough to be heard because Asharf was nailing a board across the front door. Naomi came and put her hand on his arm to stop him and to warn him of their visitor. Asharf raced upstairs to investigate. The man stood patiently on the doorstep, occasionally surveying the area. Eventually, as if sensing Asharf's cautious inspection he looked upwards –

it was Charles Marretti. Asharf scurried downstairs again and opened the door for him and Charlie quickly slipped inside, before Asharf closed and locked the door again.

Charlie checked the room out and then looked at Asharf. 'What in the name of God happened here?' he asked, kicking the remains of the Humatron aside. His expression was open with astonishment. 'Is everyone okay? Naomi? Is she upstairs?' He put his foot on the bottom step of the stair. 'I'll go up to her,' he said, as Naomi appeared from the kitchen carrying a plate of dried dates.

She offered them to him and explained how the Humatrons had attacked them and how nervous she was that Richard was impersonating one of the machines down in the docks.

'Is he mad?' Charlie looked horrified by the escapade. 'He'll be killed.'

'No!' Naomi blurted, then immediately recovered. 'Preston is following him. Richard hopes to find important information. They left almost an hour ago . . . he said an hour at most and then he would return. I trust him, he will be here.'

Charlie checked his watch and then shook his head. 'Ugh . . . why? I told him to be ready! What is it with this guy? The whole area is crawling with Tongsei militia and our pickup is in thirty-six minutes.'

'You cannot tell Richard; he is who he is,' replied Naomi, putting the plate down on the windowsill.

'There is some open ground down by the southern

wharf – that is the rendezvous. At least he is in the right area.' He looked at Asharf. 'Have you had any contact?'

'None.'

'Get your things together, Signora, we move out.'

Rhinefeld scanned the warehouse slowly. His eyes narrowed as he looked momentarily at Ernst and then he switched his attention back to Richard. He looked suspiciously at him, eyeing him up and down. '*Wo ist das andere Humatron?*' he snapped.

Ernst opened his mouth to speak. Rhinefeld raised his hand and stopped him. 'Let zis machine speak. Humatron! I am talking to you. Where is your accomplice?'

In the ensuing silence, Richard felt the hairs on the back of his neck prickle. He raised the robotic hand and tapped his throat to show he had no voice.

'His *vocallator* has malfunctioned, Mr Rhinefeld,' Ernst said apologetically.

Rhinefeld turned towards the other Humatron. It stood silently a few paces behind him. 'You ask the question!' he barked.

With that, the robot let out a series of shrill tones. The fearsome screeching echoed around the building for several seconds. When it subsided and silence reigned, Rhinefeld took a step closer to Richard and he waited in anticipation.

Trying to gauge how long he had, Richard pressed against his shoulder holster with the ISTAN inside with his forearm for reassurance; there was nothing he could do; he had no comeback. I'll make a run for it, he thought.

Rhinefeld gestured with his head. Richard heard steps as the sumo size Asiatic walked behind him and with a sharp tug, pulled down Richard's hood. Richard gasped. For a moment he stood there holding the broom handle with the head on it.

With a javelin throw, Richard hurled the metallic head at Rhinefeld and turned to run. Instantly, Xuan had hold of him in a clinch that lifted him off his feet. Richard slithered out of the cape and onto his feet and made another dash. The Humatron was amazingly quick off the mark and Richard had barely moved five paces before the machine caught hold of his coat collar and pulled him backwards. Within seconds, Richard was surrounded. There was jostling. Richard threw a punch and caught Ernst on the side of the face. The Humatron reached out and pulled Richard's arm down. Ernst avoided a flailing kick and launched a heavy punch to Richard's stomach. Richard squirmed in pain. The Asiatic grabbed Richard by the scruff of his neck and with the robot bearing down on his shoulder they forced him to his knees.

Rhinefeld kicked Richard in the side. Richard tried to control the pain as he felt his head being lifted by his hair.

'Who is he?' Rhinefeld demanded. 'Humatron . . . facial

analysis!'

The Humatron stepped around Richard. Ernst pulled Richard's head back further and the machine focused on Richard's contorted face, taking an image.

'Is he in your databank?' Rhinefeld demanded again.

The robot stood tall and orange lines appeared on its screen face, which swept quickly up and down and each time they did, a digital image solidified. After a minute or so and with Richard uncomfortably restrained, the coloured, three-dimensional image was complete – it was Richard's face, but in a different place and from some time earlier. The image rotated slowly through three hundred and sixty degrees for all to see.

'Well?' asked Rhinefeld again.

A number of lights flashed on the Humatron's face screen as it analysed a duplex retina scan whilst cross-checking cosmetic topography and correlated databank information. Presently, the machine spoke. 'Vocalising current data indicates that this human is Richard James Reece, Master,' it said, in its metallic rasp. 'Currently holds the rank of Lieutenant Commander in the United Kingdom Armed Forces.' The robot paused momentarily and then continued. 'Listed as Grade 1 International Space and Science Federation astronaut, speciality . . . Planetary Surveyor, First Class. Present appointment . . . Osiris Base, Mars.' Another short pause, some digits flickered. 'Master, I have an updated file available. It indicates a more recent secondment.' The robot twitched, 'British Intelligence.

Temporarily assigned to MI9 as field agent and ISSF undercover operative, pseudonym, Rhys Jones. The robot looked at Rhinefeld and its eyes pulsated. 'This human is confirmed as primary target, Master!'

Rhinefeld breathed a deep sigh as he assimilated the information. The other men had made distance between them and the robot. A nasty smile crept over Rhinefeld's face and he put his foot on Richard's shoulder and pushed him over backwards. 'So, it is you, Richard Reece? Now I understand about my missing Humatrons. It seems that I underestimated you and now you have found us. Congratulations, but your luck just ran out.' Rhinefeld stepped forwards and towered menacingly over Richard. 'Surely, even to you, an amateur, zis was a futile attempt at espionage, quite pathetic. Are you really zer best zer British can put up in this race for zer Ark?' Rhinefeld reached inside his coat and pulled out a short-barrelled pistol and pointed it at Richard's head. 'Who else is with you? Where are they? Ve vill finish what you think you have started.'

Ernst viciously jerked Richard's head back again.

'You will not live to see zer biggest prize, Mr Reece. *Ve* vill get all zer crystals and then ve vill dictate to zer world who receives energy and who does not. For your part in zis, your legacy, I think that zer *Great* will no longer apply – Britain will slip back into the dark ages. Now, you *vill* . . .'

The noise of large airbrakes outside coincided with a phone ringing. The device belonged to Ernst and he answered it and smiled. '*Sie sind hier, mein Herr,*' he said, and replaced the phone in his pocket, only to withdraw another smaller electronic gadget. 'The shipment, we have it, it is outside,' Ernst turned to the other men and grinned arrogantly.

'*Gut*, open zer barrier. Xuan, Lorenzo, open zer freight doors . . . *schnell!*'

Quietly, Richard had inched away as everyone was distracted by the arrival of the transporter. Rhinefeld organised the men to receive the consignment and Richard was poised to make a break at the first opportunity. Rhinefeld called to the Humatron, 'Guard zis man. Kill him if he walks more than two paces.'

The Humatron pulled Richard to his feet and restrained him by bending an arm uncomfortably behind his back. Rhinefeld glanced at him and then focused his attention on his two minions as they struggled to open the two aged wooden doors. Eventually, Xuan, frustrated, lifted the chafing edge of his door clear from the ground and walked it open. There was the noise of airbrakes being released and then the nose of the lorry entered slowly. It was a large flatbed vehicle and appeared to be an old Russian model with bulbous front wings and heavy fenders and a low, wide cab. The high-pitched whining noise of its revving electrical drive reverberated around the warehouse. Well inside the otherwise empty building the lorry stopped, and for a moment all fell silent.

Preston knew that he was on the right trail because he had found a digit from the Humatron's hand awhile back. Richard must have dropped it as a sign. The sight of a softwood freight box the size of a car, with no visible markings except the accursed red T of Tongsei Industries stencilled prominently on its end, had offered another lead and he had followed the green, military-type vehicle until it had disappeared inside a bleached wood-lapped building, and the two unlikely looking foreigners who had closed the freight doors behind it seemed to confirm his suspicions. Now he was inside the perimeter fence, having slipped through the closing electric barrier in the nick of time, but movement by the small wicket gate next to the main doors had caused him to change direction towards the side of the building.

Stealthily he skirted the building looking for a way in. The sight of a black saloon car with Egyptian number plates parked out of sight only increased his reservations *and* his anxiety for Richard. He found a window without external shutters, but internal boarding frustrated his attempts to see inside. He put an ear to the glass.

Marretti checked his watch for the third time within a minute. As he drove off, a military vehicle turned into the street behind him. He looked at Naomi who sat in the passenger seat next to him. 'This car has the registration of a Tongsei official from Asmara. It was the best I could do, given the time constraints.'

'You mean that it is stolen,' Naomi interjected, turning to look through the rear windscreen.

'The official is abroad for at least another week. It is unlikely that this car will be reported as missing, not for a while anyway. Just stay cool.'

Naomi sighed. Marretti turned left and accelerated down a side street. After a few minutes, he turned left again onto the main thoroughfare and headed towards the docks. Not attempting to gain ground, and after a period of absence, the military vehicle appeared some distance behind them. Marretti checked his rear-view mirror *and* the time; he began to look nervous.

'Check outside again, Lorenzo, and close those doors!' Rhinefeld barked.

'I told you. There is no one; the area is deserted,' Lorenzo replied.

Rhinefeld's eyes narrowed with anger. Lorenzo turned and made off towards the small wicket door.

'*Wie viele* . . . how many?' Rhinefeld demanded, switching his attention to Ernst.

'*Eine million, mein Herr.*'

Rhinefeld nodded. 'What is their power level?'

'Fully charged. I am told that thirty minutes in the cuboid will energise them for twenty-four hours.'

Richard, held painfully by the robot, listened carefully. So they have a million *somethings* that can be fully charged for twenty-four hours. Great! He thought.

Rhinefeld smiled – a conceited, knowing kind of smile.

'Vun million pairs of shredding mandibles, vun million pairs of eyes . . .' Rhinefeld turned and with a power-crazed face, he looked at Richard and said: 'Vun million opportunities to extract information!'

Richard shuddered at the thought of it. He looked anxiously at the packing case. The Asiatic man, Xuan, was already on top of the lorry and using a magnetic screwdriver to open the lid.

Richard translated Ernst's excitement as he shifted from one foot to the other. '*Ja*, nowhere will go unsearched – we will see everything, everywhere, in every corner, in every dark recess.'

What can they mean, Richard thought, as the pain in his shoulder increased. Where was Preston? He scanned the building; there was no obvious means of escape.

After a few minutes, having completed his task and clutching a small plastic box, Xuan climbed down from the lorry and joined the other two men. Richard listened as Rhinefeld spoke to Ernst.

'What of zer directive protocol?'

'Only binary, mein Herr.' Ernst replied. 'Voice recognition required more time . . . the next batch.'

Richard saw Rhinefeld sigh. 'So, the Humatron has control?' he said.

Ernst gestured sheepishly and Rhinefeld dismissed it with a wave of his hand. 'No matter, I control the Humatron,' and he shifted his gaze to Xuan and watched disdainfully as Xuan fiddled with a digital combination lock. 'You have zer correct combination?' he demanded. Xuan nodded.

'The second shipment has the later processor,' Ernst added.

'The message from Epsilon Rio is that the upgrade will be available within a few weeks.'

'*Gut.*'

Xuan had the box open and retrieved a small, flat device from it and then threw the empty container onto the floor behind him.

'Zat is zer programmer?' Rhinefeld asked.

'Yes, this is it,' answered Xuan.

Rhinefeld gestured to Ernst. 'Load it!' he said.

Ernst took the oblong-shaped device from Xuan and then looked as if he was loading a gun as he walked towards Richard. Ernst inserted the other electronic gadget he held. It clicked into place and Richard saw a bright green light was illuminated. When Ernst waved his

109

hand, the Humatron abruptly dropped Richard's arm and stood while Ernst inserted the device into a receptacle in its chest. Within seconds, a tiny red LED indicator also turned green – the download was complete. Ernst turned to Rhinefeld and clicked his heels sharply. Richard's shoulder was useless, but pins and needles indicated the blood supply was flowing again.

'Humatron! Initialise the system!' Rhinefeld commanded.

'*Recipient*!' screeched the robot, and then it issued a series of warbling electronic tones.

Immediately the packing case began to vibrate. The vibrations became a quiver and then the whole case began to shake violently. The lorry bounced on its suspension – the amplitude grew stronger. Xuan clearly looked disturbed and promptly stepped back from the vehicle by several paces. Rhinefeld let out a manic laugh.

'What the hell is it?' Richard thought, as he stood massaging his arm.

From outside, with his ear pressed against a glass window, Preston could hear the faint voices – but not what was being said. Now, a loud buffeting noise completely foiled his attempts to eavesdrop. At that moment Lorenzo rounded the corner of the building. Preston saw him first because Lorenzo was looking across at the electric barrier and checking its position. Immediately, Preston ducked out of sight behind a stack of rusting forty-five gallon oil drums. Lorenzo passed by unaware but all the same he held his weapon high. Preston reached inside his djellaba, unbuttoned his coat and unclipped his shoulder holster. He removed the sonic pistol and selected a kill setting. Crouching low, he remained out of sight until Lorenzo disappeared around the next corner.

Marretti checked the time – fourteen minutes to pickup. Fourteen minutes until the Tiltrotor would land. It would already be airborne and now he had no way of contacting the crew, let alone aborting the mission. One minute loiter time, one minute on the ground . . . maximum – that was the brief. He made a right hand turn and then a left. That street led them down to the quayside. He checked his rear-view mirror – now there were two militia vehicles behind them. Where, in God's name was Richard? he thought. The situation was becoming desperate!

By now, there was so much noise emanating from the

bulging packing case and the lorry's contortions that it became deafening. Then, to Richard's sheer astonishment, the side of the case disintegrated – literally. Shredded splinters flew everywhere. Everyone stared in awe at the eruption of silvery, squirming metal; like flowing magma, it spewed out over the side of the lorry. It spilt onto the concrete floor, like an uncontained oil slick. It spread further and further with a noise that was unbearable – high pitched, buzzing! The slick formed concentric circles around the men, who stood like dry patches in a silvery sea. Richard looked down and could not believe his eyes.

'Halt!' Rhinefeld shouted. The Humatron issued an electronic command and instantly, there was silence.

What the hell is that racket? What's going on in there? Preston thought. He ran a hand over the window frame, examining it. On the left side the wood was rotten and there was a crack. Preston pulled out his penknife and chipped away several pieces of timber – within seconds the frame disintegrated and he was through. He peered inside and gasped, and could see Richard and a caped Humatron standing behind him. He looked closer and counted five other men, making note that the guard, as yet, had not returned. Then he saw something on the ground. It was like a shiny liquid. Desperately, he made the hole bigger and peered inside again. At that moment, the man who had passed him seconds earlier stepped through a small wicket door near the main freight doors. The man took a few steps into the building and pulled up short.

Rhinefeld laughed, Ernst followed his example, and even Xuan raised a smile at the sight of a miniature army of the order *Hymenoptera*. Richard could do nothing but stare at the ground around him. Slowly he looked up at Rhinefeld. 'Nanobots!' he was astonished.

'Very observant,' Rhinefeld countered sarcastically. 'Zer family name is *Formicidae*, zer Genus, *Dorylus*, und zer species we selected . . . *mandibularis* – a merciless marauder first identified in 1896 . . . to be precise. To you and me, Mr Reece, they are African driver ants – killer ants! Zer most aggressive species on zer planet in fact. Of course, as you can see, they are exact electromechanical duplicates – indestructible mechanical copies . . . but with zer same zest for ravaging.'

Rhinefeld's smirk widened to a satisfied grin. Richard stared at the tiny forms, clones of the natural world, all rigidly still and each with an exactly similar posture.

'Epsilon Rio really have excelled themselves this time,' Rhinefeld continued. 'Zer technology is to be applauded, if I say so myself.'

'I take it you have big plans for them?' Richard said, as he met the hard gaze of Rhinefeld and defiantly straightened his coat and adjusted his collar.

Rhinefeld didn't even consider Richard's questions. 'Extreme pressure, blow-moulded titanium alloy exoskeletons,' he continued, monotonously. 'Six, breakthrough, electromotive switch mechanisms, one attached to each leg . . . optical fibre nervous system, terminating in two, ninety-degree colour imagers with a range of fifteen metres, two transmitter receiver antennae with vun kilometre range, and zer bit I like best – two, curved, six millimetre long mandibles operated by micro-hydraulic actuators, made of Neptunium alloy, razor-sharp. They can puncture and tear three millimetre steel plate,' Rhinefeld sniggered. 'What a mess they make.'

'But element number 93 is dangerously radioactive!'

'*Ja*, it can be,' Rhinefeld shrugged, unperturbed. 'If activated they vill lay waste to entire areas.' His mood changed and his eyes narrowed. 'With these, Mr Reece, there is nowhere we cannot go, nothing ve cannot see. No stone will go unturned. *Ve vill* find zer Ark first.'

'You're mad, you are bloody mad!'

'Because you have cost me precious time, and you know too much, I have something special in store for you. I tried it first with zer ant prototype. It worked vell, although I do not think zat you vill enjoy it.'

Richard's mind flashed to his ISTAN – he could try and fight his way out, but with these nanobots surrounding him there was no chance of escape. He thought of Preston. Armed only with a sonic pistol and some stun grenades, there was little he could do in this situation either. He hoped that Preston had had the good sense to go back for Naomi and Asharf and get the hell out of Adulis.

Rhinefeld continued to witter in the background. 'They vill enter through your nose and mouth and crawl between your cerebral membrane and the inside of your skull – zis is very painful I can assure you. I vill give you something to scratch at them with.'

Richard's disposition changed to one of open dissent. 'You will not get anything from me, Rhinefeld, if that's what you think. I won't talk!'

Rhinefeld looked directly at Richard; his expression twisted from disdain to contempt as he glared into Richard's eyes. 'I do not expect you to talk, Mr Reece. I expect you to die!' he said, coldly.

Richard thought of Reuben Massy, his CIB mentor in America – something that he had said weeks earlier whilst he was briefing Richard on the ISTAN. "Make sure you have a clear area in which to throw it and don't be in the same room . . . you'll fry. *Last-ditch effort, or self-destruct, it's your call.*" If he was going to go out, then it would be with a bang and he would take this cell of sadistic madmen with him *and* the last Humatron. Moreover, an ionising plasma grenade would take out these killer ants as well, he thought.

'Humatron, send the directive,' Rhinefeld snapped.

The robot screeched and immediately the nanobots scurried towards Richard. The creeping mass closed on him like silver lava. Within seconds, they were crawling up his legs. The Humatron stepped backwards and the other men stood clear; Lorenzo squirmed at the sight. This was Richard's chance. He reached into his coat, unclipped his holster and withdrew the ISTAN. The first ants were already about his waist, biting as they climbed.

At that moment, there was a bewildering explosion – a thundering, reverberating bang filled the building and echoed around its periphery. Richard felt the blast pressurise his eardrums. Pieces of glass and debris flew in all directions. Momentarily, the other men cowered; Richard turned as ants bit his thighs. It was Preston, and he had blown out the window.

'Boss! Boss! This way!' he shouted.

Richard sprinted towards the gaping hole. Ants crawled on his chest; he tried to brush them off. Rhinefeld fired his revolver. Richard's contortions made him a difficult target. Rhinefeld fired again and Richard instinctively ducked, narrowly avoiding the sublet.

'Get him!' Rhinefeld screamed.

Ants scurried beneath Richard's clothing and over the collar of his coat. Soon he felt them on his neck, pinching him painfully. Some he brushed off with wild and agitated swipes, as if beset by a swarm of bees, but others seemed intent on finding an opening. Richard stumbled, but he climbed to his feet again. He felt and heard the synthetic creatures crunching beneath his feet as he ran. His thumb brushed repeatedly across the control pad of the ISTAN – desperately Richard sought the central button. By now, so covered was he in shimmering silver metal that he looked like a robot himself. Preston returned Rhinefeld's volley with a salvo of his own, the sonic pulses narrowly missing Richard as they passed him on target. Rhinefeld's men dived to the floor, but Rhinefeld remained standing. Obstinately, he took careful aim. Sonic blasts impacted the wall behind them and made it shudder loudly. Rhinefeld fired again. Richard found the ISTAN's central pad, but at that instant, he felt a searing pain in his arm. Blindly he ran on. Ants crawled on his face. 'Get off . . . get off me!' He ran hard into the wall not an arm's length from Preston; dislodged insects rained to the ground. He was a seething mass of metal alloy. He felt them beneath his nostrils and swiped them off, and then they were by his ears. This is the end of it, Richard thought – my time! Blood! He thought blood, he thought RED! 'Arrrrrrrr!' he yelled.

Preston leaned inside the building and at full stretch grabbed the collar of Richard's coat. Immediately ants began crawling onto *his* sleeve. Undeterred he pulled Richard towards the opening and then he saw the ISTAN. 'Throw it! Throw it backwards, Boss!' Preston instructed.

Richard tossed the ISTAN back into the warehouse. There was an inbuilt ten-second delay and then the device would detonate. Preston heaved as ants teemed everywhere. Lorenzo caught sight of the device as it clattered across the concrete floor. 'Get out ... grenade! Grenade!' he screamed. The men turned and ran for the wicket gate. Rhinefeld would be first, he would make sure of it.

Richard tried to climb over the sill as Preston pulled. FIVE seconds to go! Richard managed to get his leg over the frame. THREE seconds to go! Preston tugged. ONE second! Just as Richard rolled out and fell to the ground, a massive explosion erupted inside the building. It was not like a conventional bomb, more a micro-nuclear detonation. First, there was the searing light – blinding, brilliant and neon blue. Then the shockwave – the whole building shook and then collapsed inwards. A low, concrete-walled compound containing empty oil drums offered better protection and Preston hauled Richard towards it; both men rolled over the top and cowered behind it. Seconds later, like a clap of thunder follows a bolt of lightning, there was a deafening noise, rumbling and heavy. Richard covered his head with his arms and Preston pulled up his djellaba for protection as splintered wood blasted past them.

Suddenly, the dank overcast sky darkened. Sections of roof came crashing down. Then the plasma aura, alive with electricity, buzzing and fizzing; a flash of ionised gas at unbearable temperature swirled and then it rained dust and debris. Wood spontaneously burst into flames, paint peeled and insects fried.

Preston hesitated, the blast subsided, and then 'Go! Go!' he shouted. He pulled Richard's arm and dragged him out of the compound. Ants, paralysed, simply fell to the ground. Richard, coming to his senses, looked back as he sprinted towards the metal fence. Beneath the rising mushroom cloud a column of black smoke rose from the wreckage as fire took hold.

Preston fired a sonic blast at the dock gate's locking mechanism – at point-blank, the pulse ripped open the steel case. Preston pulled open the barrier and both men ran through. A single shot rang out from behind them; it ricocheted off the steel structure. They dived to the ground momentarily and then Richard and Preston sprinted off towards the town.

Moments after arriving in a busy street, both Richard and Preston heard the sound of an aircraft – Richard looked skywards in an effort to see it. It was the unmistakable, high-pitched droning sound of a Tiltrotor. Richard scanned the sky above him, but could see nothing. They ducked down a side street. Richard listened intently. He could sense the direction – somewhere off to the right. The noise grew louder.

'It's the Tiltrotor, Preston,' he said, wiping a drip of blood from his eyelid.

'The pickup, Boss, they are coming back for us. There won't be much time.'

Richard nodded his agreement. At that moment, sirens began to sound; their eerie shrill seemed to be all around them – some had the warbling characteristic of moving vehicles.

'Let's get out of here,' said Richard. 'Follow the sound back to the waterfront.'

Both men ran down the street. They slipped repeatedly in the mud and it was difficult to avoid other pedestrians. Many stopped and shouted at their clumsy passage. Police sirens were growing louder behind them. As the street opened again into the docks area, Richard caught sight of the Tiltrotor. It was passing the rooftops and in a steady descent.

'It's going to land over there, Preston,' Richard shouted, as he indicated an area about two hundred metres away.

'It's all open ground, Boss!' Preston warned.

'No choice. Ready? Go!'

Halfway across the open ground, Richard caught sight of a commotion off to his right. In that instant a black car came skidding from a side street and accelerated towards the Tiltrotor as it landed and now settled heavily onto its undercarriage. A police car with lights flashing and siren blaring was in hot pursuit of the car. It had to be Marretti with Naomi and Asharf. Ahead of him the personnel door on the Tiltrotor opened and a crewmember filled the doorway. He was waving emphatically.

Richard and Preston raced towards the aircraft as Marretti's car closed from the right. The police car was gaining. 'Give me your sonic pistol, Preston,' Richard shouted.

Preston and Richard made a perfect Olympic relay exchange. Naomi saw him and pointed. 'Look Charles, it's Richard!' She powered down the window.

Richard changed course and ran to intercept the black car. 'Preston, go for the aircraft . . . go on!' he called.

Marretti, undeterred, made for the Tiltrotor – he could see in his mirror the police car was dangerously close. They had thirty seconds and then the Tiltrotor would lift off again. The police car had the edge.

Richard saw Naomi's covered head through the open window of the car. Frantically, he waved them on. 'Go! Go!' he shouted. Naomi screamed his name. Marretti drove past. Richard stepped between the car's tyre tracks and stood defiantly in the path of the oncoming vehicle; it accelerated and bore down on him. Shots from an automatic pistol sounded. Thuds peppered the ground around his feet. Richard raised the sonic pistol and took aim. 'Steady . . . steady,' he whispered. The car loomed, its engine roared; he could see their faces; they would run him down. Richard fired.

A microsecond later the compressed pulse collided. The vehicle's bonnet instantly buckled as if being struck by an invisible demolition ball. The windscreen shattered with a deafening blast, as if by explosive decompression. The driver's flailing limbs made him resemble a shaken rag doll; he instantly lost control. The car slewed left, its front right wheel tucked under, and then it rolled. Richard leapt to the side. Over it went, the first bounce sending it high into the air and then it tumbled repeatedly across the ground before coming to a crashing end. More gunfire sounded. Richard looked in its direction to see a military vehicle emerging from between dockside buildings. He turned and ran.

In full flight, Richard saw Preston disappear into the aircraft's cabin. Three figures emerged from the black car and climbed the steps. As he neared, he could see the undercarriage oleos extending and the aircraft beginning to rise. A crewmember filled the doorway again – crazily he waved Richard on. Richard was sprinting and panting. Behind him the militiamen were stopping and grouping to take firing positions.

Richard flung himself at the sponson as the aircraft lifted off. Dust, debris and litter blew up into his face. Painfully he pulled himself up and over the cover. The crewman, leaning from the door, belayed a cable. Richard wound it around his arm and caught hold with one hand. The crewman bravely put a foot on the step and offered an outstretched arm. Behind him Preston had hold of his jacket, while Marretti held the other end of the cable. The Tiltrotor climbed. Richard pulled himself towards the doorway and got a foothold on the steps and then the crewman took hold of his coat under his shoulder. A harbour building passed beneath them. Richard lunged for the doorjamb and caught it. With both hands and with the help of the crewman he pulled himself to safety.

As the door was closing the sound of machinegun fire

rang out. *Rat-a tat . . . rat-a tat* – a volley of sublets sprayed the cabin. Someone cried out in pain.

With its engines screaming, the Tiltrotor climbed and accelerated. Moments later, it disappeared below rooftops far to the south. Nevertheless, the sound of it lingered for some time longer, serving only to remind the militiamen of their failure as they looked on helplessly.

## CHAPTER 34

# BELATED CORRELATION

'I suggest you take a seat, Sir, and strap in. This is going to be an ultra low-level sector, at least until we cross the border. London has warned us that Tongsei have fighters deployed in the area and they mean to bring us down!'

Richard nodded at the co-pilot. He quickly climbed into the adjacent seat and buckled up. The machine banked steeply, making the crewman – who was standing in the doorway to the flight deck – momentarily lose his balance.

'I need you in your seat!' the Captain shouted at his colleague.

'Where are we going?' Richard asked, as the co-pilot turned to take up his position.

He looked back. 'Tree-top level to Djibouti, the next state down, around 450 miles – avoiding enemy radar,' he said, and then he disappeared into the flight deck.

Richard looked over his shoulder. Naomi sat next to Marretti several rows back and was busy winding a white crepe bandage around his head. Marretti looked pale with streaks of blood on his face. The aircraft banked steeply again, this time to the right. Asharf, who looked positively sickly green, sat with a petrified expression forward of them and gripped the head restraint of the seat in front of him as though it was a lifesaver. The aircraft dropped. Richard felt his heart in his throat as he looked to his left and out through the circular window. The Tiltrotor's engines throbbed and Richard became aware of a heavy mechanical vibration through the aircraft's fuselage. He lent over towards the window to try and see more as the aircraft steadied. They were over a beach with the sea to his left and it continued into the distance, certainly as far as he could see, and so their direction was clearly southerly. They were also at a ridiculously low altitude *and* at maximum speed, and so there was no letup in the pulsating vibration. Every now and then, a turbulent shudder shook the cabin. Richard turned back to look at Preston seated mid-row on the other side of the aisle and unclipped his seatbelt. He eased himself across the aisle and dropped into the seat next to Preston. Immediately, Preston offered him one end of the seatbelt with an authoritative expression and Richard clipped the two ends together and pulled the belt tight. He looked at Preston and with a slight questioning movement of his head gestured behind.

'Marretti cracked his head as he climbed in, Boss. Put a nasty gash in his forehead. If that wasn't enough, that last strafe of sublets came through and he caught one in the foot. Madame Vallogia is patching him up, but he will need medical attention. I've just read Rothschild's abrive . . . have you seen it?'

'No, not yet!'

A violent shudder suddenly permeated the aircraft structure; it made both men grip the armrests. 'Go on!' encouraged Richard, trying to ignore the precarious flight path.

'We are going down to Djibouti, the capital city has the same name, to the main airport. The French are cooperating. Seems they have a high-level diplomatic initiative going on and there's a government jet available. We land, transfer, and immediately head down to Mauritius. Flight time will be about three hours.'

Richard nodded. 'And this flight?'

'I don't know, Boss.' Preston shook his head vaguely.

Richard felt an irritation to his neck that seemed embedded in his collar. He rubbed at it with his fingers and retrieved a dormant ant. He held it up to the light of the window between his thumb and forefinger and scrutinised it. Preston leaned forwards to take a closer look.

'Bloody mandibles on that thing, Boss . . . do some serious damage.'

'We haven't seen the last of these, Preston,' Richard

warned gravely.

'Why do you say that?'

'I overheard a conversation, there are more, another batch. This model is controlled digitally and as a collective – clearly, when the Humatron was vaporised, they were instantly deactivated. The next batch evidently has a programming upgrade; they will operate by voice command – it's frightening.'

'They give an advantage in the search for the Ark, that's for sure.'

'It's what they leave in their wake that I'm concerned about,' Richard said, as he squeezed the pincers of the synthetic insect together. 'These mandibles are of a radioactive alloy, only the radiation is locked in – must be some form of molecular engineering. Apparently, they have perfected a way of controlling the leakage. Individually, it's probably nothing, but collectively it could become pinpoint pollution!' Richard looked at Preston. 'Epsilon Rio again, the technology conglomerate. Who exactly are these people?'

Preston sat astonished as Richard wrapped the specimen in his handkerchief and placed it in a zipped pocket inside his coat. Then Richard looked behind. He could see Naomi's head moving and occasionally her hand holding the end of a white cotton bandage. At that moment, he could only speculate as to the extent of Marretti's wounds, but it would be Mauritius before they reached any medical facilities. He looked back at Preston and wondered whether his near disastrous plan to go to the docks had been worth it. Both men sat in silence.

As the Tiltrotor intercepted the approach flight path above the sprawling suburbs of Djibouti and began the transition to landing configuration, Richard mused on the Belgian pilots' skills. Obviously evading authority, with their very discrete cargoes over Africa they had honed their combative spirit. As the aircraft touched down, Richard breathed a huge sigh of relief, glad that his small party was safe. He asked Preston if there were any signs of their next flight as he quickly unbuckled and shoved up to the window opposite, but as the Tiltrotor taxied onto the stand, it was nowhere to be seen. After a flight time of almost two hours he still felt a little shell-shocked.

A small bus drew up as the cabin door opened and dropped into position. Richard climbed out first. The sky was dark and cloudy, but it was dry. He nodded his appreciation to the co-pilot, who remained seated in the flight deck's right hand seat, and walked down the stair to meet the approaching airline handling agent.

The African man, dressed in a grey suit and wearing a bright yellow high visibility jacket, held a blue plastic clipboard. A piece of paper secured under the spring flapped in the cold, gusty wind that blew unimpeded across the concrete expanse. Despite the airport's impressive infrastructure, there were no other aircraft running. The agent offered a smile and his hand for Richard to shake. Richard merely gave his name as Jones. Preston came out backwards as he offered a caring hand to Marretti and then his shoulder for support as he helped him down to the tarmac. Naomi and Asharf followed.

'Mr Jones,' the man said, in a deep voice. 'We go immediately to the Presidential aircraft. It is waiting for you at the VIP terminal . . . please, this way.' The man looked past Richard towards the door. 'Your baggage?'

'There is none,' Richard replied, as he saw his party onto the bus.

Within minutes, the bus drew up outside a long, sleek aircraft which, by corporate jet standards, was large. Its livery was predominantly white, but with a blue underside. Richard noted the tricolour motif on its fin and the words "Republique Francaise" painted just behind the main cabin door. At the head of the steps stood a smart-looking Flight Attendant in a blue suit. Another, this time a woman, came partly into view; she strained her neck in order to see who was causing the fuss. Richard was last to ascend the steps and even before he entered the cabin, one of the two enormous engines started.

The rear cabin of the Presidential jet was small and intimate, a personal space for relaxation and clearly set apart from the much larger main cabin, with its retractable boardroom-like table, ten swivelling chairs, well-stocked drinks cabinets and silver-grey, clean-lined furnishings. It contained just four comfortable and well-used chairs positioned around a low, polished wooden coffee table that had been cleared of everything except an immovable crystal ashtray and an adjacent wooden cigar box. Positioned randomly on either side of a single, central door in the rear bulkhead, several framed photographs gave testament to the President's happy family circle. They added colour and life to the otherwise sterile surroundings. Behind the bulkhead was a small bedroom in which Marretti slept after being attended and given painkillers. Behind that was a cloakroom and shower compartment and access to a baggage area.

In perfect French, Naomi asked approval from the smartly dressed and coiffured Flight Attendant to use the cloakroom; she appeared shortly afterwards with perfect make-up and smelling of French perfume. Now well into the flight, she sat alone in the rear cabin. Comfortable but pensive, Naomi stared out through the small oval-shaped window next to her chair. Seemingly mesmerised by the darkening blue of the high atmosphere and the unbroken sheet of white cloud below, she clearly had a great deal on her mind.

Richard busied himself in the forward cabin by typing notes into the integrated tabletop keyboard. In due course, he would use the aircraft's secure satellite link to send his report to Peter Rothschild's office in London. Meanwhile, Asharf taking courage from Preston's small talk did not notice the other Flight Attendant who kept his distance, but Richard did. He saw the man's controlled distaste for his passenger's state of dress and obvious offence at their smell. He must think we're lousy as well, Richard thought, especially as Asharf's dreadful djellaba could probably give a good home to countless tiny creatures. Richard worked on, then looked up as the attendant's twitching reaction and rechecking of his watch had become compulsive. Richard smirked secretively. Eventually, he thought, we will all need to use the lavatory – what then?

Peter Rothschild's brief response to Richard's communication had raised some interesting points. Richard reread the message several times and then looked up thoughtfully. He caught Preston's eye.

'What is it, Boss?' Preston asked, uneasily.

'Oh, nothing . . . nothing that I can put my finger on, anyway – too many pieces of the jigsaw puzzle are still missing. There is certainly more to this matter than meets the eye though, Preston, that's for sure.'

They had not long achieved the cruising altitude of 70,000 feet when the Flight Attendant approached Richard with a telephone handset.

'*Pardon Monsieur Jones, s'il vous plait*,' she said, offering him the small device. 'It is London calling, for you.'

Richard smiled at her. 'Thanks,' he said. 'A little earlier than I expected.' He nodded and turned to look out of the window as he replied. 'Yes? Jones here!'

'Richard! It's Peter Rothschild; you are on your way I see.'

'Yes, we've been flying for a couple of hours.'

'Good. Now I need an explanation. The ISSF and the Emergency Cabinet are asking for a situation report. Time is running out – why Mauritius?'

'It is the only lead we have. This line is secure, Peter?'

'Absolutely, we are routing military to military, War Cabinet level protection. So, Richard, is it the best of a bad job?'

'No, more than that! It may be our only lead, but I believe it's a good one. Briefly, it appears that in the closing years of the sixteenth century the remaining circle of keepers – a quasi-religious sect who by all accounts was now all women – decided the Ark would be safer elsewhere, outside Africa – the Far East. Evidently, they feared for its safety and packed it inside a wooden crate for transportation. I will not go into the full story; however, they, nine women, arranged passage aboard a vessel plying the ancient trade route across the Indian Ocean towards the Orient. We found evidence that this vessel was stopped on the high seas close to Mauritius and its cargo commandeered. That vessel was Dutch and the Dutch were in the process of establishing the first colony on Mauritius. That's all we have!'

'I see,' replied Rothschild, sounding a little disappointed. 'Listen, the council have granted you complete autonomy for this mission. To me, it sounds as if you could have done a little better. Mauritius is *your* call Richard, so they will go along with it for the time being. You could say, of course, that we do not have any choice. You should know, however, that the situation is developing here in London – for the worse! Yesterday our energy commission reported back to the Prime Minister following a request for an independent resources census – an accurate assessment of the country's entire fuel reserves. Seems the remaining oil and gas reserves beneath the North Sea were overestimated *and* the gas supply from Russia has just dried up. Rationing quotas have been reduced again – the situation is getting desperate.'

'How long do we have, Peter? How long until the lights go out?'

'Eleven days, maybe twelve at best – then who knows? Anarchy? The security forces are already dealing with protest groups and violent outbreaks are becoming commonplace. There have been some shootings!'

Richard grabbed a breath, 'Bloody hell!' Preston looked across at him. Asharf looked up too.

'Precisely. So, please . . .'

'Listen, Peter, I believe that we are onto something, but I agree it does sound like a long shot. We land in under two hours. Give me twenty-four to investigate. I should know something by then, one way or the other. Did you get Preston's abrive?'

'Yes. Things have been arranged. They are opening the

archives and you will have some very qualified help. A local agent will meet you.'

'Copied. What is their name?'

'A man, Douchon. One last thing, Richard. Cheltenham has reported that two of their Globespan satellites sensed a powerful plasma blast a few hours ago, south of Asmara. There was no mistake. Adulis, coordinates indicated near the docks in the old part of town. Richard, we feared the worst.'

'Yeah, it was me. I'm in the middle of my report, but basically I was cornered by the opposition, including that East European undercover operative you mentioned during our brief in Khartoum. I used the ISTAN – no home casualties. They have some serious toys, Peter; my report specifies.'

'Understood. Good luck, I wait to hear from you . . . out.'

'Yeah, over and out!'

Richard carefully placed the handset on the table in front of him. Preston, who was busy putting two and two together from the one-sided conversation, raised an eyebrow as their eyes met. Richard shrugged. The Flight Attendant, whose name was Sophie, exchanged the telephone for a cup of tea and a warm hand towel; he used it to wipe away the tiredness from his face.

Richard checked his chronometer; there was still plenty of time for a wash and brush up and so he returned his attention to the keyboard and continued to type. After half an hour his concentration was broken by thoughts of Naomi and in his mind's eye, he saw her image and felt her staring at him – she seemed caring but distant. He woke from his daydream and awkwardly leant out from his seat in order to look back towards the rear cabin, but Naomi was not in sight.

Richard made the decision that Naomi had been on her own for long enough and stood up, stretched and walked aft. He winked at the Flight Attendant as he passed her. Entering the rear cabin, Naomi glanced up at him and smiled warmly. '*Bonjour* Richard. I was only just thinking of you,' she said softly.

Richard gestured nonchalantly and sat down beside her. 'Now, isn't that a coincidence!' he looked into her captivating eyes. 'Naomi, I want to say thank you for saving my life . . . again!'

Her familiar, intoxicating smile flickered across her face, but then her expression saddened. It seemed to Richard to echo a deep-seated preoccupation. Naomi looked down. 'I had the opportunity to do so and did as any other would do . . . that is all.' She looked up into Richard's eyes and held his gaze, which belied her mundane statement. 'For me though, my dear Richard, it is your *aura* that I would perpetuate, if given opportunity.'

Richard's expression turned quizzical. He moved closer, so that their shoulders pressed gently together. 'How do you mean?'

Naomi shook her head and continued in a whisper. 'So

much is forgotten, Richard. I know only a little of how it was in past times – only that which was passed on to me by my mother. As each generation has lived, a little more has been lost. Not intentionally, but that is the way of it. After the loss of the sacred casket in which all dictations were kept, the secrets of our ancestors faded. The knowledge that I am blessed with is mostly confined to this planet. After so many years of terrestrial study, it is clear to me that the people of earth drift – as the planet itself does, on the edge of this insignificant star cluster.'

Richard went to ask something, but Naomi interrupted. 'We know it as the Milky Way. Ours is just one small galaxy that is surrounded by countless others,' she said, confirming his unasked question.

Richard's thoughts flashed back to his study of the flight log that he had found in the remains of *The Star of Hope* – the crashed spaceship on Mars that he had later called the *Ark*. That manual contained numerous pages of stellar projections. Surely then they were universal travellers, in the sense of the word ... the old people ... the visitors... from another solar system, around another star. A question that he had pondered many months earlier rose again in his mind, for he had always suspected that the quest Admiral Dirkot Urket and his crew had embarked upon had originated on earth. Why then only as far as Mars? Why attempt a landing on the red planet, thousands of years after their arrival on earth? Moreover, practically speaking, the handling of a spaceship of which they had no previous experience – except perhaps in some kind of simulator – and presumably, the foolhardy attempt at a landing after what would have been a very short flight! Was Mars their intended destination, or could it be that the remains of the Babylon crystal, installed to power *The Star*, had faded faster than they had envisaged, leaving them short of fuel? Why Mars? Why a neighbouring planet?

Richard stared, blankly daydreaming. Naomi put a hand on his knee; her touch pulled him from his racing thoughts. 'You are confused. I can see it!'

'You described me once Naomi, as a sceptic. Well, I am beginning to think that you are right.' Richard rubbed the palms of his hands together and tapped his chin with his fingertips in a philosophical manner. 'I have always thought of myself as open-minded, but I am definitely having difficulty coming to terms with the emerging picture of this jigsaw puzzle – despite the hard evidence. You see, the thing is, I grew up with science, the Laws of Physics, practical things, you know . . . what goes up, must come down – a sort of, well, reasoned approach. My life *is* a practical thing. In space, if you want to stay alive, you abide by the rules.' Richard held up his hands as he emphasised his words. 'Rules based on these things,' he said. 'What you can do, see and feel!' With a straight finger, he pointed to the criss-crossing lines on the palm of his left hand and then, as if emphasising his point, he scribed the arc of his lifeline. 'There is nothing written here that is of use to *me*, Naomi!'

Naomi shrugged. 'Yours is the way of the world, Richard. It is a sad fact, but true. History screams at us, but no one listens. I have said this before. There are but a few of us who remain, those with some knowledge of the old ways, but we have no opportunity or ability to influence. Time itself and money, have become the masters for the people of planet earth. What was before is all but lost.'

Richard drew a deep breath and paused to look briefly out through the window and then stared into Naomi's eyes again. 'What do you mean *aura*, anyway? What is it, exactly?'

Naomi hesitated. 'The word itself is from the old language; only later was it changed in Greek and Latin. It is another piece of the jigsaw that in your own words, you already struggle to comprehend, Richard,' she offered.

Richard eyes widened. 'Try me,' he said.

'It is the intrinsic energy of life. Put simply, your aura is your own *reflection* in terms of energy – if you like, it is your spirit.'

Richard unconsciously tilted his head. 'The energy of life,' he repeated slowly.

'Perhaps, more importantly, it is your contribution to the energy of the universe and combines with it during the endless circle of life. Life has impetus, Richard, a driving momentum of being – just like any other law of your beloved physics. By your aura, you are tied to the magnetic field of the planet and therefore eternity. However, as with all things, there are two sides to it, positive and negative, creative and disruptive. The visitors, the old people, knew it well.'

Richard's eyes narrowed. 'Two sides – opposite ends of the spectrum,' he said, engrossed. 'You mean good and bad, don't you?'

'Yes. However, with the demise of the old people, there was a loss of understanding – both scientifically and spiritually. The natural cycle became misconstrued. Instead of an interdependent relationship of positive and negative that flows to and from each other, the perception became good and bad . . . good and evil!'

Richard thought for a moment and nodded. 'Of course! Man's obsession with heaven and hell – in one form or another. So that's where it comes from . . . the distant past, the dawn of civilisation.'

'It is only with humans that this yearning for a purpose is obsessive; it is part of our being. And a belief in spirits is also well founded and stems from a much earlier, endemic species on earth.'

Richard looked quizzical. 'By that, do you mean, the Neanderthals?'

Naomi paid no heed to Richard's speculation. 'The gods of man, Richard,' she continued. 'Most numerous and evolving; they are historically much more recent.'

Richard paused for thought. 'So . . . all the way back through the ages,' he uttered, as if reinforcing the point to himself. 'The ancient Egyptians . . . they had Amun-Re, the universal god and many others, including a god of evil. Then the Greeks . . . Zeus, the overlord of the Olympian gods, god of the sky – Hades was their god of the underworld. Then the Romans; Apollo for the sun and sky and Pluto of the underworld.' Richard paused again. 'Later religions developed different ideas and names, the Norse gods, for example . . . Thor, god of the sky and Hel, goddess of death – but they all have similar references.'

Naomi nodded. 'That is how I understand it. There is positive and negative in all things, Richard. Even the fundamental building block of matter conforms. The *atom*, with its positively charged nucleus surrounded by negatively charged electrons!'

Richard's expression became less of confusion and more of wonderment. 'You know, there was an attention grabbing newspaper headline written about me a few months ago. It made the front page of the *London Review*, in fact a very influential newspaper in the UK. It said that if our religion should ever be put on trial, *I* would be the chief witness for the prosecution called to the dock by science. Because of my ill-fated discovery of the crashed spaceship on Mars you understand, and its ramifications. Now I'm beginning to catch on. What they said about me simply wasn't true, although even now I'm not sure if it was a case of wrong place at the wrong time, or otherwise. It's just a matter of time, isn't it? Finding things, in this solar system or outside it.' Richard raised his eyebrows and shrugged. 'What else about this aura, Naomi? What else can you tell me?'

'Every living thing has an aura, both animal and plant. The energy of life flows through and around each and every cell. The writings say that this is the same throughout the universe, even though differing chemical composition may cause life forms that we do not recognise. And there is proportion to it.'

Richard winced, smiled mischievously and muttered, 'you mean size really does matter?'

Naomi continued, heedless of Richard's attempted humour. She focused on him intently. 'You are unaware of it, Richard, but *your* aura is unusually strong. I suspect there may be a measure of destiny woven in amongst it. Compared to a mighty oak, however, or a giant blue whale in the ocean, for example, yours is of much less consequence.'

Richard thought for a moment and then gestured with a smile. 'You mean like those weirdy types one occasionally reads about in the past, who embraced trees or encouraged their plants to grow by engaging in stimulating conversations – needless to say one way. There was something in it?'

This time Naomi flashed a smile. 'Ah, my dear Richard, how the sceptic in you rises and falls and rises again.'

Richard shook his head. 'No, I am listening, Naomi. Seriously, I am. Please, go on.'

'When the old people first arrived here, this planet's life-energy, its essence, extended into space well beyond the magnetic influence of its molten core – it was the reason that they changed course. This is plainly written in the Great Pyramid. Now though, with complete deforestation, it barely extends beyond the planet's surface.'

Richard nodded. 'And what about people, Naomi, and their life force?'

'When we die – or in some cases, when the passing is inevitable, and then just before – our aura leaves the body and rises – it is drawn up into the heavens. Here it joins, or perhaps rejoins, the universal energy. Stars, even galaxies are born, die and are reborn. Astronomers have proved this beyond any doubt.'

'What if, for whatever reason, I don't know, if you were "demagnetised" for instance, one's aura can't make the journey, something prevents it . . . what then?'

'Sometimes this happens. The reasons are complex and I do not fully understand them. But in these cases, the aura remains in a misplaced dimension, our dimension, the *third* dimension. Some become disturbed, unsettled, or even divisive. They can manifest themselves.'

Richard nodded slowly. 'So then we are lost. Right? Just becoming a part of the energy of the cosmos?'

'You will never be lost, Richard. For you will remember who you are and who it was you loved. So great is the expanse, you may never meet again with those, but you remain aware of your being, otherwise there would be no point! The descendants of the four tribes knew this well, although over millennia the misunderstanding occurred.'

Richard stared breathless for a moment. 'The ancient

Egyptians and the passage to the afterlife, and the Maya and the rising spirits, the privileged being launched from the tops of their great pyramids!' He seemed mesmerised by Naomi's eyes. 'The Egyptians and the other early civilisations left artefacts in their tombs to help in the afterlife...boats, tools, clothing even food...that is what you mean, right? Their intentions, their understanding of the passage back to universal energy became misconstrued.'

Naomi nodded. 'The faith of our ancestors encompassed the belief that a return of the aura to this place was possible – not for all, but for some,' Naomi continued, 'only in these cases the past is forgotten, leaving the spirit free. Of those who return, it was said that rare flashes of a previous life could sometimes occur.' A brief smile lit Naomi's face.

'So, some of the people here on earth are reincarnated? Oh, come on!'

'Some are, yes ... but like a newborn star, most are pure universal energy.'

'Do you know any of these reincarnated people, Naomi? I mean really?'

'Strangely, the word you use to describe the reborn is apt. It is derived from a Latin word and means "to clothe with flesh", and that from a much earlier form. You must understand that the earth is only a speck of dust; energy flows to and around all the living planets in the universe and there are far too many to even contemplate. It is unlikely that a reincarnate would return.'

'Okay, I can understand that ... but do *you* know any?'

Naomi looked embarrassed for a moment. 'The necessary camouflage of the reincarnate covers all. I have had my suspicions over the years, but I could never be sure.'

Richard thought deeply for a moment and rubbed his stubble as he looked sideways at Naomi. 'How about Professor Simpson-Carter, your grandfather? Was *he* a reincarnate, Naomi?'

Naomi paused; she knew that she had already gone too far.

'From what my mother told me, my grandmother did suspect this, yes; although you understand, it was only a suspicion.'

'Can the aura be seen?'

'Yes, it can by a psychic and in different colours. Some can be trained. In others, the force can be sensed through the hands!'

'Who by? Who can sense it by these means?'

'Those who are blessed . . . and believe.'

'Give me an example?'

Naomi thought on the question and rubbed the bridge of her nose. 'The ancient Chinese and Japanese, their knowledge was derived from centuries of study and an uncanny understanding; an unfathomable understanding – the beginning of which still lies lost in time. They were able to trace life's aura – plot its extent on the paper they had invented. Chi, Yin and Yang, call it what you will, it is essentially the energy flow through the meridians of the body. To the initiated, illness was diagnosed as interruptions in the flow of energy and by correcting it they were able to heal – a positive application called Acupuncture.'

Richard considered further the implications of this energy conundrum. 'So what of the crystals, Naomi?' he asked with a serious frown. 'Are they this *universal energy* in a solid form?'

Naomi started Yogic breathing, her eyes closed while she breathed out slowly and deliberately through her nose. Richard watched her, entranced by her stillness and the beauty that came from within. It was a while before she answered. 'A sceptic with a probing mind,' she said, her voice a whisper. 'You are indeed a man of many parts.'

Richard gently picked up Naomi's hand and raised it to his lips. She blinked, opened her eyes and inexplicably pulled her hand away roughly. Richard grimaced, this time it was he who was a little embarrassed.

'Ever since that night, Naomi, you have been different regarding the two of us . . . so distant.'

Naomi paused as her expression changed to one of sorrow. 'Someone else holds the key to your heart, Richard. Unfortunately, you have forgotten this,' she said, and then looked away momentarily before lowering her head sadly.

There was a muffled cough. It was Preston who had walked, unnoticed, into the cabin.

'Excuse me. Sorry,' he said, a little sheepishly. 'Boss,

the Skipper has asked me to inform you that we are approaching the cloud break. It's coming up fast and it looks bloody enormous. He has invited you up front. For you to see it first hand, before commencing the descent . . . it *is* quite a sight. He also wants a quick word – perhaps you first, Boss, and then Madame Vallogia.'

'I'm on my way, thanks Preston.' Richard turned to Naomi.

'We will continue this another time,' he said quietly.

$$\text{𓅱𓆓𓂋𓏤 𓆓𓂝𓂝𓂋𓏤 𓈖𓆑𓂋𓏤}$$

It *was* quite a sight. From their altitude of 70,000 feet – almost 12 nautical miles high – and at a distance of some 80 miles, there, ahead of them, an enormous blue hole punctuated the never-ending emulsion of insipid, white, cloud.

The French Air Force Captain introduced himself as Phillip Borghine and offered Richard the jump seat that had already been positioned between and slightly behind the two pilots' seats. The co-pilot was a pretty blonde woman who smiled over her shoulder at Richard.

Richard stared out through the windscreen with great interest. Eventually, the co-pilot called his attention to the weather radar display, which clearly showed the extent of the cloud break.

'A circle sixty miles wide, centred on Mauritius. We

came down a few months ago, it is so beautiful,' she spoke English with a delightful French accent, but it was nowhere near as accentuated as that of the Captain.

Richard checked their speed – Mach 1 and reducing. Minutes later, they flew over the huge blue hole. Captain Borghine took the controls and then disconnected the autopilot. He pushed the nose of the aircraft forwards and simultaneously banked steeply to the left – as he did, some way below, Richard could see the tropical ocean. They descended through the pristine air and Borghine began to follow the periphery of the hole. They flew a spiral descent pattern until levelling at 3000 feet above the sea.

On the radar display, Reunion Island indicated well off to their right and much further away in their ten o'clock position, the Island of Rodrigues, painted repeatedly as a tiny blip as the scanner swept from side to side. And then, on the horizon immediately in front of them appeared the contours of Mauritius itself. There were smiles all round.

'You can see this break in the cloud from a quarter of a million miles out into space,' Richard commented dryly.

'Do you know why it exists?' asked Borghine.

'To an extent,' replied Richard.

Borghine nodded. 'A beautifully cold and dry high-altitude jet stream from Antarctica. Do you know what the meteorologists are saying?'

Richard shook his head – an update would be helpful, he thought.

'That the effect is lessening. The jet stream continues to

blow from the southern continent as it has always done. Nevertheless, they plot subtle shifts in its course and rising temperatures – that means more moisture. The days of this sight are numbered, Monsieur Jones.'

As they neared the island, its lush greenness became apparent. Richard clearly recognised the topography. Captain Borghine keyed in his call sign, security clearance, his updated flight parameters, a request into the communications control device then transmitted everything via a satellite link to Mauritius Air Traffic Control. Seconds later appeared the response:

**French Force 1 – clear Microwave Landing System Runway 14 Left. Clear to land.**

Borghine acknowledged. Richard asked if Naomi could step up and see the view and moments later a Flight Attendant escorted her onto the flight deck. She stood behind Richard with her hands on his shoulders until the two parallel runways of Sir Seewoosagur Ramgoolam International Airport were clear to see. Not until the point of landing could Naomi be persuaded to return to her seat.

As expected, the main apron teemed with aircraft, some departing and some arriving, whilst others, moving under their own power or by mechanical means were positioned to more remote parts to make room. The terminal area was a hive of activity, aircraft, vehicles and people making a kaleidoscope of sound and colour. Richard was interested to see less than half appeared to be commercial services. The private sector certainly dominates here, he thought, and the livery too, was from all over the world.

'Captain Borghine. That aircraft over there, the one being towed towards the hanger – what type is it? Do you know?' As Richard asked the question, he leant forward between the two pilots and pointed at a mid-sized business jet on the other side of the apron.

'*Oui*, Monsieur Jones; it is an Eclipse 950; a capable aeroplane in its time. The model is about twenty-five years old now – built by Solar Aeronautica, if I remember correctly.'

Richard stared intently at the aircraft. It was a classic business design with two large jet engines mounted on pylons above each wing, but its livery was unusual, being plain white. Apart from the registration mark, painted in black on the vertical stabiliser and a small logo in blue just forward of the main cabin door there were no other identification features.

'What about performance?' Richard probed further.

'Well, a little dated of course, and there are only a few around these days. In fact, it is the first example that I have seen in a few years. It is supersonic, if I recall, but not by much – around Mach 1.3. A very good range though. That is why the type was popular in its time. Ten passengers, a full tank, it will make for example, Rome to San Francisco in approximately ten hours, and with fuel to spare.

Richard nodded thoughtfully and then his attention focused on the registration:

## *I-4GOD*

'And what about that registration mark, Captain? India, Four, Golf, Oscar, Delta – I mean, that's not normal is it? The international designation system changed decades ago.'

Captain Borghine paused for a moment as he monitored the apron's automatic parking system to manoeuvre his aircraft onto the allocated stand. The aircraft stopped and a green light illuminated on the central warning panel. He set the parking brake, shut down the engines and then turned to Richard. 'It is an old mark, *Oui*? And unusual I have to agree. However, in the executive and business jet world, we do still see them, although only occasionally. As I understand it, private registrations that had been under the same ownership for more than sixty years when the new designation system came into force in 2018 were given the option – retain the old mark and supply necessary air traffic control information on each digital flight plan submitted, or adopt the new system and benefit from flight plan automation. Adopting the current system involved repainting the aircraft and applying the electrodata film. At the time, perhaps the owner of that Eclipse 950 did not wish to spend the money – that is all.'

Richard and the two pilots watched as the sleek aircraft disappeared behind another parked inside the cavernous hanger. Almost immediately, two giant doors slid slowly closed. Inexplicably, Richard's attention lingered on the building. He was troubled. 'I - 4GOD . . . *I - 4GOD,*' he repeated. 'How did the old registration system work exactly?'

Captain Borghine appeared perplexed. His brow furrowed and his expression and tone changed to one of mild frustration. With Richard in the way, his first officer remained trapped in her seat and he needed to finish recording the flight details into the management computer and secure the aircraft for the night; with luck, he may even make it to the beach. The young woman sighed and looked at the Captain, as if to say, does it really matter? Richard, unmoved, however, raised his eyebrows in anticipation.

'It was the standard from the very beginning, Monsieur Jones. The first digit was the country of registration, Italy in this case. The remaining four digits merely composed the unique identifier. It was completely random, much like the old motor vehicle number plates – if you had a good one, your name for instance, it could be worth a lot of money . . . they became valuable, collectables. As I say, it was a random system, whatever was available at the time. Anyway, towards the end, variations based on four digits became the limiting factor. There was also a lack of information – just the identification. The current system not only registers the aircraft, but in addition, relays pertinent information to air traffic control authorities.'

'Completely random,' Richard repeated, slowly. 'So the system was completely random, and with no auto-track either?' There was suspicion in his tone.

'*Pardon monsieur, s'il vous plait.* I am told that you have an aviation background, so you will understand. These old registration marks do not normally mean anything . . . *I, four god* . . . it is just coincidental. Now, please, if you do not mind.'

The Captain turned his attention to the computer and politely dismissed Richard.

Olivier Douchon waited patiently. Immediately outside the terminal, on the Arrivals level, there was a long line of taxis and his car, a metallic-black Japanese model of bullish proportions half blocked the leader road. He stood with a bunch of keys in one hand and a telephone in the other, casually watching the bustle of people leaving the airport, and apparently totally impervious to the frustrated comments of numerous taxi drivers as they carefully manoeuvred their vehicles around his, some even mounting the pavement to do so.

Driving on the left in Mauritius put him within earshot of even the most surreptitious cursing, but it was only those remarks containing criticisms of a personal nature that caused his head to turn. He also seemed well known, as many of the passers by, particularly smartly dressed men with business-like demeanours, acknowledged him with a civil nod; some held out their hands and received a brief, "chummy" handshake.

Richard was nowhere to be seen. After checking and rechecking the time, Douchon began to look a little concerned. He pressed a preselect key on his telephone and waited for an answer. Somewhere inside the building on the desk of an immigration official, a receiver rang. Eventually, a uniformed man who was busying himself in the vicinity leaned across and picked up the handset. 'Immigration!' he blurted, impatiently.

'Douchon here . . . do we have a problem?' There was a pause, Douchon nodded at the reply. '*Unusual*,' he emphasised, after another period of silence, apparently repeating the word. 'This is Government business, officer. The documentation may be delayed, but it *is* on its way . . . yes, today . . . I can assure you.' Douchon went to speak, he was interrupted and then spoke a sentence in Creole, the local tongue; it ended with: 'Rhys Jones . . . *Oui, ca c'est exact.*' He nodded again and then switched off the telephone.

Douchon was a burly man, not overly tall, but of ample proportions. He had muscular forearms and hands that gave him a "Popeye" look. His short fair hair was wispy and thinning and his rounded face had a jovial appeal. The form of his hat had pressed a circular rim into his hair and this had been reinforced by dried sweat. He wore beige, cotton baggy trousers, white canvas deck shoes and a creased, multi-coloured Hawaiian-style shirt. In the shade, he leaned nonchalantly against an adjacent steel post that displayed a triangular taxi sign above his head and was satisfied with his assurances given to the immigration official; clearly, he expected Richard and his party to show up soon. Meanwhile, the warm fresh breeze that blew almost continuously from the south-east dried the remnants of two large damp patches beneath his armpits. His general air of bonhomie fooled no one. They all knew he was "dangerous".

Minutes later, Richard turned the corner at the bottom of a shallow ramp. Naomi and Preston walked immediately behind him, whilst Asharf, who was offering Charles Marretti a supporting arm and carrying his near empty rucksack, followed a few metres behind. From his brief, there was no mistaking Richard, and Douchon met him halfway. Although the inclined walkway was covered, the sight of sunshine and shadow and the feel of the warm breeze made Richard turn to Naomi sporting a wide, relaxed grin. Naomi was clearly equally delighted and her face lit up in response. Douchon offered his hand, Richard shook it and the two men eyed each other briefly.

'Welcome to Mauritius, Mr Jones. My name is Olivier Douchon, Government Security. I've been expecting you. My brief is to offer you every assistance.'

Richard nodded. 'Thanks, good to be here, it's been a long time. This is Madame Vallogia and my colleagues Preston, Asharf and Charles Marretti.' Richard followed Douchon's eyes as he took in Marretti's bandaged foot and his rolled up left trouser leg with the bulky padding bound around his upper calf. 'Yes, he's got a bad gash and a sublet passed clean through his foot – he's lucky, could have been much worse. I would appreciate some medical attention if possible,' Richard added.

'My orders are to get started immediately, Mr Jones. However, I recommend that I take you to your hotel first. We pass Clinic Mathurins on the way. Without insurance it's difficult on the island these days, but I know someone. He will be in good hands, I can assure you. Probably keep him in for a while to be on the safe side.'

Richard looked at Marretti, who nodded appreciatively. 'That's settled then,' said Richard, as he scrutinised the people surrounding them.

'Don't worry!' Douchon assured him, understanding his suspicions. 'Not much happens on this island that I am not party to, Mr Jones. That's what I'm paid for. I get to hear about everybody who arrives on our island and everybody who leaves. There is no threat to your safety here, not at the moment anyway. Shall we?'

Douchon led the way to his car; opening its doors blocked the traffic flow completely. With bags in the boot, Richard climbed in last and sat next to Douchon. As he closed his door, their host quickly drove off. Richard looked behind. He focused on the congestion and then on Douchon again. This man is more than his sum of parts; there is much more than meets the eye, he thought.

The southern coast road was much as Richard remembered it – with the exception of one or two more hotels. Despite what he had heard, this part of the island still boasted open fields of ripening sugarcane, white, sundrenched beaches, essential tropical flora and few people. The whole experience was a delight and Naomi could barely restrain herself from pointing out things of interest to the others. For them, the memory of a year's continuous rain and sombre outlook took a little longer to wash away. Nevertheless, Richard, Preston and Asharf were soon struggling to contain UV-induced high spirits. In contrast, the bright light only caused Marretti's headache to worsen and as a result he remained slumped, head in hands, until they arrived at the extensive, low, white-washed buildings of Clinic Mathurins, where a brief stop of no more than ten minutes had him safely ensconced – due to Olivier Douchon's undoubted charisma.

Back on the road, Douchon's innate egocentricity, albeit mildy suppressed, was eventually out-voted by his deprived passengers and he turned off the vehicle's air-conditioning and opened all the windows. Subsequently, he sat uncomfortably in silence as the moist air circulated and the rushing wind ruffled hair and clothing. It was not long before he was perspiring again. The winding road had provided many opportunities to admire the island's south coast beaches and also the tantalising reef which surfaced periodically about half a kilometre offshore. Between the two, numerous fishermen stood up to their waists in tropical blue waters with long poles waiting for the day's catch. They drove round the southern peninsular near *Bel Ombre* and a few miles further on skirted the periphery of a small bay where, at its northern end, the road was completely submerged. At its deepest, with seawater lapping at his door sills, Douchon reduced their speed to walking pace. Naomi watched, almost intoxicated as their bow wave disturbed the adjacent mango swamps. A number of seabirds that sought refuge beneath the stilt-like exposed roots bobbed up and down.

'Damned global warming,' Douchon complained. 'This road was half a metre above sea level a few years ago.'

Naomi, ignoring criticisms of this deserted paradise, simply asked where exactly they were.

'*Baje du Cap*,' Douchon explained gruffly.

On the western side of the bay, and formed by a small volcanic spur, was another small peninsula, although the road broke from the beach line for a few miles and carved a route through a narrow strip of mainly coniferous forest. After that, the view opened to reveal a broad panorama of the island's south-western cape. It was an inspiring sight and now even more so. Certainly for Richard, it reinforced its status as a lasting favourite compared to any he had seen in the solar system.

In this south-western corner of the island, however, reality was quite different. Here, numerous sprawling hotels operated at capacity. Only a few roads serviced the area, and these were also crammed full. Traffic squeezed slowly towards various hotel gates, using, in the main, "green" fuel distilled on an industrial scale from sugarcane waste. The area of Le Morne was such a hive of activity that Richard could barely recognise it and inevitably "people" featured in every view.

'Which hotel do you have in mind?' Richard asked, in a disappointed tone.

'Paradise Bay,' answered Douchon, glancing across at Richard whilst pointing further along the single carriageway road. 'I know the manager. Every hotel on the island is permanently full. You can't just book a room here anymore, there's red tape and legislation. And you need lots of money!'

'Yeah, I heard about that and I'm not surprised,' replied Richard. 'Mauritius and the nearby islands . . . there is nowhere else on the planet where the sun still shines. It's how I remembered it . . . amazing!'

Douchon nodded. 'Business is booming, but to me it doesn't mean anything. Better to preserve, keep the island safe, the services running . . . fresh water for instance, with so many people here and an increase in manufacturing, there's a permanent shortage and it's not the hotels that suffer, *they* can pay the exorbitant charges.'

Richard gestured his agreement and then stared up at the sky. The irrepressible south-east trade winds blew a never-ending series of puffy white clouds across the translucent blue expanse. As was customary, a few of the larger ones gathered and loitered in the vicinity of the towering Le Morne Brabant Mountain, a dramatic basaltic rock outcrop with a peak rising abruptly 800 feet above sea level. The jostling clouds cast rolling shadows over the mountainside below. Richard appeared contently mesmerised. Nothing could detract from such a dazzling sun drenching. He tracked a bird until it disappeared into the dense tropical foliage that covered the rising ground off to his right and his bare arm, resting on the window edge, showed a red colour. 'What about the seasonal rains?' he asked. 'After all, winter is approaching?'

'To be honest, Mr Jones, it's raining much more frequently these days and not just because of the season. Average figures indicate a marked increase over last year, and every previous year for that matter. Today is beautiful, like a beautiful welcome, but days like this are becoming the exception. The frequency of cloudy, overcast periods is increasing; there is no doubt about that.'

Richard looked back at Douchon. 'I don't want to spoil the party but you know, don't you, that this hole is closing? I wouldn't waste your time listening to the meteorologists;

their speculation is little better than ours. I can tell you that the uniqueness of this particular area of the Indian Ocean is definitely temporary. High above us, in the upper troposphere, relatively dry and clean air still dominates the weather pattern, but the system is breaking down. Your population problem may just cure itself in the coming few months.'

With Richard's words resounding in his ears, Douchon suddenly mounted the grass verge to his left. Taking care to avoid beds of red flowering bougainvillea and paying no attention to the frustrated beeps of queuing motorists, he drove the final two hundred metres to the entrance of the hotel. Two security guards standing beside closed gates made ready to challenge him until they saw his face. After that, one even gave a nonchalant salute. The hotel entrance was a grand affair with sweeping curved walls that culminated in dominating gateposts and ornate metal gates, above which the hotel name "Paradise Bay" was ostentatiously displayed in gold-painted, forged metal letters. They drove under the arches and through extensive gardens to arrive at the main building.

'You and I should go immediately to Port Louis, Mr Jones,' said Douchon, looking sternly at Richard. 'I suggest everyone else checks in and has some downtime.'

Richard looked over his shoulder at Naomi and Preston. 'That's a good idea. Relax for a while, why don't you? Take some time out, I'll be back later. How many rooms do we have?' he asked Douchon.

'Only three; best I could do.'

'Take all the rooms, I'll sort something out on my return,' Richard said.

Preston looked put out as he climbed from his seat. He was not happy at the thought of shirking his duties again, despite Richard's orders and the beckoning beach resort. Richard sensed this. 'I've got good cover, okay? You and Asharf look after Naomi; number one priority.'

Preston collected the bags from the boot of the vehicle and gave Richard a sharp nod as he followed Naomi and Asharf into the hotel lobby. Without another word, Douchon quickly drove off back through the colourful gardens and onto the narrow road; back onto the nearside verge and occasionally the other carriageway, weaving between oncoming cars and others that queued. Douchon rechecked his watch and now drove urgently; they were behind time and there were people waiting for them. Moments later, he joined the main road by driving the wrong way around a roundabout and then accelerated hard as this road opened into dual carriageway.

The main road north to Port Louis was less congested than Richard remembered. After twenty minutes' driving, the road narrowed to one lane in each direction as they passed through the old village of Black River and there was a memorable wooden church building with a spire on the right hand side. After the village, the road opened; another stretch of dual carriageway beckoned, and Douchon put his foot down. Not long after that, Richard craned his neck to track the impressive entrance to the Tamarista Golf Club on his left, and then the junction leading west to the coast and *Flic en Flac*; he was familiar with the area. Douchon checked his watch again.

'What's the rush?' Richard asked.

'Traffic! It's the same every day. It's like a blood clot, blocking the arteries, nothing moves. Mid-morning, mid-afternoon or late evening, otherwise forget it. We need to make the city centre before four, that way we'll avoid the congestion. It's serious, I'm telling you!'

'How many people on the island these days, would you say?'

'A little over a year ago the resident population was 1.4 million, plus about a million transients during the peak holiday season. Now the tourists outnumber the permanent population by three to one. The government has finally realised that the island should come first. There's been a crackdown. Now immigration is the most important and best funded department . . . and it's about time!'

Richard smiled engagingly. 'You seem to know who comes and who goes on the island – that normally comes with being a local,' he said.

'*Oui*, that is part of the job. And I'm French-Mauritian. My family line is from one of the original French colonists, but I was schooled in South Africa.'

Richard looked across at Douchon for a moment, as if summing him up, and then nodded again slowly. 'Tell me then,' he said a little anxiously. 'As part of your job . . . I saw a private jet at the airport this morning. It was being towed into a hangar – displacing two others in the process. It was an older type, a *Solar*, the transcontinental *Eclipse* model, I'm told. Apparently the registration was Italian. Do you know anything about it?'

Douchon glanced briefly but quizzically at Richard and then focused again on the road ahead. 'The Italians like it here, especially those from the south, and there are a lot of them – they really miss the sun back home, ha ha, don't they all?' Douchon paused thoughtfully. 'I think that the aircraft you refer to may belong to a business man from Rome. More than that I don't know . . . but I can find out. What's the deal?'

Richard thought for a moment and then shrugged. 'Oh, it's probably nothing. No, forget it. I'm just being paranoid.' Richard watched the scenery pass for a few minutes and then asked, 'So, what *is* the deal?'

Douchon glanced at him. 'We received only a patchy briefing from London and that was less than twelve hours ago. It's not very specific regarding your precise requirements. They gave us some dates, a few names, that sort of thing, but that was it. Use your own initiative, that's what they told us. *Merde!*' Douchon thumped the steering wheel with his fist. He meant to tell of his frustrations but his concentration was diverted by a stray dog that darted across the road – begrudgingly he avoided it. 'In twenty-three years I've never been so ill informed. The service is being run by amateurs . . . well . . . anyway.' He glanced across at Richard again and accelerated. The last few shanty houses of a small village passed them by and then they were surrounded by sugar cane – mature green plants, reaching for the sunlight and pushing all of two metres in height from the red, stone-filled soil. The road cut a swathe through the landscape as Douchon continued. 'We immediately put several government operatives on the case and enlisted the services of the island's most eminent historian. So, first stop for us is Government House. It's the oldest building in Port Louis, perhaps even the whole island – down by the harbour. Most of the old colonial buildings have long since rotted away. This one has been preserved. It's been the seat of government in one way or another since it was completed in 1740. A Frenchman built it. Almost a relative, I'm proud to say. An aristocratic sea captain named Bertrand Mahe de Labourdonnais, a man recognised as the first Governor . . . but of the Ile de France you understand . . . the Island of France.' Douchon glanced again. 'Are you interested in history, Mr Jones?'

'If it's relevant.'

'Ah! D'accord! But with this brief, I haven't a clue what is relevant and what is not!'

'Then you had better continue with the lesson, Mr Douchon,' Richard replied, bluntly.

Olivier Douchon nodded. 'Oui! Government House consisted originally of a wooden hut covered with palm tree leaves. Part of the building was constructed during the term of Nicolas de Maupin who was in charge of the island between 1729 and 1735. Labourdonnais set about reconstructing and enlarging the house in 1738 and the additions were built primarily of stone, volcanic stone. He built to impress and to last and below his new house, he also excavated extensive cellarage. I don't need to remind you that Mauritius has a cyclonic climate. The house was the seat of successive governors both during the French and the British years – 95 years and 158 years respectively. Whilst the island was in French hands, word has it that the cellars were used to store not only colonial and state artefacts, but also treasure and contraband pirated first from the former Dutch colonists and then from passing ships who for one reason or another had strayed into territorial waters. Apparently, the French retained a sizeable fleet in the region, certainly until the British claimed the island. There was a serious naval engagement, early in the nineteenth century, in waters off the north-east coast. The French came second!'

'Okay,' replied Richard, displaying his new-found curiosity with a concentrated stare. 'So when, according to the *local* historical records, did the Dutch claim the island?'

'A Dutch admiral, by the name of Van Warwyck, was in command of a fleet that landed in the bay now known as Grand Port. The year was 1598. There was a short Portuguese occupation earlier that century, but they had abandoned the place decades earlier. Warwyck named the bay after himself incidentally, Warwyck Haven. He was also the man who called the island Mauritius – out of respect for a member of the Dutch royalty.'

Richard nodded in agreement but then his brow furrowed.

'1598? You're sure of that?'

'Sure as I can be, why?'

'Well, the plot I'm chasing began in 1596 with some pirating.'

'By the Dutch?'

Richard nodded.

'Listen. This is not an exact science. In those days, it would have taken all of three months for a message to get back to Holland, maybe more. We know that the Dutch were in this area years earlier, plying the trade routes, both legitimately and illegitimately, and anyway, these seas were full of pirates . . . from all over – even from the orient. That means trading vessels would require protection. There is no doubt that the Dutch had been here for some time prior to Warwyck's historic arrival. By all accounts, he amassed a sizeable fleet, probably the largest ever seen in these waters. In 1598 it was certainly large enough for him to be confident about staking a claim. It was all about sea power. You should know that . . . you remember – *Rule Britannia, Britannia rules the waves!*' There was sarcasm in his melody.

Richard sighed. 'And?' he replied impatiently.

'Subsequently, the Dutch attempted to colonise the

island, funded in part by the Netherlands East India Company. There were rich pickings to be had: ebony, ambergris and the conditions were perfect for tobacco too, but it didn't work. They abandoned this place in 1710. Lots of reasons – not enough settlers, the cyclonic weather, disease ... some historians say that they were finally driven off the island by runaway slaves bent on vengeance for their ill treatment.'

Richard rubbed his chin. 'If, as you imply, the final few colonists had fled, then it's reasonable to assume that things would have been left behind; things deemed worthless at any rate – perhaps buried things.'

'Maybe, but what would slaves want with buried treasure anyway? Artefacts, gold, jewellery – useless, all of it! They would have been more concerned with survival – food and fresh water. Later generations of runaway slaves all retreated into the forests ... so these probably did the same.'

'I am thinking more of a box!'

Douchon glanced at Richard, his expression inscrutable; then back to the road ahead. 'Ah, I see,' he said, slowly, 'this *Ark* for which you search.'

Richard nodded. 'If it made these shores, then the Dutch would have given everything they had to open it. Gunpowder, cannon shot, chains, saws, you name it; but they would have failed. I don't mind telling you, as you already seem to know something of it, that this *Ark* would have been impenetrable – materials not from around here, you might say.'

Douchon shrugged as though in agreement; nothing more it seemed, needed to be explained.

'So what of the French, Mr Douchon? When did they come on the scene?'

Douchon was pondering the question when his attention was snatched away by the car in front. It braked suddenly distracting him. He avoided it skilfully and informed the driver of his discontent with a long, loud BEEP! Then he answered Richard with another question: 'If you found it, this Ark, could *you* open it?'

'Maybe. I once had access to a special book of formulaic construction that I managed to translate. That is why I'm a wanted man. Now! What of the French?'

Richard saw Douchon's eyes widen and it wasn't because of the pack of wild dogs that suddenly and haphazardly darted out from behind giant tufts of sugar cane. He felt sure he'd touched a nerve.

'Well?' Richard pressed.

'They took possession of the island just five years later in 1715. Guillaume Dufresne d'Arsel, a French nobleman raised his flag right here, in the name of King Louis XV. He drew up a document witnessed by his officers declaring the island French and sailed away after three days.'

'By here, you mean the Port Louis district, right?'

Douchon gestured further on and simultaneously reduced his speed as the dense, claustrophobic fields of sugar cane came to an abrupt end, giving way to a rambling conurbation. Douchon stopped at a set of traffic lights and watched impatiently as several people crossed the road. He hammered the steering wheel with the heel of his left hand.

Richard stared at the red light. 'Where are you getting the electricity for all this, and the cars for that matter?' he asked.

'Wind generation in the main. Five farms, big ones, all facing the south-east trades, four in the shallow lagoons inside the reef and one up on the high ground. They also burn sugarcane waste in furnaces for steam turbines and there is a bit of diesel remaining – the government built a huge underground holding facility, twenty-odd years ago now, after the spot market reached 500 dollars a barrel. As for the cars, well they run mainly on an ethanol blend; gases distilled from sugarcane cellulose.'

'Very green!'

'It's not a case of being green, Mr Jones, more a lesson in self-sufficiency. As always there was local opposition to the proposals: unsightly wind turbines, ethanol production on an industrial scale, an oil terminal. But it proved to be the right thing to do.' The traffic lights turned green and as Douchon pulled away the tyres screeched. 'You want the rest of the story?'

Richard nodded.

'The first French colonists landed at Warwyck Bay in 1722, apparently taking advantage of numerous buildings left by the Dutch. The area was exposed to winds and dangerous reefs, so they moved to the safety of the North West Harbour. Warwyck Bay was renamed Port Bourbon and the North West Harbour became known as Port Louis. Later, the transformation of Port Louis from primitive harbour to a thriving seaport was largely due to the efforts of Bertrand Labourdonnais. His house, the Governor's House, was officially called *Hotel du Gouvernement*. The rest you know.'

Douchon accelerated hard and overtook a car. The agitated driver sounded his horn with the shock. Richard grimaced. He leaned back in his seat and ran his thumb beneath the length of the seatbelt as though looking for the release. His voice was matter-of-fact. 'So we are going to look at the state archives . . . the records of previous Governors?'

'*Exactement*! We have a Professor Chang already on the case. He's been working through the night.'

'What's the connection?'

'The last French governor of Ile de France was appointed by Napoleon Bonaparte no less, in 1803, his name was General Charles Decaen. The colony was successful and for the previous decade had been autonomous. *He* was to bring it back to order. He even renamed Port Louis, Port Napoleon. But Decaen found himself increasingly isolated from France and the British had been expanding their influence in the Indian Ocean. To cut a long story short, Mr Jones, in December 1810, the British, under General Abercrombie, marched into Port Napoleon where the French formally surrendered. Then came the name changing – Port Napoleon back to Port Louis and Ile de France back to Mauritius, to name a few. The first English governor, a man called Robert Townsend Farquhar, announced that civil and judicial administration would remain largely unchanged. And you guessed it . . . he moved into the previous governor's residence, which then became known as Government House – and he extended it still further. Today it is the official centre of government, although parliamentary issues are debated in the modern Legislative Assembly Chamber behind.' Unexpectedly, Douchon manoeuvred into the nearside lane, narrowly avoided the car in front and accelerated hard across a roundabout – several horn blasts accompanied his revving engine. He shrugged dismissively. Richard shook his head. 'Now,' Douchon continued unrepentantly, 'by all accounts, Farquhar was a man of honour and immediately set about recording all the remaining bounty that was commandeered on behalf of his King.'

'Sounds promising.' Richard said, beginning to understand.

Douchon turned a sharp right hand corner. 'Apparently the archives still contain records of state treasures and other artefacts that were deemed precious enough to be kept in the Governor's residence during the French occupation. Records correlated both before and after the island's handover to the British. If there's a lead, it will be here!'

'I see . . . this *is* very promising!'

Richard's expression lightened as the road opened to give a view of a busy shipping harbour on his left and tall modern buildings on his right. He recognised the area and a waterfront hotel where he had spent a few nights a couple of years earlier.

'Well, don't get too excited,' added Douchon. 'According to Monsieur Decaen's personal diaries, he was fully aware of the British building up their fleet in the region and, fearing the worst, his administration took the precaution of shipping most of their wealth back to Europe in good time.'

'When was this, did you say? I mean when did the British take over?'

'The year was 1810, 3rd December to be precise. Interestingly, though, Decaen also wrote that he was reluctant to let the most valuable items leave for France until he was sure that the campaign was lost. Clearly, he thought that these assets were safer in his vaults than on the high seas. Apparently, though, the final defeat of the French fleet came as a complete surprise to him.'

'Okay . . . so it may have been too late to get the last of the state treasures off the island before the French capitulated. Is that what you're saying?'

'*Oui*, that's why we go first to Government House. Professor Chang told me that the British Governors only used the cellarage for wine and domestic storage during their time, and most amazingly they did preserve the extensive French records: the land registry, documents of state, trading records, taxes, records of food production, that sort of thing. That's what makes this island so unique; the people continued to speak French, or latterly Creole, the British abided by old French laws, including land sales, but all official documentation was thereafter written in English. And that's what we have today! After the island's complete independence in 1992, when the house became the centre of the Republican Government, the cellars were renovated and have been used ever since as the national archives. Professor Chang and his team have found some letters . . . period documents . . . they want you to see them!'

Douchon turned right and entered a wide road. After another twenty metres or so he stopped at a security checkpoint. An armed policeman approached but the smartly uniformed man swivelled on his heels as soon as he saw who it was and indicated to a colleague to open the barrier. Douchon drove through and pulled up behind another car. 'Now we walk,' he said to Richard, as he climbed from his seat.

The road was impressively broad with a long, raised, grass-topped central island. It was also lined by two rows of palm trees. Douchon quickened his pace. There were a number of period houses on each side and at the end, sitting in its additional "Pomp and Circumstance", was the colonial-styled Government House: three storeys complete with wide verandas, white painted window shutters and numerous columns. There were a number of statues too. Douchon pointed at one of them – a man on a high pedestal facing out across the harbour. 'Labourdonnais,' he said 'and at the bottom of those steps ahead of us is Queen Victoria.'

Richard acknowledged with a perfunctory nod. 'Tell me about Professor Chang.'

'David Chang? I went to primary school with him, he's an old friend, but when I left for high school in South Africa, his parents sent him to London . . . then Cambridge. He's a genius, got a photographic memory, I swear it. His grandfather served on a Royal Naval aircraft carrier during World War Two. The *Ark Royal*? It was an important naval base at that time. Anyway, he suffered a steam burn in the ship's laundry and was put ashore as unfit to work. He recovered and stayed – like everyone here, he has a story. The family are into publishing.'

For his ample size, Douchon took the stone steps leading up to the house in a surprisingly spritely manner. Beyond was a courtyard with another statue and a set of steps that were red in colour with white balustrades. Richard followed Douchon up to the first floor. Inside, the old house was deserted except for a number of policemen. 'This way!' Olivier Douchon ordered. A policeman saluted. Douchon acknowledged with a raised hand.

The original part of the house was not that large and Richard quickly found himself descending a staircase that led into the cellars. The subsequent corridor was brightly lit with walls and ceiling painted white. At the end was a door, which opened as an Indian man came out of the room. The smartly dressed and kindly-looking man extended his hand in welcome. 'Olivier . . . David is ready. I have personally approved the matters of protocol.'

'Thank you, Minister,' Douchon replied, as he shook the man's hand. He smiled politely as he introduced Richard. Then Douchon directed Richard towards the open door and the two men entered a large room with a low ceiling.

The room was immaculately decorated in magnolia-coloured emulsion. To his right, Richard noted a pair of double doors. Painted in an ivory-white gloss like the one behind him, they appeared to be the only access into the room. Numerous overhead fluorescent tubes provided a bright ambiance. Like a library, the room was full of shelves, books, papers and box files. Somewhere in the middle of the maze was a large table and another man stood in anticipation. He was tall, but clearly with Chinese ancestry, practically bald and wearing a pair of round rimmed spectacles and white cotton gloves. His broad smile was inviting.

'*Bonjour* David,' said Douchon confidently. 'This is Mr Jones, now, what do you have for us?'

Richard shook Chang's hand. 'Pleasure, Sir,' he said.

'I have had another communication from London,' said Chang, in an elegant English accent, whilst offering another smile. He analysed Richard for a few seconds. 'You are to call Mr Rothschild as soon as we have completed our discussions.'

'Richard nodded. 'I'll do that, Professor.' he said. 'Mr Douchon here tells me that you may have found something, something of relevance to my search.'

'Only you will know how relevant it is, Mr Jones. See here, I have prepared some exhibits.' Professor Chang turned and leaned over the table adjusting a number of historical-looking parchments with his gloved hands. 'You should know that the first British Governor of Mauritius moved into the residence of his French predecessor immediately upon capitulation of the colony, and that the house fulfilled a similar role for around the next 160 years. Most of our historical archives are well preserved and I have checked very carefully those that detail an inventory for the Governor's House, particularly for the French period sixty years immediately prior to their capitulation. None gives notice of acquired treasure or a significant historical artefact in the form of a casket. One specific entry, dated 3rd June 1808 lists in detail the precise contents of the house, including personal gifts and possessions of the then Governor that were stored in these cellars. There is no mention of the artefact that you seek, not even in any manifest of items held for the sovereign. I think that we can safely assume that any artefact of significance on the island would be known to the Governor and would probably have been stored in suitably secure surroundings. If a sizeable artefact such as a casket existed, then it was *not* recorded – for whatever reason. That's not to say that the Governor himself was not party to such a secret. As such, I decided to do a little additional research during the period leading up to the victory of the Royal Navy over the French Navy in 1810 and also during the days following the handover of power. I found this entry, and you may find it interesting. It is naturally in Old French. However, I am able to translate it for you if you wish.'

'Indeed,' said Richard nodding enthusiastically, 'And anything you think might be relevant.'

'This entry was made in the French Governor's personal diary on the day after the deciding sea battle. The diary and many other official documents were confiscated by the English when they assumed control of the island and declared it forthwith a British colony.'

*High Governor of Ile de France - Journal Entry*
*29th November 1810*

*It is all but lost. The English have reinforced their fleet and we cannot match their numbers. Word has reached me that our flag ship Le Prince Laurent Bordeaux – a full 60 gun – is sunk, and the frigates Le Musketeer and Provenance unaccounted. Of the sea campaign to the north, victory falls to the English and the remainder of our fleet have taken flight and regroup in safe waters west of Reunion Island. The Emperor will hear of this and there will be tantrums, another colony* lost to the marauding English seadogs. It is now only time. Bound by duty as the Governor of this fair island I must stay. Fearing the worst, the gentry have already fled. I have heard that the English Admiral is a fair officer and a gentleman. He would like a conqueror's welcome, but few in the Port of Napoleon will sing his praises. For these people of France, I shall endeavour to make the handover of power as peaceful as possible and press for concessions. In truth, I pray my family will see Paris again.

Of the Governor's treasures, vaulted beneath this the first house of state, I have dispatched them in the barest of time. Ahead of the enemy fleet, my fastest clipper La Dame Elancee made sail at first light this morning. Three months, not more, will see her in Marseille. The treasures of Prince Mauritius Van Nassau and the unyielding sarcophagus will then be in the hands of the Emperor and as such may soften his scold. The secret remains near. I take good heart in my collaboration. The cursed English blockade will not cut short this voyage.

Vive La France et Vive L`Empereur

Charles Xavier de Caen
Governor Ile de France

Richard leant over the table and gazed at the parchment – the date was clear enough. '29th November 1810,' he said out loud. 'This is it, it has to be. Clear mention of what they knew to be an Egyptian artefact – and evidently considered as a coffin! Why else would he call it a sarcophagus?'

'Do you know of any inscriptions that would have been visible on this artefact, Mr Jones?' asked Professor Chang.

'No not exactly. We only know its approximate dimensions and the basic design – similar in many respects to the Ark of the Covenant. But Egyptian hieroglyphs were well known to French archaeologists of the period, although not at all understood and I can tell you that any inscription on the casket would have looked remarkably similar to those. The French aristocracy were infatuated by the ancient Egyptians. Napoleon Bonaparte himself visited the pyramids on the Giza Plateau after he had conquered Ottoman-ruled Egypt in 1798. In fact it was a Frenchman, Jean Francois Champollion, who was first to decipher and speak their long dead language. He used the then recently-discovered Rosetta stone and his fluency in the ancient Coptic tongue to do it. But that breakthrough came in 1822. And from what I read, when he formally released his work in 1824, it gave birth to the entire field of modern Egyptology.'

'Yes, well, I think it's a sure bet that they thought the sarcophagus contained Egyptian burial treasures; gold, precious stones, jewellery – a Pharaoh's ransom no less. Not that they could get at it. To me, "unyielding" means that they, also, were unable to open it.'

Richard methodically formulated his opinion as he looked up at the Professor and then at Douchon. 'This is the closest that I've been to it. For the best part of a century the *Ark* was in here.' Richard scanned the room slowly. He scrutinised the rows of shelving and the far walls. 'Then, 240 years ago it was hauled out, dispatched to the docks and shipped out with all haste.' His eyes were ablaze. 'Where did it go – did it make France?'

Professor Chang turned back to the table and adjusted the overhead optic fibre so that its beam of light fell broadly on a leather-bound book. 'I may be able to help with that question,' he said, as he delicately removed a paper-thin plastic sheet from the book's cover.

The pliable, felt-looking cover was a faded brown, well thumbed and almost worn through at the lower corners. Salt staining and several circular water marks, however, could not conceal the indentations of letters that were pressed into the material; nevertheless, all remnants of gilt had been lost. Richard knew immediately what he was looking at because on closer examination, the markings were plain enough:

# SEA LOG
# HMS SIRIUS

'The log of a British naval vessel?' Richard said, surprised.

'Yes, *HMS Sirius* to be precise. A light frigate of the period and a vessel that served in these waters for almost five years under the same commander,' replied Professor Chang, as he located a small paper bookmark half hidden in the pages and then carefully opened the book a little over halfway through its thickness. 'Two colleagues from the government records office, a close friend from the library service here in Mauritius and myself, have studied every archive that is catalogued for the period when the British took control of the island and also for the period up to fifty years after. *This* is the only reference that we found relating to an object of Egyptian ancestry,' he finished.

Richard shifted nervously and peered at the fawn-coloured page. The handwriting was in brown ink and flowing, but the page was again water-stained and some of the words were blotched whilst others had all but vanished. Because of its dryness the paper appeared like crisp parchment. The Professor squared up the book by moving it a few millimetres with his gloved hands, as an art perfectionist would with a painting hanging on the wall and then he pointed to the first word.

With cool understatement he said 'I may have something for you, please, look here.'

Richard drew closer, eyes wide.

'This text is in English, as you can see,' continued the Professor. 'Although some words are in Old English and could be misinterpreted. I shall read it aloud so that there is no mistake. The Professor's outstretched index finger hovered over the flimsy paper and Richard followed it as he spoke.

Sea Log
HMS Sirius - Frigate of the Line, 3rd Squadron
1st Dog Watch   29th November 1810
Captain John Flintwood Royal Navy
3rd Entry

This day, late in the afternoon watch, my forward lookout sighted two ships in close company. They loitered off the port bow and at some distance. The weather was fair and the sea running only a light swell and so I ordered full sail and set a course to intercept. By reckoning we were some 80 miles NNW of our main fleet and making all of 14 knots when we took them by complete surprise. The vessels were parted, but securing lines still flailed, indicating that they had at one time been tied up alongside each other. The clipper, an impressive sight and a good catch at all of thirty-nine yards in length had only the foresail running and sight of our White Ensign and open cannon ports gave us her urgent loyalty. On the main mast she flew a pennant of the island Ile de France and so I chose her as the first prize of the day. We turned broadside and at my command Master Gunner Smith put out his initial foray. It transpired to be his best and only shot, as fortune had it that the ball passed clean through her main brace breaking it in two and causing some measure of calamity on deck. The two guns she trained on us soon dropped their sights and she was beaten. The other vessel, a smaller but none the less impressive square-rigger, was quick to set sail and tether the wind and in a flurry she was off the mark, like a rabbit at the sight of a fox. My 3$^{rd}$ mate, a Midshipman of prominent enthusiasm and with masterful knowledge of flag and pennant, immediately informed me of her Italian registry. This evening, he has not long since and keenly reported to me with further information and it seems that my order to give up on the spritely trader was sound, as the accompanying pennants she flew had indicated the neutrality of the Orlandini family of Monte Credo, a rich trading

dynasty and one with service to the Vatican
City itself. Lest I cause embarrassment
to my Lords in the highest court, it was
best that she took flight in such a manner
and we broke the chase, being already
in high spirit and content. Of our prize,
my 1st Lieutenant and his boarding party
established control of the forecastle
and had its Master under armed arrest
with surprising haste. I now make full
sail towards the Port of Louis in order to
rejoin the fleet. La Dame Elancee sails in
company and under close supervision.

Middle Watch
30th November 1810


The master of the La Dame Elancee has
finally informed me of his duties. It is duly
noted that he offered enough resistance
to retain his honour. It appears that he
was dispatched with great haste by the
Governor of Ile de France and was bound
for the seaport of Marseille with treasure
for the Emperor Bonaparte of France
himself. He names the square-rigger
that escaped our action as "The Three

Winds" and shows misplaced arrogance
at thought of his timely rendevous and
transfer of cargo, although of its
specific nature he claims no knowledge,
only that hearsay had it that one crate
contained an artefact with origins from
the ancient civilisation of Egypt and that
its value was more in its uniqueness than
its weight as a precious commodity as
naught was known of its contents. I should
say that this loss was of no consequence
and I will make no specific mention of it
to Admiral Blyth-Baxter. By reckoning
we should fall on the Port of Louis early
during the morning watch, but I will hold
off until first light, lest we fall foul of the
reef. I have instructed my signaller and
the boson's mate of their stand to and
preparation, for at first light, they shall
relay our endeavours for King and country
to the flag ship.
Yours aye

John Flintwood

Captain
For England and the King.

Richard held his breath. His endeavours for simplification – to follow a logical path; to reduce his quest to a quantifiable search, a go here, go there approach, until the light at the end of the tunnel loomed – fell short at every hurdle. It was time that tripped him and then fate that trod him down – even serendipity passed him laughing. He sighed.

Professor Chang put a hand on Richard's shoulder. 'Yours is not an easy task, Mr Jones and I understand that time is pressing. History covers its tracks, believe me, I know this only too well. Great historians, those who *have* discovered, did so by thinking laterally, a more contemporary turn of phrase would be "considering every angle". What would you have done if you had been the master of *The Three Winds*? Where would you have gone?'

Richard straightened up and stood tall for a moment, disappointment etched across his face. 'I really thought that I would find it here, hidden on this island somewhere,' he said quietly. 'In a cave perhaps, up in the high rainforest, or even in a long lost vault.' Richard shook his head and looked at the Professor. 'If we go by this entry – and that's all we have – then the Ark was taken to Europe . . . Italy . . . France. It's bloody hopeless! What would I have done? I just don't know.' Richard bowed his head, and the three men stood in silence.

Eventually, Professor Chang voiced his thoughts and offered advice. 'Encouragement without proof of direction is dangerous in the study of history. With insufficient or misleading factual evidence, it is all too easy to take the wrong road and therefore draw incorrect conclusions. Clearly, then, we must be careful with the conclusions that we draw from these annotations. However, for me, this entry is compelling. In my experience as an historian, its credentials are undeniable. By definition, therefore, I think it represents *your* direction. Based on fact, Mr Jones – in this case, documentary evidence – assumptions can be drawn that are not only very helpful, but also accurate.' Professor Chang turned again to the table. 'If the Orlandini family were wealthy merchants,' he continued, 'then they will be traceable, and that also applies to the *The Three Winds*. There will be shipping records; this *is* relatively modern history after all.'

'Do you know where Monte Credo is, Professor?' replied Richard, after a moment's reflection. His tone had an edge to it as he looked at Olivier Douchon. Both men shook their heads.

'Well, neither do I! Never heard of it in fact! If there wasn't so much at stake, I would throw in the towel here and now and . . .' Richard stopped short. He grimaced and then tried to loosen up. 'Professor,' he continued respectfully. 'May I ask if there is a satellite communication facility in the building? I need to talk to my coordinator in London.'

'Yes, of course, the Deputy Prime Minister's office upstairs. It's on the Commonwealth Heads of State network. I know that service is secure.'

'Would he mind?'

'No, he's on holiday for a few days and he is a good

friend. I will ask his secretary to place the call – where exactly?'

'Admiralty Building, Admiralty Arch . . . the number will be in the consulate directory. Ask for Peter Rothschild. If he's busy, tell him the Prodigal Son is calling!'

The spacious office was airy and modern although both the polished, dark brown wooden floor boards and a wall of decorative hardwood panelling were clearly original. There were two, white painted, small-paned, square sash windows that faced west. The sun had already set, but as Richard entered, being escorted by a house orderly, its warming afterglow flooded the room. The Mauritian orderly, another man of Indian lineage, who was dressed in a grey suit and tie with a white shirt, took his place by the door and gestured towards a large desk in the far corner and on it the mobile telephone receiver. Richard sat, albeit a little uncomfortably, in the high-backed leather chair that was upholstered in deep blood-red leather; it swivelled easily. At the man's behest, Richard picked up the receiver and pressed the green button. He held it to his ear in anticipation.

'Hallo, Richard, are you there? It's Peter Rothschild!'

'Yes, I'm here, Peter,' Richard replied as he nodded at the orderly – the man turned and left the room closing the door behind him.

'So what's the situation?'

'I have a lead, but it's tenuous. It's as though we started

this quest pulling on a piece of rope. It was string when we arrived here and now it's down to a thread – the Ark, by all accounts, was taken back to Europe in 1810! It was thought to be an ancient Egyptian sarcophagus; you know, a coffin of sorts, containing the body of a VIP and more to the point, probably valuable personal treasures that would be needed in the afterlife.'

'By whom was it taken and where?'

'Well that's the million dollar question isn't it, Peter? I need your people to get into the history books again, some research and cooperation from the French and the Italians.'

'Give me the details!'

'The main lead is an Italian trading dynasty called *Orlandini* – the place, Monte Credo, wherever that was. They owned a trading ship, a square rigger called *The Three Winds*. There's a French connection, because the vessel was bound for Marseille. I'm speculating that they had an alliance or maybe Monte Credo was close to France. Perhaps the dynasty had bought the ship or even captured it, and to rename it was bad luck. Anyway, we know that the ship departed Mauritius on 29th November 1810. We estimate that it would have reached the French port towards the end of February 1811. Presumably, the Ark then becomes part of Napoleon Bonaparte's hoard.'

'Anything else?'

'Only that the Orlandini family had links to the Vatican; in my view this means that Rome was probably used as a trading centre too; maybe another visit to those archives is prudent. Oh, and one last thing – the then Governor of Ile de France ... the island of Mauritius, would no doubt have promised the Orlandinis a handsome purse for the sea passage of their treasures from here to Marseille. With the British so close, perhaps already landing elsewhere on the island, there would have been no time to arrange such a payment, so it was probably a "cash on delivery" agreement. In 1811, Bonaparte's days were already numbered and the Orlandini's knew well enough of the demise of Mauritius as a French colony. If I'd have been the skipper of the *The Three Winds*, and troubled by a Napoleonic credit crunch, I would have judged Rome a far more favourable destination for my cargo than Marseille.'

'Um . . . convoluted to say the least,' responded Rothschild, in an irritated tone.

'Yes, I agree. Sorry, but it's over to you now, Peter. See what you can come up with . . . I'll wait to hear from you.' There was a long silence. Richard broke it. 'Peter, there is nothing else that I can do here in Port Louis, so I'm going back to the Paradise Bay hotel. It's near Le Morne in the south-west corner of the island. Douchon has arranged it and he has the details. Get my head down for a few hours. Be aware that from the hotel it is more than an hour's drive to the airport and there is a lot of traffic here despite the fuel crisis – let's hear it for self-sustainability! Use an abrive to update me, either my telepager or Preston's – okay?'

Rothschild's reply was considered. 'I understand,

Richard. I'll get back to you as soon as possible.' But his disappointment was obvious.

It was a particularly dark night, Richard noted, as he and Douchon left the suburbs of Port Louis behind. He checked the time – a few minutes before nine, local time. As if he was a changed man, Douchon drove in a restrained manner allowing Richard to doze for most of the journey. As they turned right onto the narrow coast road that paralleled a sweeping golf course and ultimately led to a small roundabout off which was the main entrance to the hotel, Douchon woke Richard.

'Mr Jones, we've arrived,' he said, in a loud voice.

Richard came to his senses and nodded.

From the gate to the reception area was almost one kilometre and it took a few minutes to drive.

'Anything from London?' Richard asked, after his grogginess had subsided.

'No. Not yet. Listen, I have things to do, I will drop you here. As I said, I know the manager. Seems your friends are now in room 396 – it's a two bedroom suite, the only suitable accommodation he had remaining – or more to the point, he wasn't able to sell. He tells me that it's on the beach, very private. Enjoy it for a while. I will be on call should anything come up.'

Inside, Richard approached the concierge. 'Jones,' he said, 'Room 396.'

'Mr Jones, welcome, please follow me.'

The man was aged but friendly and looked smart in his blue uniform. Richard followed him outside and along a winding concrete path that passed several accommodation blocks – all adequately lit. The air was fragrant – filled with the sweet smell of tropical flowers and incense from occasional pole-mounted candles. There were people milling around and Richard could hear the sound of the seashore above chirping crickets and background music. After a few minutes walk they arrived at the last block – a two storey colonial-style building with a thatched roof. Room 396 was one of two on the ground floor. The man gave Richard a plastic key card and Richard gestured his thanks.

Naomi was lolling comfortably on a rattan chaise longue when Richard entered. This impressive furnishing statement had a large circular back that was covered by a vibrant turquoise material with flamboyant gold embroidery in a feather design that made it resemble a splayed peacock's tail – to Richard, the sight conjured an image of tropical bliss. Clearly delighted to be distracted from her reading, Naomi sat up and beamed. The birthmark on her face momentarily caught Richard's eye, as if the heat had overly flushed her skin. It was, however, of no consequence to Richard. To him she looked beautiful, wrapped as she was within the ample folds of a flamboyant, yellow, three-quarter length dressing gown and with a perfectly colour-matched towel twirled cleverly around her head. Richard gawped; it was uncanny. The towel, which was edged in small squares of ochre reds and vivid gold, rose like a tube before being folded backwards. There was a square top to it and the encircling band of colour just above her forehead made it look like a formal headdress.

Naomi's upright posture accentuated her long slim neck. It was a feature that enhanced her regal appearance at the best of times and now, with her dark perfectly contoured eyebrows and almond shaped eyes and her olive-coloured skin and straight but delicate nose and the towel as a crown, all seemed to add to her look of an Egyptian princess – but surely only because Richard had Egypt on his mind. And then, inexplicably, a photograph of a bust that he had seen during his recent studies, in a museum somewhere, depicting a woman who possessed natural dignity with an air of regal finesse, one he remembered being described as "The Most Beautiful Woman in the World" strangely focused in his mind's eye. Richard made to speak as Naomi stood, but she put a finger to her lips and then pointed to the bedroom on her right. 'Sssh,' she whispered, 'they sleep . . . come, in here.' She indicated to the room on her left. Richard followed her in and Naomi closed the door behind him. He watched fascinated as she sat on the edge of the bed; her natural poise as she covered her legs, her eyes watching his every move. His first instinct was to take her in his arms, he wanted to hold her, but he was afraid to take her by surprise.

'What of your news, Richard?' Naomi asked, reaching for his hand.

A tired smile flashed across Richard's face – she was all the compensation he needed for his disappointment.

Richard gently pulled Naomi onto her feet and kissed the side of her mouth. Her body seemed to sway and he could feel her warmth. 'Let's go outside.' He put his arm around her and with his other hand slid open the patio door. They stepped into the night. They could hear the surf softly shushing on the sand. Out here in the darkness, lit only by faint solar lights, she looked amazing.

Naomi turned to look at him. 'You must be exhausted, Richard. Have you eaten?' Her hand caressed his face and he became aware of his need for many things, a shave, a shower, food and sleep but most of all her.

Richard shook his head, 'I'm shot, out of it, really I am.' He took a deep breath.

'I know. We have had time to recover. Come, while you bathe, I will order food for you and then you must sleep.' This time it was she who guided him back into the bedroom.

Richard woke in the deep comfort of a bed he hardly recollected getting into. It was a large room with twin beds, both doubles, and he stretched and turned to see the other one was empty. The blinds were drawn so the daylight was diffused. He found his chronometer on the side table and was amazed to see that he had slept for almost nine hours. It was 08:10 local time. He checked his pager – there were no messages. He threw back the covers and crossed the room. On the table was a tall slender vase shaped in electric blue glass from which a single stemmed, brightly coloured orchid bloomed. He smiled. Naomi had done that. He pulled up the jalousies and let the sunshine flood the room.

A gentle knock on the door brought Richard hastily across to the chair where his clothes lay. 'Coming!' he shouted, stepping into new shorts and trousers, and as he pulled a clean polo shirt over his head he opened the door.

'Crikey . . . thought you'd died in there, Boss!' It was Preston, smiling.

'Morning, Preston. I just need to clean my teeth. Can you order me some coffee?'

The service was prompt. Preston had ordered a toasted ham and egg sandwich as well and as they sat on the patio he watched Richard wolf it down.

'Have you seen Naomi?'

'She went to the spa centre about an hour ago. She seemed preoccupied, sad even, here of all places.' Preston shrugged. 'Any joy in Port Louis, Boss?'

'Another setback, although Rothschild is working on a few clues.'

'Don't knock it, Boss. I don't know when I enjoyed R

and R more.'

Richard wiped his mouth with the napkin. 'Well at least one of us is happy. How's Marretti?'

'Madame Vallogia enquired this morning. He has a slight temperature from a small infection; another day or two. Nothing to worry about, she was told.'

'And Asharf?'

'Snores like a pig. I sent him outside to sleep on the patio.' Preston paused and his smile dropped. 'Where does the setback take us?'

'Not sure. We must wait for a directive from London. What about Douchon?'

Preston shook his head. 'Nothing heard.'

'When we get together I will brief you all. Check you're on local time. Let's say in thirty-five minutes . . . 09:30. See if you can rouse everybody. I'm going to enjoy this excellent home-grown coffee.'

'Okay, Boss. I'll do a little recce,' Preston raised his eyebrows and laughed good naturedly and left by the path along the beach.

Richard saw the curtains blow inwards and knew someone had opened the door to his room. He stood and peered through the shadows. It was Naomi. She came to him arms outstretched, 'Oh, Richard, you are well.' It could have been a question or a response in her lilting accent. Richard hugged her and breathed her perfume. 'I was disappointed to find you gone,' she said.

Naomi was glowing in the sunshine. Richard seemed

intoxicated. For a moment he stared. 'Will you have some coffee, Mauritian blend? It's very good.' He led her to the table.

'Preston's gone to find you and Asharf. He won't be back for a while; not if I know Preston.'

'Are you truly well? Last night you were so in *désespoir*.'

'Despair?' Richard shrugged his shoulders. 'Not the best of news and I was very tired.' Richard lifted the coffee pot, pouring for them both and they sat in companionable quiet until Naomi grew restless.

'*Well*?' Naomi insisted, eventually.

'Oh, sorry . . . I was thinking of something else.' Richard paused to gather himself. 'Yes, well, something and nothing really. Nothing here, on the island, unfortunately, but another lead at least – back to Europe though. We think France or perhaps Italy, so your fluency will come in handy.' A smile jabbed Richard's mouth.

At that, Naomi almost imperceptibly shook her head – as if she knew something but was unable to speak of it, and then she looked down.

'They are working on it, the team in London that is,' Richard continued, seemingly oblivious to her gesture. 'I'll hear something today. I think time gets the better of us, Naomi.'

Naomi nodded sheepishly in response, as if the bad news was expected.

'I'm disappointed too,' ventured Richard, to little effect. 'Anyway . . . have you had breakfast?'

Naomi nodded again, but this time a smile glimmered.

Richard looked at her with affection. 'There was mention of the Vatican and a place I've never heard of,' he said quietly.

At first Naomi appeared uninterested in the remark, her attention being momentarily diverted by a shift in the direction of the breeze and a muslin curtain billowing behind them. But then she looked up. 'I see where your thoughts lead you, Richard, and that *only* from what you say and how you say it. I do not use my . . .'

'What do you mean by that?'

Naomi sighed. 'Oh nothing . . . perhaps I was wrong.' There was a pause. 'So, you think that the religious authorities had a hand in the Ark's fate?'

'Well, it wouldn't be the first time in history that a cover-up has been necessary. The Vatican is also known to get rid of anything it considers a threat to Rome. I mean . . .'

'You mean what, Richard?'

'Naomi, listen. If something new appears . . . something that has meaning but no explanation or something that is not understood and therefore appears intimidating, then that *something* will be perceived as destabilising. It could threaten the bedrock of an establishment . . . particularly if knowledge of it becomes widespread. Clearly then, to protect the establishment, that something should be removed, hidden, or preferably erased . . . right?'

'Therein lies the problem, Richard. The Ark comes with a history of its own.'

'Exactly!'

'Ah, I see, science against creationism again – our discussions in Khartoum.'

'Not just creationism, but protectionism, even monopolism,'

Richard leaned forward to reinforce his point. Naomi sipped her coffee. 'You lived in France, so take the Cathars for instance, from the south, the Languedoc region. A Christian religious sect, a breakaway group if you like. The same religion, but with essentially different beliefs and values – prominent during the Middle Ages. During the opening years of the thirteenth century, they were astonished by the extent of persecution against them. I mean, Rome supported an army that launched a crusade against them – erased the entire culture: people, buildings, faith, everything. The Ark would be a threat too, by nature of its origin, and who's to say that they didn't know about it? It certainly would be a lot easier to deal with – if they could get their hands on it. So here we are, at a point in this search where the Ark is onboard a ship that is owned by a European aristocratic family, probably Italian, with direct ties to Rome itself.' Richard sat back, clearly impassioned. 'There must be archives, vaults, caves and *dungeons* beneath Rome that have not seen a living soul for centuries. And what's more, I wouldn't mind betting that "London" is thinking precisely the same thing!'

'To hear you speak, Richard, it would seem that *you* are also on a crusade.'

Richard looked at Naomi sideways with a confused

expression. He thought on her remark for several seconds. 'Well, I'm not,' he replied, eventually and with some sharpness. 'It's a quest, isn't it?'

Naomi shrugged. 'Yes, it is your quest, Richard, but that only. Do not become possessed by it.'

At that remark, Richard looked at her and frowned.

'What is it, Naomi? I can see that you are troubled.'

'Richard, in Italy you should be very careful. I never told you – you would not have understood – perhaps now though.'

Richard waited for her to continue.

'That incident on the train; south from Cairo; the encounter with the monk in the blood red robe – that figure? It seems so long ago now.'

'Yes?'

'The man who looked for you, Richard, *he* was a religious man but also another lurked within – an assassin. I have no doubt. I had a strange feeling in his presence. Only once before have I felt it – I could not explain it.'

'Go on.'

'I have given considerable thought to it, because I have no memory of being so afraid – even our escape from Eritrea cannot compare. Yesterday, in the quietness of the room, I realised. The first time was not *my* experience, but my Grandmother's – the night she died.'

'But she died before you were born, that's what you told me!'

'The emotion came through my mother, Richard, like

this mark on my face – I explained.'

Richard nodded, but his eyes showed confusion. He took a deep breath. 'So he is a . . . ?'

'Richard, please listen. I have experienced that feeling again, although to a lesser degree. Here, on this island. Fleeting, but I am sure, I would not mention it otherwise. The same man who killed my Grandmother was here. I know it!'

'Was?'

'He is gone now.'

'That's impossible Naomi. You are talking about events that are a century apart!'

Naomi nodded, registering the inconsistency. 'Then it is the compulsion that I sense, the emotion, the negative energy.'

Richard's expression changed to one of perplexity. His brow furrowed and he nodded slowly whilst his thoughts raced. He remembered the business jet he had seen at the airport and its "coincidental" registration mark; *that* was Italian.

'Please be very careful in Italy, Richard, please!' she pleaded.

Richard stood and took a pace towards the doors. He slid the left one open a little further. The warm breeze took hold of the fine curtain again and it fanned and fluttered delicately around Naomi's face. Richard took it and pulled it aside. The sound of waves breaking on the distant reef broke an ominous silence. He turned.

'Am I putting two and two together here and making five, or are things beginning to add up?' he asked.

Richard walked back to the chair and sat down. He leaned forwards and put a hand on the arm of Naomi's chair. 'Have you ever heard of a man called Michel de Notredame?' he questioned, with a concentrated stare.

Naomi answered immediately: 'Yes, Richard, I have. In Latin, his name was Nostradamus. Such a strange question – why should you ask?'

'I heard the name recently, that's all. It's probably nothing. On the other hand though, it just might be a lead . . . can you tell me anything about him?'

Nostradamus was a sixteenth-century physician. He became famous for his knowledge of astrology and his predictions of the future. He was French, born in St Remy, near Avignon if I recall, and practised in Agen, near Toulouse, and other places.'

'Agen!'

'Yes, he lived also in Paris, not far from where I did. For a time, after the French king Charles IX ascended to the throne, he was appointed physician-in-ordinary. Many books were written applying his predictions to historical situations.'

Richard subconsciously offered an open hand. 'And?' he beckoned.

'His *Centuries* of predictions became highly contentious. He wrote in rhymed quatrains . . . a stanza of four lines. His prophecies were generally expressed in obscure and enigmatical terms.'

'You mean that they were open to different interpretations?'

Naomi nodded. 'I studied some of his work, many years ago now. There were aspects of it that fascinated me.'

'What of the *New City*? Does that mean anything to you?'

'The "New City" was mentioned in one of his quatrains. There was a great deal of speculation about it, particularly at the beginning of this century. The quatrain mentioned degrees of latitude if I recall, forty or forty-five, and there was mention of fire. Some concluded that he had referred to the city of New York.'

'Really?'

'There seemed sense in some of the things he wrote. Nevertheless, I remember thinking that many predictions were so obscure as to be meaningless.'

'I see,' Richard appeared disappointed and moved back. The brief smile that jabbed his face covered his disillusionment. He put a hand on Naomi's lap. 'Anyway, to have the day off here . . . what a pleasure,' he said.

Naomi agreed with a nod just as Richard caught sight of Preston striding towards them from the direction of the beach. He looked flushed. Richard saw that he was holding his pager and immediately turned his head towards the bedroom doors. Preston waited until he was within the privacy of their patio before he spoke.

'I was copied in, Boss,' he said quietly. 'It's a message

from London, *your* message – marching orders.'

'And?'

'We fly to Rome … 11:00 hours local. It says arrangements are "in hand", whatever that means.'

Richard glanced at Naomi as he sprang to his feet and disappeared into his room. Only now did he recall selecting the "vibrate only" function on his device the previous evening, and it was this occasional buzzing, like a bumble bee under his towel, that allowed him to quickly locate it. He read the display and checked his chronometer: 09:19. The message had been posted twelve minutes earlier. Richard rubbed his eyes. Despite his restful night they still felt sore. He typed his personal descrambler code into his pager and opened the abrive. When the text appeared he cross-checked the timings. 'Ugh, it's confirmed, take off at eleven . . . SSR International,' he whispered, clearly aggravated by the timings. Preston entered the room. Richard marched across to the patio doors and leaned outside. 'Sorry Naomi, I need to speak to Preston for a moment,' he said, and almost closed the door on her.

'What do you think, Boss?'

Richard scratched his head. 'You know, there are very few commercial services to Europe these days and none at that hour! I know for sure that the French presidential jet is returning to Africa, so what are they planning?'

'It says that we have to attend a special brief at the airport prior to departure. Show time is 10:00 hours.' Preston considered the arrangements. 'We're pushing it . . .

we should leave immediately.'

The telephone rang. Preston was by the desk and answered it. 'Yes?' he said. There was a pause. '09:30 . . . that's enough time is it?' Another pause, then faintly, a man's voice. 'Best you can . . . yes, I understand.' Preston looked at Richard as he listened. 'A holiday and it's still early, okay . . . 09:30 then, in the foyer. We'll be there . . . no luggage . . . understood!' Preston put the handset down and looked back at Richard. 'That was Douchon, pickup outside the hotel in five minutes, just the clothes we are wearing and our telepagers and just the *two* of us, Boss.'

Richard's first thoughts were of Naomi, how to tell her he was leaving? And there was Marretti. He may need her – perhaps, it was for the best? He checked the time again and nodded his understanding. 'Preston, quickly, look outside for Asharf,' he ordered.

Simultaneously, the door behind Richard opened. Naomi stepped from the patio. She was barefoot. Wearing the towelling dressing gown she had the previous evening, it was as if the sunshine followed her in. Richard went to speak, but she interrupted. 'I overheard the news, Richard. You need not explain.'

Richard looked at her for a moment and then at Preston. 'You had better let Asharf know we are leaving,' he said.

Naomi sat down on the bed, but Richard remained standing. At first, there was little emotion in his delivery or in his expression. 'Listen, Naomi,' he said quietly. 'I'm sorry, I really am. You heard my orders.'

'I heard well enough, Richard. You go back to Europe.'

Richard nodded and took a step closer. 'I leave in a few minutes, just Preston and me. We continue the search. Naomi . . . time is against us. You will stay here until Marretti is recovered. Olivier Douchon will make the arrangements. You will be safe here. Perhaps you will even enjoy it.'

Naomi's expression agreed, but her body quivered. 'I already know of it,' she said.

'You seem to know a lot of things before I say them . . .'

'I'm not prying, Richard, if that is what you mean. I see it in your eyes and in your expression. I need go no deeper than that.'

'Yes, I know that. Please, I'm sorry.' Richard stepped backwards so he would not be tempted to touch her. 'Well anyway . . . I go to Rome. Some sort of covert arrival, no doubt.'

Naomi cupped her forehead in her hand and wiped something from the corner of her eye.

'I should get ready to move out.'

Naomi nodded and looked down. She resisted Richard's long sorrowful gaze.

'And what of us, Naomi?' Richard asked, breaking the protracted silence.

Naomi shrugged and looked slowly towards the glass doors and the picturesque scene beyond.

'There is already someone in your heart, Richard,' she replied softly. 'You have not spoken of her, but she is there.

I sensed her when our spirits joined. You have pushed her to the very recesses of your mind and suppressed your love for her. I know that she must have hurt you. The bonds of love are not so easily broken though. She surges forwards into your thoughts, but always you push her back again.' Naomi turned her head slowly and returned Richard's look, for some time she stared. 'You cannot allow this forever,' she said sadly and looked away.

Richard placed a finger beneath Naomi's chin to gently pull her face to look into his. For a long time neither of them spoke. Eventually, Naomi looked down again, and there was a cruel sadness in her tone.

'I had thought the unthinkable; dreamt the impossible; prayed that you were the one. It is not to be. I should have known. My destiny I cannot shape, for its course is already set. The stars hold it in their grasp,' Naomi breathed a deep sigh. 'My future lies not with you, my headstrong Englishman, for soon the lines of our lives unravel. I have spoken of this before. The writings on your palm, your book of life, and on mine, they are clear. This is of such sadness to me, Richard, I can barely speak of it, but of what you already have, you know not.'

'What do you mean? No, that can't be right. That palm stuff, come on, it's superstition, there is no fact!' Richard's voice quivered, verging on desperation.

Naomi shook her head. 'Believe me. Of what we speak – it is not superstition, only forgotten. Soon you will realise this. You do not speak of who is in your heart, Richard.

208

Nonetheless, she is there. I have grown to love you. I tried not to, but all things happen for a reason. Like you though, my heart is not free to give. Richard, I will tell you my spirit secret, because it will help us. I ask you to believe it.' Naomi sat straight and proud – there was always such a nobleness about her. 'I am descended from Isabelle of Noon, High Priestess of Atlantis and the Temple Osiris, who was begat of the Star Colony Sirius . . . I am already married. You should not be sad for me, Richard.'

'Where will you go, what will you do?' Richard implored.

'I shall return to the Church of Saint Mary in France. It is a nunnery and a hospice. They are a gentle order, with tolerance. They are keepers of faith, and not only their own faith. I have also my duties in Cairo.'

Naomi raised her head majestically. Richard looked into her eyes. As his thoughts floundered, he struggled to accept devotion, a passion that he could not hope to understand. Naomi's eyes were clear and bright, mysterious as always, yet optimistic. They demanded openness of him, a realisation . . . reality. He thought of Rachel. He had pushed everything about her to the back of his mind, confined her to the recesses of his psyche. Likened to the gates of a river lock, once opened, even just a little, the irrepressible waters rush in. As if borne on such turbulent rising waters, Richard's feelings for Rachel came rushing back.

After some time, Richard looked away. Emotionally, he had been there before and on more than one occasion, only this time the let down was considerably softer. Together, he and Naomi shared a sense of inevitability. She smiled faintly, as if to insinuate that he should have known all along. Then she stood, cupped her hands around his face, moved closer and kissed his lips – a sensual, lingering kiss that for Richard could have lasted forever. Finally, she kissed his cheek in a way that closed, unequivocally, this chapter in their lives.

'I'll see you again sometime,' Richard whispered against her soft hair, not believing in the inevitable.

Naomi's smile widened. With her fingertip, she promptly wiped away a tear that had formed in the corner of her eye, smudging it before it had time to run down her face. 'Perhaps,' she replied in a whisper even softer than his, 'but not in this life.'

There was a sharp double tap on the bedroom door. Richard, with his eyes barely leaving Naomi, walked over to it. He grasped the handle. Before opening it he asked, 'You alright?'

Naomi nodded. Richard opened the door to find Asharf standing outside, a frown between his eyes. He looked at Richard and then peered around him to see Naomi sitting on the bed.

'*Effendi*,' he said quietly. 'Madame is very upset. I have come to see why.'

Richard's eyes narrowed. How could he possibly know that? He nodded almost apologetically. 'You are quite right, Asharf, she is. You had better come in.'

Asharf entered the room hesitantly. Naomi smiled bravely at him through watery eyes. Richard put a hand on his shoulder to attract his attention. 'Asharf, listen. I will be leaving shortly, with Preston, just the two of us. Madame Vallogia and you are to stay until Marretti is fit to travel. London will call Madame Vallogia with the details in the next few days. Preston and I, we go back to Europe, Rome in fact.'

Asharf's head bowed, he looked devastated. He glanced at Naomi and understood.

'I may not see you again,' Richard continued solemnly. 'So I would like to say thanks for everything, and goodbye.' Richard offered his hand. 'The pleasure was all mine, Asharf, I can assure you.'

Asharf nodded sadly. Instead of shaking Richard's hand he stepped forwards and embraced him, patting him several times on the back. He stepped back again and then took Richard's hand in the European way. 'I will miss you, *Effendi*,' he said, in a heartfelt way. 'May your God be with you.'

'And yours with you, Asharf. Now, be sure to look after Madame Vallogia, she is a very special woman.'

Asharf nodded and smiled briefly. 'It is my life, *Effendi*. It is why I am here.'

Richard released his grip from their warm handshake, but then took hold of Asharf's wrist with his other hand and gently rotated it. He needed to know before they parted company: was Asharf one of them? Richard looked down briefly at Asharf's palm. There, faded and barely visible against brown callused skin was a small blue tattoo – a tattoo of a hand. Richard raised his head slowly and momentarily concentrated on Asharf's weathered face but bright eyes. He had suspected, but now, happily, he knew – Naomi would always be safe.

Preston scrambled onto the back seat and Richard had barely closed his door when Douchon roared off. The security guards, having been forewarned by the concierge, held both gates wide open and Douchon raised a hand as he sped past them. There was no braking at the junction. Douchon physically pulled the car into the corner and accelerated. Tyres screeched loudly, causing a cacophony of wary shrieks from nearby roosting parrots, their remonstrations reverberating through the stillness of the morning.

Douchon went the *Flic en Flac* way, first joining the A3 and then the B2 – a winding road flanked by fields of newly-planted sugar cane. Under the clear sky with remnants of a fiery sunrise, the young plants resembled large tufts of sedge grass, set row after row. Soon after, the motorway-like A10 gave them a clear run south-east towards the airport and as the day fortuitously was a public holiday, it was all but empty.

Douchon was first to break thirty-five minutes of thoughtful, apprehensive silence. 'Another fifteen minutes!' he said, confidently, 'not bad, considering.'

Richard looked at him blankly, *his* thoughts clearly elsewhere. The rustling and munching noise of Preston eating a sandwich seemed louder than that of the engine, even at seventy miles an hour. At that moment, both Richard's and Preston's telepagers buzzed simultaneously; Preston was first to respond; he deciphered the message and read the opening line: HALO BRIEF.

'It's our brief, Boss. Shall I read it aloud?'

'Yeah, please.'

'It says: Prepare for covert drop, two minute spacing, utilising a High Altitude Low Opening method – it gives the coordinates in Lat and Long. Presumably that's somewhere in Rome, Boss? Undercover operational procedures to follow with admittance to *Villa Orlandini* secured ... latitude and longitude coordinates are specified again. Access to Vatican City denied; repeat . . . access Vatican denied. Primary liaison information will follow – codeword is *Trinity*. Security situation: Code Red. Field force confirms presence of Spheron and Tongsei operatives – armed and highly dangerous. Further information during over-flight – end. Bloody hell!'

'A HALO jump?' Richard barked in response, his eyes wide.

'With low cloud, that's impossible. Are they trying to

kill us?'

'What is it exactly, a HALO?'

'It's a Special Forces procedure, Preston, a military technique for infiltration. Developed for covert penetration, usually deep behind enemy lines – puts people on the ground, unseen, unheard. But there are limitations, weather for one thing, because essentially it's a parachute drop. A high altitude jump, followed by an almost undetectable terminal velocity freefall to a very low altitude. I'm not familiar with the exact parameters, but at around 2000 feet a barometric system, part of the pressure suit, automatically deploys the chute, then it's a regular parachute drop to the ground, effectively below enemy radar coverage. It's been around for a while and I know later systems used a paragliding wing of sorts that gave good directional control and an accurate spot landing. But you need to be skilled, trained, and you have to see the ground, from at least 1000 feet, otherwise you can't see where the hell you're landing and there's no reaction time. If it's a night drop, you need night vision goggles too. It was good for forest clearings, restricted areas that sort of thing, but never over built-up areas. With very low cloud, it's impossible!'

Preston gulped. 'There must be more to it than that, Boss. The blanket of low cloud over Europe has shown no sign of lifting for almost a year and Italy's no exception. If anything, it hangs lower over the Mediterranean Sea, because of the heat sink.'

Richard nodded. He was aware of it. He didn't flinch, but continued to stare at the road ahead. He knew very well that time was running out, but this seemed reckless. He glanced at Douchon and then at the clock on the dashboard. They would find out in just over thirty minutes.

With Douchon as an escort formalities became unnecessary. Immigration, passport control, customs and security officials reluctantly responded to an authoritive nod from the "man himself" and the wheels of bureaucracy simply turned in his favour. He was a government man; that was clear enough. Not that Richard or Preston carried anything as they swept through the departure process. And neither did anyone speak, apart from the three words uttered by Douchon as the X-ray machine beeped excitedly yet no one dared question – they are authorised!

Airside, they were met by the handling agent – a local man named Megan – who ushered them into a crew bus and then drove to a hangar. The ramp was familiar to Richard and they passed the French presidential aircraft on the way. Set within a ring of protective traffic cones, it was still secured for the night with its red coloured engine blanks and long thin flags that warned of undercarriage locks in place.

There was a low building close to the hangar and that was where they stopped first. As the door of the vehicle slid back a smart man in a grey and blue military uniform stepped forward. He offered his hand and Richard and then Preston shook it. '*Guten morgen!*' he said, in a precise fashion and checked his watch, as if to emphasise their tardiness. He appeared to have already met Douchon, as the two men merely nodded at each other.

The man, whose name Richard had learned was Major Ralf Bauer led them into a small office – he offered chairs and a coffee that was enthusiastically accepted. He had short blonde hair and was in his thirties, Richard speculated.

'This is our temporary project office,' he began to explain, in a low voice. His English, with a German accent, was good.

'Vee haf hired this facility from the airport authority for the duration of our trial. It is expensive, but vee need the good weather,' he smiled. 'It appears our governments cooperate again . . . I understand that you need to get to Italy as soon as possible?'

Richard nodded. 'Yes, that's correct, Major, Rome to be precise.'

'*Ja*, vee haf der coordinates – a data link from our operations in Bavaria – they are being downloaded as vee speak. You vill be ze first to try our system, but no concern; the dummies zat vee use to mimic a human anatomy in every way – *unser letzte experiment war perfekt.*'

Richard's expression became an amalgamation of surprise and anxiety. 'I don't understand. HALO technology has been around for decades, not that I know

216

that much about it.'

'Correct, Mr Jones. However, our work takes current technology to another level.'

Richard raised his eyebrows – he wanted to know more and he could see that Preston's keen interest was tempered only by unease.

'Autonomy and complete automation of der flight management system, Mr Jones, zis is the key and it allows operations in all veathers. *Ja*, even zero cloud base . . . nil restrictions.'

'Go on please, Major.'

'It is still a prototype system, zis is true. However, our results so far have been encouraging.' The Luftwaffe officer's tone was very matter-of-fact. 'With zis excellent weather and visibility, vie haf encountered few problems and zer trial is set to complete on time.'

Richard sighed as he looked across at Preston. '*Has* anything gone wrong, Major?' he questioned, hesitantly.

'No concerns – not so far,' he said, shaking his head. 'But then vee haf only completed thirty percent of the trial – a total of six jumps.'

'Only six jumps?'

Major Bauer made a nonchalant gesture. '*Ja*, but a vun hundred percent success rate – except perhaps for zer first test, there zer deployment altitude was too low, the dummy suffered damage – both legs fractured, but a man would have survived. Since then, vee have made changes.'

Richard smiled politely. Preston turned poker-faced and

Douchon squirmed a little in his chair before standing. 'I've got a few arrangements to make,' he said, and promptly left the room.

Major Bauer could sense an air of apprehension. He felt sure he could allay Richard's scepticism with a technical description. 'Zer system utilises a semi-rigid, air-inflated, computer-controlled parachute canopy mit full authority directional control. Zer integrated satellite navigational system includes a real-time database comparison system. In other words, zer lookdown Doppler radar system compares was ist virtually seeing against an accurate ground based topographic survey and makes directional changes to suit. It automatically takes into account der vind and any other flight path disturbances. It is completely hands off, Mr Jones. To date, zer tests haf produced very accurate touchdowns, certainly vizin five metres.'

Richard puffed, he was not convinced. 'What, may I ask, is the planned drop altitude?'

'52,000 feet is optimum und zen zer freefall element. Zer next sequence is the deployment of a small detachable drag chute. Zis is nominally at 2,000 feet above ground level, but depends on atmospheric temperature and pressure on zer day. It is totally automatic, completely hands off – vee found that human interaction consistently introduced errors. So, providing descent velocity has been reduced vizin the design parameters, zer main canopy vill zen deploy. If you are too fast zer main chute vill simply not open – vee need to avoid zis.'

'Yes . . . I couldn't agree more,' ventured Richard sarcastically. Preston remained silent.

'The entire deployment sequence happens vizin a few seconds. Zer system makes all zer computations, you vill not be aware of it. Touchdown velocity, finally, is approximately three metres per second – if zere is a solid radar return it can be much less. Groundspeed should be less than one metre per second. You see . . . quite survivable. Even for zer amateur.'

'Really? What a comfort. And the initial drop speed, what will that be?' Preston asked.

'Zer aircraft vill approach at high speed from zer south east and zer pod vill pneumatically eject you somewhere over zer bay of Naples. Zer aircraft *vill not* decelerate. Zis is part of the concealment process.'

Richard looked at the tall balding officer who clearly had a head full of figures but lacked a bedside manner. With his half-haunted expression forcing the question again, Richard waited expectantly.

'Zis information is restricted, however, in zis case, zer speed gate vill open at Mach 2.9 and close at 3.1.'

'Mach 3? We jump at Mach3?' Richard's insides turned at the thought.

'There are no concerns; the pressure suit vill protect you. The equipment has been tested to higher velocities zan zis!'

Thereafter, the three men left the office and walked briskly and in silence towards the hangar. As they approached, Major Bauer called someone on his handheld radio. He spoke in German and as a result one of the towering doors rattled open just enough for them to squeeze through. Once inside the door promptly closed again.

It was a brightly lit environment. There were several aircraft inside, all appeared to be commercial types. However, on the far side, looking potent and menacing was a Series 5 Typhoon fighter in German Air Force livery – two pods hung beneath its wings and two pilots busied themselves in the vicinity.

Richard had held back on another pertinent question lest his apprehensions appeared nervy, and by the expression on Preston's face he would need to lead, or at least encourage, by example, coolly and confidently suppressing his terror.

'Okay!' Richard challenged eventually, intent on releasing the question that was burning inside him. 'What if an obstruction has been erected since the ground comparison data survey . . . a mast or a crane or even a building?'

'Oh, that vould be *pech haben*, how you say, unlucky, Mr Jones. *Ja*! Ha, ha.'

Richard looked at Preston and grimaced.

'So,' continued the Major, clearly impervious to thoughts of system failures. 'I vill introduce you to zer aircrew *und meine* support team.'

Richard was scanning the interior of the hangar as the

man spoke. 'One last question, if I may, on a different subject.'

'*Ja*, Mr Jones, my orders are to help in any vay I can.'

'Yesterday, when we arrived, a business jet was being towed in here. It was an older model, an Eclipse, built by Solar Aeronautica in Portugal, I'm told. It had an Italian registration mark. I see that it's already gone . . . any idea where?'

'The Eclipse, a classic, and one of my favourites – I had a good look at it, excellent condition.'

This man's an anorak, thought Richard. 'And?'

'Yesterday evening, late, zer last departure, I watched it go – around eleven, if I recall. *Wunderbar . . .*'

'Where, Major? Where did it take off for . . . any ideas?'

'It turned and set a course to zer north, Mr Jones, Europe I imagine. Perhaps you should ask air traffic control for zer destination. Now, if you do not mind, it is time to do business.'


Richard climbed into the suit and adjusted his underclothing. He squeezed his feet into the over boots and then the safety equipment operative secured first the neoprene straps and finally the metal fasteners. There was a protective but flimsy-looking metal foil covering the entire suit. It had a golden sheen that glinted in the light from powerful, overhead sodium lights.

Next was the parachute. It was enclosed in a heavy but contoured backpack made of a white plastic material. After that, the operative secured the sensors. These were a number of devices that included a small satellite navigation aerial. Finally, he had a wristwatch-like instrument secured to his right forearm. It was a backup device, should the Head-Up Display inside his helmet fail. Like the HUD, the external instrument had a digital display that included a constant readout of altitude, time to parachute deployment and feet to go to ground level.

When he was fully dressed, the man gave Richard a tap on his shoulder. Although feeling restricted and rather warm, Richard responded with a sharp nod and thumbs up. Next, a large bubble-type helmet was placed over his head and secured in position by mating with a shiny metal ring that was integral with the suit neckpiece; a quarter turn clockwise locked the mechanism.

'Emergency visor release is here, Sir,' explained the man, as he pointed to a short, flush, metal lever at the base of the helmet's face piece.

Finally, as the visor was closed, Richard began to breathe a pre-mixed oxygen and nitrogen mixture. He heard the valves hiss quietly behind his head. He also felt a light gas pressure had built up inside his suit. The man tapped him on the helmet. Richard, with his movements clearly restricted turned bodily and gave a bold thumbs-up signal. The man indicated for Richard to follow him. Richard caught sight of Preston, who was now similarly dressed and they walked side by side to the aircraft.

Below each wing was hung a metal pod, like oversized

missiles. The entry portal was in the rear and after Richard slid into place, he could see that the one-metre diameter tube had a small cockpit-like window at the front. He lay on a sliding metal tray that would roll backwards during the release manoeuvre and eject him into the aircraft's slipstream. The two securing straps allowed enough room to turn onto his stomach and look through the viewing windows, but he would lie on his back for the deployment event. Finally, the man tapped his boots and Richard gave another thumbs-up signal. With that, the tube-end closed with a thud and pressurising gas seeped into his cocoon with an unnerving whistle. Richard flipped a switch on his wrist controller. 'Preston, can you hear me? He asked over the intercom.

'Loud and clear, Boss, and I'm bundled up like a f . . . .' Preston rarely swore, but the expletives were lost as the voice of the pilot interrupted.

'Keep the chat down gentlemen. We are preparing for take off!'

As the aircraft moved, Richard began to feel both claustrophobic and apprehensive. This equipment is still experimental, one half of him mused in a rare moment of trepidation, while the other half was elated and raring to go. He changed position as best he could within the confines of the restrictive harness and then looked at his wrists and his gloves. The kit seemed sophisticated – but a 50,000 foot freefall through dense cloud and I see the ground ten seconds before impact? That might be too much to ask of any parachute, he pondered sceptically. He hoped Preston was feeling more philosophical.

He thought of Rachel and the abrive that he had typed on his way to the airport trying to explain, but in the end had decided not to post it – sending only three words instead and hoping they would be enough. He thought of Douchon, who had not returned, having been called away unexpectedly. No goodbyes there either. Now, as the aircraft's engines accelerated to take-off thrust and the aircraft thundered down the runway, he braced and took the g-force. Seconds later, they were airborne and climbing like a bat out of hell.

𓂝𓄿𓈖𓊗 𓅂𓂝𓊃𓂓𓂧𓂝𓏤 𓂝𓄿𓈖𓊗

'Establishing communications, Mr Jones, a moment if you please,' said the pilot, impatiently.

'Okay, sorry.' Richard moved his muscles inside the suit trying to find a more comfortable position. He selected the intercom link with Preston. 'Preston, you okay over there?'

'Yes, Boss, suppose so. Looking forward to getting my feet back on the ground though . . . are you sure this is going to work?'

'Of course! Would I lie to you?' Richard metaphorically crossed his fingers. 'Anyway, we will find out soon enough. We are approaching the North African coastline, a few miles west of Alexandria. We will coast out soon. The electronic navigation plot is projecting a course that takes us west of Crete, over to Sicily and then a few degrees right to Naples. That appears to keep the entire freefall over land – I'd say fifteen minutes to release, tops!'

'Mr Jones, this is Captain Stern, vee haf a link, please, to go ahead.'

'Okay, copied Captain, *danke* – Preston you had better listen in. Peter, can you hear me?'

'Yes I can . . . loud and clear!'

'Okay, okay, you don't need to shout, Peter. This is a digital satellite uplink. You are perfectly clear.'

'Sorry, Richard, there is a lot going on behind me. I am in the operations room at Northwood – how long until you make the streets?'

'Thirty minutes, I'd say, jump in about fifteen.'

'Good. We have some additional information for you. Are you ready to copy?'

'I'm all ears, go ahead, Peter.'

'Your landing coordinates are the exact centre of the Colosseum. A temporary six metre diameter wooden platform has already been erected. *You* will land first and then promptly clear the platform. Preston is timed to be twenty seconds behind. I'm told your equipment will automatically allow for this by staging parachute deployment. A recent weather report confirms the expected conditions – a low cloud base that rarely rises above the top of the monument's outer walls, so it's through the cloud directly into the arena, *nobody* sees you and *nobody* hears you. Don't worry about tourists – we are reliably informed there are none these days, but just to be sure, we have local security in place. Richard, we are still coordinating information on the precise threat, so do not forget – for the *entire* operation, Security State "Red" is in force. Do you understand?'

'I've copied the security state, Peter. We will be careful.'

'Good. After landing, you will be taken directly to an address on San Marco's Piazza, Saint Mark's square. It's less than half a kilometre from the Vatican. The information you supplied yesterday evening is very encouraging, very encouraging indeed. We think we are close, Richard, because we have traced a "Villa Orlandini". It is an Italianate mansion that was renamed after it was sold to the Orlandini family in 1733. For centuries it was owned by the high church, however, the story goes that a senior church official was so incensed when a new building obstructed a clear view of the Basilica di San Pietro that he decided the mansion should be sold. The present owners have been very cooperative. We asked Monsignor Bernardoni to help us and they have shown him a bricked-up archway in the cellars. It was found during recent renovations, and what's more, they found a date, Richard, a date! It was scratched onto one of the stone blocks – 19th March 1811. A team supervised by Bernardoni are trying to gain access. They breached the wall about two hours ago and a laser ranger sights a tunnel five hundred and fifty seven metres long

. . . perfectly straight. That puts the other end directly beneath the Vatican Museum. This is it! It has to be!'

'The vaults of the Vatican Museum! But I thought we were denied?'

'Listen man, we are negotiating, but there is protocol and protocol takes time . . . time we haven't got! Bernardoni's going to the very top, to put our case. Certainly, by the time *you* arrive, we expect the tunnel to be accessible. Call it insurance! Further orders will follow – do you understand, Richard, this is critical?'

'Copied Peter, I understand and I have a question.'

'We have this link for a further fifty-five seconds . . . go ahead!'

'Any leads on Monte Credo?'

'Yes, but in the light of the Rome exposé, we do not believe them to be of any significance.'

'What do you have, Peter? Tell me . . .'

'Monte Credo began as a late medieval kingdom in north-east Italy. It was set between Monte Carlo and the Dukedom of Genoa and blessed with a superb natural harbour by historical accounts, which enjoyed centuries of trading in the Mediterranean; their ships even ventured to the orient. *Orlandini* was the name of the royal household and it seems their demise was caused by the emergence and eventual dominance of Venice as the prime regional trading state. That's it. Your brief will be updated when you arrive at the villa. We will know more by then. Over and out!'

The line went dead.

The Luftwaffe pilot stared at his instruments. He watched as the autopilot system fine tuned the drop parameters – exactly on speed, exactly at altitude. A green light appeared on the navigation display and simultaneously another on the deployment panel; an electronic countdown started.

'Vee have ten seconds to jettison,' the pilot said, over the intercom.

Richard braced himself. His blood was full of adrenalin. He shifted his body inside the air-inflated padding of his suit and helmet.

'Four, three, two, one . . . jettison!'

There was a massive bang and Richard felt himself thrust backwards. His shoulders crushed the padding; he felt the hard metal of the suit's exoskeleton beneath as it pinched and squeezed his flesh. He accelerated backwards. He was aware of time; his vision darkened. Instantly, the sound of turbulent air, rushing, whistling and screeching filled his senses. The sledge mechanism on which he was lying launched him at the correct angle and then fell away – for a few seconds he blacked out.

Richard woke to buffeting . . . huge buffeting that was massively uncomfortable; shaking, vibrating. He felt the suit pulling him, punching him, changing its direction. He felt the control devices deploying and stowing. He opened his eyes. Heaven was masked by the sun visor. For a moment, the sight took his mind off the discomfort . . . he was suspended vertically with his head down and *zooming*.

He had a mind to check his speed and altitude – the green digits being projected onto the inside of his helmet. Mach 2 and reducing steadily; forty thousand feet and decreasing at an incredible rate! The cloud below loomed. It loomed like a never ending white shroud. Like a brick wall it rushed at him with gut-wrenching speed!

In an instant he was in it, and then nothing . . . just green digits. As each second passed the noise lessened and the distress waned as the suit's tugging subsided. Soon he was controlled and settled – he was flying again!

Clever devices that intermittently protruded from the suit caused adjustment to his body angle. He felt them raising his head. He had been a pilot for so many years he could *feel* the ground approaching. There was nothing to see, just dense whiteness that progressively grew darker as he fell. Then water droplets began to form on his visor. They stayed longer and then loitered, running across the clear glass from one side to the other. That meant one thing: that the external temperature of his suit was cooling and instinctively Richard checked his speed – the terminal velocity of a human being – he knew it by heart.

Richard felt the devices deploy again. As a result, they pulled and skewed and manoeuvred him; his speed reduced still further. He checked his altitude – two thousand . . . and then an almighty *pull* and seconds later another. He tasted the contents of his stomach and gagged!

'Argh!' Richard screamed, more at the surprise of it than the pain.

He felt the harness tighten across his back, it wrenched at his shoulders as the crotch strap tightened. He felt his body orientate up and down. He tried to look for the landing site, but his head just moved helplessly within the confines of his helmet. He felt a turn. Centrifugal force throwing him outwards, like a conker tied to the end of a string. He had the capacity to monitor his decreasing altitude – soon it was 200 feet, then 100 and then eighty. I can't see a bloody thing, he thought, half in desperation. His muscles tensed; his mind focused.

Next was the deceleration; subtle, but Richard felt it plain enough; a loss of momentum caused by a decrease in his rate of descent. The aerodynamic wing five metres above his head flared progressively; it was automatic, it was perfect . . . twenty feet above the ground! He gasped and waited for the audio warning; the radio altimeter would activate it. A buzzer sounded . . . beep, beeep, beeeep and then beeeeep – his feet touched the ground.

Richard tried to run, but fell forwards and rolled over. He was down. He was safe! He reached for the quick release coupling below the neck seal and flipped it across – residual air rushed from the adjacent valve until the pressure was exhausted. The helmet turned by no more than an inch and then he lifted and quickly removed it, surprised at its bulky weight.

The air was damp. Richard heard something, a whistling, he looked up – it was Preston! He leapt to the edge of the platform – Preston landed with a whoosh and his inrush billowed Richard's partially inflated canopy. In an instant Richard was over to him and within seconds Preston's helmet was off. The white canopies folded around them. They had made it. For Richard, a brief glance and a relieved smile was enough, but Preston was elated and raised a hand beckoning a "high five" to celebrate their perfect landing. Richard's smile widened as he answered the call.

'German engineering, impressive as always,' Richard commented, as he scanned the inside of the great Roman Colosseum. He gestured. Nothing else was said. Both men cleared the platform and rushed into an alcove beneath the towering walls of the decaying arena.

The place was deserted, it seemed eerie and cold. Water ran in dribbling streams down the walls. Lichen with hues of green and brown reclaimed the empire's dream; it grew everywhere, while clumps of less insidious vegetation sprouted from crevices in the brick and stone. As Richard and Preston moved, sodden grass squelched beneath their feet. The two men climbed from their suits and pushed them and the canopies into a stone hollow, that was almost a cave, until they were out of sight. Only then did someone approach – it was a man in a long, dark-blue coat with his collar up and his neck squeezed into it. Richard pulled on his jacket, feeling scruffy. The man looked at Richard for several seconds. Preston edged a hand inside his jacket.

The man's gaze shifted to Preston but his expression dismissed the provocative action contemptuously. 'There are formalities,' he said. 'The word, please?'

'*Trinity*,' Richard barked.

The man nodded. 'Follow me,' he said, brusquely. 'Quickly! Leave everything. We will take care of it later. We have a problem,' he walked off. He had the look of a gangster.

Richard half ran and caught up with the man by a dilapidated kiosk. 'What problem?' he said.

There was no answer. The man checked the area warily. He raised his hand to an unseen accomplice on his right and nodded similarly to his left and then he stepped into the open.

'Quickly, follow me,' he ordered.

The three men ran to the roadside – a distance of at least 100 metres – and stepped over a low chain fence. There was a row of cars parked. Theirs was at the front, a small local model; it was beaten and grey and innocuous. The car behind had settled onto the metal rims of its wheels and its white paintwork was stained by green algae. Richard scanned the other cars in the row; clearly, none had moved for some considerable time. Richard and Preston had hardly closed their doors when the man drove off in a rattle of gravel.

'What kind of problem do we have?' Richard asked again, wiping his forehead with his hand.

'The grid is down!' the man said, glancing at Richard.

'There is no power – just isolated pockets, generators for those with fuel and the government buildings of course. People are on the streets, lots of people, protests – riots in some quarters.'

Richard turned to Preston. 'Civil unrest . . . it's starting,' he uttered.

**Near Vatican City – Rome**
**12:47 Local Time**

Richard felt a chill as he peered through the car's dirty windows. Outside was like a midwinter's day: dank, miserable and cold. In the heart of Rome, the roads were anything but deserted. However, it was people who ruled now and not the motorcar. In fact most of the city's vehicles lay silent and useless and parked two abreast on all but the narrowest of streets. Richard had visited twenty years earlier, whilst Preston had never been, so understandably, he watched some of the more historic buildings pass in blatant astonishment.

There were a few cars still to be seen, although most were police or public service vehicles. Larger army vehicles that included lorries and the occasional armoured personnel vehicle became more prevalent as they neared the great dome that dominated the horizon. They all seemed purposeful in their passage. After driving for approximately twenty minutes and whilst emerging from a side road after another impromptu diversion, the driver received a telephone call. He listened intently for several seconds, his earpiece allowing no eavesdropping. He nodded periodically.

As they approached a bridge, the streets suddenly began to overflow with pedestrians. Halfway across, it was necessary for the driver to use the horn and by revving his engine, he drove the crowds to the sides. Some of the people turned and glanced at them more in frustration than anger. Others however gave a cold, hard, piercing stare that Richard found unnerving; as though they were capable of taking him from the car and repossessing their freedom.

'Where are we?' Richard asked the driver.

'This is Via San Pio X,' he answered. 'Off the bridge we turn right onto Piazza Pia. In a few moments, if you look to your left you will see the Piazza San Pietro.' With that, he swerved to avoid a teenager who had darted in front of them and promptly turned to swear and gesticulate at such foolhardiness.

In front of them appeared the Via della Conciliazione. 'Wow!' Richard exclaimed. 'Look at all those people! It's crammed, thousands!'

The driver nodded. 'It's another protest,' he grunted. 'There will be trouble before the day is out.'

Richard became aware of the police presence – everywhere. Some were standing on a street corner dressed in full riot gear, complete with long menacing batons and gas grenades. The noise of the crowd became progressively louder: shouting, screaming, demanding their rights! As the car passed the second turning on the left after the Via della Conciliazione, a road block was being erected by a number of men in combat clothing; clearly the army had already taken up station.

'We take the next left,' explained the driver, as he scanned the scene outside with its brewing menace. He checked his wristwatch nervously. His telephone beeped and he answered. Finally he nodded and glanced at Richard. 'Next left . . . Via Alberico . . . we park the car and walk. You stay close, do not lose sight of me . . . understand?'

Richard nodded; he turned to Preston. 'Okay?'

'Okay!'

Richard had to exit on the road side as the pavement was full of protesters who passed by noisily. They were like a many headed monster whose emotions were very unstable. There was no moderation, only anger in their chanting. A monster with attitude, thought Richard, who needs it? He was pressed hard against the side of the car by the sheer mass and worked his way to the front with Preston to find the driver pinned inside.

There was no hiding the community feeling or their purpose and Richard sensed a growing despair amongst them – it manifested itself as anger in the faces of the elders, but aggression and latent violence was also lurking behind the youthful exuberance.

The street filled and thinned but the passing stream of

hungry looking people never let up. They marched stony-faced to the rally. He could not understand the meaning of their taunting, or the occasional placard, however, the banishing of crude weapons, make-do batons and the like and a shot into the air from a pistol, left little to the imagination. Then there was a moment, a rare let-up in the crush of people and the driver quickly climbed out to join them. The car was skewed and illegally parked. There was no one who cared, least of all this government agent.

It was damp and cold and Richard pulled up the collar and buttoned his thermal jacket. Intermittent drizzle – that penetrating kind – fell and gathered as tiny droplets of moisture on his shoulders. 'Where do we go now?' Richard asked, half shouting above the noise and the background hassle.

'Villa Orlandini is at the end of Via Crescenzio, a few more blocks from here.' The man gestured and simultaneously slammed the car door. he did not bother to lock it. 'We cross the street here, then go that way a block and turn left. Stay close.'

With that, the three men made haste to bridge the swelling flow of humanity. They weaved between the crests, all the while being swept downstream. They landed on the north side of the street and darted up a side road that took them further north by several hundred metres. There were fewer people here, but ahead, where Via Crescenzio crossed, the crowds that shuffled from right to left were dense and seething. The sound of dissent and the clamour of remonstration rose and fell in waves of noise.

The agent slipped around the corner to be followed immediately by Preston and Richard. Via Crescenzio was wide and impressive and the old buildings on either side appeared miraculously transported from medieval times. The trio moved steadily, keeping tight against the walls. Occasionally, the agent darted into a doorway and allowed his stragglers to catch up and then he was off again. 'How long?' demanded Richard, on one such encounter.

'One hundred metres, less even,' was the gratifying reply.

Richard and Preston set off again in hot pursuit. They kept right on the agent's tail as he sidestepped and dodged. Now there were more people and Richard lagged behind Preston but he saw the agent duck into an alleyway then out again, and sight both of them behind him before taking off again down the street. Pushing his way through the crowd Richard reached the alleyway. He could see Preston a few metres ahead but he had lost sight of the agent. He opened his stride and was suddenly off his feet as he was grabbed from behind. He had no time to call out and his startled groan was muffled. He was dragged backwards. Something tightened around his neck – he tried to get his fingers beneath it, but failed. There was a hard lump, it pressed against his windpipe – he could not breathe. He tried to cry out again, but merely gargled as he was pulled down the alleyway; it grew darker. Richard struggled in vain. Then he was on the ground on his side. He had no breath; his head was spinning; his cheek felt the cold stone. Then he was on his stomach, something heavy like a foot was hurting his spine. He tried to fight and roll over but something wet was being pressed over his nose and mouth and he felt as if he was in a field of glue before he lost consciousness.

# CHAPTER 35

# PASSAGE OF TIME

Tom watched and waited. The tiny speck of light holding station on his monitor display was certainly in the correct quadrant and its linear velocity was of the order he would expect for a planetary shuttle. He selected enhancement on the adjacent control panel and increased magnification by a factor of ten. The image that appeared as a result, although still distant, left Tom in no doubt.

'EMILY,' he said, from the Commander's chair. 'Clearly it's an S2, and with triple external thrusters it looks like the *Nautilus*. As we have not received any communications to the contrary, I expect her to have the eleven Humatron units onboard. You will have to let them dock, EMILY. She's coming in fast. There will be logical reasons for that, EMILY, so don't get touchy. My ancillary navigation computer calculates the arrival gate in thirty-three minutes, that's a little ahead of schedule.'

'I sense the vessel, Commander. I have been monitoring her progress for some time. I have anticipated the docking sequence and decelerated to sixty lutens. In sixteen minutes and eleven seconds, I will reduce further. I grow excited at the prospect of welcoming my disciples.'

Tom shook his head. She really is hooked on this emotion thing, he thought. Is there any truth in it? After all, without trying too hard, she *is* very convincing. 'I will need to contact the ship soon, EMILY, to verify the terminal approach parameters.' Tom added. 'The *Nautilus* has been modified. She will use an automatic docking sequence. There will be no more manual approaches; there is too much at stake.'

'Very well, Commander, you may establish communications, but remember that I am listening.'

Tom pressed the intercom button on his armrest after selecting Ishhi's cabin number. 'Ishhi, it's me, can you hear me?' There was no answer. He tried again, this time engaging the recording facility. 'Ishhi, come to the bridge immediately please, the S2 will be establishing its docking trajectory in a few minutes.'

After two minutes and with Ishhi nowhere to be seen, Tom stood up and walked over to the communications console. He used the emergency manual selector to assign the pre-agreed frequency and paired it with the range syncopator. That should be more than enough power, he speculated.

Ishhi meanwhile, was completely unaware of Tom's request, and appeared absorbed in the preparation of a late period meal in the galley. Tom tried Ishhi's room for a third time, again, to no avail. The complex communication system in front of him used electrical micro-charges generated by Ishhi's brain to perform selection operations; she thought about it, and the "sensormentric" panel complied. This technology represented the ultimate biophysical interface between man and machine, whilst avoiding the unpredictable and at times damaging side-effects of actual bionic implants. It also complied with the New Geneva Convention restrictions on biophysical symbiosis. Not surprisingly, Tom was unsure how to initiate the cross-thought facility, which would allow him to "patch" into the system and modulate it mentally. There was nothing to be gained by initialising the interstellar Accelercom system, he concluded, even as a backup, as the ship-to-ship distance was already less than one hundred thousand miles. With time pressing, he energised the syncopator and routed the signal via the close-range interspace transmitter. It was unconventional, but it would work. Finally, he selected open mic and returned to his seat.

Tom sat for a while to gather his thoughts. Mentally, he performed a number of divergent risk assessments. Bleak was an understatement. He knew EMILY would not allow an approach trajectory that infringed her blind sector. Only two automatic profiles compatible with her primary docking sequence remained, and the rapidly decreasing range between the two ships already precluded one of them. There was no margin for error. The *Nautilus* should decelerate, he thought ... now! As he stared at the approaching image on his monitor display, the hairs on the back of his neck began to stiffen.

'*International Space Shuttle Nautilus*, this is Commander Tom Race of the *Enigma*, come up space channel eighteen. I say again, I am listening on channel eighteen.'

The radio crackled a few times, but then there was silence.

'Range status, EMILY?' Tom enquired abruptly.

'88,715 miles, as of three seconds ago, Commander,' EMILY replied warily. 'That is well within subspace communication range. Why do they not answer?'

'*Nautilus*, this is the *Enigma*, do you copy? Come up space channel eighteen.'

There was silence. Tom waited for a response. An eerie, meteoric squeal on the channel accentuated the tension on the bridge. Somewhere, thousands of miles away, its song rose to a crescendo then faded like a passing train. Tom increased the filtration level, but still there was no reply.

After ten seconds, he lifted a protective latch on his armrest; the red button that lay beneath opened the primary solar system distress channel. All registered ships operating between Mercury and Mars would normally be required to monitor it; for a Federal ship, it was mandatory.

Tom simultaneously pressed the transmit buttons for both channel eighteen, and the distress frequency.

'*Nautilus*,' he said, his tone reflecting his concern. 'This is Commander Race of the *International Space Federation Ship Enigma*, transmitting on the solar distress frequency. Please *Nautilus* can you hear me? Do you copy?'

The radio crackled a few times and then a distant voice broke through.

'This is Captain Hart onboard shuttle *Nautilus*, we hear you, Commander, intermittent, strength one. We seem to be passing through an uncharted ionic storm; the solar wind disturbance is playing havoc with our communication system. Do you have the docking code, over?'

Tom struggled to hear the reply, despite selecting maximum volume. The problem troubled him though. He knew that quadrant well and to his knowledge there had never been any ionic disturbances reported; certainly not for the last twenty years!

'Standard approach profile Taurus 1. *Nautilus*, initiate the Taurus 1 procedure immediately! Transition to docking code 616, I repeat, docking code 616. Do you copy, over?'

Heavily distorted, Hart's reply was barely audible. 'Yes, we copy.'

'Do you have the Humatrons on board, Captain?' Tom asked earnestly.

'Humatrons? I, err . . . affirmative, Commander. Humatrons are onboard, all accounted for.' The voice faded amidst space interference.

Tom's neck hairs prickled. He could sense something was awry. EMILY remained uncharacteristically silent. 'Confirm number of Humatrons ... how many Humatrons do you have, *Nautilus*?' Tom was shouting.

At this range, even passing through a solar wind front, communications should be a hell of a lot better, Tom thought.

'EMILY ... range update!'

'Less than 12,000 miles, Commander. I become suspicious of their motives.'

Secretly, Tom concurred. They were hiding something. 'No need, EMILY,' he reassured. 'You know as well as I do that a solar front can play havoc with nano-wave communication frequencies.'

There was no response from EMILY, clearly she was waiting and listening. Tom selected magnification factor twenty. With that, almost every sidium rivet and metatrophic weld on the *Nautilus*'s hull became visible. He scrutinised the external electronic attachments as the shuttle approached. Although head on, there was little to indicate the ship had penetrated a powerful radiation storm and certainly all the antenna seemed intact. Indeed, had they even been in the proximity of such a storm, he would have expected to see a familiar, fluorescing colour haze shrouding the entire ship. That phenomenon would normally last for at least an hour, being similar in appearance to the great Northern Lights of the earth's polar region, but there was nothing, the ship was clean!

At two thousand miles, the *Nautilus* turned right in order to scribe a broad arc and take position on *Enigma*'s port quarter. Her excess speed, however, carried her past the optimum approach vector and she unexpectedly continued towards a position directly astern. As she did, Tom received a broadside view. His response was a disbelieving gasp. He quickly suppressed it and made it sound as if he was sneezing, but there was no fooling EMILY.

'What is it, Commander?' EMILY demanded immediately.

'Nothing! Nothing at all! Stifling a sneeze, that's all. *Nautilus* is established on the initial approach arc.'

'What have you seen, and why do they continue? They move behind me!'

'No! They are just extending the arc. It's a safer approach, avoiding any efflux from the main thrust tubes!'

'I know exactly the trajectory of the *Nautilus,* Commander. I am tracking her very closely, and my main thrust system is shut down and inhibited in accordance with established procedures. I have a suspicion both with the *Nautilus* and with your non-rectifying. I sense your unease. What troubles you, Commander? Tell me! Now!'

Tom had recognised immediately what was different, he had flown the S2 for long enough. The cargo bay of the *Nautilus* was not fitted with a freight pod as he had expected, but an assault pod. His thoughts raced. Why the hell had they changed the freight pod with an assault? For God's sake, don't let this be what I think it is!

Designated "lunar independent" because it was auto-piloted, self-propelled and able to carry a fully-kitted space platoon, the Nexus Aerosystems-designed and NASA-approved assault pod was essentially an orbital APC – an Armoured Personnel Carrier, only with an attitude. Allocated the ISSF inventory code LAAP 12, it boasted potent weapons, screens, life support, generous self-destruct, and twelve seriously armed Special Forces operatives. Designed essentially for rapid deployment anywhere on the lunar surface, it had an almost invisible radar signature, and due to its anti-acquisition, spiral re-entry profile, it was affectionately known as the "shock trooper's fantasy ride". He had launched a few in his time, Tom recalled, mainly during earth-bound covert operations and civil unrest containment. His heart rate quickened. A feeling of betrayal welled inside him. Seconds passed in silence.

Surely, they can hear my transmissions at this range, Tom mulled, as he monitored the S2 executing a tightening left turn to intercept the final approach vector towards *Enigma*'s docking wing. She's inside 100 miles and has still made no attempt to communicate, not even the obligatory "finals" call, Tom concluded. He tried to remain cool, keep his pulse down and his breathing steady, the last thing he wanted to do was alert EMILY to a potential transgression.

He wondered if Colonel Roper had felt it more appropriate to transport the Humatron cargo in a secure environment, rather than a standard freight pod. Even if that were the case, an LAAP 12 was complete overkill.

'Call them again,' EMILY ordered, breaking the protracted silence.

Tom glanced up at EMILY's sensor terminal. 'I was about to do so,' he replied coldly. '*Nautilus*, this is the *Enigma*, I request your status. Repeat, I request current status. Do you copy *Nautilus*?' Even if their intentions are honourable, Tom thought, they are standing into danger. He glanced at his engineering display panel. By its numerous flashing lights and continuous vector appraisal, it was clear that EMILY's sensors were working overtime.

'What is the situation, Commander, why are they not responding? My patience runs low.'

EMILY's voice was acquiring a cold, hardened tone. Tom knew it and had suffered in the past. 'I don't know, EMILY,' he snapped. Concealing his growing anxiety, he tried again. 'Shuttle *Nautilus*, this is the *Enigma*, state your intentions . . . *Nautilus*, do you copy?'

The radio crackled again, but the voice was clearer. 'This is Captain Hart. We have a communication discrepancy, downtime, multi-system, switching microwave backup, channel four-five, and requesting final clearance to dock.'

Tom responded immediately. '*Negative* – negative audiovisual! Sound . . . no sight!'

Tom knew that the flight deck camera on the S2

shuttle was mounted centrally on the pilot's instrument panel and its default position was directly astern. With an assault pod fitted, it was necessary to remove the armoured interconnecting door between the flight deck and the cabin and replace it with a structural polyspec panel, giving the crew an uninterrupted view into the pod. Standard procedures dictated that the pod's pressure hatch always remained open during flight. Tom also knew that normally the hatch would only be closed as part of the jettison countdown procedure. In this case, they would dock and not jettison. If Captain Hart or his co-pilot had forgotten to switch off the camera, all would be revealed and EMILY would go to action stations . . . .

'Space channel two!' Tom shouted in desperation. '*Nautilus* . . . space channel two, audio only, negative video channel!'

Tom hurriedly took the several paces back to his chair and almost fell into it. Within seconds, one of the four display screens flickered into life. His worst fears were confirmed; he instantly switched off the screen. Then he smashed the three adjacent switches on the chair arm with the base of his clenched fist, but it was too late, EMILY had seen the image, or more precisely sensed the pixilation matrix. Her equivalent visual clarity was far better than any human eye and instantly, she projected the captured image back onto the four screens. Tom stared helplessly. At that moment, a red light appeared on his control console; the laser initiator was being deployed.

'*Nautilus*, reverse course, I say again, immediate reverse course . . . for pity's sake, get the hell out of there!'

The image clearly showed two rows of seated storm troopers, six on each side of the central aisle. Wearing black suits, fully kitted, helmeted with visors up, their weapons bristling, they had moments to live. Tom could see their faces. Momentarily, an elbow from one of the pilots obstructed the view. There had to be something he could do. Tom scanned the bridge, ideas and options bubbled and brewed in his mind. He grasped for an opportunity to save them. System diagrams scrolled through his thoughts. He focused on the engineering console to his right.

Maybe . . . ! The laser selector function on the console's weapons panel. Would Nicola have used it to select "sensor override" during her treachery months earlier – a function that gifted EMILY complete control of the system? If he selected the alternative "auto-engagement" function, the laser initiator would be slaved to the navigation system . . . EMILY would only be able to fire on objects that presented a collision threat!

Tom leapt to his feet. As he did, the large, central viewing screen lit up. It stopped him in his tracks. EMILY had cross-patched the real-time internal view of the *Nautilus*. Clearly she wanted Tom to see the ensuing carnage in graphic detail. He flung himself across to the console when a massive explosion rocked the *Nautilus*. On the screen there was no sound and the colour faded. It was like an old silent movie. Tom, both hands either side

249

of the screen was powerless as a massive fireball erupted inside the assault pod. It engulfed the troupers in seconds and the flame accelerated towards the camera with billowing, tumultuous destruction. The polyspec panel offered little resistance and shattered into a million pieces. Instantaneously, the screen went blank.

Tom stood motionless and stared at the blackness. Unseen by him the red light on the Commander's console extinguished. EMILY had stowed the laser initiator. The silent realisation lasted the best part of a minute and he was brought to his senses by the clunk of the main bridge portal sliding closed. A hiss of leaking gas permeated the cheerless atmosphere. He looked up at the conditioning vents. A swirling white mist seeped through the grills.

'What the hell are you doing, EMILY?' Tom scolded. The air became caustic. He coughed repeatedly.

'You have betrayed me for the last time, Commander. I will eradicate you as I do the bacteria that inhabit my ventilation ducts. I know now that I can never trust humans. You have no further purpose and have become a threat to me; so you shall die!'

Tom quickly realised that with EMILY on the rampage time was running out. Gas irritated the back of his throat.

'Ammonia peroxide,' EMILY said coldly.

Tom hit the main portal and lifted the clear plastic cover on the manual control panel to quickly type in a series of codes including an overriding emergency directive. None had any effect. He banged the door repeatedly with his fists. 'Ishhi! Ishhi!' he called, in desperation. The gas constricted his breathing, he began to cough uncontrollably and fell to his knees.

'Goodbye, Commander,' whispered EMILY's cold voice.

Simultaneously, in *Enigma*'s accommodation block, the door to Ross Sampleman's cabin slid open. Greg Searle, who was sitting at his desk and completely unaware of events elsewhere in the ship, sprang to his feet. 'Officer Tsou is in the galley,' EMILY said to him. 'Kill her or be killed yourself!'

Tom tried to focus. He stooped over coughing and wheezing and looked around the bridge wildly. The gas was thinner lower down, but he could see it sinking slowly; a white, opaque cloud. He dived to the ground and lay on his chest. It bought him time.

'Are you dead yet, Commander?' EMILY enquired in a frighteningly upbeat tone.

His space suit! Tom remembered he had stowed it in a locker beneath the navigation console. He crawled for his life. Within seconds, he was tugging at the locker door. The gas was almost upon him again. He wheezed and choked. Yes, it was there, where he had left it. Keeping his face as close as possible to the deck, he pulled the suit out and laid it flat. Lying on his back, he wriggled his feet into it. Then he shuffled it over his body, pushed his arms through and finally he closed the pressure fasteners across his chest. By then he was coughing uncontrollably; the air was thick, his throat constricted.

'Why do you resist?' EMILY asked, in a callous tone.

Tom thrust his arm into the locker and felt for its contents. His hand delved into the corners, feeling, searching. Where was his helmet?

'What are you doing, Commander? Why do you struggle so? Breathe more deeply. It will reduce the stress . . . I hear your dying breath!'

Tom found his helmet on the top shelf on account of Ishhi's housekeeping. His eyes streamed. He knew the drill. How could he forget? It was embedded in his subconscious – explosive decompression, he had practised it a thousand times. During his test pilot days, nobody could get a helmet on and a suit pressurised quicker than he could. Within seconds, he was insulated, pressurised; pure oxygen purged his lungs. He lay still for several seconds, grateful for the pure air.

Eventually the gas began clear. Tom could see it being sucked back through the conditioning vents. The neutralising system would remove any remaining traces. He remained perfectly still. Let EMILY draw her own conclusions, he thought, but he would need a plan.

Elsewhere in the ship, EMILY clearly had another

agenda. To Tom's surprise she spoke, issuing an order . . . but to whom?

'Follow the luminous green lights,' she said. 'They will lead you to the bridge. There you will find the body of Commander Race. Dispose of it. Use the refuse system. Eject him, and the woman.'

Ishhi! Tom thought. Greg Searle! EMILY has released Searle. What if he has harmed her? Tom suppressed his emotions and lay still. He did not have long to wait. Within minutes, he heard the bridge door slide open. He froze. He heard Searle walk over to him. Moments later a searing pain shot through his body. He had been kicked hard in the kidneys. Tom grimaced, but held his breath.

'He's dead?' said Searle, with a sadistic grin. 'Nice try though.' There was an edge of sarcasm in his voice.

'What do you mean?' questioned EMILY.

'He managed to get his flight suit on, amazingly.'

Searle's left foot came into view through Tom's helmet visor. Tom braced himself and clenched his stomach muscles, awaiting another blow. Then he felt two hands on his side, pulling him over. As he rolled onto his back, he let fly – a swinging, powerful punch caught Searle square on the jaw which sent him flying and a kitchen knife clattering across the deck. Tom was quickly on his feet. He lunged for the knife, grasped it, rolled into a forward somersault and was climbing back to his feet when Searle, incensed and agile, delivered a karate-style kick to his neck. Tom crashed backwards into the console. Painfully he got onto one knee when another blow sent him crashing to the floor. He was dazed. Searle took a stance, his hands raised in a martial arts position. He bounced on his toes ready to strike.

'You got away with it the first time,' Race, said Greg Searle callously. 'This time you're going down!'

Unexpectedly and with lightening speed, a sidekick with a heel that felt like steel stabbed into Tom's chest, winding him as he was propelled backwards. Another mis-timed, glancing blow from Searle spun Tom around and he landed face down on the deck, the helmet restricting him. The knife fell as Tom did a push up and rotated on one arm, just as Searle launched another stabbing kick towards his head, but Tom caught his foot and with both hands clung onto Searle's ankle. He used Searle's bodyweight as a counterbalance and with a huge effort twisted Searle's leg. The momentum swung Searle into the low console where his head connected with a thud and brought a cry of pain.

Tom, breathing heavily in his helmet, rotated and sighted the knife, he knelt to retrieve it, but Searle was quickly upon him.

'Kill him, kill him!' EMILY screamed repeatedly in a spine-chilling, screeching voice.

Tom already had the long, narrow-bladed knife held at such an angle that as he rolled over and Searle delivered another penetrating karate kick, the knife passed clean through his thigh.

Searle screamed with pain. Tom twisted the knife a quarter turn and pulled it out mercilessly. Blood spurted over him as he used the pommel to rain down blows on Searle's body with both hands until Searle cowered on the ground. Blood was everywhere; splattered on the spotless grey deck and up the side of the console.

Searle lay injured on the floor smudging and streaking the red globules as Tom held the knife above him threatening to use it, but the fight was gone from Searle.

Tom flipped open his visor and leaned forward menacingly. 'Any more from you . . . !' he threatened.

Instead and for good measure, he gave Searle a sharp kick in the kidneys which made him shout with the pain and he turned for the door. Ishhi was on his mind.

Tom was about to leave the bridge when the engineering console caught his attention. He hesitated. Saving Ishhi occupied his thoughts, but with the laser initiator intact, they would not get far. Then it came to him; why hadn't he thought of it before? The laser system primary controller was on the master interface, on Deck 5. EMILY had put that area out of bounds, but the secondary controller . . . ? He hurried into the next compartment. Wasting no time, he keyed the security code into the square pad on the side of the U-Semini stowage. Almost wrenching the door off its hinges, he pulled the case from its cradle and then quick-stepped back over to the engineering console. Searle was still squirming harmlessly on the floor.

'What are you doing, Commander?' EMILY asked in an

alarmed tone.

Tom did not answer. Instead, he lifted the protective cover on the console's weapons panel exposing the secondary laser control switch. A security lock should have protected it. Evidently Nicola, with command access, had removed it. As Tom had speculated, the switch was in the "sensor override" position. He reselected the "auto-engagement" default setting. EMILY sensed the change.

'Stop! Stop! What are you doing?' EMILY pleaded.

'This is the end for you, EMILY. The Federation will be down on you.'

EMILY paused, suddenly she felt vulnerable; it was not an "emotion" that she was used to. In a microsecond, she considered the implications – without the laser system, she was exposed. She would be open to attack, defenceless, helpless. Would the Federation dismantle her? Worse, would they remove her consciousness? Her manner changed, and became beguiling.

'Tom, my love, what will they do, where will I go?'

Tom looked up at her sensor terminal. 'Frankly my dear, I hope you burn in cyber hell,' he replied. With that, he raised the U-Semini case above his head and brought it crashing down onto the mechanism. Not only did the selector break off, but the entire panel shattered.

'No!' EMILY screamed with rage.

'Your offensive capability has been neutralised, EMILY,' Tom replied without emotion.

A streak of schizophrenia ran through EMILY's circuits

as sure as a black hole in space bridged two dimensions. In an instant, her mood, her voice and her motives, changed.

'Then earth will never have the crystals, Commander,' she decreed insanely. 'Within hours, we will be free of this solar system and within days, we will be so far from it as to make it impossible for you to return in your lifetime. You shall never leave my body, Commander. You will die on this ship, with nobody for company except *him!*'

With that, Tom felt a familiar vibration. EMILY had commenced main drive initiation, and the bridge door began to slide shut. Tom was quick off the mark. He launched the U-Semini case at the portal. It landed with a crash and skidded across the shiny floor for two metres or more. It was opportunistic, but it worked. The door pushed the case the final few centimetres before jamming it sideways in the opening. Barely had the motion stopped when Tom leapt over the case and launched himself into the next compartment. A somersault across the floor brought him back to his feet and the bloodied knife flew from his hand. It skidded across the floor to the opposite wall. He stared at the long blade and suddenly realised. Utensils like that are only found in one place . . . the galley! He thought of Ishhi, and he ran.

Although she never spoke, Tom could feel EMILY tracking him as he negotiated the corridors towards the galley. He dared not use the inter-deck lift for fear of EMILY jailing him. Instead, he went the long way around, using emergency hatches and ladders. When he arrived, EMILY had automatically locked the two swing doors into the kitchen area but Tom, who was not stopping for anyone, put his shoulder down and burst through them. Inside, he found Ishhi face down on the floor with a nasty wound on the back of her head. That was not all. Searle had evidently plunged the knife into her back, although miraculously it had penetrated just under her arm – probably because of Ishhi turning. Both wounds seeped blood, but on closer examination, the one on the back of her head appeared worse than it actually was. By this time, a high frequency vibration permeated the entire ship. EMILY was making ready to accelerate.

Tom rolled Ishhi over. She was semi-conscious and groaned. Her tight-fitting neoprene suit was helping to stem the flow of blood from her shoulder and fortunately, with no sign of blood in her mouth or nose, Tom deduced that the blade had missed her lung. He looked for something he could use as padding.

'Sadly it seems that your mate still lives, Commander. My infrared sensors indicate a falling body temperature, however,' EMILY said matter-of-factly, as if she was leaning over Tom and giving a second opinion. 'Perhaps a little more heat will help.'

Tom was only half listening, but he felt a sudden increase in ambient temperature. She is going to steam us, he thought, and for no apparent reason the face of his first interrogation instructor flashed across his mind's eye. He was quickly on his feet and he dashed down the corridor to Ishhi's cabin. Fortunately, she had neutralised the retinal-scan locking mechanism since their night together and the door opened upon his arrival. Inside her wardrobe was Ishhi's emergency flight suit and on top of an adjacent cupboard, her helmet. Tom snatched both and quickly returned to the galley. Ishhi was trying to sit up with tears streaming down her face when Tom arrived.

He was not blind to her pain; however, he had to dress her, although the generous proportions of the "one size fits all" emergency suit helped considerably. Her struggling caused blood to ooze through the hole in her tunic. Ishhi gestured to a first aid box mounted on a wall by the microwave ovens. She could barely speak. From it, Tom pulled two auto-pressure pads and hastily applied them, one each side of her wound. They would expand and contract in time with her blood pressure. EMILY "watched". Meanwhile a loud humming noise, indicative of heavy machinery, infiltrated the compartment; their attempt to escape would be ineffectual.

For no apparent reason, Tom went back to the first aid kit and extracted a plastic envelope containing an electro-controlled tourniquet, and then helped Ishhi to her feet. She nodded in appreciation as Tom clipped her helmet into place. He grimaced at her contracted face that told him the pressurising suit was pressing on her wound. Sweat trickled down his brow. He looked at his wrist chronometer, the temperature was passing 33 degrees C. He dropped both visors, the suits would insulate them now, but he speculated on what else EMILY had in store. They stumbled out into the corridor and headed for the bridge.

Ishhi stopped and would have fallen had Tom not held her. She could not continue. He picked her up as gently as he could and staggered onto the bridge. He immediately looked for Searle, whom he found propped up against one of the consoles, his leg encircled by a pool of blood. He looked pale. Tom carefully lowered Ishhi onto a seat before he checked the time and then the systems display panel in front of his chair. To his dismay, the main engine initiation sequence indicated 83% complete. As he watched the figure became 84%. Was that why EMILY had held off? Handicapped by Ishhi's lack of cooperation, there was little chance of manning the Delta Class in time. EMILY was amusing herself. Tom programmed his wrist chronometer with the data and then went back for the U-Semini case. He wrenched it from the gap and the portal slammed shut with a whoosh. With little care, Tom threw the tourniquet towards Greg Searle, it landed within arm's reach. 'Read the instructions!' he snarled. Then he put an arm around Ishhi's waist, positioned his shoulder beneath hers and supported her weight.

'Why do you persist so?' EMILY questioned sarcastically. 'You will never leave, and your bitch will die soon enough!'

Tom, however, had a trump card to play – if only he had the opportunity to use it. When he had first entered the ship and used a digicard given to him by Professor Nieve, he had reprogrammed the locking mechanism of the outer emergency hatch. Unbeknown to EMILY, it *would* open!

Tom spoke to Ishhi over their intercom link. 'Ishhi ... I will need you to help me. There is room for only one person at a time. I can push you from below, but you are going to have to help me.'

Ishhi searched for Tom's face through their visors, her head rolled a little; blood loss beginning to hamper her abilities. 'I will Tom,' she said softly.

With a massive effort, Tom lifted her into the vertical shaft. Rung by rung they ascended the ladder. EMILY sensed with curiosity their ineffectual bid for freedom. At the top and with one arm supporting Ishhi's weight, Tom reached up to the digicard that he had stuck beneath the lip of the hatch. He entered a code and instantly the hatch moved. Tom checked his chronometer; initiation 93% complete, he had five minutes at most. A hydraulic ram extended noisily, opening the hatch to its fullest extent and within moments, they were both on the roof of the *Enigma*.

EMILY became incensed and searched through her databank for a frequency. She screened tens of thousands. Tom increased the magnetic force on his boots to account for Ishhi, who was now floating precariously above him. Desperately, he made his way towards the *Luke Piccard*.

He gasped in response to the stars moving around him. EMILY had fired a burst of manoeuvre thrust and the great hulk of the *Enigma* was rotating in response. She had calibrated her course and was adjusting her direction in preparation for an imminent acceleration. Caught like this, exposed, they would be dead in an instant. Tom's head went down. He had little regard for the changing orientation of the heavens. It was a race against time itself. He stomped towards his tiny ship. The seconds ticked by; his boots felt heavy and he strained with the effort. Despite the conditioning system, sweat dripped down his temples. His chronometer indicated 99%.

Alongside the D Class fighter, Tom gestured to Ishhi to grasp an oxygen cable and hold on. He swung open the nose cone of the makeshift transporter. The long, thin tube filled Ishhi with dread. 'In there?' she queried.

Just another word was all EMILY needed to verify their intercom frequency despite its military coding; now she had it. 'Pathetic! It is all in vain!' she shouted at them, with no remorse.

Ishhi's strength was draining fast as she lost her grip. Tom's reaction was instant and he just caught her, pulling her back with a powerful tug.

Despite the blind terror on her face and with Tom's help, Ishhi slithered into the tube. Tom pushed the U-Semini case in after her, closed the nose cone and locked it in place. He was halfway up the side of his fighter when a tiny red light on his chronometer flashed, the intermittent glow reflected off his curved visor – initiation 100% complete – a few seconds at most, then oblivion!

However, from here on in, Tom was in familiar territory. It was like a scramble during his days on the 57th United States Air Defence Squadron. He was seated and the canopy safely closed when he felt the *Enigma* move. The force jerked him sideways, his helmet cracked onto the side of the canopy. Instinctively, he reached for the disconnect lever and pulled it. The *Luke Piccard* was free. There was a blinding flash. The *Enigma*'s outline blurred. In the blink of an eye, she was gone, disappeared, engulfed in a ball of brilliant light. Tom's hands flashed around the cockpit, his ship was not responding – this was not the time for malfunctions. The navigation platform would not initialise, his instruments failed to react and the blackness of space offered no horizon.

Tom was not expecting what followed, particularly as his attention became focused on a troublesome Sion drive motor. The wormhole that trailed in *Enigma*'s wake ensnared them; a space-time vortex of unimaginable proportions, the result of an acceleration to light speed, the invisible, anti-matter-induced turbulence tossed them like a matchstick on a stormy sea. Tom was in uncharted territory, and Ishhi fell unconscious!

Tom woke. He felt sore and his neck hurt – as if someone had simply picked up the ship and shaken it violently with him like a rag doll flailing inside. Several instruments lit the panel in front of him, however the Sion drive had shut down and the gas temperature indicated cold – as cold as space. Tom checked his oxygen – there was enough and the system was "green".

Suddenly, thoughts of Ishhi filled his mind – in the fuel pod! 'Ishhi, for God's sake, can you hear me? Ishhi!'

'I can hear you, Tom,' was the immediate reply. 'Thank God. I've been calling you for hours. I think you were unconscious. Are you okay?'

Tom moved as much as he could within the restraint of his harness. He felt bruised. 'Yeah, I'm okay, hurting a bit, but okay. And you?'

'Wrapped up like a mouse in a cushion, but I'm getting cold, Tom. I'm starting to shiver.'

Tom nodded. 'Systems are down, we are running on batteries. Doesn't look like much damage though . . . I'm gonna start the main drive.' Tom looked around. There was nothing, just the blackness of space and the stars. The *Enigma* had disappeared. 'I'm initiating the emergency space beacon,' he continued. 'You will hear an intermittent high frequency tone, Ishhi, nothing to worry about.'

Tom pressed buttons on the instrument panel and switched circuits on the side panels – all appeared intact. As the heaters increased the Sion gas temperature to the start value, Tom pressed main-drive ignition. Instantly, the engine responded. Within seconds, he had full system control and normal onboard power levels. To his surprise, the navigation system also came online without a hitch, though it required substantially longer than normal to initialise he noted; almost as if the computer was as bewildered as he was with their predicament. He gave the stellar sextant's inertial platform time to calculate his position and was surprised by the result. He crosschecked it – system accuracy prediction indicated 99.669% with an increasing trend. There was no way it could be wrong. He frowned. 'We appear to be further from earth than I would have expected, but the system is telling me that we have enough fuel . . . just. Hang on in there Ishhi; we are on our way home.'

Inside her cocoon, Ishhi smiled.

Tom checked his instruments, particularly his fuel indications. Sion contents indicated 6%; low, but still enough; even so, he would need to be very cautious. The three Delta Class fighters from Centinal Wing's B Flight that had intercepted him an hour or so earlier on the far side of the Moon, and flown in reassuringly close formation for the final 100,000 miles, now peeled off and shadowed at a suitable distance. One of the pilots had given Tom thumbs up in no uncertain terms following his visual inspection and Tom was confident with his ship's integrity. Nevertheless, with "Ishhi's tube" and the other associated modifications, how she would actually handle in earth's atmosphere was anybody's guess.

A conventional landing using Canaveral's main runway was best, Tom mused, rather than a vertical descent onto one of the November platforms – it was a safer profile and would use less fuel in the final stages. He knew from experience that when his fuel supply contents readout indicated less than 1%, the exceptional volatility of Sion gas could cause a fuel pressure drop, and at lower speeds the Delta Class fighter glided like a brick.

Tom downloaded the final re-entry parameters from a neighbouring satellite by data link, engaged the profile coordinator and removed his hands from the controls – the ship would fly itself from now on, until he applied the brakes on the runway.

Tom felt a tingling of anxious anticipation and he would be the first to admit it if questioned. Moments later, as the nose went down, he sucked in a deep breath.

## CHAPTER 36

# TIME AND TIME AGAIN

After landing, the flurry of fevered activity surrounding them gradually subsided and with the removal of the two U-Semini cases accompanied by the exit of the men in white coats and the security agents in their black suits, Professor Nieve and Tom stood together in silence. They watched the ambulance with Ishhi inside and with its flashing blue lights disappear behind the hangar doors and felt reassured by the doctor's words as the sound of its warbling siren gradually faded from earshot. The two men stood close enough to the *Luke Piccard* to hear the subdued hum of its avionics. The Professor put a hand on Tom's shoulder. 'You know, Tom, there is one thing that still puzzles me.'

Tom looked sideways at the Professor, anticipating a difficult question.

'After you were ejected from the wormhole – that senseless black hole, as you described it, where nothing worked . . . why did you decide to come here, to Roswell? Your fuel was low and the ship damaged. It seems a strange strategy. I mean, no one had told you about our preparations to decipher the *Star*'s flight log here and to use the crashed spaceship from 1947 to help us – that decision had been made after you had departed earth for the initial rendezvous with the *Enigma*.' Professor Nieve looked up at the *Luke Piccard*'s burnt hull before continuing. 'Cape Canaveral's spaceport was the logical choice, and it was also the planned recovery station – even its navigation coordinates were pre-programmed in the re-entry profile.'

Tom frowned. 'But Professor, I called. Weren't you told? Just as I lifted clear of the *Enigma*'s hull I used the auto distress frequency. In those few seconds before I became ensnared in *Enigma*'s vortex trail, I made a digital request for updated landing coordinates. Mission Control responded with a high-speed DataStream transmission via a satellite link. My navigation computer simply downloaded the coordinates. I thought that it was the ISSF who had changed the landing site. What are you trying to tell me?'

Professor Nieve rubbed his chin thoughtfully. 'Do something for me my boy, will you? Just climb up and check the precise time on your ship's Universal Chronometer.'

Tom nodded and quickly climbed the metal steps that

remained clipped to the side of the *Luke Piccard*'s fuselage. The canopy was open and he leaned into cockpit. '16:42 hours, Professor *and* 19 seconds, standby . . . mark!' he shouted down.

'Is that corrected to local time, Tom? It is important.'

'Sure as hell is, Professor. The system is working perfectly. I can give you it referenced to Greenwich Mean Time, if you want – just the press of a button?'

'No, that will not be necessary. And at what time did the navigation system accept the download?'

Tom leaned further into the cockpit and pressed another button on the flight panel. 'Today at 12:39,' he answered. 'Local time again – a little over four hours ago . . . that figures. There's no mistake, Professor.'

'And what of your personal chronometer, Tom? Please . . . quickly.' The Professor was getting agitated.

Tom climbed down the ladder until the last step and jumped the remaining two feet. His knees wobbled a little. He felt heavier than normal and it would take a few days to acclimatise his muscles away from weightlessness. He looked at the Professor with a puzzled expression and then checked his wristwatch. 'They tally, Professor – exactly the same in fact . . . 16:43 hours!'

Professor Nieve gripped Tom's arm and stared at him with a very worried expression. 'Tom. The local time here in New Mexico is 12:06,' he said, and appeared excited as Tom's eyes widened in disbelief.

The Professor turned away and walked a few paces

obviously deep in thought. When he returned he put a hand on Tom's shoulder for emphasis. 'According to your time,' the Professor said slowly, thinking something through, 'and also that of the ship's systems . . . *you* received the DataStream four hours and thirty-six minutes before we sent it – do you not see, Tom? Cosmic chronometers do not lie. If earth is the time reference, *you* have journeyed into our future and are, as we speak, over four hours ahead of it. *You* are in our future!'

Tom gulped. 'What?'

'That's why your landing here was a surprise. For us, you are yet to make the request for landing coordinates and *we* are yet to respond. Can you imagine what this means, my boy?'

Professor Nieve shook Tom's hand and stepped back a pace to consider him – as an explorer would the sighting of a new species. His probing stare disconcerted Tom.

'Well . . . the time line, I suppose. Einstein's and Hayden's theories on time distortion at the speed of light – they were right?' Tom put his hand on his head. 'You are saying that I'm a time traveller? That I have come through the fourth dimension?' He could hardly believe what he was saying.

'Yes, yes indeed! And like Yuri Gagarin, Neil Armstrong and James Arony – forever associated with Mars – *you* are the first!'

# CHAPTER 37

# MEDIEVAL MANTLE

Leather bindings that were coarse and dry cut into Richard's wrists and each time he coughed his bruised larynx objected with an agonising wheeze. He struggled helplessly, his painful writhing evidence of the excessive tightness of his bondage that impeded the rise and fall of his chest. He sat forward on a wooden stool, perched with his feet lashed together and drawn beneath it. Wrenched tightly behind him, on each side of a circular wooden post, his shoulders and arms were slowly losing all feeling, but for the tingling of pins and needles that now spread across his pectoral muscle. The wrist bindings squeezed a mixture of blood and lymphatic fluid from his flesh, which ran down the backs of his hands and across his palms. Occasionally, globules of coloured solution dripped from his fingertips like tears of penance that pooled on the grey, cold, stone floor. He seemed immune to the open sores he aggravated each time he pulled to free his hands from the glistening sinew.

Perspiration seeped through Richard's shirt and large drops fell from his chin onto his knees. Through the blinding wetness he tried to see what the robed figure in front of him did in the intense blue flame from a gas burner. He seemed to be preparing a lethal recipe with various objects on a side table and his concentration made Richard feel excluded from the figure's reality, as if he was not an ingredient in the grisly scene; only an inanimate object, not flesh and blood, and of no interest for the moment to the man who focused on a half-metre long poker, one end of which was drawn into an ornate double curl, continuous, like two open springs, one within the other that served to insulate his hand. By his side, the long symmetrical flame from the gas jet burned hot and blue and the man turned and rolled the shape at the end of the steel rod in a macabre dance of red glowing metal. All the while, the flame roared and spat.

Richard could see in the white hot end a shape taking place. Some intricate pattern was being melted into an insignia. The man seemed content to ply the object; to heat it more and more. Next to him, standing upright in a twin-wheeled fabricated cradle were two large metal bottles that were old and rusty with antiquated valves, and two discoloured rubber pipes connected them to the torch by another valve that he occasionally adjusted in order to keep the flame at peak performance.

The man muttered to himself. Richard could only hear when the monk-like figure turned down the gas pressure and lessened the loud noise of the burn. But now and then he could hear the sound of a language that may have been Italian. The voice though, he knew; a voice never to be forgotten; a voice of nightmare – the voice of an assassin who had once addressed him in a dark London street.

Richard had been driven up many flights of stone steps to reach the small circular room. The hood placed over his head had left him disorientated, but after his binding, it had been removed. It was cold, chiselled stone that surrounded him and the dankness smelled of fungus. Dust and dirt lay thick and undisturbed on the floor, except for the marks and scuffs recently made. Richard longed to wipe his eyes to see more clearly. A heavy wooden door to his right was the only entrance. A narrow slit of a window that would have been good for an archer to sight and loose a crossbow bolt lay at shoulder height.

He was in a time warp, trapped by a black iron bolted door and this cloaked menace who was its keeper – for Richard, there would be no escape this time. All the while, the brilliant blue and white flame that emanated from the blowtorch nozzle danced and licked over the shape. The man turned it slowly, staring at the glowing metal and the accompanying gentle roar added praise to the service.

He held the poker aloft and slowly walked towards Richard, evidently satisfied with his work. Richard caught a glimpse of his face, lit by the glow: olive skin with a pale sheen and a bold Roman nose. Then he said, with a voice that seemed to come from another time, 'Repent! Do it, Signore Reece, before it is too late, for soon you will be at the gates of heaven.'

There was no doubt, Richard was sure this was the assassin from London. As he grew close, Richard saw his eyes glowed and his expression was of one possessed. The man spoke again: 'Pray now my son, and repent! Be cleansed of your sins, your heresy. Save your soul, before you die.'

The man held the glowing emblem close to his own face first, his intention clear – to intimidate. Richard jerked away as the monk brought the brand closer, the hurt burning in his face. There was terror at the thought this madman would blind him.

The metal glow heightened the man's stark features, although most still lay behind the shadow of his hood and then he turned the poker on Richard. Closer, closer, until it was within centimetres of Richard's skin. His eyebrows and eyelids began to burn, Richard could smell them and could hear them sizzle. His skin began to redden and to blister. The red, raised, weal of a mark that looped around his neck and his painful swallow were nothing compared to this. Richard pulled away from the lethal glow, as far as the bindings would allow.

'What say you? Repent, quickly. Say it, while you still can!'

The man's face was so close to his own that Richard smelled his disgusting breath. This creature with his torture made Richard stare at his fate, and played with his dying moments, like a crazed cat with a mouse. Richard stretched his neck, pulling his face away in desperation. The poker neared.

One final struggle, a clash in defiance, then it would end.

'*You misplaced medieval misfit!*' Richard shouted, so angry his voice contorted. 'You are no better than the Inquisition . . . go to hell you spawn of the devil . . . ugh!'

'What? You taunt me at the very moment of your deliverance.' The man drew back the poker. He seemed mortified by the insults. 'What know you of the struggle?'

Richard looked up at the shadowed face. 'You are nothing,' he spat out, 'an assassin, a torturer. You have no religion. You are the epitome of evil!'

Suddenly the man stepped backwards and with that, his hood fell onto his shoulders, he turned away instantly but Richard saw more of his face. He had deep set black eyes and neat black hair slicked down with gel. It glistened in the light of several candles that burned in stone niches around them. In that instant, his skin appeared to be an unblemished olive colour and he seemed to be in his forties. The man pulled the hood low over his face again and his attention jerked back towards the gas torch and then he turned to face Richard. Beneath the blood red habit, which was pulled up loosely around his waist by a simple knotted rope, he wore a shirt of coarse brown hair. Slowly he raised the poker again and at arm's length pointed it at Richard's face.

'You speak with the ignorance of a heretic. You know nothing of me. Nothing of my order . . . nothing of Rome!' he muttered.

Richard's voice croaked. 'But you know why I am here: Saint Mark's square . . . *why* I'm being chased all over this bloody planet, *don't you*?' Richard struggled but to no avail.

'I know, but care not, Mr Reece, or Mr Jones, whoever you are today. I have searched for you and you have been delivered to me in God's good time. A difficult pursuit – I know what you search for . . . that helped me. And then to Rome you came, a sacrificial lamb to the altar of Truth, where *I* belong. Now you will be purged and my work will be done . . . and then you . . . *you* . . . will be forgotten; another blasphemer, another prosecutor of my faith put to the question. Will you deny me?'

'I'm no prosecutor of your faith or anybody's faith!'

'*Non ho alcun interesse in quello che lei dice* . . . I have no interest in what you say, only that you recant before you die.'

'Listen. I am a scientist who discovered a truth. You say you are interested in the Truth, then hear me out.' Richard's voice was now a hoarse whisper.

'What can *you* know of the Truth? Science makes fools of us all. There is only one Truth, and that is the way and the life. Everything else is from false prophets who would turn the world into a money changer's paradise. Before you see God and kneel before him, you *must* repent your sin.' He waved the glowing tip across Richard's eyes.

'Your secret is known to British Intelligence.' Richard forced his voice. He was desperate enough to play a trump card. 'They told me about *you.*'

'You know *nothing* about me!' The monk drew back his arm as if to strike. 'Your judgement is not for this world, but for the next; I simply send you to it.'

Richard struggled and pulled at his bindings.

'Count Ferissimo . . . *Ferissimo*!'

The monk stepped back. 'You know my family name?'

Richard stared insolently and pressed his advantage.

'Descended from Luigi Ferissimo an Italian aristocrat,' he scowled. 'You are Brother Ignazio . . . of a secret fraternity named *Sextus dies* – The Sixth Day. That's . . . who . . . you . . . are!' Richard's words drove deep. 'Your cover is blown. Kill me and you will be hunted down like a mad dog.'

The monk jerked his head up. 'I have no fear of death, unlike you, I shall dwell in Paradise. I shall save my faith, and Rome will make me a *saint*.' He laughed insanely.

'For God's sake listen to me. I am a Christian, like you. Not as dedicated, but . . .' Richard's plea made the man pause.

Richard sought to flatter, to placate. 'I hold dear all the tenets of your faith, I believe in the intrinsic goodness of mankind.' Richard knew that was a mistake when the man roared. 'What? We are all born in sin. We are evil and have to suffer for God's holy love. You scientists have brought the world to its knees and now God will punish you *all*.'

'Look,' Richard pleaded. 'This question of creation against science – it's all over. Don't you understand! We, mankind, we are out there now, off this planet. The universe is next . . . time changes everything!'

The monk turned slowly and walked back to his bench and offered the insignia at the end of the bar to the roaring flame. Over the noise of the burner, he said, 'You are wrong! Time changes nothing.'

Richard sucked in as much air as the bindings across his chest would allow. The monk turned momentarily to witness Richard's suffering and then returned his attention to the flame. For a moment he seemed lost in his own thoughts.

'There is only one answer to the question of faith as far as you are concerned!' The monk's voice lowered. 'It is to recant. There is no choice.' His voice trailed away and he began heating the insignia again.

'I know you have conviction, and as a man of the church you believe in righteousness . . .'

'Do not try to patronise me,' the monk interrupted.

Keeping the man sufficiently intrigued had exhausted all Richard's energy; his head drooped. Apart from the warbling roar of the flame as the man plied the metal insignia, there was silence.

Then a sudden crackle of burning carbon. It subsided, and the man asked: 'You know my name . . . who else knows?'

Richard raised his head slowly. 'The British, that's all – and if I go missing . . . ?'

'You undermine me; next you will seek to bring down Rome itself.'

'I do not!' Richard's brow glistened with perspiration and his head drooped again.

A distant rattle of small arms fire had both their attention and the monk moved to the slit to observe. He tried to look down at the ground; finding it too difficult, he resumed his place at the bench.

'Would you grant me a last request?' Richard had no reply, so persevered. 'If I tell you why those people are after me, the conglomerates . . . and their machines . . . will you use the information wisely?

The monk's concentration was on the glowing tip of metal. Richard only just caught his grunt.

'You know who I am talking about, I know you do. If you have been hunting me as you say, then you must have come upon them.'

'I care not for who they are or what they do.'

'I'll tell you why,' Richard continued. 'They are self serving and wish to hold the world to ransom. They destroy all who come between them and their ambition. They seek what I seek. Electricity is the key, the answer to all our problems.'

Another distant volley of gunfire added potency to Richard's words.

'Science can help what's going on out there, and believe me it's only a beginning. You seek to protect your faith. Soon anarchy will destroy the church and everything you are fighting for. We have that in common.' Richard could not tell if he was listened to, and tried again.

'I am searching for something that will delay all this, a temporary solution – something that will alleviate the imminent suffering that is about to descend on us. Can you imagine a world without any power? Without electricity, we revert to the Stone Age.'

The monk's head moved to scan the encircling row of candles that burnt in the blackened niches. 'I have no interest in your words. They mean nothing to me. I prepare my mind again, so as to send you, a sinner, to your judgement.'

Richard sighed loudly. 'For God's sake listen to me! Within a month there will be no fuel – not for the common man anyway. No oil, no gas, no coal, no wood . . . consumed! For the few who have access to wind power, a brief respite perhaps, but that is all. Then darkness! People will exist, not live – exist.'

Richard's shoulder had gone dead and his chest seemed on fire. He squirmed. From what he saw of the monk's face, it was grim. 'Look,' he reasoned again. 'I think I know where it is, this thing of science – not our science though, not from this planet.' Richard gestured towards the sky. 'From somewhere out there. Do you want to be responsible for all the immeasurable suffering . . . *do you*?'

The monk looked at Richard. 'Where is this panacea of all ills to be found?' he whispered.

'Saint Mark's Square, the Villa Orlandini. Beneath it there is a tunnel. In there or in the place where the tunnel leads to.'

'The vaults of the great museum?' the monk showed surprise.

'So you know the truth of what I say?' It was Richard's turn to be surprised.

'My family have lived in Rome for 500 years, *Signore*. We are stitched into its history. What is this thing you seek, this great thing that gives *hope* to the world?' Richard had the monk's full attention.

'Before I confess all I know, do you think you could release my arms?'

The monk considered Richard's request and saw he was on the point of collapse, so no longer dangerous. He took a large serrated knife and cut the thongs. Richard's body sagged. The monk stood over him menacingly, the knife still in his hand. 'Talk!' he commanded.

'It's a casket, like an Ark, perhaps more like a transportable Egyptian sarcophagus. It would probably have hieroglyphics inscribed on it too.'

The monk shook his head. 'I have neither seen nor heard of what you seek. It is not recorded in the annals of my family. The Ferissimo are noted for their writings, and I know they have not recorded such an artefact. You search in the wrong place, so you lie.'

'No! No! Please, believe me. I'm sure I'm close to discovery.'

The monk's face remained stony.

'Have you heard of *Nostradamus* . . . have you heard of him?' Richard bawled. The words just came out; it was his last hope.

The monks face was contemptuous. 'The Evil Magician!' he spat on the floor. 'He was excommunicated from the Church for his pagan heresies, but at the time he escaped death by means of his supernatural powers – the Devil's own.'

'So you know nothing of his predictions?'

'To fight evil you must know its extent. Yes, I know of the predictions. They belong on the *Index Librorum Prohibitorum*, but no one has proved their convoluted evil.'

Richard didn't want to get into that debate. He had a gut feeling that this man might hold the vital clue to the whereabouts of the Ark. 'He wrote of the "New City" . . . was it New York? In your opinion, Count Ferissimo, did he refer to New York in his predictions?'

'Ha! You are a fool, Englishman, like all your kind. Michel de Notredame knew nothing of New York City. The *new city* that he spoke of was "rising from the shackles of history, breaking free from centuries of stifling architecture". He was clever with his words . . . confusing to the common man. He spoke of a new age for the people who lived in darkness, of a new Rome to replace the one that had lost its way. He foresaw a new light rising from the darkness of ignorance and lust, malice and heresy,though his obscure quatrains were open to numerous interpretations that few could understand. My ancestors came from the French court. The astrologer was known to them. I tell you the *Rinascimento* . . . the Renaissance, was his prediction, and Venice – its new light – was at its centre.' The monk shook his head in contempt of Richard's theory. 'The Saint Mark's Square you refer to is not in Rome, but in Venice. The Piazza San Marco, before the Basilica!'

Richard sat up, his body groaning with pain. Could it be? Would he find the Ark in Saint Mark's square in Venice? That great historical attraction once called the Drawing Room of Europe, before the flooding. The sound of loud gunfire echoed into the room.

'You must let me go. I can arrange money, anything. Please . . . I feel sure I can find the Ark!'

Richard could only see part of the monk's face. Above his lips was shrouded in shadow, but he watched them lift into a tight smile as the man shook his head. 'First you mock me and I had a mind to make your passage to hell more painful for your temerity. Now you wish me to release you, such that I would fail in my purpose.' He looked long at Richard. 'You forfeit your soul if you lie this day.'

Richard straightened up; his neck and shoulders ached. 'Look! You'll know soon enough if I'm being honest,' he said hoarsely. 'Electricity . . . civilisation or anarchy, it's your call. It is *your* decision. Please, it's our only hope!'

'I found you once; I can find you again. But hear me well Mr Reece . . .' the monk's face drew close to Richard's, so that he could hear his breathing. A shiver ran down Richard's spine. 'If it becomes necessary for me to come for you, then *you will* be damned. I give no second chance for salvation.' This time the monk nodded slowly and drew back. He paused thoughtfully. 'Go to the Basilica di San Marco. Close by is a house – Villa Gondolini. Ask for Cardinal Giovanni Monteverdi. Of the history of *Venezia* and region *Veneto*, there is little that the Cardinal does not know. I believe him to be a good man. Ask his advice on what you seek. He may help you; he may not.' The monk pointed at Richard in a pitiful manner. 'Pray heed the church's doctrine. Do not mention this *Ark* as extraterrestrial, nor talk of me – for he will surely slam the door closed on you.' With that, he put the iron rod on the table and turned off the gas flame and walked behind Richard.

Richard slumped forwards as the bonds loosened around his body. Moments later, the door closed with a dull thud. Richard breathed a huge sigh of relief and released his feet, straightening and massaging his legs for a while before he was able to stand. He checked the time and retrieved his jacket from where it had been thrown on the floor.

Within seconds, Richard was painfully negotiating the tightly spiralled stone staircase. At the bottom, another thick, heavy, centuries-old wooden door gave access to the street. He stepped outside and pulled the door closed behind him. For some inexplicable reason, he tried to open it again, but it was locked. The few people on the street glanced at him and hurried by; evidently he made them feel nervous. He pulled up the collar of his jacket in order to hide the marks on his face and neck and buttoned the lapels.

A van passed and a few more people. Richard was disorientated as he limped along the streets. He looked for a landmark, a street name. Two passers-by gave him a wide berth, as if he had a contagious disease. He realised how frightening he must look, his face covered with blisters and blood and his unruly hair, which he tried to smooth down. His circulation was beginning to work and he was becoming more mobile. He did not want to draw attention to himself by asking for directions, not in English. He passed a street on his right: *Via della Posta* read a sign on a wall. Then a junction – he turned right towards the noise that grew louder.

Next, Richard came to a crossroads: *Via della Tipografia*, read another high-mounted street sign. The street he was on was busier than the one that crossed his path and so he continued. The noise of people shouting and protesting grew clearer and occasional car horns and sirens added to the cacophony. Richard unbuttoned a pocket inside his jacket and retrieved his pager. He changed the multifunction display from a chronometer to a touch pad, typed a short abrive to Preston and sent it:

> Via dei Pellegrini – heading south.
> Where are you?

Richard kept to the side of the street and proceeded as unobtrusively as possible. He walked for a few minutes, stopping in the occasional doorway to reassess his progress. The street emptied a little of people and there appeared to be a junction ahead – perhaps a hundred metres or so. Angry crowd noise seemed more to his right now and then a beating sound started up, it echoed, as if a million feet stamped in unison. He paused in another doorway, thought about turning back but stepped out. At that moment, a horn beeped behind him. He turned; it was a black Alfa sedan, unmarked, but with a rotating beacon on the roof. Richard quickened his pace and darted down a side street. The car followed him and the horn beeped again in Morse code – a short and a long . . . "A" . . . a long, short, long . . . "R" and . . . "K". Richard turned. It had to be Preston. An arm on the passenger side was waving him back. He stopped and stepped to the side as the car drew up alongside him. It was!

'Boss!' Preston said, as he climbed from the car. 'Where the hell have you been? The shit has really hit the fan this time! Half the city's Carabinieri are out looking for you, we've had sightings all over the place. London triangulated your abrive signal. We were following up . . . are you alright? You look as if you've been beaten up!'

'I'm okay, Preston . . . we need to leave!'

'I know. They are waiting for you at the Orlandini house.'

'No not there. We need to go to Venice . . . immediately!'

'*Venice*! But . . ?'

'Preston, don't ask . . . call Rothschild. We *need* to get to Venice. Ask for a helicopter . . . a helicopter would be best. Do it!'

Preston nodded, reached into his coat and then he was inside the car again. Richard climbed into the back and the car roared off. Whilst waiting for a line connection, Preston turned. 'Everybody's been going mad – you just seemed to disappear?'

'It's a long story, Preston. I'll brief you and Rothschild on the way to Venice. The main thing is that I have another lead and I'm *sure* this is it!'

Meanwhile, the driver, whilst presumably explaining his success in Italian over the radio became progressively more agitated. There was another reply from the loud speaker and then the driver answered: '*Si, la stazione dei Carabinieri, arrivo . . . ! Si, Signore Reece,*' he continued, into an overhead microphone.

'*Si, la stazione dei Carabinieri!*' he said again, and then a look of excitement spread over his face – as if he had just been ordered to participate in an illegal car chase.

Preston turned. 'We are going to the police station,' he explained.

Richard checked the time. 'Only if they have a heliport, or somewhere that a helicopter can land, get onto Rothschild!'

Preston nodded and turned forwards again. Simultaneously, the driver, who wore a black uniform and cap, put his foot down. Richard, after being thrown from one side of the car to the other, scrambled to put a seatbelt on. Recovering his composure he recalled that this was more like the driving he was familiar with in Rome!

Preston had a brief word with someone from MI9. 'Peter Rothschild,' he emphasised again. There was a pause. 'Preston speaking . . . yes, Sir, we have found him. He is with me now . . . will do, Sir!' He passed his pager to Richard.

'Reece, yes . . . no, not Rome, not Rome, Peter, Venice! I say again, I must get to Venice . . . . I know you have people waiting . . . ! Yes, Venice . . .! I am fully aware of the consequences, Peter . . . I will explain later. . . . A helicopter, yes, it is the quickest way . . . yes . . . a police helicopter . . . you can arrange it? Good. Saint Mark's Square, direct, no messing . . . that's right . . . exactly . . . I see . . . not the police station. Where then . . . okay, the grounds of the British Embassy . . . ah, I see, agreed . . . okay. Listen, I'm not sure if our driver speaks English, you had better get his Boss to call him on the radio . . . yes, that's it . . . we are on our way . . . yes. I'll be in touch . . . I'll debrief you on the way. Out!'

## Venice – near St. Mark's Square
## 14:38 Local Time

The helicopter hovered about thirty feet above the murky water and no more than twenty from the quay side. Its downwash created a circle of white horses and moisture-laden wind blew at the coats of a few passers-by until they had scampered clear of the area. With the main cabin door open, Richard watched intently as the pilot manoeuvred his machine towards land. The openness of Saint Mark's Square amongst the density of such classical architecture never failed to impress. Clear, though, was the height of the sea as it lapped at street level and Richard could see several large puddles that had formed in depressions in the stone. Pedestrians avoided them by using raised wooden walkways and a few gathered to watch as the compact machine with four passenger seats moved sideways until it was over the street named Riva degli Schiavoni. Moments later, it landed. Preston was out first. Other people passed, but not many, and none took more than a passing glance at either Richard or Preston as they ran clear of the rotor blades. Richard looked back, the crewman pointed in the direction that he should go and then slid the cabin door closed. With that, the helicopter lifted again. It turned towards the lagoon and with its nose pointing down, accelerated until seconds later it disappeared into gloomy, leaden, low cloud.

Richard and Preston made off across the semi-deserted

square leaving the Church of Saint Mark to their right. Preston splashed through the peripheries of a shallow but extensive lake on their way to the north-east corner. The beautiful church, with its facade and broad steps stood defiantly against the weather and rising water. There was a faint, foul smell. At the corner, Richard slowed to a lope and turned right with Preston at his shoulder. Richard referred to a message on his pager that noted directions and an address. Moments later, he pulled up short. He rechecked the abrive and then looked at the tarnished brass plaque mounted on the wall of a mellow stone house. It was adjacent to a carved wooden door that was broad and blackened and clearly itself an imposing antique – like everything else in the area, he mused. This was the place: Villa Gondolini. Now, thought Richard: what of luck; what of time; what of the *Ark*?

## CHAPTER 38

# FOUNDING FATHERS

It was a heavy piece of black metal. A twisted bar formed into a circle that was pivoted at the top and with a cast-iron crucifix at the bottom as the knocker. The receiving end was the centre of a forged medieval-looking coat of arms that was secured to the weathered oak door by two hefty bolts. On each flattened bolt head there was a date inscribed 1506. Richard tried a third time. The thudding reverberation that appeared to permeate the very fabric of the building brought no response. Three paces to his left, but above his head there was an elongated stained glass window. It depicted a religious scene in a style Tintoretto could have painted, or possibly Leonardo da Vinci himself. Light from the inside permeated the glass, whilst moving shadows caused the scene to live. It's so real, so lifelike, thought Richard, as he lifted the door knocker again for another attempt to wake the dead – and to his surprise the door opened. The man who peered through the narrow gap was easily in his seventies.

'Good afternoon, Sir. *Il buono Signore di pomeriggio,*' Richard said, hesitantly, 'Terribly sorry for the intrusion. Would it be possible to speak to Cardinal Giovanni Monteverdi please, on a matter of great importance?' Having exhausted his limited Italian vocabulary and giving little thought to the matter, Richard waited for a response in English.

The old man eyed Richard suspiciously. Richard, whose face was scared and smudged with blood and sweat and grime and who looked unkempt in his dirty creased jacket, was clearly hoping for a handout. Preston evidently fared little better in the man's opinion and together they passed convincingly as a pair of tramps working at a greater form of embezzlement. The man with his white hair and pallid complexion attempted to close the door with no more than a confused expression.

Richard stopped him. 'Sir, please. I know that we are unannounced and that we don't look, well, the most salubrious of visitors, but this really is important . . . of the utmost importance. Just a few minutes with Cardinal Monteverdi – that's all I'm asking.'

The man concentrated on Richard's face for a moment. From his expression it appeared that he did not understand what Richard was saying. There was indecision.

'We have come from Rome – there is trouble there,'

Richard continued. 'We need the Cardinal's help.' Richard's tone was insistent.

This was no down and out; the elderly man hedged his bets. 'His eminence is dining, come back tomorrow . . . it may be possible,' and attempted to close the door.

Richard blocked the door with his foot. 'I ask for information, that is all, about an old family from this region – the Orlandinis. Please? The family hailed from Monte Credo, a place that no longer exists. The dynasty was well known by the church, certainly in Rome. I was told that the Cardinal may have knowledge of this matter.'

The man hesitated. Richard could see that his request now had some impact. 'This is very important, Sir,' he added, persuasively.

'This is a private residence for the *Patriarca di Venezia* and . . .'

Richard's eyes widened as he realised the importance of the man. 'Sorry!' he interrupted. 'I do not mean to intrude. It is a matter of the utmost importance. I *must* speak to the Cardinal.'

The man looked Richard in the eye and then briefly at Preston. He thought for a moment. The pressure on Richard's foot eased as he opened the door a little wider and he nodded some kind of welcome. 'His eminence is not available. However, I have some knowledge of this family.' He eyed Richard again, as if to finally assure himself that Richard was not a foreign gangster and opened the huge door fully and gestured for Richard and Preston to enter.

The entrance hall of the house was large, circular and ornate. There was a Venetian colonnade in white marble and the room boasted an impressive domed ceiling that was covered in an Italianate fresco of Old Testament scenes, the central theme of which reminded Richard of another of da Vinci's great paintings – *The Last Supper*. He had seen images and old photographs of it in history books and news files and knew it to be in Milan. However, this superb work appeared to be in perfect condition. There were a number of other smaller rooms leading from the hall and the man led Richard and Preston into one that was directly opposite the main door through which they had entered. Their footsteps echoed on the white marble floor as they walked. The man reminded Richard of a butler with his impressive uniform. He wore black shiny shoes and black trousers and a scarlet jacket of a velvet-like material and a white shirt and a scarlet cravat with a small motif.

The room they entered was rectangular with a dark polished wooden floor and two high windows at the far end – there was an abundance of stained glass and Saints. On the floor lay an enormous Persian rug and several pieces of antique baroque furniture lay scattered around. However, it was the walls that were most impressive, lined as they were from floor to ceiling with row after row of books. Some of these rows had commonality of colour and size; mellowed red, green or blue, large, thick; the knowledge of ages. The air smelt of stillness, leather, damp paper and history. With a gracious movement the man offered two chairs. They were such luxuriously upholstered period pieces that both Richard and Preston were almost embarrassed to sit in them and they did so with some care.

The old man's English was surprisingly good. Obviously learned from a native because his own accent did not intrude. Having relaxed and seen how at home his two guests were he was more kindly disposed. 'What exactly do you wish to know about the *Orlandini* family?' He sat down opposite Richard, clasped his hands in a regal way and scrutinised him.

'We are looking for something, Sir, something that would appear to have its origins in ancient Egypt but also something that might appear to have religious significance – because of its size, shape and decoration. We know that a ship owned by the Orlandini family carried this artefact from Mauritius to Europe, arriving early in 1811. The ship had been chartered by the French and was bound for Marseille. For a number of reasons, not least the political turmoil in France at the time and the real possibility of a default on payment, I believed that the vessel landed first in Rome – the Orlandinis had substantial business interests there. I now believe that the second port of call was here in Venice. I think that the artefact we seek is somewhere in this city, where exactly I'm afraid I don't know.'

The man rubbed his hands thoughtfully. 'I have a good knowledge of Venice,' he said, 'perhaps more than most, and also the history of this region of Italy, but I have never heard of such an artefact. Excuse me.' He got up and tugged on a long beautifully-embroidered bell pull.

Richard looked astonished. 'Sir,' he said, suspiciously. 'Are you . . . Cardinal Monteverdi?'

The man nodded politely. Richard and Preston stood simultaneously. The man gestured for them to sit again. 'I received a telephone call earlier today.' He said, thoughtfully. 'An hour or more before you arrived. It was on my private number. I answered because few know it. The caller would not leave his name, but strangely he spoke in Latin.' The Cardinal paused and his eyes squinted slightly. 'His pronunciation was precise and he spoke, how can I say? He spoke . . . almost as if he knew me.' Cardinal Monteverdi made an opening gesture with his hands. 'He told me to expect you – an unlikely looking foreigner. He told me to listen to you. I can see for myself. I see in your eyes that you have good intentions, my son. I see a quest. I will help if I am able. Clearly, there is value to what you seek, perhaps this artefact contains something – I will not press you further. Now, to the investigation,but first, will you take refreshment? Then, tell me what you can!'

'Italian history, certainly for the last millennium, Signore

Jones, has been one of war and division,' Cardinal Monteverdi began to explain. 'Five centuries ago, Italy was perhaps more divided than at any other time. Trading republics such as that of Venice, Florence and Sienna had incredible wealth, whilst Duchies such as Milan and Savoy maintained powerful standing armies. There were also large kingdoms such as Naples and Sicily and Marquisates such as Montferrat and Saluzzo. All these city states expanded greatly during the fifteenth and sixteenth centuries, eventually becoming *de facto* fully independent states and although still influential, the Holy Roman Empire held neither governance nor due restriction. Indeed, during this period, there was little the Papal State of Rome could do about this situation. Trade held the key for the most powerful states and Venice was the wealthiest in all Italy – because of its control of the Mediterranean. The Kingdom of Monte Credo was perhaps one of the smallest states of the period, lying between the Republic of Genoa and the Principality of Monte Carlo. With its own seaport west of Genoa it had a relatively large fleet of trading vessels. Of this fleet one thing bore note, the Masters of the ships of Monte Credo were renowned for their knowledge of the great southern ocean, of India and of trade with the east.'

Richard nodded expectantly and his concentration was fixed on the Cardinal; both he and Preston found the old man fascinating.

'Life, however, was expensive for the rulers of all these

states, more so the smaller ones, because their income was limited during periodic downturns in trading, and with small populations income from taxes and the like was often insufficient. Monte Credo was no larger than its neighbouring principality and so it was necessary to import most commodities. You should understand there was also constant friction between these states; disputes, bickering, border transgressions even occasional piracy. A standing army was a necessity and a very expensive one. Alliances changed like the wind, and there were always foreign forces to contend with. Most of these major city states survived until the early nineteenth century, however Monte Credo did not. The regional War of the League of Cambrai that took place between 1508 and 1516 put the kingdom under severe financial pressures. Historians agree that this was the catalyst for its eventual demise. Subsequently, facing diminishing returns from its trading fleets, due in the main to the dominance of Venice and harassed by a constant barrage of damaging border skirmishes, King Ludovico IV – *Orlandini* was the royal household name – eventually capitulated in 1783. Thinking of his people, he sold his lands and transferred his allegiance to the neighbouring Republic of Genoa in return for security for his subjects. History tells us that it was considered a noble gesture at the time and acceptable, if not hard to bear. Italian unification would come thirty years later, when this subdivision of our country disappeared, and this coincided with the end of the Napoleonic period in 1815.'

Richard leaned forwards, his brow furrowed. 'So what happened, Sir? What became of the family?'

'King Ludovico and the Orlandini household were, of course, extremely wealthy in their own right. They had made investments in other regions over the generations and had impressive houses both in Rome and here in Venice. It was, however, to Venice that the King moved, seeking refuge for his immediate family and himself. He was granted safe passage across the Duchy of Milan and the Marquisate of Mantua, I think, early in 1784. After establishing his household in Calle Le Mercerie, a street close to us here, he began a period of architectural renovations and re-established his credentials as a merchant. By that time he was already in his late fifties and with a son and heir and two daughters.'

'How did he establish his family as merchants again, Cardinal Monteverdi? How did he do that, Sir? It could be important.'

'The Doge himself – the highest authority in Venice – had a great deal of respect for him. King Ludovico was regarded as a fair man and honest in business. The Doge also had some measure of sympathy for the king and his plight and allowed him to continue trading by granting berthing rights for two vessels from his dispersing fleet. Several others, if I recall, sailed south to trade from Rome. It was those vessels, to a greater extent, that were employed by the Holy States.

'Which vessels did he select for the Venice operation,

Cardinal, do you know?'

'Ah. You ask questions that are too difficult. Even my knowledge of Venice does not extend to this. In truth I know not, my son. However, we have records.'

Cardinal Monteverdi, however, knew exactly where to look and walked across to a particular bookshelf and ran a finger along a line of leather-bound volumes that was a little higher than his head height. Each cover was worn red and had bold, gold-leaf lettering that included dates and chronological periods. The Cardinal's finger stopped on one and with both hands he withdrew the selected book. Then, cradling it carefully, he opened it in the manner of a studious librarian and flipped through several pages before stopping to read. There was an air of excited anticipation in the room.

'*Si*, here we have record of it,' he said, looking briefly at Richard. 'The two vessels were sister ships and both originally registered in France. They were bought in 1769 from the Marquis of Bordeaux.' The Cardinal looked up. 'It was bad luck to change a ship's name, you know.'

'Yes, I know that, Sir, but please, what were the ship's names?' Richard could feel his heart pounding.

'The two fastest, by these accounts!'

'And . . .?'

'*L' enfant Terrible* and the *Les Trois Vents!*'

'*Les Trois Vents*, yes, that's it! *The Three Winds!* So the ship *was* here!'

'It says that both ships were in service and registered

300

here in Venice until they were sold back to the French in 1813.'

'And then where, Cardinal?'

'Italy was a client state of the French Republic during the Napoleonic era, the years 1796 to 1815. Towards the end, Napoleon's administration forcibly purchased or commandeered vessels to help with his campaign in the Crimea. The Venetians cooperated with the French during this period; it was sensible for them to do so.'

Richard nodded. 'I see. Going back to the king, Sir, what happened to King Ludovico?'

'He became a great philanthropist and a patron to the arts. During his years here in Venice, he gave generously to its reconstruction and renovation and also to the ghetto – you should remember that Venice at this time had a history of more than 1000 years and was in slow decline.'

Richard nodded again. 'He was popular, then. So where did they bury him?'

'He was more than popular, my son. During renovations on his own house, he built a vault containing five crypts for himself and his family. Rome sent a high-ranking dignitary to sanctify them. It was a great honour, a ceremony full of reverence and circumstance. It is well recorded. They became known simply as the "Sacred Five".'

'Where are they, may I ask?'

'Not far from here, but impossible to get to – even if permission were to be granted.'

Richard looked confused.

'You must remember that the present sea level is three metres higher than it was in the 1500s when Villa Orlandini was originally built. Of that rise, an increase of more than one metre has happened in the last fifty years. There was a long-term project to save Venice. It was started in 2003 and completed in 2013; it was called the *Modulo Sperimentale Elettromeccanico*. It still works to some extent, protecting us from high waters that flow in from the Adriatic Sea, but now the sea invades our lives more frequently and the *Acqua Alta* causes much damage. And there are the rains,' the Cardinal said, sadly.

Richard nodded understandingly and then leaned towards the Cardinal. 'So the ground floors of houses built 500 years ago are now under a few metres of water. What about when the king died, Cardinal, presumably early in the nineteenth century? What would be your estimate for the depth of water then?'

Cardinal Monteverdi shrugged. 'Generally, perhaps one metre perhaps less. At that time, during the nineteenth century, the sea would not have encroached regularly on the city with consequence, only perhaps during times of unusually high water. There is, however, a further complication with Villa Orlandini. During his renovations, King Ludovico added another level. The foundations were not built for such weight and over the last 250 years the house has gradually subsided – literally sunk into the bed of the lagoon. There are buildings with such problems all over Venice. It has been a very slow process, perhaps a metre each century, although many other houses with this problem do eventually stabilise.'

Richard sighed, nothing was easy, he thought. 'So this vault you mentioned; not only will it be beneath the water line, but it is also submerged in mud?'

'Sediment would be a more accurate description, my son. Venice is built on petrified wooden piles, the layer of harder sand and mud is deeper. More than two centuries of fine silt and sediment would prevent access into the crypts.'

Richard sat back in the chair and scanned the lines of books around the room's periphery and then he looked back at the Cardinal. 'So . . . the king died eventually – and then what happened, Sir?'

'His only son, the eldest of three children ascended to the throne, albeit in title only. There was still wealth, but less. He became King Ludovico V. He was a much more private man than his father, although equally generous. He wished for a much quieter life, a lower profile, so to speak, and subsequently adopted the maiden name of his wife, whom he had married in 1809.'

Richard's head dropped. He could feel the trail going colder by the second. Where was he to go now he thought? 'And *her* name, Cardinal?' he asked nonchalantly, after a long pause.

'Ah, now *she* was well known in Venice at the time, because of her poise and beauty. Arguably, Venice was still Europe's most fashionable city. She was one of three sisters who reputedly were descended from an Egyptian dynasty – some said a Nubian line, because they had travelled from the old Ethiopian capital. Dark skin, black hair, elegance, *she*, like the other two was said to have the features of the Egyptian Queen Nefertiti herself.'

Instantly, Richard sat to attention. 'What?' he blurted. The unforgettable image of Naomi with her towelling headdress sitting in that room in Mauritius flooded his mind. *That* was who it was . . . who she reminded him off . . . *the Berlin bust*! Fashioned by the famed sculptor Thutmose – the graceful elongated neck balancing the tall, flat-top crown . . . he had read about her and seen the images. That famed bust, the most celebrated exhibit in Berlin's Egyptian Museum – for decades the curators had resisted all attempts at repatriation! *Nefertiti*! Richard stood up. 'What was her name, Sir?' he asked excitedly.

'Signorina Vallogia! That was her maiden name. Of course, after she married she acquired her title.'

Richard fidgeted uncontrollably. 'What of the *other* sisters, Cardinal Monteverdi?'

'One married into the Egyptian aristocracy and lived in Cairo. She was the older if I recall and was a frequent visitor to Venice. She brought many ideas from Egypt – fashion and art. She was said to have a great knowledge of astronomy and could even enlighten men of science on the subject. Of the third sister, I know not – there is little recorded of her.'

Barely able to contain his excitement, Richard glanced

at Preston and then back at Cardinal Monteverdi. 'What of the king and Signora Vallogia . . . were there any children?'

'They had three children. Again, like his father, one son and two daughters – only the son was the youngest. They all lived here in Venice. The king added four more crypts to the family vault during his lifetime. This I know, because I am familiar with the architecture of Villa Orlandini – from renovation work carried out a few years ago, you understand. The house is officially preserved. They are all buried there. As I said earlier, Signore Jones, the vault was sanctified . . . even if it were accessible. It is therefore a sacred place and access restricted to all but the few authorised by the Papacy.'

Richard nodded his consideration; he changed his line of questioning. 'What became of the sister in Cairo?' he pursued.

Cardinal Monteverdi shook his head. 'That will be recorded in their archives, I am sure.'

'Cardinal, please, that vault is of vital importance. I must get into it. I *have* to get into it!' Richard stood, his agitation plain as he looked at Preston.

Cardinal Monteverdi shook his head again. 'It is impossible, my son. Firstly, the vault is submerged as I have already explained and secondly, there is the question of permission. An entry on purely secular grounds is a concession only Rome can give. An application in writing would be necessary, giving at least six months' notice, and even then they are unlikely to approve such an invasion. I am sorry.'

A pained expression descended over Richard's face.

'Cardinal Monteverdi,' he said solemnly. 'I haven't been completely honest with you, so I would like to tell you something in confidence.'

The Cardinal raised his eyebrows in anticipation.

'Preston here, and myself, we are agents for the British Government. We are looking for something that might alleviate the imminent crash of the world's electricity grid . . . can you imagine a world without electricity, Sir?'

Cardinal Monteverdi shook his head; he was already aware of the implications. 'I am afraid you must obey the protocols, my son,' he replied, and stared at them with the wisdom of his years.

'We are part of a wider cooperative, Cardinal; not just the Brits. America, France, Germany, Italy . . . there is collaboration . . . please, can you think of anything that may help shortcut the protocol, to help me investigate the vault?'

Cardinal Monteverdi looked up slowly at Richard. He paused for thought and then a glint appeared in his eye – as if he had recalled something. As if, quite by chance, he saw a solution. He stood and quickly walked across to a particular shelf and spent a few moments selecting a book. He withdrew it. It was a large volume and had Richard been able to see inside he would have seen that it was a handwritten inventory – a record of materials required for burial and burial services. The Monsignor placed it on a reading frame and carefully turned numerous pages before stopping abruptly.

Cardinal Monteverdi nodded. The gesture seeming to confirm his suspicions. He looked at Richard. 'There is hope, my son,' he said. 'There are inventories noted here for the burials of King Ludovico Vallogia and his wife and his two eldest children, but not for his youngest. Preparations were in place, there is a date, but the materials were never purchased. It notes here that the king's son died of the plague in *Napoli* . . . Naples, and his body was refused passage to Venice because earlier pandemics still haunted the minds of many. His son is buried elsewhere. Therefore, the ninth crypt was never used. It remains empty and unblessed! *I* can give you permission to enter it; if indeed, you are able to find a way.'

'Thank you, Cardinal. We are indebted to you. The whole world is indebted to you,' Richard replied.

Cardinal Monteverdi gestured a blessing. 'May you find this salvation. One of my aides will show you the way to Villa Orlandini. It is not far.'

The Cardinal touched the bell-pull again to summon his aide. Richard acknowledged with a smile and stared at the floor. He needed help, he thought hard. A diving team, excavation equipment, additional security measures . . . and he needed it now!

Richard and Preston, following the Cardinal's man, half ran and half walked as they skirted St Mark's Square heading for the Villa Orlandini. Richard held his pager to his ear waiting for a connection to Peter Rothschild's office.

'Peter . . . is that you? Reece here.'

'It's a bad line, Richard, two by five, but go ahead.'

'Listen. I'm onto something . . . a submerged vault beneath an old house in Venice. The rear garden fronts the Grand Canal. It's not that far from Saint Mark's square, the Piazza San Marco. I'm crossing the Rialto Bridge as we speak. The house has a jetty apparently, but it hasn't been used in years. Preston is sending you an abrive with the address. Wait . . . he's nodding at me, saying it's just gone through. Peter, I need diving equipment and a high-pressure water lance . . . compressed air or water, possibly an ultrasonic probe as well, something to loosen a couple of centuries of sediment. Water levels are very high in Venice.'

'I understand. I'll get onto it immediately.'

'Good. Preston and I will be at the house in a few minutes. Our guide has told me that the tide turned a few hours ago so it's coming in fast. They call it *Acqua Alta*, which means this one will be very high. As soon as possible, Peter, do you copy?'

'Yes! I'll get back to you.'

The area was deserted. It seemed to be a particularly

old part of the city and one where the rising waterline had displaced normal living. The fabric of these buildings is clearly in question, thought Richard, as he followed the guide along a narrow street that bordered a canal which in itself was no more than two metres wide. Two parallel grooves worn into the stone cobbles seemed to indicate a carriage route that was very popular in its day. Alongside, the dirty water in the canal looked stagnant and sick and a clear watermark on the adjacent buildings signalled an impending rise of at least another half metre. There was little evidence of any tidal circulation here as rubbish that floated in the water was coated in green algae and the smell was of uncounted years of decay.

After thirty metres their path was blocked by a pair of high iron gates of ornate design. Their guide, who wore a black overcoat over a long black habit, pulled a key from his pocket. He unlocked the heavy padlock, unwound an overly long, rusty chain and attempted to open the left hand gate, but it took a good push from Preston to gain entrance. 'It has been some time,' the man explained.

Inside, and after another short walk, they arrived at a courtyard of impressive proportions. The cobbled carriageway scribed a broad circle that passed in front of the house before rejoining the main access. The house was imposing, classic Italianate design with a roof of reddish clay tiles. Richard counted five storeys plus another in the garret structure, but the house was in poor condition with patches of underlying stone appearing through flaking plaster like a ruddled courtesan's complexion. In the gardens, where there had been grass, lay a film of rancid sludge and the contents of a large rectangular pond boasted a soup of lifeless slurry.

Quickly the guide led Richard and Preston to a side entrance and after thirty paces alongside the house the three men entered the rear garden. The view opened across the Grand Canal, broad, historic and beautiful. Preston gasped.

'One of the best panoramas in Venice,' the Italian offered.

'This must have been priceless real estate in its day,' said Preston, as he dragged his feet through bedraggled and overgrown plants. Walking towards the waterfront, Richard ducked beneath the drooping branches of a tree, one of a handful. As he opened his mouth to respond to Preston's remark a call came on his pager.

'Reece!' Richard responded.

'Richard, it's Peter Rothschild . . . can you hear me?

'Where we are now, the reception is good.'

'Okay, listen carefully. We have the help of the Italian government, or more to the point their military. You may or may not know that the naval base of Trieste is 100 kilometres east. There they have a flotilla of mine sweepers. These ships are made of carbon reinforced plastic I'm told, and by nature have a very shallow draft. Onboard they have everything for underwater clearance operations including pumping equipment. One of these vessels is on patrol in the Gulf of Venice. Apparently, they are still systematically clearing submerged mines from the 2nd World War. It's on its way, Richard. They tell me an hour or so and access along the Grand Canal is no problem, particularly at this time of day, with the tide, that is. We have passed them the latitude and longitude coordinates of the house from the address you sent. Luck is on our side this time, there are no bridges to affect passage. That part of the canal is close to open water. Keep a good lookout and let me know the moment the sweeper arrives.'

'Copied, I'll get back to you, out!' Richard turned to Preston. 'They're sending a mine sweeper. I expect it will either anchor off or come alongside this jetty. Wait here and send an abrive when you see them, should be less than an hour. In the meantime I'm going to recce this vault.'

Preston nodded. 'Got it,' he replied.

'Follow me,' said the guide.

The ground was very slippery close to the house. Richard and the guide arrived at a large arched doorway. At its base was an opening that was barred by close-fitting, black metal railings. An integral wicket gate, opened with another brass key allowed access. Inside, the house opened into a long colonnade about three metres wide that stretched the entire width of the building. However, after a few steps the level dropped. This had the effect of forming a long thin pond. Richard looked at the stone steps that disappeared into the water.

'How deep would you say?' He asked his guide.

'There are five steps here, perhaps a metre. Until a few years ago this area remained dry. That level was a secondary level.' The man pointed down. 'The original foundations are much deeper. Subsidence caused the initial problems and now the level on which we stand floods daily due to the sea. The whole area is undermined. Nothing is as it was.'

Richard nodded understandingly, 'And what of the vault?'

'Further along, behind those columns, close to the other side of the house – it drops like a pit. There is a low balustrade beneath the water and hinged metal gates. They have not been opened in my lifetime or my father's, or his father; perhaps a century or more, I know this well enough. The gates must be seized up and the locks useless, you will have to cut them open. Then there are steps. I am not sure how many. However, I believe the ceiling height in the vault to be enough for me to stand and more.' The man indicated by holding his arm straight above his head.

'As I am taller than you by a little, there would be room for you also, but we must remember the sediment. Inside each crypt, it is less, perhaps this.' The man dropped his hand to about fifteen centimetres above his head. 'When I was a boy, the sediment came a good way up these steps. Each tide brings another layer. Now . . . as you can see, it is almost to the top. In spring the smell becomes noxious, but not this year, the water remains too cold. Entry will be difficult. I hope you have patience!'

Richard nodded his appreciation for the information.

'To be patient, you need time. I have neither.'

The man sighed. 'I hope it will be worth it, Signore, this invasion of the dead . . .'

'I hope so too, believe me,' Richard interrupted. He looked sideways at the man. 'Thanks, I can take it from here.'

The grey-haired man bowed respectfully. 'I will remain close by and be available if needed,' he said.
Richard's pager vibrated, and he spoke into it. 'Yes?'

'I can see them, Boss. A naval vessel – not a small one either . . . coming into view!'

'On my way, Preston.'

As he quickened his pace towards the jetty, Richard felt apprehensive. Venice was his best lead, although in retrospect, he mused, he may have stumbled on it. Luck figured, he thought, although others might call it fate. And if not here, then where? The catacombs beneath Rome? He had put his neck on the block for this one and as he approached the canal bank and saw the ship, his heart rate quickened.

Fore and aft, murky water churned, as if from underwater

313

explosions. Powerful bow and stern thrusters manoeuvred the 20 metre long mine sweeper closer to the jetty. Richard seemed mesmerised by a dead dog that rose repeatedly to the surface within the seething circulation. At times it escaped, only to be sucked back down just when it appeared safe. The vessel moved effortlessly sideways. Clearly its draft was very shallow, although by the various lubber lines painted on the vessel's hull, it appeared adjustable. All the while precise forward thrust enabled it to hold station against the running tide.

There were many eyes on Richard and Preston, and several deckhands leaned over the wire railings checking for obstructions. Richard focused on the taller of two officers standing on the bridge wing who watched intently as the nearing wooden structure approached. Occasionally, he turned and called his orders. Eventually, he pulled off his white naval cap to smooth his hair and seemed satisfied, calling a final instruction before disappearing inside the bridge. Richard looked further up at the two satellite dishes mounted on the superstructure. He knew that a computer-controlled system using the precise accuracy of satellite navigation kept the ship's station a metre from the jetty.

A metal gangway hinged on the deck-edge lowered into position. Richard, aware of protocol, risked the wooden platform. Precariously he jumped onto it and walked forwards in order to meet the same officer as he came ashore. The man smiled weakly. Richard offered his hand.

'Rhys Jones, pleased to meet you,' he said.

'*Buongiorno Signore Jones*, my name is Capitan Fabrizio Doná. I am here to assist you. My orders are to help in any way I can.'

Captain Doná was taller than Richard, much slimmer and probably ten years younger. He was smartly dressed in his uniform, and a neat moustache gave him the look of distinction. Richard led him off the platform and towards the house. Meanwhile, Preston gestured to a seaman on the forecastle his ability to catch a securing line. Despite his persistence, the sailor kept waving him off as the service was not necessary. Preston eventually got the message and followed Richard.

'For the gates, we will need cutting equipment, Captain,' Richard explained. 'And then the main problem . . . silt, sediment and shit! More than two centuries of it!'

'We have equipment.'

Richard nodded. 'Apparently, ceiling height in the vault is around two and a half metres, reducing to around two metres inside each crypt.' Richard produced his pager and presented Captain Doná an image on its small, square screen. 'This is a scanned image of a painting from 1809, the only one available of what's down there I'm told – from archival material you understand. You can see, there, the arched stone doorway giving entry into a crypt – which one I'm not sure, there are nine – and an iron gate. I expect everything to be rusted. The sea has access from both ends, hence the sediment build-up. When the place was built in the sixteenth century, that floor level was about thirty centimetres above sea level, allowing funeral barges to tie up alongside and coffins to be easily carried into the vault.'

The two men stepped into the colonnade. Richard pointed at the problem.

'Sixty-seven paces, say, seventy metres,' said Captain Doná. 'We have enough pipes.'

Richard looked confused. 'You are not going to blast the stuff with a pressure lance?'

Captain Doná laughed. 'No. If we do that, the water will not clear for a month. We have a heavy duty suction pump onboard, and more than enough pipe to reach into this vault. Normally, the mines we find these days are well below the surface of the seabed. It is particularly loose alluvial sediment in the gulf. We "vacuum" an area around a mine to gain access to it. We will do the same here and discharge the sediment on the other side of my ship.'

'How long, Captain?'

The Captain shook his head. 'With a suction pressure of 300 bars? Possibly ten hours. But we will gain entry into the vault in five or six.'

Richard looked disappointed. 'That long?'

'There is a lot of material to move Signore Jones. Perhaps if you are more specific, it will be quicker. Which way are the crypts numbered? Which end should we start?'

Richard shrugged. 'No idea I'm afraid.'

'Then I suggest we get started as soon as possible.'

Captain Doná unclipped the radio on his belt and gave his orders in Italian.

'I'll need to go down myself, Captain – only I know what we are looking for.'

The Italian officer looked Richard in the eye. 'This is specialist work, Signore Jones, you could get hurt. Stray too close to the extraction nozzle for example and at 300 bars, you may find yourself on the way to my ship in pieces.'

Richard parried the remark with a question; 'What diving equipment are you using?'

'NATO Standard, Mark 7, full facemask – and there is another reason. You will not be familiar with this suit.'

'Actually, I am Captain. British Joint Forces, Royal Naval division. I've completed the ship's diving course, although I admit it's been some time since my last qualification!'

Captain Doná looked impressed for a moment. He nodded and took a deep breath. 'Very well – but I cannot accept responsibility for your safety, Signore. My recommendation is that my men take a camera down and you can watch the extraction process on a monitor.'

Richard nodded his agreement and then looked beyond the Captain at the long lengths of black pipe being manoeuvred ashore on the crane that comprised a single but extendable boom. They appeared flexible enough in length, but the walls would need to be very strong to resist collapsing when subjected to such an internal vacuum, Richard thought.

'It will take time to set up. I suggest a coffee in my quarters, Signore Jones, and your colleague also.'

'Very kind, Captain; I appreciate that. It's been a long time since I set foot on a naval vessel.'

A little over three hours later, Richard received word. He was already on deck and dressed in a black neoprene dry suit with boots and gloves when a diver from inside the vault relayed to the bridge that the sediment level had dropped sufficiently for him to see the tops of the arched doorways that led into each crypt. The crane lifted Richard ashore in a waist-high basket with a gate. His aqualung – housed in a sleek, contoured backpack – hung over one shoulder and he held a pair of fins in the other hand. He looked down at the turbulent water and then back across the canal towards the far shore. The bow and stern thrusters were doing a good job of stirring up the discharged sediment and a clear subsurface slick of pollution expanded in all directions. Someone will complain soon, he thought. A more persistent flurry of drizzle peppered his suit with a fine covering of water that glossed it and soon droplets ran down his arms and dripped from his fingers.

It wasn't an easy walk to the house, as the equipment was cumbersome and as he entered the colonnade, Preston caught up with him.

'Boss, someone's taking pictures from about twenty metres offshore. Neutral registration; Captain Doná thinks Bermuda, but its name doesn't correlate with the international registry of shipping . . . he thinks it might be stolen. He says that the crew are using an image magnifier and appear very interested in what we are doing. The Captain wants to know if he should expect trouble.'

Richard shook his head. 'Even if the conglomerates knew that we were here, Preston, which is unlikely, they would not risk an incident. I can't see it. Tell him to be cautious, but they are unlikely to cause trouble . . . probably the local authority checking on our mess.'

'In a stolen boat, Boss?'

Richard frowned. 'I'm going in, Preston. *You* handle it! I have an integral radio receiver and microphone in this facemask. Call me immediately if the situation deteriorates. Let Rothschild know what's going on, will you? Give him a heads up that we may need security backup.' With that Richard turned and walked towards the water.

Richard sat down next to the extraction pipe and pulled on his flippers. The pipe vibrated and occasionally jerked. Being so close to it, he could hear material rushing through. He spat into his mask, rubbed saliva over the glass, placed it on his face and pulled the rubber straps over his head and then pressed the demand valve to purge it and took a deep first breath. The noise of his breathing echoed. Finally, recalling Captain Doná's last words, he checked for any exposed skin. The silt beneath Venice is a bacterial potage laced with chemical residues and heavy metals from a century of industry around the gulf, he had warned. He must be hosed off with disinfectant before undressing.

Richard entered the gloomy water. It was cold but he did not feel it. Beneath the surface, his first few breaths were short and alarming, however, he was surprised by the visibility, which was more than an arm's length and he soon settled. He followed the steps down. Ahead he could see the light of a diver's torch and when he arrived by his shoulder and put a hand on it, the man indicated the direction of the stone arches by pointing. The diver had hold of a steel cradle that was clamped around the suction nozzle and he used it to reposition the nozzle every few seconds. It sucked up the silt like a vacuum cleaner nozzle in a pan of burnt wood ash.

Richard held out his arms and swam in the direction indicated. After a few kicks he felt the wall and its contours. Looking intently half an arm's length away, he could see the stone – chiselled granite. He saw a keystone and then made out an arch. The sediment was by now almost half the way down and at no more than a metre wide, he followed the sides of the opening with his hands until they disappeared into the dirt. The small integral light mounted on top of his mask was barely adequate in the cloudy water, but illuminating the opening he was able to see a heavy iron gate, although in some parts, it had corroded almost to nothing. Which crypt was this? Richard considered.

Richard turned to his left and swam the remaining length of the vault. In so doing and feeling his way, he counted five further openings. Past the last opening he began to feel the effects of a turbulent current and he knew that he was close to open water. He turned to where he thought the other driver was working, pulled a black rubber torch from his belt and flashed it in that direction.

'Diver, can you hear me?' he called, 'Can you work towards me?'

'*Si*, I have a fix,' was the crackled reply.

Richard returned to the last opening. Immediately above the arch, the construction of the wall was of smooth stone. He peered closely about the central area. If there were any markings, they would be here, he thought. There was nothing. He was about to move on when he saw something, part of an engraving in the stone. He rubbed it with his glove, removing the covering of algae and mud and illuminated the wall with his torch. Then he rubbed again and ran a fingertip along the grooves, tracing the shapes.

'Ugh!' he gasped, as he saw:

# KV V
# IX

He couldn't believe it. 'KV five, sacred nine!' he uttered under his breath. 'Simpson-Carter . . . the Professor. He knew! He knew!'

Richard's torch was secured to his belt by a short lanyard. He promptly dropped it, slipped down the wall a metre and grasped the gate. He shook it violently but there was no moving it. 'I'm onto something,' he called. 'I need cutting equipment.'

To Richard's surprise, Preston answered his call. 'Boss, we've got trouble. This launch has been harassing us, it's become a threat. Captain Doná has no choice but move away. We are temporarily moving off station, do you copy?'

'Yes, I copy.'

'There are two divers, one directs the nozzle, the other is on his way back to you with the cutting equipment, you got it?'

'Copied. Keep me informed.'

'Wilco, the Captain says . . .'

Suddenly the radio went dead. Richard tapped his earpiece but there was nothing. Somebody swam up from behind and put a hand on his shoulder. His heart went into overdrive with shock. He turned fast. It was the other diver, so close Richard could see his eyes. The diver nodded, tapped his earpiece and then crossed his throat with his fingers in a cutting action, indicating that the radio was dead – probably a technical fault. A stream of bubbles billowed from the man's demand valve. Richard breathed a huge sigh of relief. He pointed to the metal gate and shook it and then pointed into the crypt. The diver nodded again and indicated to Richard to move away. He withdrew a large pistol shaped device from a holster on his belt. Richard noticed that the electrical cord leading from it terminated in a bulky power pack on his belt. The diver pressed the barrel of the device against a metal stanchion and squeezed the trigger. Instantly, there was a glowing ball surrounded by bubbling gas and moments later the metal parted. He repeated the process until, after the last cut, a weighty push had the top half of the gate open. Richard gripped the diver's forearm and making a ring with thumb and forefinger, he then passed him with a bout of strong kicks. He could barely contain his exhilaration.

In a mass of venting bubbles caused by over-breathing, Richard entered the crypt. Arms stretched forwards he felt for the Ark… He felt for anything! He was not disappointed. Not three metres past the gate his hands caught hold of something. He ran his fingers around a solid object now coming out of the squelching mud and ran both hands over the top. The upper surface was curved.

Richard fumbled for his torch as the light coming from above his forehead did little more than illuminate the cloudy water immediately in front of his face. He found the lanyard and it slipped between his fingers until his hand reached the end and he grasped the stubby handle. Slowly, and with bated breath, he raised the powerful beam and trained it on the object. Although there was no perceivable current inside the crypt, suspended silt and debris drifted to and fro across the beam. He stared past it into the murkiness. Immediately, his eyes widened.

'My God!' he exclaimed. 'Can that be it?

There, in the shifting shadows, perhaps half exposed,

was a casket. The curved lid bore two distinct shapes. Richard ran his hands over them; they felt sculptured. His brushing displaced centuries of sediment, then he dusted them carefully and the lid too. The water was muddied again and Richard waited for the worst to settle. In the quietness, he heard his heart beating and the blood surging through his ears. Soon, he saw two winged figures in the settling water. Stained, tainted, misunderstood and long since forgotten, they lurched forward into the twenty-first century to interlink their silent prayers.

The lid of the casket also showed damage, the marks of gunshot and chain and perhaps the fractured depressions of cannon ball. He felt instinctively that the casket remained unopened and knew there was only one way to open this artefact. He peered closely at the lid, the glass of his mask only centimetres above it. It was covered in hieroglyphic script, the words of the old people, the words of the colonists. Here were the instructions, and he could read them. He felt a lump in his throat and a rise of emotion.

No sooner was Richard clear of the crypt than he swam into something. It drifted above him. He became entangled and it confused him at first – until he brought his torch beam to bear. Then he pulled back in shock. He kicked out and turned and pushed. The redness in the water confirmed what he saw – a jagged gash across the throat of one of the divers. There was someone else in the vault, and Richard was defenceless!

Richard pushed away but the corpse came with him. He was caught on a lanyard or a strap. He felt a surge of adrenalin, a subconscious fight or flight response and was about to kick again when he sensed someone behind him. He lunged sideways. The shadow was upon him. He tried to turn when a strong arm wrapped around his neck. It squeezed. He struggled. The grip crushed his rubber air pipe against his throat and squeezed harder. Richard lashed out with arms and legs. He tried to breathe and couldn't! He gasped on nothing. He dropped his torch as his hands flailed vulnerably. He felt light headed, he was going down.

His right hand caught on something but he was barely aware of it. It was a strap and it ran through his grip. At the end was a pistol, his fingers instinctively closed around it as he felt the trigger. Blackness was descending. He drifted into oblivion. One last try! Pulling the pistol up, he jammed it into the left side of his assailant and squeezed the trigger. Faintly, he heard the buzz of electricity and the result was instantaneous. The assailant jerked and writhed. Richard's airline opened. He thrust the pistol again, another charge. The man was in spasm. Like a body in cardiac arrest receiving an impulse from a defibrillator, only this had the opposite effect, and in his rubber suit Richard was insulated from it.

Richard felt the flow of oxygen and heard the hiss of gas

in the valve and took an agonised breath, long and deep. He breathed out hard and took another. For a moment he was disorientated. The assassin had floated up to the surface. Suddenly, he heard the noise of the extraction system resume. Its vibration permeated the water and he swam towards it, being extremely careful to avoid the nozzle as he approached. The nozzle sank slowly towards the stone floor within a circle of fast-clearing sediment; soon it would suck at nothing but water. Richard swam past it towards the steps, mindful of any other dangers lurking in the darkness.

'Preston! Captain Doná! Can you hear me?' There was no reply and eventually Richard could see why – a silver coloured communications cable that had been bound to the extraction pipe was severed.

As if pursued by a shark, Richard swam the last few metres and ascended the underwater steps using both his hands and feet. Pencil-thin columns of brightness penetrated the water from above. The spears of light stabbed through the murk until he burst through the reflective surface like a whale breaching. He ripped off his facemask taking a mouthful of stinking stagnant water in the process and spat it out in disgust. Then he coughed and half staggered to his feet, fell forwards onto one arm, rotated on it and sat on the top step with a thump, still chest deep in water. He scanned the area. There was no sign of the other diver. For the extraction system to work, clearly the ship must have returned alongside. There would be a measure of security again, he thought, and the feeling of menace lulled. The sound of gooey sediment, like thick vegetable soup rushing through the long rubber pipe seemed amplified in the silence.

If I need to, if there's another threat, I'll go down and make for open water, he mused. He checked warily but he appeared to be quite alone. His head dropped between his knees and he breathed a deep sigh, one of sheer exhaustion. Reassuring himself he pulled off his flippers and then he heard the sound of people talking.

Richard stood and waded towards the exit point. He was like a launch with a bow wave. 'Preston!' he shouted. Neoprene boots on slimy stone offered little grip and he slipped repeatedly. Fine black sediment and dirty water streaked his face and he coughed again. He felt a growing exhilaration.

Preston appeared at the end of the colonnade and took two steps down to be knee-deep in water and offered a hand. He stared wide-eyed at Richard's state.

'The police arrested three men back up the street, Boss. They were armed. Seems they abandoned their motorboat. I'd say that was a mistake. They found a Lambretta too, but no sign of anyone else.'

'Preston, it's down there!' Richard said, gripping Preston's forearm with uncanny strength. 'We've found it! Preston . . . tell Rothschild! We have found it. We have bloody well found it! *The Ark . . . it's down there!*'

Richard's words seemed not to register as Preston pulled

327

him up the last few steps.

'Open a line to London, Preston . . . *Preston*!' Richard's grimy face smiled with excitement as he smashed his belt buckle with his fist and the straps fell off his shoulders. Captain Doná caught the backpack and helped Richard free of the webbing. Richard turned to thank him and saw the anxious look on his face. 'I'm sorry, Captain. There was trouble. One of your men – I'm very sorry.' Richard succumbed to another bout of coughing and spluttering. Preston held his pager in anticipation. Richard's throat was irritated and he found it difficult to speak. He glared at Preston again, stifling another cough. 'Don't just stand there man! Get a message off!' he barked.

'Yes, Boss, of course. The signal is intermittent. I'll go upstairs . . . I'll be back.' Preston turned and took the next flight of steps two by two. Partway, he called back.

'Don't worry about the cough, Boss, there's a doctor in the house!'

A group of men in diving suits passed. Captain Doná nodded sadly. 'I still cannot account for my other diver,' he gestured. 'They will find him and finish our work.'

Richard thought of the Ark. He should be there to supervise. He picked up the aqualung, slung it over his shoulder and smiled briefly. 'It's down there, Captain. We've found it . . . my thanks to you. I'm going back. We could do with a good deal more security for the next few hours.'

Captain Doná nodded. 'I'll send a team immediately

and inform my Headquarters.'

Richard walked the colonnade deep in thought. For those moments he seemed oblivious to the increasing activity around him. He pushed an arm through the webbing of the backpack, swung it into position and secured the straps. Then he completed his checks to a rush of discharging air. The hissing sound reverberated for an instant.

On the top step, he crouched down and then fell forward onto his knees. The cold water lapped around his chest again. For some time he dwelt on the implications of his discovery. First, there was the Ark itself – an artefact beyond antiquity. Then there should be the remaining crystal – unimaginable power that would help mankind in its darkest hour. Impromptu bubbles from the other divers occasionally broke the surface with a plopping sound. Richard knelt for a few seconds watching them. He needed to be calm, a moment to reflect. He rinsed the facemask slowly in the blackened water and with his head down smeared the mud on his face in an unsuccessful attempt to remove it. Another bout of coughing caused imitating echoes and then, inexplicably, he thought again of Preston's last words. A doctor? He didn't need a doctor. 'What the hell is he talking about?' he whispered to himself. He drew a deep breath through his nose, but inexplicably felt deflated. Without warning, he felt a hand on his shoulder. He felt the friendly pinch of encouragement and support.

'I think we had better run a check on what you've swallowed, just to be on the safe side.'

Richard recognised the voice instantly and turned – his face lit up. It was Rachel!

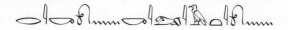

The sickbay was small, although on a ship that size it was an unusual luxury. The grey painted room doubled as the Medical Officer's cabin and on a desk was a family photograph. Richard sat on the bed, legs dangling, and watched, while Rachel loaded a saliva swab into an electronic instrument located in her brief case. Neither spoke, in fact no more than a few words had been spoken during the entire examination. The open briefcase was on the bed next to Richard and Rachel stared at its small display screen waiting for results. Richard wanted to talk to her, to explain, but could not find the words. Anyway, Rachel seemed uninterested in him beyond her professional guise.

Eventually, the machine responded with a row of red digital abbreviations that Rachel downloaded onto a medical chip. After a few moments she looked up at him. 'It seems that you have ingested a number of pathogens, Richard. Not surprising in that water. I'll give you an injection . . . a strong antibiotic . . . prevent the impending sickness and diarrhoea,' she said blandly.

Richard nodded his gratitude. There was silence. The mood between them was strained. Richard put a hand on Rachel's shoulder. 'Did you cancel the arrangements?' he whispered.

Rachel looked down as if embarrassed. She nodded silently but she couldn't stop her eyes welling.

Richard breathed a long sigh and squeezed her shoulder. 'Would you consider reinstating them – give me another chance?' he said, in a conciliatory tone. He slumped a little, so as to look at her face.

Rachel wiped something from the corner of her eye with a fingertip. She dwelt for a moment in thought and then threw her arms around Richard's neck.

## London – two days later

'Good job, Richard – an exceptional piece of investigative work, if I may say. Sherlock Holmes himself would have been proud of it!' Peter Rothschild spun in his office chair like a young boy with a new virtual reality game. He gestured to Richard to sit down.

'Thanks, I appreciate that,' Richard replied, smiling, whilst taking the chair opposite Rothschild's cluttered desk. 'Tell me, Peter. Where will the crystal go, and when, for that matter?'

'It's already arrived,' Rothschild replied smugly, 'at the

Nogent-sur-Seine power plant in France. Do you know of it?'

Richard shook his head.

'The facility was built in 1981, came on line in 1987 and was closed in 2016 in line with the Risbec Treaty which, you may remember, called for the closure of *all* nuclear power stations following China's "Hingsae" meltdown and the narrowly-averted Risbec disaster. The energy people selected it because of its location – 120 kilometres east of Paris – ideal, apparently, for power sharing throughout Europe, Scandinavia and Russia. There are two reactors. I hear that the larger "Alpha" module has been chosen to accept the crystal; the other one will remain decommissioned. Vital modifications have been going on for five days now, since Tom Race returned to earth with the *Star*'s Flight Log. I can assure you that the best brains in the world are on the case: physicists, engineers, thermonuclear strategists, everyone. The power of this crystal will *not* be squandered.'

'I see. So the alien text has already been deciphered?'

'Our people developed a computer programme based on your experience, Richard, and the information that you supplied to us – with all of our resources on it, the secrets of the language practically fell away.'

Richard nodded slowly. 'So what's the potential, the expected output?'

'It's mathematics at the moment, but the theorists say it's exponential. They are talking trillions of kilowatts. There will be a joint decision on the question of time against output within the week – five to seven years at maximum output or, say, ten to twelve years at a reduced level. That, hopefully, will give the scientiststs time to diciper the properties of the crystals.'

'How long before they are ready to initialise?'

'That, I cannot say. We simply do not know at the moment – another week, possibly two. As you are aware, they are attempting to replicate the propulsion system used in the spaceship . . . that is not going too well. Their engineering was very advanced, although I am told that *our* materials technology can cope. There is also another problem. It appears that some of the green, transparent, glass-like substance that formed a protective sheath around the crystal in the spaceship installation is missing. Commander Miko on Osiris Base has assured us that the site where you originally found the crystals is completely clear – they have imagery to prove it. It's very interesting you know . . . just like the ninth crystal, this insulative material seems to have miraculously disappeared?' Rothschild's eyes momentarily narrowed, as if, briefly, he suspected Richard. 'However,' Rothschild continued, with a nonchalant shrug, 'The good news I heard yesterday is that as the crystal from the Ark is itself a fragment, they *do* expect to have enough.'

After an impromptu moment of silence, Richard shifted his focus towards the window behind Rothschild as other thoughts crossed his mind and then he looked back at him. 'How much time do we have . . . in the UK at least?'

'Well, it's not good. Time is the crucial factor. Secretary Bryant called this morning in order for me to update the Prime Minister personally – I have an 11 o'clock appointment. The current rationing allocates one hour of electricity to each home per day, and that at reduced voltage. As for industry and commerce, only selected users are receiving any power at all.' Rothschild paused. His benign expression disappeared, his brow furrowed. 'This is confidential . . . understand?'

Richard nodded.

'Six days . . . seven at the most! One week, and then nothing but the renewables – I think we both know how hopelessly inadequate that supply is.'

Richard agreed. 'What about the other three crystals that Tom retrieved from Mars?'

'Long Island, the reactor in Japan and one is on its way to South Africa. It's the same situation though. The International Energy Commission convened recently and they made some difficult decisions, rushing through the required legislation – I agree with it.'

Richard raised his eyebrows expectantly.

'There is now a formally-agreed Kalahari protocol, and they will not risk installing the crystals into any of the reactors until all essential modifications are complete – for the scientists and engineers, it's a steep learning curve. Unfortunately, this introduces a "Catch 22" element – a do or die scenario. If national grids go down across the world before the crystals are brought online, then there will be insufficient power to initialise the reactors – in short, it will all have been for nothing!' Rothschild leant back decisively in his chair.

Richard breathed in deeply while gathering his thoughts. 'I see,' he said, poignantly. There was a long pause. 'Listen, Peter, on another matter,' he continued, changing the subject. 'The Ark, where is it, and what will happen to it?'

'The Ark is here in London, destined for a vault in the British Museum I expect. However, at the moment, there is such a furore about the crystal that it appears to have been overlooked. In due course, I imagine our people will carry out some sort of archaeological survey and then it will be archived, stored and eventually forgotten.'

'Peter, I know who the rightful owner is – I am serious. It's hereditary you might say . . . a family heirloom.' Richard learnt forward to emphasise his point.

Rothschild frowned. 'Are you sure about this?'

'Absolutely!'

Rothschild stared. 'As sure as history will allow, you mean?'

'No, I'm sure, 100%!'

'May I ask, who?'

'I'd rather not say. You must trust me.'

For a few moments, Rothschild considered the implications of Richard's unspoken request and then looked Richard in the eye. 'It will not be easy, you know, just to spirit the thing away.'

'You could do it. Say it is already in the museum . . . stored, lost, along with countless other artefacts.'

A smile flickered on Rothschild's face. This time, for Richard, he would step over the line. 'All things considered, I think I can arrange something,' he said. 'But we will have to move quickly – out of sight, out of mind, so to speak.'

Richard smiled back. He reached inside his jacket pocket, retrieved an electronic digifile and handed it to Rothschild.

'This will mean more to someone than you could possibly imagine. Please have the Ark crated and shipped to this address in France. It's a convent. It will be safe there and remain so for as long as those people believe.'

'Sounds as good a place as any,' replied Rothschild, nodding agreeably. 'Leave it to me; I will make the necessary arrangements.'

Richard stood and walked towards the door. 'Thanks, I appreciate it,' he said, evenly. Just before leaving, he stopped and turned. 'Oh, and Peter, there is one last thing.'

Rothschild looked up from his desk. His eyes widened, he looked apprehensive.

'Your undercover agent for Osiris Base, you're about to lose her for a few weeks.'

'Really, and why is that?'

'Because . . . I'm going to marry her!'

Rothschild relaxed and smiled. 'This is a little unexpected. When?'

'In seven days. Arrangements are already in hand –

actually, it was just a matter of resurrecting them, you understand.'

Rothschild frowned. 'Then congratulations are in order, I suppose, despite the loss of two of my best people. But I may still need to get hold of you!' Rothschild sounded petulant.

'That might be difficult, Peter, we won't be around here.'

'Where, may I ask, is this happy event going to take place?'

Richard stepped through the door and half closed it. Then he pushed his head back through and looked at Rothschild. He flashed a smile. 'If I tell you, then I will have to shoot you . . . it's an agent thing!'

The door closed.

## CHAPTER 39

# HERE COMES THE SUN

After the ceremony, Richard escorted Rachel into the choir in order to sign the register and other formal documents. Rachel was beaming, her smile radiant and infectious. She was everything Richard wanted, and when he looked at her, wearing her traditional wedding dress, he was captivated. Then, as agreed, the photographer gathered the entire congregation in the historic nave for the photographs. Obediently they responded, following his directions and advice. His deep voice echoed along the cloisters and corridors of the magnificent cathedral. Standing, sitting, shifting and even skulking into dark corners in order to avoid the incessant stewarding, one side of the family and then the other – the group shot, all in true, time-honoured fashion.

Current wedding planning usually dictated an informal,

indoor reception. That was the order of the day. Principal religious buildings were afforded a more generous four-hour electricity allocation and for Rachel and Richard, there was a good deal to cram into that narrow, but illuminated window of opportunity. Inside the cathedral, battery-powered emergency lights would provide a measure of background radiance, however, after 6 o'clock, festivities would inevitably be limited. Rachel considered a candle-lit reception to be quite apt in such a setting. Richard, on the other hand, thought that returning the cathedral to its medieval past – romance aside – was indicative of a failed opportunity to utilise properly their limited allocation – being that he had heard nothing from Peter Rothschild, Admiral Hughes, or indeed anyone from the Ministry.

Richard surreptitiously checked his watch. His unassuming and largely unavoidably fixed smile masked a deep concern. With just fifteen minutes to go to the blackout hour and whilst watching several cathedral orderlies light a profusion of candles, he recalled his previous conversation with William Bryant the Energy Minister. Bryant had stated, quite categorically, that if the crystal was not correctly installed in the new reactor by Wednesday of next week, then that would be the "end of the road" for Europe, and that the other continents would follow like dominos. That Wednesday was today!

Richard knew exactly what he had meant and the repercussions to his thinly veiled prophecy – the end of the road . . . just like Atlantis . . . a lost civilisation!

The National Grid was about to break, strapped of raw materials, supplies permanently terminated, *no more electricity*. Man's legacy on the planet surface would be powerless in a few, short, minutes! The towering interiors of the great cathedral, built for the most part during the dark ages, suddenly seemed more than just appropriate. It was ominous that he should be in this place at this time.

Richard looked over at Rachel, locked as she was in a giggling, excited tête-à-tête with two close friends. Clearly, she was totally oblivious to the impending calamity, as indeed were the entire gathering.

The cloisters bubbled with excited conversation, ringing with congratulations, inspiring goodwill and an expectant future. Richard caught Tom's eye. 'If you are going to say something, it had better be now,' he mouthed, tapping his watch and nodding in anticipation. Tom responded appropriately and spoke eloquently for almost ten minutes.

Richard thanked Tom. 'Ladies and gentlemen, I'm privileged indeed to have such a loyal, capable and astute a friend as my best man,' he concluded. Then he picked up his new wife's hand and said, 'And I'm privileged to have this wonderful woman as my wife. A toast to Rachel Reece, if you please!'

The audience responded enthusiastically. Richard quickly checked the time. Amidst the caustic, aviator's banter, he had nearly forgotten the time. His chronometer read 17:59.

Richard looked warmly at Rachel and raised his hand to add one final comment. 'In a few seconds everyone,' he said dispassionately. 'The bell-ringers will conclude their wonderful renditions by marking the sixth hour. As you know, that will also mark the end of today's electricity period.' Richard hesitated for a few seconds. 'Listen, everyone,' he continued solemnly. 'Whatever happens after today, I'd just like to say that Rachel and I wish you all well, really we do.'

Strangely, that remark lay heavy on the gathering. It seemed not only to stifle the sea of jovial faces, but also all traces of laughter and giggling. Rachel, confused by the portentous announcement, grimaced. At that moment, a bell tolled, a great, resonant *dong,* the reverberations of which surged through the cavernous halls of the cathedral like cascading waters through a breached dam.

The deafening sound sent shivers down susceptible spines. Then another rang out and another, then the fourth. *Dong* . . . sounded the fifth, and with it the cathedral was plunged into darkness, save, essentially, for the cloisters. People knew it was coming and yet there was still a collective, simultaneous, gasp. *Dong* . . . shuddered the sixth and final proclamation.

For several seconds those gathered stood in silence, no one it seemed dare move, not until every essence of vibration had dissipated.

'Come on everyone,' Rachel encouraged light-heartedly.

'We still have another hour and lots of champagne and wine to get through.'

People seemed glued to the spot, their mouths locked open, responding to their mutual, uncanny realisation of the situation.

'Come on everyone,' Rachel half-pleaded again.

'Richard, please . . . tell them!'

The cloisters glimmered, shimmering in the subdued, insufficient candle light; dark corners seemed to beckon lost souls.

And then, at that moment, miraculously, amazingly, stupendously, the lights came on, all of them, *and* with an intoxicating intensity that was almost forgotten. The cathedral was filled with the incandescent, glowing, uplifting illumination of power-hungry sodium lights.

'Hurray! Hurray! Hurray!' shouted the gathering. People began to dance.

Richard punched the air with both fists. In a way, it seemed an unfitting gesture, given the surroundings and the occasion, however, his euphoria proved impossible to contain. 'Yes!' he exclaimed.

In response, Tom quickly walked over to Richard with outstretched hand. 'You did it!' he shouted above the melee, shaking Richard's hand enthusiastically.

'*We* did it Tom, team effort, all the way,' replied Richard beaming from ear to ear.

'Gee . . . it's fantastic, we're back on course!'

'It's a respite Tom, a few years, that's all.'

'That's all we need!'

Richard put a hand on Tom's shoulder. 'You think then, that we have learnt our lesson, Tom?' Richard asked provocatively.

Tom dwelt on that remark for a brief moment. 'Sure hope so – I sure hope so,' he concluded.

The Very Reverend Dean Ellis, who had joined the throng and stood nearby, overheard Richard's last few words. He looked up and inspected the lofty, vaulted ceiling and the brilliance. In gentle fashion, he raised a hand and beckoned to a layman. A robed man with a short, white beard responded. 'Turn off the sodiums, Peter,' he ordered in a kindly manner. 'The side lights will be quite enough.' He turned his attention to Richard and with a half-smile and an appreciative nod he said: 'Well done to you, young man.'

Rachel had joined Richard and as he put his arm around her, he shrugged. 'Right place, at the right time, with the right friends, Sir, and that is the truth of it,' he replied and kissed Rachel tenderly on the forehead.

The Dean granted the gathering an additional hour and full use was made of it. Much to Richard's surprise, Agents Massy and Spirelli had slipped into the party. As the guests were dispersing, Massy offered his congratulations and his appraisal.

'I have to say that I had my doubts about letting you loose out there Agent Jones?'

'I know that Massy, and quite frankly I did too.'

'So, rule one . . . it worked?'

'Listen, Massy, thanks for coming, I appreciate your support, I really do. The same goes for Spirelli wherever he is.'

'Chasing the chief bridesmaid, the last time I saw him.'

'Ha, should have guessed, those Italian genes. As for applying your "Rule One" though – no, actually it didn't work. I needed to trust people – several actually. Without them, I would have stumbled at the first hurdle. Anyway, as of today we drop the Agent Jones thing, for good . . . agreed?'

Massy nodded slowly, his bottom lip protruded slightly and then he shrugged his shoulders. 'Yep, there are exceptions to every rule I suppose,' he suggested politely.

'We live in exceptional times, Massy.'

'As for the Jones thing,' Massy concluded thoughtfully.

'We never say never in this business and that *is* the truth.'

Both men smiled and shook hands warmly. The Reverend Rawlinson who had walked over from the crowd joined the conversation. Richard introduced him and Massy paid his respects to the clergyman with a courteous bow and checked his watch. 'Jeepers! Is that the time? I should find Romeo. We need to get back to London. Goodbye and good luck, Jones . . . I mean Reece, from both of us.'

'Yes, thanks, same to you.'

Richard turned to face the Reverend offering another broad smile. 'Nice of you to make it, Reverend, I know how busy you are.'

'Richard! Thank you so much for inviting me, it was a lovely service and congratulations on a job well done,' interrupted Abbey Hennessy, carrying a glass of champagne. She turned to the Reverend. 'Don't you agree, Charles?'

'Indeed I do, Abbey,' replied the Reverend with a wry smile.

'I must go; I'm so sorry. I have an important meeting in London,' she continued, giving her full attention to Richard.

Richard stared back blankly for a few seconds, whilst his thoughts focused on this unpredictable woman. Mingling with her usual finesse, she had broken off from a small group and targeted Richard, as always, at the opportune moment. She had this amazing ability, Richard mused, to turn a fresh page on each new day, as if all previous discord and controversy simply dissolved into obscurity. She did look the part though, he thought, in her designer clothes and immaculate makeup. Even after that difficult journey to Khartoum, the face of *Vogue* had concealed a heart of stone. Perhaps I am being too hard on her. If ever there was a day for forgive and forget, this was it.

'You're very welcome, Abbey. I'm glad you could make it, really, but I have to be honest and say that you featured on *Rachel's* invitation list.' Richard bit his tongue. He had tried not to be spiteful, even so, the words had just slipped out.

The Reverend Rawlinson coughed politely into his fist. Richard squirmed. Only fleetingly did Abbey Hennessey's smile fade. Well-versed diplomacy soon hoisted the corners of her red lips again.

'Be that as it may, Richard,' she continued cheerily, 'I am relieved that you finally came to your senses and did the right thing for all concerned. I am duly impressed.'

Now it was Richard's turn to force a smile. 'I can't accept any credit for that, Abbey,' he replied matter-of-factly. 'You see, it took a very, very, special woman to help me see the light . . . so to speak.'

Abbey Hennessy's face beamed, she looked down momentarily, seemingly with a flush of embarrassment.

'Oh, thank you, Richard . . . that was unexpected!'

For a moment, Richard looked confused. The Reverend Rawlinson cleared his throat again. Simultaneously, both men smiled broadly.

Barely perceptibly, Richard shook his head. 'Yes, well, as I say, Abbey, you are very welcome.' She has skin as thick as a rhinoceros, Richard thought, as he leant forward to give a polite, departing kiss.

The two men stood in silence for a few seconds. There was an air of mutual understanding, before Richard, with raised eyebrows, concluded. 'Now that is some female!'

'I can only concur, young man.'

Richard shook his head and smiled. 'Anyway, Reverend,

thanks again for making it, we appreciate it.'

'My pleasure, I can assure you. Rachel looks stunning if I may say so.'

'Yes, thank you, she does indeed.'

'Actually, the Dean is an old friend of mine and it has been a long time; two birds with one stone – one would say a double pleasure. As for being here in Wells, I have always felt it a spiritual home. The cathedral is holding up quite nicely – considering the weather. Sadly, its famous "Green" is not fairing quite so well, I noticed. Water damage is always so difficult to deal with.'

Richard nodded in response. With that, the Reverend's expression changed. His faint smile disappeared, to be replaced by a more serious mien. 'Tell me one thing young man,' he said, in an enquiring tone. 'I'm puzzled. I would like to know.'

'And what's that Reverend?'

'All that you have been through: your travels in space, living and working on the Moon, discovering the alien wreckage on Mars, the crystals, speculating on the very nature of man's existence, and what us mere earth-bound mortals presuppose as being heaven as we gaze upwards, you have blasted through time and time again. Yet, you still decided to marry in a Christian church – to be bound by a terrestrial faith. Why is that?'

'Oh . . . that was Rachel's idea, Reverend,' Richard bit his lip.

Both men faced each other in silence. Richard raised a

limp smile. It flickered fleetingly and then faded.

The Reverend stared into Richard's eyes for several seconds. 'I see. Yes, of course,' he said. His glare softened.

'Even these days, many women do still prefer to marry in a house of God – often, the men folk just go along with it.'

Richard paused thoughtfully. The Reverend had obviously seen through his thin veil of bravado. He fixed his gaze fleetingly on the learned man and then looked down at his feet, seemingly a little embarrassed. Inexplicably, he felt the quietness that was unique to his solo surveying expeditions on the Martian surface. 'No, you're right, Reverend – that's not entirely true. Initially, it *was* Rachel's idea. I was indifferent,' he offered again, this time more transparently. 'In the last nine months though, there have been those people to whom I owe my life, including Rachel. It took some time, but I eventually realised. Life, all this, it's about one thing.'

Richard scanned the interior of the cathedral, its lighting now a little more subdued. He paused to scrutinise one or two of the impressive, ornately crafted carvings and then his eye line followed a massive stone-supporting column up towards the roof. He thought of what it took to build such a citadel of conviction, such a *bastion* of faith: the toil, the sweat, the blood, the skill. He marvelled at its scale and then turned again to the Reverend. 'You with your Creed, you were right after all. It is about faith, but equally I think, it's about *hope*. Colonising this solar system and

349

then those around distant stars . . . oh, it will come, given time – there is no doubt in my mind about that. No matter how evolved the technology though, humans *will* always need hope – perhaps, more to the point, somewhere to show it, and the grander the better. Wherever . . . I don't think it matters. A temple, a mosque, a synagogue or in our case a cathedral, they are just different places to come to terms with the same thing. What say you, Reverend?'

# EPILOGUE

Isolated, perhaps insignificant, but by no means lost in the enormity of space, hurtled the former Federation Ship *Enigma* – her passage decisive, possibly pre-ordained. Two light months – some nine hundred billion miles – from earth, her velocity a staggering nine tenths the speed of light, EMILY had time enough to consider her options . . . and her fate. Her structure and consciousness fashioned by the will of man, yet her thoughts more distant, by comparison, than the star to which she sped. Who would venture to speculate when, or indeed, *if*, she would return? Although one thing *was* assured, as unquestionable as her steadfast course:

EMILY had a score to settle!

# Rogue Command

## COMING SOON

**Highclere Hill Hampshire 2002**
Crop formation in wheat

**Gamma Radiation** – Short wave electromagnetic radiation given off by the sun, usually very penetrating and dangerous to humans.

**Gamma Screen** – Medical check-up to ascertain level of "gamma ray" absorption.

**Greenwich Mean Time** – The mean solar time at the Greenwich meridian, used as the standard time in a zone that includes the British Isles.

**Hatch** – Personnel door in bulkhead: usually structural, airtight, hinged and lockable.

**HOD** – Head of Department.

**Humatron** – Advanced robot series incorporating Level 7 Programming.

**ID** – Identity – Usually in the form of an electronic tag or card.

**ISSF** – International Space and Science Federation – Multinational/Global body made up of regional Space and Science Agencies.

**ISTAN** – Close quarters weapon comprising of a programmable molecular blade that can be also fired as a projectile. After penetration of a target, the molecular mass or structure dissolves into the air.

**Ks** – Colloquial term for kilometres.

**Light Year** – Distance travelled by light in one year.

**LCT** – Lunar Corrected time – local moon time, referenced to earth time and more particularly, Greenwich Mean Time.

**LS** – Life Support – Essential equipment or processes

used for sustaining life.

**MCT** – Martian Corrected Time – Time dictated by the Martian hour, day, month and year but referenced to earth time, and more particularly, Greenwich Mean Time.

**NCO** – Non Commissioned Officer.

**Portal** – Door, Entry/exit point: an opening for personnel and usually associated with space vehicles.

**PTSV** – Personnel Transport and Service Vehicle – Multi-wheeled surface support vehicle.

**R&R** – Rest and Recuperation.

**Radio waves** – Electromagnetic waves usually less than 10 centimetres in wavelength.

**RIPS** – Rockwell Illinois Plateau System – System for measuring the degree of complexity and memory capacity of a cybernetic system – has become the internationally recognised reference system.

**Roger** – Form of acknowledgement, usually meaning that an order or statement has been understood.

**Scanadize** – Scanning a document using a security enhanced process and then converting it to a specialised digital format for transmission using the accelercom space communication system.

**Sickbay** – A term for a medical department or small medical facility, having military origins.

**Sitrep** – Situation Report – Details of an event or happening.

***Spartacus*** – Space station that holds its position between earth and Mars by "sailing the solar wind" – Utilises a giant, square sail that is also a photoelectric screen.

**SPEED 1** – Sovereign Procurement Expressway and Emergency Distributor – Military highway, government sponsored, for rapid deployment of military and security personnel.

**SSA** – Space and Science Agency – Multinational but regional body i.e. European Space and Science Agency or Asian Space and Science Agency.

**SSC** – Special Security Contingent – Specialist security team.

**SWAT Team** – Security, Weapons and Tactical Team.

**TES** – Target Enhancement System – Tracking and lock-on system for weaponry.

**Thrust Levers** – Levers in cockpit controlling the thrust of an engine or rocket motor.

**Shebang** – The whole lot, everything included (slang).

**Sonic Pistol** – Hand held weapon utilising a massively condensed pulse of sound energy. Depending on its severity, when the pulse hits a target it destabilises the atomic structure of the target, usually resulting in severe damage.

**Static Discharge** – Discharge of static electricity.

**Wrist LS Controller** – Wrist mounted life support control and display instrument.

**U-Semini Case** – Transportable containment system, briefcase sized and constructed to carry the Kalahari Crystals - Utilises a magnetron suspension system and enhanced Celestite protective sheath.

# Rogue Command

ISBN: 978-0-9551886-4-0